The men and women who fought and won World War II, and truly made the world safe for democracy, come together in these thrilling stories of war as it was really fought by these great and bestselling military writers:

Stephen Coonts
Ralph Peters
Harold Coyle
Harold Robbins
R. J. Pineiro
David Hagberg
Jim DeFelice
James Cobb
Barrett Tillman
Dean Ing

VICTORY

ON THE ATTACK

EDITED AND INTRODUCED BY
STEPHEN COONTS

RALPH PETERS

JIM DeFELICE

DEAN ING

JAMES COBB

FORGE®

A TOM DOHERTY ASSOCIATES BOOK
NEW YORK

VICTORY: ON THE ATTACK

Copyright © 2003 by Stephen Coonts
Introduction copyright © 2003 by Stephen Coonts
"Honor" copyright © 2003 by Ralph Peters
"Wolf Flight" copyright © 2003 by Jim DeFelice
"Hangar Rat" copyright © 2003 by Dean Ing
"Eyes of the Cat" copyright © 2003 by James Cobb

All rights reserved, including the right to reproduce this book, or portions thereof, in any form.

A Forge Book
Published by Tom Doherty Associates, LLC
175 Fifth Avenue
New York, NY 10010

www.tor.com

Forge® is a registered trademark of Tom Doherty Associates, LLC.

ISBN 0-812-56169-4
EAN 978-0812-56169-2

First edition: May 2003
First mass market edition: June 2004

Printed in the United States of America

0 9 8 7 6 5 4 3 2 1

To all the men and women who fought
for Liberty during World War II

CONTENTS

Introduction ix

STEPHEN COONTS

Honor 1

RALPH PETERS

Wolf Flight 71

JIM DeFELICE

Hangar Rat 157

DEAN ING

Eyes of the Cat 269

JAMES COBB

INTRODUCTION

I was born in 1946 on the leading edge of the baby boomer generation, one of the sons and daughters of the men and women who fought and survived the greatest war the humans on this planet have yet experienced, World War II.

Early in the twentieth century Winston Churchill noted that the wars of the people were going to be worse than the wars of the kings—which was prophecy. There have been other wars since World War II, horrific wars such as Korea and Vietnam. And yet, terrible as they were, they did not become the defining experience for an entire generation, as did World War II, World War I, and the American Civil War. At the dawn of the twenty-first century our wars are fought by volunteers, professional soldiers, and not very many of them. There are those who say that this is progress. In any event, it insulates the vast bulk of the population from the rigors and emotions and risks that define war.

I don't think that the age of general warfare is over. The biblical admonition to be fruitful and multiply has been blindly obeyed by the world's poorest people. There are now over six billion people on this modest planet, one that must provide the wherewithal to support all the creatures that live upon it, including the humans. Too many people and not enough land, food, and jobs has always been a prescription for disaster.

Today nations around the world are busy developing weapons of mass destruction, a handy term to describe nuclear, chemical, and biological weapons that kill indiscriminately. In the early months of 2002, India and Pakistan, two of the world's poorest, most populous nations, went to the brink of nuclear war and stared into the abyss before backing away. As I write this in the final month of 2002, United Nations' weapons inspectors are again searching for weapons of mass destruction in Iraq, an outlaw nation led by one of the worst despots on the planet. What will happen next in Iraq is anyone's guess.

If that weren't enough, one of the world's major religions, Islam, has grown a perverted branch that holds that murdering those who don't believe as you do is a holy duty. Worse, some of the clergy of this religion teach their acolytes that suicide while committing mass murder is martyrdom that earns the criminal a ticket to paradise. This isn't a new thing—Islam has gone through these paroxysms before. Mercifully, most of the other religions that demand human sacrifice are no longer practiced on this planet.

And finally, there is the planet itself. These six billion people have arrived on earth during what many climatologists feel is a rare period of unusual warmth. The only thing we can say for certain about climates is that they change. If the world cools or suffers an extended drought, the planet's ability to support its present population will be severely impaired. But we don't have to wait that long for disaster to strike: If a supervolcano (such as Yellowstone) blows, or major earthquakes inundate populated coastal regions, or a cosmological disaster (such as a meteor) strikes, our happy, peaceful, post–World War II age will come to an abrupt end. Man may survive, but not six billion of us.

And man may not survive. Despite our best efforts our species may well go the way of the dinosaur and the woolly mammoth. The tale has yet to be written. In any event, armed conflict will probably be a part of man's experience as long as there are men.

As I write this fifty-seven years after the Japanese surrender aboard USS *Missouri* in Tokyo Bay, World War II is fading from our collective memories. Currently about one thousand veterans of World War II pass on every day. All too soon World War II will be only museum exhibits, history books that are read only in colleges and universities, black-and-white footage of Nazi troops, and thundering *Victory at Sea* movies that run late at night on the cable channels. Some of us also have knickknacks that our parents kept to remind them of those days when they were young and the world was on fire, yet all too soon old medals and fading photographs become merely artifacts of a bygone age.

The sons and daughters of the veterans understand that they are losing something important when their fathers pass on. Many have approached me, asking if I know of anyone who would help them write down their father's memories while he is still able to voice them, capture them for the generations yet unborn. Alas, except for a few underfunded oral history programs, these personal memories usually go unrecorded. Diaries have long been out of fashion, and the elderly veterans and their children are usually not writers. Even those who could write down their memory of their experiences often get so caught up in the business of living through each day that they think no one cares about their past.

Perhaps it has always been so. From the Trojan War to date, personal accounts by warriors are few and far between. Other than the occasional memoir by a famous general (often one out to polish his military reputation), the task of preserving the past is usually left to historians who weren't there . . . and to writers of fiction.

Historians write of decisions of state, of fleets and armies and the strategy of generals and great battles that brought victory or defeat. Fiction writers work on a smaller scale—they write about individuals.

Only in fiction can the essence of the human experience of war be laid bare. Only from fiction can we learn what it might have been like to survive the crucible, or to die in it. Only through fiction can we come to grips with the ultimate human challenge— kill or be killed. Only through fiction can we prepare ourselves for the trial by fire, when our turn comes.

STEPHEN COONTS

HONOR

RALPH PETERS

RALPH PETERS is a writer and a retired U.S. Army officer. He is the author of eleven critically acclaimed novels, an influential book of strategy, as well as many essays and articles on conflict, culture, and military reform. During his military career, he served in Germany for a total of ten years. In addition to writing the introduction to recent Modern Library editions of Clausewitz and Sun Tzu, he translates German classics as a hobby.

Herr Oberstleutnant im Generalstab Draus *Freiherr* von Borchert pissed in a ditch. The autumn twilight captured the high fields and surrounded the groves, leaving Borchert alone on the darkening road. As if he were a battle's sole survivor.

He scanned, warily, from left to right.

The plateau above the Rhine lay hushed, as if a fearful world were holding its breath. The shadows stretching from the horizon gave the landscape an illusion of endless depth. Borchert might have been back in Russia, where everything had been endless. Everything but victory.

He finished his business, closed his ragged trousers, and stepped back onto the farm road. The fields were as bare as the Jews stripped down in the marketplaces of White Russia. As naked, and almost as pale. Glancing about one last time, Borchert nodded to himself, satisfied that he had not been observed. Even now, after all that had happened, it would not have done for some cackling farmwife to see an officer of good family relieving himself by the roadside.

Walking northward, he scratched at the rash beneath his tattered uniform. He had left the camp, but the camp had not left him.

The road was narrow, with a grassy ridge at its center. The packed earth of the ruts lay half a leg lower than the surrounding fields. Borchert strode along, bullying himself. Trying to ignore the soreness of his feet. Thin as cloth, the leather of his boots had cracked open, and the ball of his right foot had worn through the sole. The cardboard that filled in the gap had been torn from an American ration box. It did little to protect him from stones and nothing to keep out the wet. He had replaced the cardboard twice since leaving the camp and had enough scraps in a pocket to close the hole a few more times.

Borchert had never imagined that he would descend to hoarding trash, or that his uniform and boots one day would look like a vagabond's rags. So much had been lost, so much more taken away. He had come within seconds of pulling a better pair of boots from the corpse of a comrade who died in the camp, but, fingers inches away, he had restrained himself. To take those boots would have gone against his code of honor, and that code was all that had sustained him. That, and the thought of his wife. So he hesitated.

Other hands grabbed the boots. The man who got them grinned in Borchert's face. And the American guards taunted them both from the victor's side of the wire.

The Americans had no sense of honor, no inherent dignity, though they were better by half than the Russians. Now they ruled. Borchert had seen the effects of defeat on his fellow prisoners, their last pride vanquished by the triumphant, ever-present smirks of their captors. Men who had been good soldiers groveled and cowered. They begged. Demeaning themselves. For nothing. The Americans lacked elementary human sympathy, as well as proper respect for officers. They did not shoot their prisoners. But they did not mind starving them slowly.

In the weeks after the surrender, the prisoner-of-war camp outside of Bad Kreuznach had filled with a hundred thousand men. Then more arrived. In the unseasonable cold, under late snow and whipping rain, they had no shelter or sanitation, and what little water they received was foul. The prisoners went for days without food while the Americans only shook their heads, strutting about with their carbines and clipboards. Men who had survived the war died needlessly. Cringing against one another for a hint of warmth.

Borchert had joined a delegation of officers protesting these violations of the Geneva Convention and the fundamental laws of war. The American captain who met with them stammered excuses for his military's behavior, claiming that the supply system was overwhelmed by the German collapse and that the available food had to go first to the local civilians, who were starving. But when a German brigadier general, a proper man with good decorations, pointed out that, surely, captured officers must be fed without delay, the American dropped

all pretense of civility. In mongrel English that annoyed the educated ear, the captain said, "You son-
sofbitches are just getting what you deserve."

Men lived in holes scraped from the earth and
woke drenched by a downpour. Sickened prisoners,
too weak to support themselves, fell into the latrine
trenches at night and drowned in filth, their final
cries ignored. Later on, toward the end of the summer, conditions had improved. The starvation
paused, though every mouth craved more than it
received. But the camp never approached a level of
appropriate decency, and the Americans humiliated
the officers among the prisoners through sheer ne-
glect. There was only the sameness, the lack of news,
the denial of the right to send or receive letters, the
endless indignities, and the slow corruption of the
body.

It had occurred to Borchert during his days in the
camp that dullness might be the chief characteristic
of Hell. As a prisoner, he had to struggle against
despair, which he had never had to do during the
war. In war, you were too busy for despair. But in
the drab impotence of the camp, his spirits had
threatened to quit him. The world seemed pared
down to nothing, and even the thought of his wife
sometimes failed to lift his mood. He feared he
would die amid the squalor, the last of his direct
line, and he submitted without protest to being
sprayed down along with the other prisoners as a
preventative measure against typhus. You tasted and
smelled the chemicals for days, clinging to you like
the odor of death. The way his Russian mistress had
clung to him, begging to be taken along when the
Germans were leaving, not in love with him but only

terrified for her life. He rarely thought of her any-more, and never willingly. She had been an edu-cated woman, a beauty after the Slavic fashion. And she had made the mistake of believing that beauty and education would save her.

Nothing in this life could save a man or woman except strength. And sometimes even strength was not enough.

The camp had shamed him. As nothing in his life had ever shamed him. Nonetheless, when the interrogators combed through the prisoners, look-ing for officers with experience fighting the Rus-sians and promising special treatment in return for information, Borchert had kept his knowledge to himself. Others tumbled over themselves to please their captors, hoping to extricate themselves from the camp. But not him, not a von Borchert.

He never lost his honor. He had been tested, but had not failed. In time, his own release had come about as a matter of justice. Even a matter of honor, you might say.

Borchert breathed deeply, savoring the fresh night air and his freedom. Scouring the camp out of his lungs. The smell of shit had filled his nose for almost half a year. It was cold along the high track, and his overcoat had gone missing in the first days of captivity, along with his iron cross and his father's watch. The latter two items had been stripped as he slept—by a fellow prisoner. So he was cold now, in his ragged tunic, but Borchert embraced the chill. Reveling in the good German air.

The night seemed so pure when he drank it in that he had a sudden vision of his wife, his Margar-ethe, on skis. He saw her smile, white as the long runs plunging down between the evergreens, her good skin pinked by exertion and the winter's bite. In memory's photograph, she wore her red sweater. That would have been in Switzerland, the last time they went, before the border closed and the days of generous leaves for officers ended forever.

Now his leave would be permanent. Unless the Americans fought the Russians. Then they would find that they needed the Germans, that they needed officers with experience, men of courage and honor. Borchert had thought the matter through: He would only serve if Germany were allowed its own units. He would *not* serve, under any circumstances, under the immediate command of an American or British officer. And certainly not under a Frenchman. That would have been like eating out of a camp latrine.

Suddenly, he thought of von Tellheim. Unwillingly. Von Tellheim, who had betrayed his class. Who deserved what he got.

Borchert pushed the thought of his old comrade off into the darkness.

It felt very cold now.

Why wouldn't von Tellheim let him alone? The man had brought everything upon himself. Every bit of it. It would be impossible for anyone to blame Borchert. He had behaved with honor throughout the whole affair.

Borchert folded his arms across his tunic and pushed his weary legs to a quick march. Warming himself to the extent he could. He had known greater cold than this, far greater, but his body had forgotten its experience. And he had been ill intermittently in the camp. Not so ill as others, but sick

enough to emerge a weakened man. Now his legs
felt withered beneath him. Pared down. As his life
had been pared down. He recalled the hard, white
cold of the steppes and the wind cutting through
his greatcoat like a thousand razors, and he told
himself this German autumn was nothing. But his
body would not be persuaded.

The flesh forgot. Perhaps wisely.

His feet ached to slow their pace, but Borchert
ordered himself to go faster still. The right foot was
the bad one, the one that had begun to freeze when
they had to fight their way out of the Russian trap
on foot. You could not give up, that was the thing.
In Russia, men simply gave up. And they died. In
the morning, you found them covered in white and
stiff as stones. You dared not give up, not ever.

But he understood it now, the delicious appeal of
quitting. He understood it so well it frightened him.

He thought again of his wife, his beacon. With
the unique red-blond hair that ran through her family. A von Sassen girl was always unmistakable. Margarethe had left their estate in Pomerania the
autumn before, grasping the cautious hints in his
letters. He had needed to write very carefully. The
Stauffenberg affair, a disgraceful mess, had put
everyone on their guard, and letters were scruti-
nized by the authorities for any hint of defeatism.
Even the letters of officers. *Especially* the letters from
officers. Thank God, he thought, he had managed
his transfer before that pathetic business blew up.

They had all known the Russians were coming. He
had known it at least since the summer before, in
White Russia, and now he suspected that he had
known it even longer, at least since von Paulus lost

his nerve. It was the blockheads like von Stauffenberg who were slow to grasp that the war was lost. Then, when they did grasp what was happening, they went into a panic, with the Red Army threatening their family holdings. Oh, none of them had turned when the going was good. And when they did turn, they had proven ineffectual.

Borchert grimaced as he marched through the darkness. He had known the family, and that alone might have incriminated him, had he not been so careful. The von Stauffenbergs thought themselves so fine. But the truth was they didn't have a pot to piss in. And the fool couldn't manage to place a briefcase where it needed to go. That sort gave all the old families a bad name.

None of them had conspired when the going was good. And Borchert would not turn just because the going grew difficult. And the business had struck him from the first as stupidly dangerous. He had rebuffed the first—and last—overture made to him. Honor and good sense had gone hand in hand.

It had been enough for him to save his wife. Heeding his warnings, she had made the journey westward long before the Russians arrived, taking refuge with her sister in Cologne. Now the Russians were on the land that had belonged to his blood since an ancestor was ennobled by the Swedes, by Gustavus Adolphus himself, for service in the wars against the Poles. In the camp, he had mourned the loss of the land as he might have mourned a father. Perhaps even more deeply, since his father had died leading his regiment at Gumbinnen, in the opening days of the first war, and Borchert had been too young to feel the loss.

Yes, the estates were gone, perhaps forever. Unless the Amis drove the Russians out. But whether or not the land came back to him, Borchert was determined to survive and rise again. His line had known reverses before. And plenty of deaths. Nor was this the first time that the Russians had come. And the family had always endured. Outfacing even the occasional disgrace. Such as the minor scandal his wife's younger sister had created precisely a decade before.

A baron's daughter, the little fool had married a Rhineland Catholic from the middle class. Borchert did not like Rhinelanders, in any case. They were calculating and sly and hardly German. With the taint of French blood. But to marry a businessman and a Catholic, even a wealthy one, was unforgivable among the landed families who retained the old virtues. Waltraud might as well have married a Jew.

Better to be poor than stained. Of course, some good had come even of that matter in the end. With her own husband off commanding an artillery battery, Waltraud had welcomed Margarethe into her villa in an outlying district of Cologne uninteresting to the Allied bombers.

Margarethe's last letter had reached him in March, when the heavens were falling. Waltraud had been notified that her husband had been killed near Geilenkirchen, a Sunday drive from home. Ever theatrical, the young woman hanged herself, leaving Margarethe alone.

He had not allowed himself to think of the things that might have happened to his wife when the enemy arrived. He forced himself to imagine her as healthy, unsullied, and smiling with her good white teeth. Waiting for him. He knew that the Americans had been the first to reach Cologne, and they did not have a reputation as rapists. That was something in their favor, however little. He could not bear to think of his wife dishonored.

She would have killed herself over such a disgrace.

They had been a perfect match, he and Margarethe, both wellborn, with interests in common, from riding to music, though their childlessness had been a disappointment. But Margarethe was barely thirty, and he was only thirty-seven, after all. There was still time. He only needed for her to be safe a little while longer, just as long as it took a man to walk from Kreuznach to Cologne. Then they would begin to rebuild their world, their own world, excluding all the tawdriness, the shabbiness, of life outside their walls. Refusing the defeat that stretched around them. Even if the land was gone, the blood remained. Margarethe was strong and brave. Together, they would regain their lost world, all of it that mattered. Children *might* come, there might be an entirely new beginning . . .

He smelled the smoke before he saw the house. Woodsmoke, wandering through the night like a lost patrol. Cresting a swell in the wintering fields, he saw the bulk of a house and barn in black shadows. The courtyard's walls shone pale against the edge of a forest. The windows of the house had been shuttered, but cracks of light shone through.

His empty stomach filled with acid.

Borchert had mastered hunger to the degree a sane man could. He knew its varieties, the bite of the empty belly early in the day, and the hollow ache that replaced it as the hours passed. The sudden, useless rages, the urge to hurt and tear. And the growing physical weakness, the temptation to give up. He knew the thoughts that made a man ashamed, that threatened any sense of honor he might possess. The night thoughts. And the sunlit thoughts, as well.

He *knew* hunger. And the resentment it spawned. With the overfed Americans lounging beyond the wire, or patrolling lazily among the prisoners, always smirking, their weapons slack in their hands or slung over a shoulder. The Americans would never have survived on the steppes. Or during the awful days in the swamps of White Russia, before he and his staff had been rescued and brought west for one final effort. Only their uniforms made the Amis seem like soldiers at all. It was a disgrace to have been defeated by such men. With their abundant cigarettes, making a sport of flicking the butts through the wire. Immeasurably bitter, he recalled the amusement of his recent captors as the prisoners scrambled for the shreds of tobacco. The Americans could eat in front of a starving man, cold-eyed.

Borchert despised the Americans, but he had never hated them, and he could not understand why they hated him.

Making his footsore way down the slope toward the farm, Borchert smelled manure, warm and sweet and unlike human waste. The woodsmoke thickened, teasing him with visions of a hearth and a warm supper.

There was no dog. That was a bad sign. A farmyard always had a dog. Did it mean the dog had been eaten? Had the Allies starved these people, too? He knew the French had moved into the area behind the Americans. The French were capable of anything. A nation of whores. He had heard that the English had relieved the Americans in Cologne. That, at least, gave cause for hope. Their better officers were gentlemen. He had gotten to know some of them quite well before the war, on visits to his wife's cousins in Surrey. Good horsemen, most of them.

He made his way through the archway that led into the farmyard, watchful for a silent, lowering dog. Even in the dark, the place looked untended. Almost Slavic.

Borchert struggled to push back unworthy thoughts. Perhaps the poor conditions meant the man of the house had not returned from the war? Perhaps a wife had been left alone to tend the farm? Women were easier to persuade, and more generous, than men. Most of the time. Women would feed you. Even the enemy's women. Black bread and sour milk. Widows fed you and wept, remembering their own. At times, they wanted something in return.

He heard low voices within the house. He *thought* he heard them. His hearing was far from perfect now, and he would never hear music clearly again. Sometimes his ears tricked him. He imagined things. In the night, he heard the screams of dying men. And begging voices.

He knocked on the door. Firmly. Three times.

The voices fell silent.

Finally, footsteps came toward the door. They were heavy enough even for his ruined hearing: a man.

The farmer opened the door partway. Cautiously. Firelight burnished his left cheek. He had a peasant's features and the thickness of an old company sergeant. His right sleeve was pinned up at the shoulder, where an arm should have begun.

The man looked Borchert over. And his features shed their hint of fear, passing to burnished spite. Then on to venom.

He did not give Borchert a chance to speak.

"Go to hell," he said. "I've got nothing for you. Or for any other shit-boy officer."

The farmer slammed the door the way a gunner slaps shut a breech during a barrage.

Borchert passed back under the archway and turned, again, onto the farm road.

Scratching furiously at the raw skin under his sleeve, he burned with shame and outrage. The time had not been so long ago when such a man would not have dared to speak to him that way. To him. A lieutenant colonel. Or to any officer. Or to any von Borchert. Had one of the tenants spoken in such a tone, his grandfather would have taken a whip to the man. As he had whipped the leftist vermin off his land when they dared to bother his villagers with their nonsense after the first war. Oh, yes, they had thought that everything had changed, the little, grasping men. But they had found out. As Liebknecht and Luxemburg had found out. Facedown in a Berlin canal. His uncle in the *Freikorps* had described it cheerfully. And that was how it would be again, Borchert was convinced. The world would come to its senses. The common man needed an orderly regime. Proper men would take charge and provide that order.

Hitler and his pack had been common men, that was the problem. Yes, the great Führer. A shabby little Austrian nobody. That was at the root of the disaster: commonness. Men with no sense of honor. Creatures of the lower middle class. And worse. Scufflers. Touts. Adored by their own kind for their strutting theatricality, all barking and blaring. And kitsch. Bad taste had nearly destroyed the world. His own kind had been fools to go along.

He smiled bitterly. Yes. But it had been easy enough to go along.

Limping now, Borchert walked along the long, long road through the cold. He was ablaze with indignation, his hunger almost forgotten. When next he came to a farmyard where no dog howled, he slipped quietly into the barn and filled his pockets with animal feed. Even in the dark, he could tell by the feel that the grain was low in quality and cut with straw. He knew the world of stables and barns, as a landed gentleman was obliged to know it, and he could move so that no animal took alarm.

He hurried into the woods with his harvest. When he came to a stream, he lit a fire with a pack of American matches he had taken up from the floor as he waited for his release papers. Even their matches were weak and cheaply made, and the fire was hard to start. Borchert picked out the straw, then cooked the feed in a tin cup for as long as he could stand to wait, boiling it soft to spare his loosened teeth. After he gagged down the mush, he took out a scrap of paper and a pencil. He wrote down the approximate location and estimated what he had taken. He would have to return, of course, to pay the farmer. As soon as possible. As soon as

he had recovered a bit. Even if it was only a few
pfennigs. He was a German officer, a von Borchert.

His bowels began to rebel at the slop in his belly.

It all had begun so well. In Poland. He had been
Hauptmann von Borchert then, leading a company
of infantry, as his forefathers had done in the good
years and the bad, at Kunersdorf and Leuthen, Jena
and La Belle Alliance, Königsgrätz and Sedan. He
remembered how troubled by secret fears of failure
he had been, since he had not yet seen combat.
Hehad been sent to Spain too late, when the battles
had already given way to executions, and he had
worried to himself as he led his men from the order
of Silesia into the ripe, unkempt Polish fields . . . oh,
the harvest had come, the harvest had come, indeed. He had been relieved to find himself calm of
voice, though his heart had thundered within him
at first sight of the enemy. He had given clear, crisp
orders to nervous men in field gray as the sun
caught the tips of the Polish lances across the valley.
He positioned his machine guns personally.

He had rather admired the Poles. At least their
cavalry. They had dash, for all the good it did them.
As he watched them unfold into long lines and trot
forward through the sun-washed fields, he had told
himself, "*That* is how it should be. War should be
that way. An affair for gentlemen. Not this grinding
of machines."

His men had been well trained. Although there
were only two old veteran noncoms in their ranks,
no one opened fire prematurely. Very much the officer, Borchert watched the Poles through his field
glasses as his men lay in wait on the swell of foreign

ground. He recalled the rumble of the hooves, how it grew until you felt it in your knees, and the gleam of the sun on the leather and the hot, wet coats of the horses, the glint of the medals on a white-haired officer's chest, his mustache ends willowing in Borchert's lenses.

Where he stood that day, the world had assumed a wonderful stillness, reduced to buzzing flies, lazy with the advanced season, and the occasional clinking of a soldier's kit. A clarion call, then another, punctuated the cavalry's advance, and the horses took the meandering streambed that divided the low valley. After crossing, they quickly dressed their ranks and shifted to a canter. Borchert did not need his field glasses anymore.

The officers rode beautiful horses. He always remembered the horses.

He could feel his enemy's senses straining toward him, just as he could feel the earth shaking under the thousands of hooves. Perhaps soldiering truly was in his blood, for he knew what they were thinking: *Let the Germans hold their fire just a little longer. Just a little while longer.*

Borchert called out the engagement range. The lieutenants and sergeants repeated it along the line.

He raised his hand.

The Polish bugles cried again. Angry now. The first of the long, rippling lines of riders lowered their lances.

Just a little longer.

He understood it all. The timing. The yearning. The huge, peculiar longing to kill that had nothing to do with hatred.

It was a deeper, richer thing than hatred.

His rhythms were theirs. As if it all had been arranged. As if all things were in harmony.

The Polish commander tried to spare his horses as long as possible, to marshal their strength for the uphill charge into the German positions. But he waited too long. As Borchert had known he would.

The Poles looked fine and brave, and he longed to kill them.

Just as the first line of horsemen broke into a gallop, shouting a hurrah, Borchert dropped his hand, and barked, "Fire."

The world changed irrevocably.

The Poles came on furiously. But horses tumbled, spraying blood, shrieking and throwing their riders over their necks as they crashed to the earth. The machine guns cut them down with an efficiency that made Borchert wince. For just an instant, a child's fear overtook him. As if he had done something horribly wrong that would be found out. Something unforgivable. Then the fear was gone, and he was shouting, and he could not hold still for the elation bursting out of his skin. He strutted along the line, almost running, screaming at a machine-gun crew whose weapon had jammed.

"Kill them, damn you. Cut them all down!"

The earth shuddered. Other companies of Borchert's regiment had come into line while the Poles were advancing, and cross fire tossed men and beasts into the air, hurling them sideways, exploding their flesh. Artillery rounds, crisp observed fire, found the rear lines of horsemen just as they reached the stream.

No book he had ever read, no story he had been told, had prepared Borchert for the beauty and exhilaration of slaughtering his fellow man.

The Poles were valiant. But backward. Unimaginative. Suicidal. They pressed on, a handful of horsemen coming so close it seemed a perverse miracle. One lancer, facing his death with an expression of rage, hurled his shaft into the German line in the instant before a dozen rifles brought him down and turned his horse into a writhing fountain of blood.

His men did not stop firing when the Polish remnants turned and stumbled back toward their own shrinking world. Borchert would not let them stop. And he cursed the unseen artillerymen when no more splashes of earth and fire, of dust and smoke, pursued the retreating enemy.

He only came to his senses when the company's senior sergeant, the *Spiess,* a veteran of the Western Front, put his face close to Borchert's, and said, "They're out of range, *Herr Hauptmann.* They're out of range now. It's a waste."

Reluctantly, he gave the order to cease fire.

Then Borchert did the other things a leader must after an engagement, but he did them mechanically. All he wanted to do was to stare out across the valley. At the confused, meandering horses' streaming gore. At the wounded and crippled men trying to limp away. The dead horses were visible, for the most part, their bulk pressing the grass flat, but the dead and badly wounded men had disappeared into the yellow fields.

Nothing in his life had ever given him such a feeling of accomplishment, and he wondered if anything would ever make him feel so alive again.

He felt sorry for the horses, though.

Borchert woke just after dawn, shivering and itching, with his guts still quaking from his attempt to feed himself. He rubbed his face with his hand, feeling the shabbiness of whiskers, then slapped his flesh and got to his feet. Dancing absurdly to chase the cold. As men had done in Russia, even when a campfire was allowed.

No, it was not so cold as that. A field surgeon had described it as "paralytic madness," the way some men simply gave in to the Russian cold. This was warm as August in comparison.

His body would not listen. It shivered.

He would have liked a cup of coffee. He could not remember the last time he had held a cup of real coffee in his hands. It was a torment to think about it.

He followed the road into a grove. Sluggishly awake. In the morning stillness, he could hear motor vehicles down through the trees, on the good road along the river. His chosen path was little more than a forester's trail now, following the edge of the high ground. But he did not want to go down into the valley until it was absolutely necessary. The soldiers would be in the valley, in all the towns, and the French might not honor his American parole. They might send him to another camp. He did not know if he could bear that. Not with his wife only a few days' walk away.

He would have to go down at Koblenz, of course, to cross the Mosel where it joined the Rhine. There was only a military bridge now, he had been warned, and it would be guarded by the French at one end and the British at the other. They were fickle about

letting Germans cross, even those with valid docu-
ments. But Borchert had no choice. The river lay
between him and Margarethe. Still, he did not want
to test the authority of his American papers before
it was absolutely essential.

And what if they sent him back to the same camp?
He knew that some of his former comrades would
not understand what he had done. They would not
recognize the dictate of honor in his actions. They
might even try to kill him. Although it was all von
Tellheim's fault, from first to last. He had sensed
weakness in von Tellheim the first time they had
met, years before, on the road to Smolensk. But he
had not recognized the power of that weakness, or
the danger it posed.

Now he knew.

But he could not go back to the camp.

And if any of them pursued him later on, after
they all had been released? In a misguided quest for
vengeance? Borchert snorted. Let them. He would
have the law on his side then, and not the law of
the camp.

Von Tellheim was the only one to blame. They
would have to see that.

He walked through a swamp of fallen leaves,
smelling their wet rot. Then he smelled something
else, and it stopped him cold.

Meat. Cooking.

He began to move again, with his pace quicken-
ing on its own. The road made a bend, and Borchert
stopped, startled. Confronted by the ruins of a castle. A long-shattered bit of history, a reminder of
other defeats.

Burned by the armies of Louis XIV? By Turenne

himself? Or broken earlier, perhaps? During the Thirty Years War? Or earlier still?

So many defeats. And still the strong endured.

He saw her then, the little, round witch of a woman. Laughing silently at him as she stirred a battered pot over a fire. Even from a distance, he could see that her big chunk of face was mole-scarred and mannish. Cropped gray hair spiked from beneath a knit cap. She did not seem dressed so much as layered over with an accumulation of rags.

A huge gray cat lay flopped at her feet by the fire.

He had to restrain an urge to wrest her food from her.

She laughed again, but no longer silently.

"Come out of the woods, they do. Look, Manko. Like bugs out of the walls."

Borchert crossed the open space between them. Watched by the cat.

He stopped half a dozen paces from her fire. Unable to move his eyes from the hand that stirred the contents of the pot.

"I'll pay you," he said. "For food. For something to eat. I'll come back and pay you. My wife's in—"

She laughed out loud. As though he were the funniest thing in the world.

"Got a cigarette?" She gestured toward the pockets of his tunic. "Any cigarettes in there?"

He shook his head.

"I'm an officer," he said, shamed by the pleading tone of his voice, "I'll come back and pay you. I'll—"

" 'An officer!' " She nudged the cat with her foot. She wore soldier's boots. They were in better condition than Borchert's. And too large for her by several sizes. "Hear that, Manko? He's an officer! We're safe now, aren't we, boy? He'll defend us, sure."

Her tone was not respectful.

"My boys weren't officers," she continued. "No, sir. But off they went. Wherever the officers told them. And now they're dead. And my husband. The old idiot. The ass. Out drilling with the *Volksturm*. Everything for the Führer!" She raised her right arm in a mock salute. "Old cretins. Senile, all of them. And little boys. You know what the Russians did to them?" She cackled, almost howling. "No worse than they did to my daughter, anyway. God knows where she is." A demonic smile passed over her face. "Maybe she's with an officer? If the Russians are done with her? Would an officer take up with a woman after the Russians finished with her?"

The woman was mad.

"All the way from Liegnitz, I've come. All that way," she went on. "Every step. Leave the dead behind, I say. Just leave 'em. All of 'em. Leave 'em for the crows."

From Liegnitz? If she wasn't completely mad, if any of it were true, the woman had crossed three-quarters of Germany. And the Rhine. But it was impossible for someone like her to cross the Rhine. The Allies would never have let her cross one of their military bridges. Not without papers.

The smell of the food made him feel as mad as the woman on the other side of the fire. He wanted to plunge his hand into the churning brown broth, grab what he could, and run.

He thought he truly would go mad from the burning in his belly. It seemed to him that he had never before been so hungry. But he knew that was not true. Hunger was like the cold: new every time.

"You . . . came all the way from Silesia?" he asked. Trying to pacify her, to please her. "To here?"

She roared. "I'm not done yet! I'm going farther. To Paris! I'm going to be a dancer in the *Folies*. Lift up my skirts and get me a handsome Frenchman." She nudged the cat again, and it stretched, yawning. "Right, Manko?"

"I'm sorry about your losses, madame."

She grunted. "Why? It's over for them. They're better off."

"The Russians are barbarians."

She looked at him. Cannily. Not half so mad of expression now. "*Are* they? *Are* they now? Unlike the high-and-mighty German *Volk*, then?" She made a face as if she had tasted gall. "Why should I blame the Russians? What have they done?"

He was baffled. "You said . . . your daughter . . . your husband . . ."

"If I was a Russian, I would have done the same thing. What business of ours was it to go off invading Russia? Or anybody else? We had work enough on the farm. A hard enough life it was. But not such a bad one." She reached down and stroked the cat. "Plenty of fat mice, right, Manko? We didn't need any Russian mice. Now they're all over the place, those little Russians. Just like mice. Eating everything up." She looked up into Borchert's eyes, and he saw that hers were of stunning cornflower blue. "My youngest boy wrote me from Russia, my Franzerl. He said it was the poorest place he'd ever seen. What did we want in a place like that, I ask you? Why couldn't we let them alone and eat our own soup?"

Of course, it was no good speaking of glory or strategy to a madwoman. But her eyes demanded an answer. With their immaculate, inhuman purity.

Perhaps she once had possesed her sliver of love-liness. A village beauty. And now she was nothing but lumps and rags. It happened commonly in the lower classes. A few short years with a bountiful girl, then a lifetime with a hag.

"We asked for it," she said, in a low, harsh voice. "And we got it. *Sieg Heil!*" She lifted her hand, wear-ily, and cackled again, forgetting the spoon in the pot. "Weren't my boys proud as could be, with their short pants and armbands and all that marching up and down? That's how it started, that's how they twisted them up." She wrinkled her mouth at her memories. "I said to my husband right off, I said, 'You watch out for that one, that Hitler. He's a wormy little turd, not a man.' But would he listen? Not if the beer was free, not my Fritz." She shook her head. "Nothing but turds and fancy boys, all of them. Dirty buggers, and not a decent, healthy man among 'em. With officers by the thousands to lick their boots." Suddenly, she smiled. "Well, they're all in Hell now, and good riddance. To Hell with 'em all. And to Hell with the Fatherland, too. Just give me my soup."

Unbidden, the old fears of dangerous speech rose in Borchert, a reflex from the years when many things could not be uttered. Involuntarily, he said:

"That's treason."

The old woman looked at him. Staring with her mad, blue eyes.

Finally, she wrinkled her mouth, and said, "I knew it was all up when they came for the Jews. What country can get on without its Jews? You think the Lord didn't put the Jews here for a reason?" She smiled at him. "Land in the shit and blame the Jews. And now we're in it up to our necks, and who do we have left to shovel us out?"

Borchert refused to think about such matters. He had had nothing to do with the handling of the Jews. Nothing at all. In Russia, when his unit was tasked for personnel to help round up the yids, he had sent only enlisted men, not officers. The Jews had not been his business, but preserving the honor of his subordinate officers had been, and he had behaved with due propriety. Anyway, everyone knew something had to be done about the Jews. Perhaps not anything so excessive. Deportation, perhaps. Deportation might have been a perfectly sound solution.

Borchert had avoided the entire issue, refusing even to listen to the rumors, although he had felt an unavoidable, human satisfaction when he learned that old Engelmann and his brood had been rounded up. But that was only to be expected. Engelmann had made enemies. Margarethe had written from their estate, telling Borchert that the local Party officials had made it clear that all debts owed by those of pure German blood to Jewish moneylenders and bankers were erased, as were all Jewish liens on Aryan property, although a small contribution to the local Party coffers would be welcome as a sign of gratitude and confirmation. All Borchert knew was that he would never again have to face the indignity of going to the old Jew, with his throbbing pink tongue, to ask for an extension on the payments for the property he had mortgaged. No, the fact was that Germany was well rid of the Jews.

After all, a man didn't have to be an anti-Semite to find the Jews a pestering lot. And those in Berlin had been even worse than those back home. With their cultural pretensions and their social ostentation. Burrowing like rodents into the best positions in the universities and elsewhere. Always laying claim to a higher position and making a great show of their abilities. Grasping. Even turning up at a man's tailor. It was laughable. What nobility could you derive from owning a department store? Or an underwear factory? Hadn't the Jews brought it on themselves, in the end?

At night, in the Russian towns and villages, he had heard the firing squads. But his men had not been involved, except when matters became urgent. And he had always demanded a written order from a superior before he would send a single soldier to that sort of duty. Some of the men had rather relished it, of course. But others were demoralized by the tasks they had to perform. Really, he had done his best to avoid the matter. Better for the unit that way.

Sometimes, you saw them. The bodies. Still unburied, as you marched on. At other times you could not avoid running into a pack of Jews being driven along the streets toward a pit or, perhaps, a rail siding. Clutching their paltry belongings. With terror in their eyes, or simply bewilderment. The old men always looked stunned. With their shabby gabardines and their steel-rimmed glasses askew. Their hands pawed the air, as if to soil it.

He recalled the old Jew with the overloaded suitcase. A shriveled creature with a stained beard, the Jew had lagged behind a pack of yids herded along by local turncoats. Dragging a big suitcase through the dust, obviously incapable of managing the burden, the old man had a useless, stinking look. The Russian *Hilfstruppen* driving the filthy bunch of them to the siding kicked at the old man, cursing him, telling him to get along, but the yid would not leave his suitcase behind. Then the German captain in charge of the detail, an SS man, strutted back to see what the delay was about. Barking. What was the problem? What was holding them up, damn it? The Russian volunteers went timid as mice at the SS man's approach. They stepped back, letting the officer see the old man and the suitcase. "Break it open," the officer ordered. "He's probably got a fortune in there. That's all these bloodsuckers care about." The *Hilfstruppen* tore the suitcase from the old man's clutches, and the Jew wailed. Then he tried to fight them for it, but landed in the dust with his jaw smashed. The Russian volunteers emptied the suitcase onto the road: nothing but books. The old Jew threw himself on top of the volumes, gathering as many as he could to his breast, until the exasperated officer shot him and walked away.

"I don't know anything about the Jews," Borchert told the old woman. "They're not my affair. I swear I'll come back and pay you, if you'll give me something to eat."

"Sit down, *Herr Offizier*," the woman told him. Smiling queerly. "Sit down and eat your fill. There's more than enough. We don't have to feed the Jews anymore. So there's lots for everybody." She grinned. "Right, Manko?"

Scratching idly at his thigh, Borchert sat down on

a stone block long since fallen from the castle wall.
The sky had lightened to gray, but would not color.
He sensed rain coming.

From behind her skirts, the old woman drew a
clamor of tin plates and cutlery. The sight of the
plates, filthy though they were, punched up the
hunger in his stomach again. He wanted to grab, to
cram food into his mouth.

"None for the Jews, lots for the *Herr Offizier*," the
woman sang. She dished two clumps of gray meat
onto a battered plate and held it out to him.

He did not, could not, wait for anything. Picking
the meat up in both hands, he gnawed at it with his
unsteady teeth, burning his fingers, his lips, his
tongue. When it grew too hot to bear in his mouth,
he swallowed the meat unchewed, scalding his in-
sides. Eating with his eyes closed. Dripping juice
over his chin. It was the most generous portion of
meat he had been served in a year. At last, he
opened his eyes in wonder at the ineradicable good-
ness of the earth.

Across from him, the woman ate with the slowness
of the aged, glancing over at him as she fed morsels
to the cat.

Borchert cleaned the bones and sucked the last
flavor from them. He was out of breath from the
effort he had put into eating.

His stomach felt wonderfully warm. Almost full.
He licked a bone one last time.

"I think," he said generously, "that was the best
rabbit I've ever had."

That set the old woman going again. Howling
with unreserved glee. When she finally calmed
again, she told him:

"That wasn't rabbit. That's rat. Manko catches them in the ruins."

It had been miserable going through the Ardennes. The tanks pushed ahead, leaving the forest tracks a sodden mess, and higher headquarters was never content with the progress the infantry made. Borchert felt as if a whip had been applied to his back, and every other officer in the regiment felt the same way. There was too big a gap between the *Panzer* spearhead and the rest of the invading force, and the gap seemed to grow by the hour. The infantry slogged on, and the horse-drawn artillery bogged down in the narrow river valleys, with the engineers played out after getting everyone across the Meuse. The tanks were already at Sedan, and the infantry was still in the woods. Then the tanks passed Arras, and the infantry had barely reached Sedan. All the glory went to the *Panzertruppen* in those days.

As always, the infantry did most of the actual fighting. Not that the French put up much resistance. Small units fought, but their parent units failed. After the long stalemate of the last war, the French commanders were bewildered by the speed of their own collapse. The sharpest encounter involving Borchert's regiment had been fought against troops holding the far bank of a canal. The French were surprisingly dogged, unwilling to surrender even when German forces outflanked them on the right and the left. Borchert almost admired them as the shells wrenched apart the grove where they had dug themselves in.

Then, suddenly, a white rag went up across the canal. Borchert was the first officer of his regiment

to enter the French position, where the fallen far
outnumbered the able. The French battalion commander was dead, and the major who had taken his
place, arm limp and bloody at his side, fought back
tears.

A German officer never would have behaved so
weakly. Officers did not weep.

"You fought well," Borchert had told the man,
speaking the polite French that had been whipped
into him by a succession of governesses and tutors.
"You did all that could be done. There's no shame
in it."

At that, the French major's tears exploded. But
they were tears of rage, not of sorrow. "*I* never
would have surrendered to you," he said, almost
spitting. His face was swollen with anger and blood.
"We were *ordered* to surrender. By cowards . . . cowards . . ."

After that, the sun had stayed with the regiment,
and the marches were long and dusty, but mostly
peaceful. Each village had its own soul. Sometimes,
the houses and shops were shuttered and silent as
the Germans marched by. Elsewhere, the French
showed themselves submissively—curious and already anxious to please their new masters. The summer had come early and full, and the best roads led
between lines of shade trees, with green fields
stretching off toward church spires. In Lothringen,
lindens scented the air. It hardly seemed like war at
all.

The regiment's officers were furious when they
heard that the British forces surrounded at Dunkirk
had escaped, though the English had shamed themselves by leaving the French behind on the beach.

Oberst von Elmerdingen listened quietly, glass of wine in hand. Then, when the junior officers had all had their say, he simply told them, "That's what we get for putting our faith in tanks instead of in our feet. I wish you a good night, gentlemen."

But if Borchert's regiment did not get to Dunkirk, they did get to Paris. The French wept when the Germans marched in. The French always seemed to be crying. Borchert found it distasteful. Had they fought harder, they might have spared themselves the tears. Really, the French were weak, a played-out people.

But the women were fine. In their own shameless way. He had been elevated to a staff position, in Paris, of the sort for which he had been trained before the war. Margarethe was able to visit, and Borchert took her to hear Mistinguett and Chevalier. And when his wife was not on hand, Borchert spent his spare evenings in an elegant bordello where any sort of French patriotic nonsense stopped at the front door. He had even grown quite fond of one of the girls. Emma, a slender blonde from the countryside near Rouen, shameless to the point of inspiration. They had enjoyed their time together. The little slut had the gift of making a man laugh and want her furiously at the same time. And she understood, intuitively, the things he liked, and never mocked him. Those had been lovely times.

Until the silly fool greeted him publicly, a block from the Opera, while Borchert was strolling the boulevards with a pair of fellow officers. The whore sent him a little wave, followed by a "*Bonjour, monsieur.*"

Borchert slashed her across the face—twice—with

the riding crop he had carried in those days. What
on earth had the idiotic tart been thinking? He left
her on the pavement, bleeding and shivering between two friends—doubtless whores themselves.
He did not bother to look back.

At the next corner, one of his companions observed, approvingly, "They have to learn. They really
have to learn . . ."

A few days later, Borchert remarked, idly, to an
acquaintance serving in a specialized department
that the woman appeared to have Jewish blood. He
never knew what happened to her, of course. It
wasn't any of his business. But whatever might have
come her way had been fully deserved.

He despised the French.

Borchert received his promotion to major shortly
thereafter. He was bored with Paris and with the
dullness the war had taken on. Through the good
offices of friends in Berlin, he received command
of an infantry battalion, a position that rightfully
should have gone to a lieutenant colonel. But the
army was expanding again, and properly bred officers already were in short supply.

His battalion was waiting for him in Poland, not
far from Soviet Russia's new border with the
German *Reich*.

It was in the glorious days of the advance, with the
Red Army broken and surrendering in the hundreds of thousands. Just short of Smolensk, a sniper
fired from a village, killing one of Borchert's lieutenants. The boy had not been of good family. Still,
he was a German officer. Borchert ordered his men
to surround the settlement. Then they went from

house to house, searching for the sniper.

They never found him. So Borchert gave the order to burn the place to the ground.

His men had just gotten to work when an officer arrived from the staff of Borchert's new regiment. Von Tellheim had been only a captain then, but he had not been shy about confronting his superiors.

"What do you think you're doing?" he demanded of Borchert.

"I don't 'think' I'm doing anything. I'm burning out the rats and lice. As you see."

Von Tellheim stared at him for a moment. As arrogantly as if their ranks had been reversed. "You have no right to do such a thing."

"No right? A sniper killed Lieutenant Kantner. Firing from the village."

"And your response is to burn the place down? God in Heaven, man, that's exactly what the Russians want! The fanatics want us to take reprisals. To turn the population against us."

"Well, then," Borchert said, "I intend to give them what they want. If you don't approve, *Herr Hauptmann*, I suggest you take it up with the regimental commander."

And von Tellheim had done just that. The colonel backed Borchert, of course. Warning von Tellheim never to question the authority of a commander in the field again.

And the Germans found far more imaginative ways to turn the population against them than merely burning villages. Even so, to the very end, many of those who had endured the Soviet yoke preferred the Germans as the lesser of two evils. It amused Borchert, who considered himself a student of the human condition. And the local inhabitants were always glad to help with the disposition of the Jews.

Borchert did not believe in unnecessary cruelty, of course. Personally, he did not find the least appeal in burning villages and the like. But war required a certain sternness, and a man could not indulge his own emotions. Especially when fighting an uncivilized people. You had to demonstrate your strength. Every day.

Von Tellheim turned out to be a dutiful, capable officer, if overly excitable, and a truce arose between the two of them. Over the summer and into the early autumn, they even learned to banter with one another. Drunk with victory. After all, the von Tellheims were a fine, old family, though the captain's father had married a middle-class girl, a Lessing. Most likely to get the family debts paid down.

The snow came early and hard, and neither Moscow nor Leningrad had fallen, and the plains seemed more endless than ever, with the great rivers freezing over beyond them. Even then, in that first winter, Borchert had begun to doubt the wisdom of the campaign in the east. Unable to draw winter equipment, his men's feet froze in their hobnailed boots. Lacking winter overcoats, soldiers fell to the frost and to pneumonia. Frostbite struck the tall, lean men hardest, and Borchert might have succumbed himself, had he not been able to have his own kit sent out from a military tailor in Berlin. It was hard watching the men suffer, though. And the snow brought the Russians back to life.

They swept through the darkness, in mad, bar-

barian attacks against the German trenches. Driven on by their commissars. Perhaps, even by patriotism. Neither side had enough of anything but bullets, so prisoners became an immediate liability. And both sides stopped taking prisoners.

It was not war as Borchert would have liked it. But the Russians had brought it upon themselves. Through their savagery. And their obstinate unwillingness to surrender.

Moscow did not fall.

Leningrad did not fall.

The machine guns froze up.

And the men behind the guns froze, too.

When the spring returned, there were seas of mud at first. Then the earth dried and the offensive swept forward again, toward the Volga, toward the Caucasus. Again, Russian prisoners were taken by the hundreds of thousands, the cheapest commodity on earth. German arrows swept across the map.

Borchert got his iron cross.

But something was gone. The edge of confidence that carried you forward when you were already tired out, or sick, or low on ammunition seemed ever so slightly dulled. The battles were more intense than those of the year before and, on paper, the triumphs seemed even greater. The division to which Borchert's regiment belonged was assigned to the Sixth Army, which had closed on Stalingrad. But Borchert was ordered back to Berlin, to the Army High Command's staff. He was not sorry to go.

He flew out on the same plane as von Tellheim, who had been wounded in the legs by Russian shell fragments.

*   *   *

Borchert marched northward under a steady autumn drizzle. In the murky, dissolving afternoon, mud oozed through the gap in his sole. His feet had gone from pain to numbness, and he was afraid to remove his boots and look at the flesh. Then, daydreaming about the past—almost hallucinating—he stumbled on the wreckage left by a skirmish where two farm roads crossed. Any damaged Allied equipment had long since been cleared away, but a litter of German vehicles and upended guns lined the roadside, where they had been pushed to clear the way. It appeared they had been taken by surprise, perhaps while retreating. In the cab of a shattered truck, a corpse hunched over the steering wheel. Picked over by animals until the remaining meat grew too foul even for scavengers, a face half skull and half leather lolled beneath a helmet. On the flapping door of another vehicle, someone had scratched, "Kilroy was here."

By the time he reached the high ground above Koblenz, Borchert was soaked through. Even if he had been able to summon the courage to remove his boots, he had no cardboard left with which to fill the gap in his sole. There was still sufficient daylight for him to cross the small, ravaged city and present his papers to the guards on the bridge. But he stopped, unable to go another step. Not because he was tired, though he was weary enough. Because he was afraid.

He told himself that it wouldn't do to approach the guards in the rain, since the poor weather would have put them in a bad mood. And he did not want to draw out his precious parole in the rain and have the papers ruined. And he really was worn-out. But the truth of the matter was simply that he was afraid.

If the guards at the bridge turned him back, what would he do? Where could he go?

He had to reach Margarethe. Nothing else mattered now. And he was afraid of the thousand mistakes and misunderstandings that might stop him.

He took shelter in a ruined house above the city. It was impossible to start a fire. The world was too wet. So he huddled in a corner, where a remaining bit of upper floor kept the rain off him. The only good thing was that the wetness of his clothing calmed the itching that had spread all over his body.

The house had been destroyed long before, likely by an errant bomb from one of the Allied planes attempting to destroy one bridge or another. The giveaway was the lack of personal effects. The ruin had been picked over countless times, until there was nothing left of the least utility or identity.

The rain strengthened. Hammering the bit of flooring that drooped above his head. Leaking through in spots.

Thunder exploded. Borchert flattened himself, an automatic response. Then, ashamed, he gathered himself together again and settled back into his corner. Wet. Cold. Weary. And already hungry again, despite the grim breakfast that had come his way.

It sounded like bombs. The thunder. The rain that had begun to pound.

All nature had gone over to the attack.

It sounded like bombs.

Always the bombs.

At night.

His first sight of Berlin after a year and a half shocked him. The Allied air raids had become earnest and routine. The beautiful city, with its gardens and grandeur, looked like a mouth with half its teeth knocked out.

More and more of the important work moved underground, into bunkers. The staff officers were well trained, and experienced now, and their work went smoothly. But it seemed to Borchert as though there was an unreality to their actions, as though all the endless staff work was a pretense. After von Paulus betrayed the Fatherland and surrendered his army, the atmosphere grew worse. Nothing was the same after that. Even though the next summer brought a last smattering of victories, and no one spoke of the possibility of defeat, a secret despair permeated the Army High Command like a gas.

And the bombing continued. Hamburg. Frankfurt. Hannover. Mannheim. Bremen. Every corner of the Ruhr. Hanau. Stuttgart. Nuremberg. Munich. Kiel. Cologne. One city suffered after the other. Borchert could not believe the barbarity of it. The Allies had no moral justification for what they were doing. It wasn't only factories and docks that went up in flames, but treasure-houses of history. Churches. Palaces. Countless homes. German civilians perished by the thousands. The brutality of it all stunned him, and made him glad that Margarethe was safe on their estate.

And the bombing continued. The *Luftwaffe* did what it could, bringing down American and British bombers by the hundreds. But the Allies seemed to have an endless supply of planes. Goering began to speak of wonder weapons, but the army had never trusted him and didn't believe him now. It was difficult enough producing tanks.

The folly hadn't been fighting the Russians, of course. That was inevitable, although the initial offensive might have been better timed. As Borchert saw it, the folly lay in Germany's inability to avoid a war with the Americans. With their factories and assembly lines that were proving more than a substitute for courage.

The Allies seemed to have as many bombers as the Russians had infantrymen.

The Führer's rages became legendary. Officers who once had flocked around him avoided him when they could. And the generals lied.

The poisonous thought had arisen in the Army High Command that the war in the east might fail, but no one believed—not yet—that the Russians would ever set foot on German soil. There would have to be a peace settlement. To give the *Reich* a chance to catch its breath, to consolidate its gains.

To give Germany a chance.

Borchert was promoted to lieutenant colonel and offered a brigade back on the Eastern Front, in Army Group Center. At the beginning of the war, the position would have gone to a one-star general, later to a full colonel. Now it was his, if he wanted it. But *General-major* von Klenstein, an old family acquaintance, let Borchert know, without needing to use words, that he could remain in Berlin if he preferred. Without so much as lifting an eyebrow, von Klenstein communicated his belief that it was all futile now.

The old man was a defeatist. And not the only one.

Borchert took the command, although his appetite for glory was less than it had been a few short years before. After all, it was his duty to serve where he was needed. The von Borcherts had never shrunk from their obligations to the Fatherland. And there might be a colonelcy, or better, at the end of it.

Despite the debacle that overtook them all the next summer, in White Russia, taking command of the brigade proved a wise decision. Von Klenstein and several others with whom Borchert had worked in Berlin were implicated in the von Stauffenberg affair. Von Klenstein shot himself to save his family, while two other officers from Borchert's department were hanged. By then, Borchert had been evacuated from the Eastern Front, along with dozens of other commanders and staffs. By the autumn of 1944, he was in the Taunus Mountains, just east of the Rhine—almost directly across the river from the ruin in which he found himself now. He had been tasked, though still a lieutenant colonel, to serve as the number two for a new division being raised for service against the Americans and the British, who had reached the Siegfried Line.

The overage men, teenage boys, and weak-limbed support troops sent to fill the *Volksgrenadier* division had appalled him at first. But Borchert never lacked a sense of duty. And he had gotten to see the Ardennes again, this time in winter.

The rain pounded down, and Borchert could not sleep. He shivered in the ruined house in his ruined country, telling himself his courage would return in the morning.

The morning came cold and gray, but the rain had stopped. The earth smelled heavily of autumn, and sounds carried. Borchert could hear heavy trucks down along the river road, their engines turning over steadily as they moved in convoy. The city drowsed under a gray blanket.

His soldier's instincts saved him. He heard them sneaking up on him and just had time to pick up a fallen board and swing it against the lead boy. The pack wielded primitive clubs and stones, but Borchert was swift and unsparing. He went for their heads and dropped three of the children amid the rubble before the rest drew back. They would have killed him for what little was in his pockets, he recognized that much by the feral look of them. Moving quickly, he got back to the road, chased by stones and curses worse than those of dying soldiers.

When he had gained enough distance to relax his pace, something collapsed inside of him. This is what Germany had come to, after all that had been sacrificed: wild children murdering their elders. He wanted to sit down by the roadside and rest his head in his hands.

Instead, Borchert gave himself orders to march down into the streets of the city. More than anything else, he would have liked a dry pair of stockings. Even more than food. His feet felt tender and shriveled, and the chill climbed up his legs to his groin.

Women worked in the ruins, shifting rubble in wheelbarrows. Picking up broken bricks with their hands. German women. Working like slaves.

It got worse as he approached the confluence of the rivers. Closing on the bridgehead, entire blocks had been flattened, one after the other. Where doorways stood, women shifting as prostitutes waited for their morning customers. And the customers

came: black men in French uniforms. African
troops. Borchert watched one of them disappear
into a hallway with a young girl who should have
been in school.

The French were doing this to humiliate Germany. It was clear. It wasn't necessary to occupy
German cities with their black barbarians. Even in
the camps, Borchert had heard gruesome stories of
the behavior of the French colonial troops in the
south, in Baden. Now they were here.

At least Cologne would be free of them. The British were in Cologne. Perhaps Margarethe had been
able to contact her cousins in England?

The prostitutes, thick as lice, did not even look at
him. Their attentions were all on the French soldiers. Then, turning a corner, Borchert smelled coffee—real coffee—brewing in a cellar. He almost
broke down and wept.

But it was unthinkable for a German officer to
shed tears in public, and he mastered himself.

The river was running high with the autumn
rains, high and gray. A convoy of American-made
jeeps and trucks, with British markings, snaked over
the temporary bridge. On the near bank, by a guard
post, a line of German civilians stood quietly, waiting their turn to cross.

Borchert got in line.

The old woman ahead of him carried just-roasted
potatoes in her bag, he could smell them. Her
midday meal, no doubt. Borchert pictured fire-
blackened potatoes, broken apart, salted, and but-
tered. It made his gut ache.

He almost opened his mouth to ask if she would
sell him a portion on trust. But there were too many

people about—a half dozen more had already joined the line behind him—and he was afraid he would shame himself.

The smell would not let him be.

The convoy cleared the bridge, and the crowd pressed forward. Two Africans in uniform stepped from the guard shelter, and a clamoring began. Taking their good time, even arrogant, the Africans, a junior noncom and a private, inspected papers. Sometimes they laughed. And they turned one old man away, giggling like children as they watched him limp off.

Borchert would have liked to shoot them down.

What had Germany done to deserve this?

A young woman with a child of six or seven excited the attentions of the guards. They held up the line, toying with her. Finally, she went into the shack with the noncom, leaving her little girl in the care of the old woman who was next in line. After a few minutes, the NCO emerged without the woman, and the private went inside. In less than five minutes, the private came back out, trailed by the woman. The expression on her face was set, and she didn't look back at anyone, only took her child by the forearm and dragged her out onto the bridge. Only then did the child begin to cry.

When Borchert's turn came, the soldiers played with his papers and spoke in a jabbering language. Smiling their huge grins.

"It's a parole authorizing me to travel," Borchert told them in French. "From the Americans. It must be honored by all Allied forces."

The noncom ignored him and, for a moment, Borchert feared the man would toss the papers into the river. Instead, he handed back the sheets and said, in an accent Borchert could barely understand, "Cigarettes? Money? What presents did you bring us, *monsieur?*"

"I have nothing," Borchert told the man. "The pass authorizes me to go to Cologne. I'm entitled to cross this bridge . . ."

"No presents, no bridge, *monsieur,*" the NCO said. He and his companion giggled again.

Borchert stepped forward. But the private unshouldered his weapon, and the giggling stopped.

A jeep pulled up, with a French officer in the passenger's seat. Another African sat behind the wheel. The guards came to attention and saluted. It appeared the jeep would simply pass by, but the officer ordered it to halt. He stepped out and walked over to Borchert. The Frenchman was a colonel, and his right arm hung limply in the sleeve of his uniform.

The colonel looked oddly familiar. But, then, there was a sameness to the French.

"What's going on here?" he asked the noncom.

"He wants to cross," the NCO answered, in a voice made simple.

"Does he have papers?"

The NCO shrugged. "Not in French."

"Pardonez-moi, monsieur le colonel," Borchert said, in the most respectful voice he could muster. He held out his papers. "I've been paroled by the Americans. To go home to my wife. The papers are in order."

The French officer looked at him hard. After a moment, he said, "We'd all like to go home to our wives." But he took the papers.

After scanning the sheets, the colonel wrinkled up the side of his mouth, as if in disgust.

"Let him pass," he told the guards.

Borchert stepped forward to thank him, one officer to another, but the Frenchman had already turned back toward his jeep.

"Move along," the noncom told Borchert, as if it were all a matter of routine.

British soldiers manned the far end of the bridge. They let the civilians go by without interference, but stopped Borchert.

" 'Ere now, you there," a corporal called him over. He and his men wore berets with red-and-white brushes fixed upright. *"Papieren? Versteh?"* he added, in a dreadful accent.

Borchert handed over his papers.

A sandy-haired private with bad skin and bad teeth said, "Ask 'im if those black buggers give 'im one up the arse before they let 'im come over. And ask 'im if 'e liked it."

"Versteh English?" the corporal asked Borchert.

"Nein," Borchert lied. Wary of the further insults his comprehension might bring.

"About bloody time 'e learned it," the sandy-haired private said. "Ain't that right, Corporal Jones? Time they all bloody-well learned it."

"Oh, piss off, Alf," the corporal said. "You can see the poor bastard's all in." He handed the papers back to Borchert, telling him, *"In Ordnung."*

"Danke," Borchert said.

But as Borchert stepped away, the corporal called after him.

"Halt!"

Borchert's heart pounded. He saw Margarethe as clearly as ever he had seen her in the flesh, a vision

almost religious in its intensity. And he feared what
was coming. With his fate—their fate—at the mercy
of this lowest of noncoms, a man who wasn't fit to
shine a German officer's boots.

He was about to protest that his papers were in
perfect order, when he saw the corporal was holding
out a pack of cigarettes, offering him one.

" 'Ere, you sorry bugger. 'Ave one for the road."

Borchert took the cigarette. *"Danke. Vielen Dank."*

As he walked away for the second time, Borchert
heard the corporal say, "You look at a poor, sodding
bloke like that one, and you can't 'elp wondering
'ow the Jerries gave us such a time of it. Makes a
body wonder, don't it, Alf?"

Borchert did not light the cigarette until he was
on the high ground again, beyond the last houses
and out of sight. Then he stopped and struck a
match with an unsteady hand.

It was a good cigarette, with real tobacco. He had
not tasted anything as good since the previous De-
cember, in the Ardennes, in the snow, when he had
taken a packet of American cigarettes called Lucky
Strikes from a captured vehicle.

The Americans had cost him his promotion to
colonel. But they had paid for it.

Borchert walked along a gray road, under a gray
sky, with bald fields right and left. In the high ridges
of the Ardennes, the snow had been packed to ice
on the trails, tamped down by thousands of boots,
but in the forest it might come up to a man's waist.
Snow had an odd effect on inexperienced soldiers,
as nearly all of the men and boys in his division had
been. When they sank down in it, they imagined it
would protect them, as if it were a wall of earth. He

had seen men try to hide from bullets by crouching down behind a snowdrift. When they first were hit, their blood was as crimson as a red silk scarf. Then it soaked in, sometimes pink at the edges of the pools, but finally brown. Almost the color of shit. As though everything within a man was foul.

Crows sat on a gate and watched him pass: a man smoking as if a fire burned inside him. Borchert drew on the cigarette one last time and burned his lips. Still, he hated to let it go. And, yes, there was a fire inside him. It flared anew whenever he thought of that last great attempt, the winter surprise the Allies didn't expect.

He scratched his groin and remembered.

His division, green though it was, had been given a position of honor. At the cutting edge of the attack. Ahead of the tanks this time. The intelligence reports had promised that the first troops they would hit would be the broken men of the American Twenty-eighth Infantry Division. The unit had been torn apart in the autumn fighting and had been shifted to a quiet sector for rehabilitation. Borchert's own reconnaissance section, led by a veteran of the Eastern Front, confirmed that, for once, the intelligence reports were correct: The Americans before them wore the Twenty-eighth Division's red-bucket patch on their sleeves, and they were spread thinly across a huge sector. Punching through them, especially with surprise on the German side, would be only a matter of hours, if not of minutes.

Things began to go wrong the day before the attack was set to begin. The tank troops positioned to exploit the attack's initial success moved up too far too early. It was hard for Borchert to believe that the

Americans across the valley had not heard them. And
the tanks cut the communications wire strung along
the roads and trails. Rations failed to arrive, and an
inspecting colonel from the high command told
Borchert that the roads were clogged with military
traffic for eighty to a hundred kilometers behind the
front lines. Before the skies closed in, American aircraft flew over the jump-off positions. Despite all the
camouflage efforts, the pilots had to have seen some
of the activity on the ground. The German troops
were green and meandered past their assigned positions, their young leaders unable to read maps or
lacking maps entirely.

Still, Borchert was accustomed to such confusion.
Everything behind the lines always seemed a mess,
he knew that much. It was only as you approached
the edge of battle that things began to make sense.
The rear of an attack always looked so chaotic a civilian would have mistaken it for a defeat. And the
Americans were few, and tired of the war. Borchert
felt confident. He would see Brussels again. Perhaps
even Ostende and the sea.

The infantry moved out in darkness, then the artillery began to pound. The first reports were encour-
aging. Despite everything, the Americans appeared
to have been surprised, indeed. Their positions were
surrounded and quickly overrun. Pockets of resistance held out, but their destruction was only a matter of time. All that mattered now was opening the
roads.

A crucial point of resistance lay at a crossroads
hamlet on a forested bluff. Given the thickness of the
surrounding trees, the angle of the slope and the
depth of the snow, it was impossible for vehicles to by-

pass the settlement. The hamlet had to be taken
swiftly and the roads opened so the tanks could pass
through and strike deep before the Americans could
organize their defenses.

The morning passed into afternoon, and the
hamlet still was not in German hands. The first inquiries came down from corps, then from army
level. Was the road open? Could the *Panzer* forma-
tions move through? What on earth was the problem?

Borchert went forward himself to crack the whip.
He arrived as the early winter dusk began to
thicken. A fellow lieutenant colonel should have
been on the scene to meet him, but the man had
gone missing. A major, recently transferred from an
antiaircraft-artillery unit to the needy infantry, was
in charge. He began to salute before Borchert
slapped his arm down.

"What's holding you up? Why isn't there any artillery? Why don't I hear any artillery, for God's
sake?"

"The land line's broken. We're fixing it."

"Send a runner, you ass."

"I did, *Herr Oberstleutnant.* The artillery say we
don't have priority of fires."

"This is the division's main attack, man."

"We're trying, *Herr Oberstleutnant.* We—"

Borchert had heard enough. He relieved the man
on the spot. With the threat of a court-martial. Taking charge personally, he sent a written order to the
division's artillery regiment, organized a second
team to trace the communications wire and find the
break, then went forward to get the troops moving
again. If the artillery hit while they were attacking,

too bad. The crossroads had to be opened. Immediately.

With the hamlet no more than a cluster of masonry farmhouses glimpsed through black tree trunks, Borchert found the surrounding snows littered with his infantrymen. Lying there as random as casualties. But they were healthy enough, these old men and boys, former *Luftwaffe* ground crewmen, and even sailors without ships—all magically transformed into infantrymen by the stroke of a pen. Most of the sergeants were better suited to be air-raid wardens than to lead infantry assaults.

"Get up," Borchert shouted. "Move forward. This is nothing. You. Sergeant. Get your men moving or, by God, I'll shoot you myself."

He worked his way along the line, fighting with the snow that did its best to slow him or topple him over. Pressing the men forward, he saw that, as soon as they took fire from the hamlet, they went to ground again. The best of them fired their rifles at the buildings. But even those lacked the will to drive home an attack.

It was an hour before the artillery struck. Then the shells fell behind the houses. Borchert stormed back to the headquarters that had been established in a hollow. The only good news was that the field telephone was working again.

Borchert corrected the artillery fire himself. Soon, the shells were crashing down on the roofs of the buildings and into their courtyards. Borchert pressed the gunners to keep firing, to eliminate any resistance. He knew how difficult it was to blast defenders out of well-built dwellings. But the Americans were tired, and few. A barrage should be sufficient to teach them their lesson.

When the artillery officer on the other end of the line insisted he had to shift fires, by order of the corps commander, Borchert went back up to the line of troops. With the darkness compressed under a thick, low sky, the high ground was illuminated only by a pair of fires in the hamlet. Desultory rifle cracks punched the night.

It was cold.

The infantrymen had begun to huddle together, for warmth, drawing back instead of going forward. Borchert tried, again, to drive them into the attack, but the most he got out of them was a fifty-meter advance, leaving a distance of over a hundred meters between the nearest cluster of German troops and the outbuildings.

He had never seen anything like this: German troops unwilling to attack. There were two battalions, the better part of a regiment, spread over the slopes, and they had taken no more than a few dozen casualties.

Legs exhausted from a day spent fighting through snowdrifts, Borchert went back to the field headquarters and called the division commander to ask for fresh troops—and better ones, if possible. Before he could state his case, the division commander lashed out at him, demanding to know what in Heaven or Hell could be holding up the German advance. Doubtless, the man had taken his own whippings from his superiors, but Borchert could only feel resentful. He had put everything he had into trying to move old men and boys to attack. If the mission was so vital, why hadn't they been given at least one seasoned infantry regiment? Or even a single battalion of veteran troops?

At last, weary of shouting, the division commander agreed to commit the division's last infantry regiment.

But the troops arrived piecemeal, confused by the darkness. By the time Borchert could organize an assault, the sky had begun to pale again. The fires in the hamlet had burned themselves out, and the buildings looked empty and still. Perhaps the Americans had withdrawn during the night?

Borchert got elements of two fresh battalions moving through the gray-flannel light. The forward companies reached a point hardly fifty meters from the houses, and Borchert thought, *Yes, by God, the Americans are gone.*

A machine gun opened up.

Gray overcoats tumbled backward, or twisted and danced and dropped. In seconds, the entire attack had burrowed into the snow. Borchert personally directed machine gun fire toward the sources of the American bursts, but the Americans only shifted and opened up again as soon as the Germans tried to move, whether forward or backward.

Borchert called for more artillery. Additional batteries joined the barrage, and some of the shells fell short, among the German troops. Men tried to run, only to be blown into the air, sailing through the trees like kites swept away by a storm.

When the artillery fire lifted, Borchert sent forward the fresh regiment's last battalion, which was missing a company that had gotten lost during the night march. Some of the new men had watched the earlier attack. They told their recently arrived comrades what had happened, and their attack was tentative, at best. This time, the American machine gun opened up at a greater range, surprising the attackers again.

Even with the casualties they had suffered, Borchert knew he had well over a thousand able-bodied men in the ravines and draws surrounding the hamlet. And how many men did the Americans have? How many had they had to begin with? A company?

Borchert heard rumbling. Familiar, heavy, earth-shaking rumbling.

Fifteen minutes later, in the milky light, a huge whitewashed tank came up the road. With another just behind it. And another.

As soon as it had a direct shot at the hamlet, the lead tank paused in the middle of the road. The following tanks in the forward platoon deployed where the woods were thinnest.

An officer in a black uniform jumped from one of the tanks and eventually found his way over to Borchert.

The tanker was a colonel. He started out cursing and never really stopped. Borchert had to use every bit of his self-control not to strike the man. No German officer, no veteran, no von Borchert deserved such insults. It was a gross violation of the officer's code of honor.

All right, Borchert thought. *You do it, you sonofa-bitch. Open the road for yourself.*

"Do you think you can at least get these shit-boys of yours to follow my tanks?" the *Panzer* officer asked.

The black-clad colonel went back to his tank. Moments later, the armored vehicles fired a salvo and began to grind forward. One tank slid sidewards into a ditch, and its track broke, writhing like a snake and slashing through the snow into the earth. But the others closed toward the village.

The Americans did not fire back now. Perhaps they saw the futility of it at last. Perhaps they had slipped off the moment they saw the tanks.

The tanks blasted walls away. Beams spared by the artillery cracked as masonry collapsed. Dust and smoke rose from the hamlet.

Borchert did not need to drive the infantrymen now. A substantial number of them rose up on their own and followed the tanks. Then the lead tank penetrated the cluster of buildings.

Fire burst on the side of the tank, and the American machine gun opened up again, from an oblique position, cutting through the advancing infantrymen. But, this time, one of the tanks, then another, used their main guns to blast in the building where the American weapons crew had positioned itself.

But the lead tank was burning. Then it shook with an internal explosion. None of the crew emerged.

The division commander appeared by Borchert's side. Borchert winced even before the cursing could begin.

But the commander was a changed man. In place of the fury of the night before, there was only weariness, almost resignation.

"I've come to tell you," he said, "that I've been relieved." The elder man smiled wryly. "The division is yours now, *Herr Oberstleutnant.* Perhaps you'll be more successful."

Borchert looked up through the snow, blackened in oblong patches by the hot waste of muzzles or by bodies, wounded and dead. The tanks were grinding on, blasting into the buildings at point-blank range. But the infantry had frozen again.

A white rag on a stick began to wave from a smoking window.

The smile on the face of Borchert's former commander grew even tarter. "Ah," he said. "You're in luck. A lucky officer is a treasure. To be prized." Then he walked off.

Borchert hurried toward the hamlet. By the time he could make his way through the snow and the litter of casualties, enough of his men had recovered their self-possession to take the American surrender.

The *Panzer* colonel was directing, personally, the removal of the burned tank that blocked the road to the west. He wrinkled his mouth at Borchert, looked at his watch, and said, "We're almost thirty hours behind schedule. Thanks to you. *Herr Oberstleutnant.*" Then the path was clear, and the colonel remounted his tank. Standing in his hatch, he pulled on a headset and began to speak into it. The tank moved, followed by others, and the stench of exhaust thickened the cold air.

Borchert's men had gathered the Americans in a courtyard. Only five of the prisoners could stand upright. A dozen more were too badly wounded to keep their feet. Their breath steamed.

At first, Borchert was taken aback. He had expected to see the remnants of a company, at least, with American bodies littered about.

The senior American was a sergeant, with his arm in an improvised sling.

For once, Borchert found himself at a loss for words.

The American watched him approach. Unshaven and cold-eyed, the sergeant's skin looked swarthy underneath the grime of battle.

An Italian, perhaps. Maybe even a Jew.

Still bewildered by the fewness of the Americans, Borchert summoned his English and said, "You . . . were wise to surrender. Your efforts were futile, you know. You—"

"Stick it up your ass, Adolf," the sergeant told him. "We just ran out of fucking ammo."

Borchert had never seen such hatred in a man's eyes. The red patch on the sergeant's sleeve looked like a bucket of blood.

Remembering his position, Borchert pivoted, doing a perfect about-face. Returning to his own language, he approached a lieutenant standing nearby, the only other German officer present.

"Shoot them," Borchert said.

A look of astonishment passed over the lieutenant's face.

"I told you to shoot them, damn you."

The lieutenant began to stammer. "*Herr Oberstleutnant* . . . they've surrendered . . . they . . ."

Borchert tore a submachine gun from the grip of the nearest soldier. He turned it on the Americans who were still standing, cutting them down before a single one of them could react. He emptied the magazine into their bodies.

Tossing the weapon back to the soldier, Borchert

told the lieutenant. "Make sure they're dead. All of them. Or I'll have you hanged."

Dreaming of his wife and the future, Borchert crossed the Ahr. In the lowering hills to the north, he had a stroke of luck. After a night spent shivering in the loft of a barn, he saw an old woman with an empty sack leaving the farmhouse across the courtyard. She looked around to make certain she was unobserved, then slipped into the woods.

Borchert knew what that meant. He had learned it first in White Russia, then in the miserable expanses that led toward the Volga. The peasants always hid what food they had, careful to appear half-starved to all combatant parties.

He waited until the woman reappeared with the sack filled and slung over her shoulder. Once she was back inside her house with the bolt shot, he slipped off and circled toward the spot where he had seen her enter the trees. The old woman had grown a bit careless, perhaps because of the peace, and Borchert found a well-worn path. A Russian peasant would have gone a different route to his or her cache each time to avoid leaving a trail.

Nor had she covered up her digging very well. Where she had closed the hole, churned, wet, matted leaves showed darker than the surrounding copper froth. After a brief look over his shoulder, Borchert began to dig with his bare hands.

Potatoes. He filled his pockets with them, but he wanted more. Despite the chill, he stripped off his undershirt, doing his best to avoid the sight of his scratched-open flesh, and made a sack of the yellowed rag. Hastily, he filled in the dirt and kicked fresh leaves over the spot.

He forced himself onward for half an hour before permitting himself a cooking fire. He did his best to note the location of the farm from which he had borrowed. Still, it would not have done to be discovered. In time, he would make amends. For now, he did not choose to explain himself to anyone.

And to whom did he owe an explanation? For anything? After all he had done for these people? While they sat safely at home, gorging themselves? They were cowards. All of them. Like those sluggish old men in the snow in the Ardennes, who would not get up and do their duty. When, Borchert asked himself, had he ever done anything but his duty?

He didn't need to explain himself to some old farmer's hag. No more than he had to explain himself to the men in the camp after the Americans took von Tellheim away.

Borchert tried to eat one of the potatoes before it was cooked through, but his teeth were too loose in his gums. So he sat, aching, and let the potatoes roast. Finally, he broke the hot skins apart and made a mush in his palm, devouring the white paste until he was sated.

As he pushed on north, Borchert had to travel along paved roads. The British drove past but never stopped to question him. Finally, he gave up on his efforts to move by stealth and went down to the good road along the Rhine. In the gray river, the cabins of sunken barges broke the current and, here and there, a bow or stern protruded from the water. All of the old bridges were in ruins, replaced, for now, by military pontoons.

When he reached Bonn, it was a shock to find the little city almost intact. A dreary university town, it must not have seemed important enough to bomb. So something was left. Of the old Germany. Something remained. Something, however slight, on which to build.

In the market square, the Red Cross had set up a soup kitchen. Borchert joined a line hundreds long.

His feet had gone numb again. But it wasn't far now. Only a fair day's walk to the other side of Cologne, where Margarethe would be waiting. Where she had to be waiting. With her red-blond hair, that von Sassen hair, and her white teeth. And a sense of self-worth and honor that matched his own.

Then, drinking from the can of soup handed to him, an awful thought pierced him. He had not thought about any practical details. What if Margarethe had nothing to eat herself? How would he provide for both of them? In Cologne, where he knew no one? Where the Rhinelanders were little better than Jews themselves? He had not thought beyond their reunion, unless it was to dream of a distant future into which they had made a successful leap. What if a hungry man returned to his wife and found her hungry, too? How would he bear that? How would he bear his inability to provide for her?

He left Bonn a frightened man.

Just short of Cologne, a jeep with two Americans passed him by. He had grown accustomed to seeing only British soldiers, and the sight of the Americans launched him into a fit of panic. He almost threw himself into the ditch by the roadside. Afraid they had changed their minds about his parole, afraid

these Americans had come to take him back to the
camp.

The notion was absurd, of course. The Americans
drove on, oblivious of his existence. A liaison officer
and his driver, most likely. Enjoying the chance to
lord it over a conquered people.

Borchert never regretted killing the Americans
who had surrendered in the Ardennes. They had
earned their fate, and the sergeant's insolence had
sealed it. Prisoners had to surrender more than
their weapons. Still, the incident had not turned out
well. The lieutenant who had been so reluctant to
follow orders turned out to have been a mere eighteen years of age—and the son of an industrialist,
the sort of imitation Jew who always survived and
always had influence. Within a month, Borchert had
found himself relieved of his command, rather than
promoted, and condemned to the task of defending
a town along the Rhine that had no bridge and no
strategic value. Unless you counted the vineyards. It
was a mockery, an insult. And that was where he had
surrendered to the Americans. Surrendering the pathetic old men and children he commanded—less
than a hundred of them, all drafted into the *Volksturm* from the local area—and ignoring the last orders he had been given: *Fight to the last man. Heil
Hitler!*

The men had made it clear that they would not
fight and that they did not want their homes destroyed. The local Party officials disappeared in the
night. Borchert dressed in his best uniform, with all
his decorations, and went out into the raw, late-
March weather to meet the American armored column approaching along the Nierstein road. But the

Americans were not interested in a formal surrender. A sergeant took his Luger for a souvenir. Dis-
missively, the man told Borchert just to wait by the
roadside with his men until the military police came
along. So he sat in the cold for the better part of a
day, at the edge of a muddy vineyard, watching an
endless parade of war machinery go past. His own
"soldiers" slipped away and went home. Then the
military police came by at last, in well-pressed uniforms. And that was the end of his war.

But the camp had been worse than the war. A
humiliation. Nonetheless, he had never compro-
mised his honor. Not in the ways that mattered.
When the difficulties arose with von Tellheim, it had
been his duty to do what had to be done. Other
officers, men of higher rank, should have acted. But
all of them had turned into sheep. Or into collab-
orators. And cowards.

Von Tellheim had broken every code of honor
imaginable. Organizing a ring of thieves the way he
did. The American medical services had been overwhelmed by the squalor of the camp and the ill
health of the inmates, so they had begun to use med-
ically qualified prisoners as trusties, first in the tents
that served as the camp's clinic, then, as the skills of
the prisoners became evident, even in the medical
system that served the Americans. That was where
von Tellheim had seen his opportunity.

The Americans had marvelous new drugs, capable
of curing serious illnesses virtually overnight. But
these were in short supply—or so the Americans
said—and they rarely were expended on German
patients. Von Tellheim, who had no medical attach-
ments of any kind, nonetheless managed to con-

vince the prisoners who served the Americans as
orderlies and medical assistants that it was their duty
to smuggle out the wonderful new American drugs
in order to save their fellow prisoners. Von Tellheim
set himself up as the arbiter of fates, and it soon
became evident that he always had been a traitor to
his class, perhaps even a traitor to his country. He
ignored matters of rank, insisting that the war was
over and they all were equal now—as if he had become a Bolshevik or, perhaps, had always been one
in secret—and he gave no more priority to a sick
colonel than to a sick private. He even encouraged
the lowest-ranking men to address him by his first
name, telling them that all the army's nonsense was
finished. It was unthinkable.

But the issue of theft was worse, by far, than von
Tellheim's social boorishness. German officers did
not steal, not even from their enemies. Officers did
not consort to bribery and corruption, cloaking
themselves in claims of nobility and service. Officers
had to set an example as model prisoners. How else
would they retain their authority in the peace that
lay before them?

Inevitably, the Americans discovered that they
were being robbed. Major quantities of drugs could
not be accounted for. So they began their interro-
gations.

Borchert had already decided to tell the truth
even before the Americans called him in. He didn't
know all of the details, of course, since he had re-
sisted taking any part in the affair, but he knew von
Tellheim was at the center of it. A Communist, obviously. A fifth columnist. An infiltrator. How else
had the man survived the siege of Berlin and made

his way to the West? The sleight of hand with the medicines was obviously no more than a way to win over the lower ranks, to seduce them with Leftist ideas.

He even recalled von Tellheim saying, "If Germany's ever going to pull itself up from the shit again, it won't be thanks to the generals and colonels."

Who but a Communist would talk like that?

And the Americans had become quite interested in Communism since the war's end. They took von Tellheim away immediately. Rumor had it that, after a brief interrogation, the Americans had driven him over the hill to Kirchheimbolanden, where they shot him and buried his corpse in the forest. Rumor also had it that Borchert had been the one who had talked to the Americans.

As a reward for his assistance, the Americans released him with a parole. Borchert took it, since he saw nothing dishonorable in his actions. Or course, those with no sense of honor of their own might not understand why he had informed on von Tellheim, so taking advantage of the release was only sensible. If Germany were to be rebuilt, it would be men like him, not traitors like von Tellheim, who would do it. He, and men like him, *had* to survive. And several of his fellow prisoners had already hinted at threats.

All that was behind him now.

Whatever had or had not happened to von Tellheim did not weigh on Borchert's conscience. Von Tellheim had made his own fate. Borchert had merely upheld the honor of the German officers' corps.

*   *   *

Cologne was a wasteland. The center of the city had been flattened. The devastation was grimmer than anything Borchert had seen, far worse than Berlin the autumn before or even the condition of Frankfurt when last he had passed through. For entire city blocks, not a single wall had been left standing, and the ruins stank of decay and collapsed sewers. Almost half a year after the war's end, not all of the streets had been cleared of rubble. The cathedral's walls remained standing, massive and scorched, but the roof had collapsed and the great windows had been blown to nothing. A treasure of German civilization had been destroyed. Doubtless, the Allies excused the bombing of the cathedral because it stood next to the main train station. But Borchert suspected the destruction had been done on purpose. To punish Germany.

The human beings at work in the rubble looked as beaten down as Russian prisoners. Most worked in silence. Old men wandered about, as if the disappearance of lifelong landmarks had made them lose their way forever. The warren of the old city's streets had become a new labyrinth, one of open air, that confused its former inhabitants.

Once, when Borchert asked his way, a woman in a head scarf answered, "What does it matter where your Graulillienstrasse is? One street's as good as another now."

But Borchert found his way as the afternoon withered. By dark, he was almost there, suddenly cast among streets of pleasant villas, scarred by war only to the extent that their shade trees had been cut down for winter fuel. Children played outdoor games, and cooking smells drifted through the gardens. It seemed miraculous.

Yet, his pace slowed as one street passed into another and the darkness came down. What if she wasn't there? What if a single bomb had fallen here, and that bomb . . . ? What if she had gone off looking for him?

He still had three potatoes in his pocket. They were all his willpower had let him save.

At the last corner, he turned around and began to walk in circles on his ruined feet. Afraid. It seemed to him now that all he wanted in life, all he had ever wanted, was a decent, honorable life with Margarethe. His Gretchen of the red-blond hair.

Yes, his Gretchen. Goethe's good girl. Imbued with the sacrificial power of Woman. In the camp, he had thought, bitterly, of other lines from *Faust*: "He'll eat dust, and like it."

Staub soll er fressen, und mit Lust.

He had eaten dust. But he had not liked it.

Now he only wanted a chance to begin again. With Margarethe. A chance to build their world anew.

She had always understood him. The bloodlines told. Some things could not be taught, only inherited. It seemed to him now that he had never been fighting for some abstract, idealized Fatherland, or even for a real Fatherland of earth, blood, and borders. Margarethe was his Fatherland, his essence, his purpose.

She was all that mattered.

He found himself standing under a weak streetlamp, a few blocks from the villa where Margarethe had to be waiting for him. Unable to move another step.

A mother and daughter hurried across the street, bundled against the cold and coming home late. The little girl pointed at Borchert, and asked, "Mama! Who's that? Why is that man standing in front of our house?"

The mother looked over, first with a hint of panic in her eyes, then with a dismissive expression.

"That's the *Sensenmann,*" she told her daughter in a harried voice. "He carries off bad little girls and never brings them back."

The little girl drew close to her mother, pushing away from Borchert, until the two of them disappeared behind a gate.

Struggling to gather his courage, he walked until midnight struck in a parish steeple. And, somehow, he found himself in front of the house at last.

It looked completely unscarred. A single, faint light glowed deep in the interior. As if he were expected.

He ordered himself to go forward.

The bell didn't work—at least he heard nothing when he tried it—so he knocked. But no one answered.

He tested the door.

It was open.

Borchert let himself into the house, gathering his bearings for a moment before he began to step, quietly, toward the light. He had not been inside the house since a last visit to Margarethe's sister and her husband before the war, a visit he had made only to please his wife. But he remembered the feel of the place now, how the rooms were arranged. The light came from the kitchen, toward the rear of the house. Just beyond that, there was a small maid's apartment, as he recalled. And here, along the hallway, the dining room was to the right, just there, and the library to the left, past the formal sitting room The hall was gloomy, but, toward the end of the passage, there was enough light for him to mark the normalcy of its condition: Paintings still hung on the walls. The furniture remained in place.

It made him want to weep. For the beautiful commonness of it all. But officers did not cry.

The first thing he saw in the kitchen, just beyond the lamp, was a quarter loaf of bread, lying on a breadboard with a knife. A covered butter dish stood beside it.

Then Borchert heard the sounds. He jumped at the first noise, an abjectly human murmur. Coming from the maid's room. Next, he heard the bed.

The maid was up to something. Entertaining visitors. In Margarethe's absence.

He marched into the maid's room.

A lamp burned in that room, too. On the nightstand. A British officer's uniform had been arranged, neatly, over a chair.

Then he saw Margarethe. With her unmistakable red-blond hair. And her pale skin.

The Englishman turned about with a look of annoyance. "Do you mind, old boy? I mean, really. You might wait your turn."

Margarethe said nothing.

Somehow, Borchert pulled the door shut again and made his way as far as the kitchen table. He dropped down in a chair. And sat. Unable even to lift a hand to scratch his ravaged skin. Refusing to hear. Refusing to think.

Refusing.

After perhaps an hour, he heard other sorts of noises. Despite himself. Low, intimate voices, and the rustle of clothing.

The Englishman came out, correcting the line of his mustache.

"Sorry if I was cross, old boy. You understand, of course." The officer tugged his jacket straight under his leather belt. "Anyway, you'll find old Margie's worth the wait."

The officer left, and Borchert closed his eyes. Shocked by the wet, salt taste on his lips, he realized he was crying.

After an eternity or two, he heard lighter footsteps. He opened his eyes and, through a wet blur, saw Margarethe, hair awry, wrapped in a velvet robe.

"Our honor . . . *my* honor . . ." Borchert whispered.

His wife looked at him for a moment, then lit a cigarette. "You can't eat honor," she said.

Borchert didn't close his eyes again. He stared at the floor. He had not known that a man could feel so empty, or so alone. Even in Russia, he had never felt so alone. Not even in the camp. What was left for him? What was left of his world?

His wife put her hand on his shoulder, and the gray morning light came in.

WOLF FLIGHT

JIM DEFELICE

JIM DEFELICE is the author of several techno-thrillers. His latest, *Coyote Bird,* is now available in paperback from Leisure Books. He can be contacted at jdchester@aol.com

Memory changes everything. It adds color and tones, reshapes hues, arranges backgrounds. Much of this is trivial. Whether the sun shone a particular way last June matters to no one, least of all to the man who was there. But memory also undertakes acts of treachery. It confuses action with intent. It makes us into heroes, larger than the life it invents.

And yet, we must remember. Without memory we cannot place ourselves in the world, cannot see the distance we have traveled, nor the places we have left to go. We cannot know if we deserve God's mercy, or must be denied it. So we wrestle with memory, remembering, correcting, remembering again. The stories our memories tell are refined over and over, and so are our selves. If in the end we are left with truth—if it lies at the bottom of the grave like bones after the worms have made off with the flesh—then we will know what God Himself knows, our own souls.

I have struggled with my memory long enough to know I am not a hero, though I knew one once. But this knowledge, like all knowledge, has not been without cost.

As for the hero, memory has taken its toll there, too. I can close my eyes and see his face, but I am no longer sure that what I see is truly his face. I have gained certainty over the years—I believe that he really was a certain height, that his hair really was jet-black and his nose slightly misshapen. But I have learned that certainty is often an illusion, in my case a sweet bribe for growing old.

And so I admit, in my long-winded way, that bits of the story I tell may be wrong. But its bones are as true as my own.

We called them Butcher Birds. And that's what they were—swift, violent birds of prey that flashed from above without warning, singling out the weaker members of our flock. And we were all weaker members in their gunsights. In the late fall and early winter of 1941, the Germans unleashed a new fighter against the British, the Focke Wulf Fw 190. It had a radial engine and could easily outperform the Spitfire V, the most advanced plane in the RAF inventory at the time. In its first encounter with Spitfires, an outnumbered group of Butcher Birds took down three RAF planes without a single loss. The lopsided victories increased as the planes began pouring off the production lines, until by early spring 1942 they threatened to wrest control of the air completely from the RAF, even over southern England. In one typical encounter, a large flight of Fw 190s took on a wing of Spitfires, downing eight and sending five home with serious damage, to no losses of their own.

Mine was among the planes damaged in that encounter. I cannot describe the fear I felt when the first German plane dived on me, for it seems to me now that I wasn't afraid. It seems, as my memory tells it, that I held my position on my leader's tail, protecting him as he pursued a German fighter. Whether that is true or not, today I cannot say. What I do remember clearly, what I feel strongly, is the fear moments later when I was forced by a second Fw 190 to break from my position.

It is no less noble for a fighter pilot to run from an enemy when he is in his sights than it is for him to press home an attack when he is on his opponent's tail. In the swirling swarm of a mass dogfight, such situations constantly present themselves. I was trained to get away, and had done so many times before, dipping down and pulling into a sharp turn, zagging back, easing up on the stick and leveling off to take on another fighter.

Except that day, the bullets continued to cross my wings even after my maneuvers. I flailed left and right, then, with my panic building, I nosed downward into a dive. It was then that my opponent's machine-gun bullets finally struck me. My heart raced; I felt as if a pair of fists were pummeling my temples. I pulled back sharply, hoping that the enemy plane wouldn't be able to change direction quickly enough to destroy me.

It was not the best strategy, and by rights I probably should have had my tail shorn off by my pursuer. But instead the Focke Wulf broke off, and I was able to escape.

I don't know even now why he did that, and didn't then. I have guessed that someone else jumped him, or that he thought I was a goner and went to take someone else. I have guessed that he was caught by surprise. I have even guessed that he ran out of ammunition. But none of the answers is really satisfactory. I know only that he did break off, and that I was able to wrestle my plane back into level flight more or less on the original course.

Two or three hours later, I was in a pub not far from our air station. And it was there that I met Captain Clark Peterson.

"Hey, Yank," he said as I leaned in for a beer. It was not surprising that he knew me, or had a rough idea who I was. I was the only American in the wing, originally a volunteer who had joined the RAF with the help of Canada; strings had been pulled somewhere along the line to allow me to remain while giving me American lieutenant's bars, though I still wore the British uniform.

Peterson also had a reputation. I knew of him vaguely as a man who had been caught with the daughter of some local official, though how important the official or daughter was didn't register. He bought me my drink, then began plumbing for details of the 190. Memory tells me now that we didn't speak long and that what I did say was useless, but the important thing is that somehow we became friends that night.

Somehow.

I can tell you how, or at least why I wanted to be his friend. Peterson was everything I wanted to be. As a pilot, I don't believe he had a peer. He'd shot down more than three dozen planes. He had also lost at least one plane himself; for me and many others, the fact that he had survived the shootdown was in itself an accomplishment.

But it wasn't his skill as a flier that impressed me so much as his confidence and smoothness. And yes, the way he reveled so much in sin—women and booze, specifically. He reeked of both.

My father was a minister; I grew up in the shadow of a small-town church. Truly I believed strongly in God—then, and now as well. But sin, or at least such sins as Peterson seemed to embrace, had an attraction for me. Then, and now as well.

The exact sequence of events over the next few weeks are boring and even a little confusing when laid out, but exactly thirty-six days after my encounter with the Fw 190, I found myself in the hold of a Handley Page H.P. 57 Halifax, a boxy, four-engine bomber that at the time was the mainstay of British Bomber Command. Except that this plane had been detailed to RAF Special Duty Operations, an arm of the Special Operations Executive, to which Peterson and I had recently been attached. The plane carried no bombs; Peterson and I were its only payload. The seven-man crew were under strict orders not to speak to us, and they obeyed those orders perfectly.

The takeoff was routine. We were over the Channel in a matter of minutes. I persuaded myself that I wasn't nervous; I remember, or believe I remember, thinking to myself how incredibly strange it was to be so calm.

There were windows on the side of the fuselage, and as I looked through one I saw an AAA shell cut a triangular hole in the sky, stamping through the blackness to the white words of the universe. In the next moment the plane began to stumble as flak exploded all around us. I thought for sure that we were going in, and I was calm no more.

"They're shooting at us!" I yelled. I lost my balance as the plane shuddered. I grabbed desperately to try to steady myself as the crew door was opened nearby. Peterson grabbed me by the arm, all grins, and helped pull me forward to the door.

"They're shooting at us," I told him.

"Yes," he said. He added something, but it was lost in the roar of the engines and the wind. Then his smile broadened, and he stepped out of the plane.

We'd boarded the plane wearing our jump gear and packs, though when I think back now I remember myself in just my uniform. I see myself standing at the door. I have trouble breaking my grip on the frame; wind buffets my body the way a river pours on rocks at the foot of a massive waterfall. Shells burst outside. I take a step and my knee snaps tight, refusing to budge.

I think anger made me overcome that fear. I was angry at myself—maybe for volunteering, maybe for chickening out, maybe for both. Somehow, I managed to throw myself into the chaotic wind and the dark night.

I forgot what I was supposed to do, forgot to tuck in my legs and curl down my head, forgot even to reach for the ripcord. God reached down and did it for me, pushing my hand against the rimmed handle in the center of my soul. My shoulders flew upward, and as my head jerked back under the spreading canopy, I regained control of myself.

The moon was nearly full. I could see the stone fence of a farmer's field ahead, and for a while I thought I was going to land precisely on the stones. I kicked my legs, then saw a tree close by. Preferring the wall to the tree, I stopped kicking. In the next moment something kicked me hard in the back and I found myself rolling sideways, tangling in my lines.

It was a horrible landing, far worse than any of the dozen or more I'd practiced. My mouth was full of dirt, and I smelled the metallic taint of blood in my nose. But at least I was still alive.

Peterson, laughing, pulled me up.

"Been waiting for you, Yank," he said. "Good jump."

"I didn't jump, I dived. How did you find me?"

He laughed even louder. "Well, I was watching."

"Why were they shooting at us?" I asked. "We're in bloody England, aren't we?"

"I imagine no one told them we were coming," said Peterson. He probably smiled indulgently at my using English slang; he usually did. "Come now. Let's gather your parachute, then ring the commander, shall we?"

The phone we found was in a pub about a half mile up the road. Along the way, I realized that my knee hadn't locked out of fright; I'd banged it in the plane and gashed it somehow.

" 'Only joy, now here you are,' " said Peterson.

I shook my head, not getting the reference.

" 'Fit to hear and easy my care,/ Let my whispering voice obtain/ Sweet reward for sharpest pain.' " Peterson smiled. "Sidney. Sir Philip Sidney."

"Oh."

"Poetry, lad. You really ought to study it. The stout will fix that," he added, pointing at my knee. I nodded and took a sip of my beer.

"You Yanks don't study much at school, do you?"

"Poetry, no."

"The art of seduction," said Peterson. He took my drink and added a shot of Scotch from a flask as part of the prescription, and by the second gulp I had completely forgotten about the cut, my knee, and my momentary hesitation.

The room was empty, except for us. The bartender explained that a German aircraft had attacked nearby and been shot down. All able-bodied men were out searching for the crew.

"Good job, that," said Peterson, hoisting his beer as a salute to the absent pensioners.

Until that night's final orientation, designed to get us—me—used to parachuting in the dark, the mission Peterson had suggested and volunteered for had been—how can I put it? It was like listening to someone else's dream.

We were to steal a Focke Wulf from one of the airfields in France. On the day he met me in the pub, Fighter Command as well as SOE had approved the plan. All that was needed were arrangements with the French Resistance.

And a second man to tag along, a backup and assistant in case things went wrong. Air Chief Marshall Sir Sholto Douglas himself had insisted on it, Peterson told me.

" 'Two heads better than one,' though to my mind he just knows too much about me."

I'm not positive that Peterson knew Douglas, the head of Fighter Command, or vice versa. He could have, and in fact if I had to make a judgment I would say he did. Peterson seemed to know everyone.

Approving the mission had been controversial, but in the end the toll being taken by the Fw 190s made it obvious that something had to be done, even if it were a desperate shot. Selecting Peterson for the mission, on the other hand, made a great deal of sense. For one thing, he'd come up with the idea, and he volunteered. For another, he spoke excellent French and decent German; he'd spent a year in Hamburg as a young man studying classical literature. During the early days of the German blitzkrieg he'd had engine trouble and landed behind the lines in France. He'd managed to slip back to his unit with only a few small tears in his uniform for grief. He may also have had some sort of commando training—he hinted as much, but never said so specifically.

What my qualifications were, I'm not sure. I, too, volunteered, though it seems to me that there would have been no lack of volunteers, even though the mission seemed suicidal when explained by anyone other than Peterson. I'd like to think that my piloting skills had something to do with it, or at least my ability to adapt to different planes quickly—my record *was* good there, though probably a dozen chaps were just as flexible. I did speak, or thought I spoke, French. I had also taken two years of German in high school. Before volunteering to help the British, I had been in the Army and took some Ranger training, which probably looked more impressive in the dossier than it was in real life. I'd made a dozen parachute jumps, but none had been at night.

Peterson liked me, and that, too, probably counted for a lot. But in the end I think I was picked to go, or allowed to go, because no one really had much of a hold on me. As an American I was always the tenth man on a nine-man team, an afterthought who had somehow managed to wander into the locker room and onto the playing field after the sides were chosen. Losing me would matter less to most commanders than losing someone else.

In fairness, the man in charge of the mission, a Colonel Maclean, gave me a way to bow out gracefully the morning after Peterson and I took our jump under fire. Maclean, part of a commando group working with SOE, had his headquarters in an old school building whose upstairs rooms looked as if they'd only just been abandoned by the kiddies for the weekend. We met in one of those rooms that morning to go over some details; our place had already been secured on a bomber due to leave the next night.

A large map of the world hung at the front of the room in place of the blackboard. My eyes wandered to it constantly, searching among the letters and lines for my hometown in northern Pennsylvania. Peterson sat on one of the desks nearby, arms folded, listening with a grin as Maclean talked about recognition codes and the weather. The colonel spent an inordinate amount of time on the weather, perhaps because someone had told him once that pilots liked to hear about it.

"Tomorrow evening, then," he said finally. "Pilot knows, but the rest of the crew won't be informed until just before takeoff. Security. It's a Lancaster, part of a regular flight, not one of ours, so keep it dark, right?"

Instead of answering, Peterson made a joke about receiving six of the best in a room like this. "Six of the best" was a beating. The grammar school teachers apparently used to break their rulers and straps on the pupils' backs.

"Off with you now," Maclean told him. "Lieutenant. A word."

Peterson got to his feet, his manner somehow suggesting swagger while expending a minimum of effort. He wagged a finger at me.

"Naughty, naughty, Preacher Boy," he said.

Maclean said nothing, waiting for Peterson to leave. The colonel had a certain grim efficiency about him, but then a lot of the officers I met in England had the same quality. They said confidently that they would beat Jerry—that was how they often put it—but privately they realized that things might not work out that way. Even if they did, most knew they might not survive the war. I suspect most had been utterly shocked by how quickly the Germans had brushed aside the French. Whatever contempt they held their onetime allies in, to see them so easily and utterly beaten couldn't help but weaken their own confidence.

Before Maclean began to speak he reached into his pocket and pulled out a lighter. He turned it over in his hand a few times, running his fingers along the smooth skin. Then he took a pack of cigarettes from his shirt pocket and offered me one.

"I don't smoke, sir."

"Yes. Quite." He lit the cigarette and took a long pull. He reminded me of a member of the lay council in charge of my father's church, waiting to examine the books.

"This mission has been authorized and approved by all the important men," he said at last.

"Of course," I said, nodding.

"It's a voluntary mission. Strictly voluntary."

He looked at me like he had something else to say. I waited, and when he didn't say anything else, I shrugged.

I think—but this is only looking back through the long telescope and fog of memory—that he did not believe in the mission and wanted to scuttle it if he could. Peterson would have been delayed if I backed out. But maybe the colonel had taken a liking to me and wanted to save me.

Or maybe not. Maybe he thought I was too skittish, or maybe he'd noticed that I'd done poorly in the small-arms trials. Maybe one of the crewmen in the bomber noted that I had frozen. In any event, he said nothing else for nearly a full minute. I glanced over at the door, then back at him, then at the door again. He continued smoking his cigarette. Then, finally, I said something inane like, "The weather will be good, I hope."

He answered with: "We don't order someone to go behind the lines."

"Of course," I said.

"You are liable to be shot if you're captured. You will definitely be shot."

I nodded. Maclean was the first person to say that specifically, though it was obvious enough. I would jump in a flight suit so that it would look as if I'd bailed out of a plane, but after that—and even then, frankly—I expected that any German who found me would kill me as a spy.

After torturing me, naturally. It wasn't exactly something I dwelled on.

"I want you to know, son, if you change your

mind—if you have any reservations, there's no shame in it. There will be other opportunities."

"I won't change my mind."

Maclean narrowed his eyes into a squint, trying one last time to peer into my skull and see what sort of madman I truly was.

"Very well," he said finally. "Dismissed."

I spent the night—well, how would you spend the night?

Sometime the next morning I got up from the barracks—actually another part of the converted school—and went out to get my bike and satisfy a curiosity I'd had since coming to the village a week before. That was how I thought of it—a curiosity. There was a large stone church in the center of town, and I wanted to go inside it. Not, I told myself, to make peace with God or nurse my nostalgia for home; certainly not to make a fleeting connection with my father, whose life's work was so intimately connected with such places. I felt instead that I wanted to see the inside of a real English church, something I hadn't done in the nearly eighteen months since I'd been there. And so I nodded at the sergeants at the gate, and rode on into town.

The churches of my youth were predominantly small, plain affairs. Their interiors were washed by yellow and green hues, and while there were a few fine touches—I remember particularly a handsome rail of intricately carved wood—on the whole there was nothing in the interior to distract the mind from the business at hand.

This church, however, was an English church, Anglican, or Episcopalian on my side of the Atlantic.

The Catholic heritage was obvious, at least to an out-sider. Where the doors of my father's churches were light, this one was ponderously heavy, so slow to give way that at first I thought it must be locked. Inside, the cool dampness of the stones mixed with the lin-gering perfume of incense—or so it seems now in my memory. There were no lights on, but the morn-ing sun streamed through the painted glass windows sufficiently to color the inside an orange-yellow. The apostles stood in all their glory and shame on the glass—Peter denying Christ, Thomas being pushed to touch his wounds.

I sat in the next-to-last pew, soaking it in. My head hurt a bit, despite the aspirin I'd taken, and my stomach had the metal hollowness one feels a few hours after it has been forcefully emptied. I thought of Maclean offering me a way out; I wondered if he had a cure for a hangover.

I also wondered if he knew that I was scared. I was afraid of being afraid then. I didn't have enough experience with it.

Until the year I'd left home my greatest fear was being caught doing something wrong by my father. He didn't beat me, and actually rarely punished me. His lectures were more collections of silences than tirades. And yet his disapproval weighed like iron on my back.

I began to think of him there as I sat in the church. It was not, by any means, the sort of church he would serve in, yet I saw him walking to the lec-tern with his worn red book, his favorite service book, carefully sliding the ribbon back and begin-ning to speak.

A noise from the front startled me. A light came

on—I thought, honestly thought, that through the side door near the altar my father would appear. He did not, of course, only a priest in black garb who talked to himself as he went about his business, inspecting some lights near the side. As I watched him silently I realized he was about my age and build, a short man, not overly athletic, self-absorbed as I often was.

While his calling had perhaps prevented him from joining the military, I realized as I watched him move that there could have been another reason as well. He dragged his right leg slightly, and after he knelt for a short prayer had trouble rising.

He turned and started. His features were similar to mine and for a moment I felt as if I were looking in a mirror.

He nodded.

I nodded back.

"If you'd like something, my son—"

It is always amusing how putting on the collar makes a man instantly older. Many a twenty-year-old minister has called a grandparent "son" or "daughter."

"No," I said.

He smiled and walked toward me.

"Difficult times," he said. "You're an American."

I nodded. I was wearing my RAF uniform, but even one word could give me away, and it had.

"Would you pray with me?" asked the priest.

Why not, I thought. I told him I would and got down on the kneeler. He bowed his head and began the Lord's Prayer. Just as I joined in a car horn beeped outside the church. I knew instantly it was Peterson, and I rose in mid-sentence.

"I'm sorry," I told the priest. He looked up at me, possibly shocked that I would get up in the middle of a prayer. But when you have been praying all your life, one prayer or another is not particularly important, or so I felt at the time. In any event, I had to answer Peterson; it was not in my power to resist.

"I have to go right away. Sorry." I kept repeating the word "sorry" as I left. The bright light outside temporarily blinded me; when I focused, I saw Peterson pulled halfway out of his car through the window, waving at me. Inside his coupe were two women; I could smell their perfume from the church steps.

"Hello, Preacher, knew I'd find you at work. Come, we've got a good six or seven hours yet," he shouted.

We had less than four before we were supposed to report to the airfield, which was a good distance away.

"I have my bike," I said. "And a hangover."

"Leave the bike," he said. "You don't need it now. As for the hangover—"

He slid back into the car, implying that the cure lay inside. Shaking my head, I went to find out.

After we came over the Channel and made landfall, the sky lit with the sweeping arcs of searchlights. The crew had told us to expect this; they'd been on the raid to Lübeck just a few nights before, setting the medieval German city on fire with a bellyful of incendiary bombs. The city had been chosen because so much of it was made of wood. They claimed it was still burning, and if they had pointed to a spot in the distance and said that was it, I would have believed them. The defenses that night seemed far less ferocious, though they would still have a good distance to go after we left. They had told us of the Me 110s, which would "have a good go" at the Lancaster's unprotected belly if they could get into position. The two-engine night fighters, generally vectored to the intercept or making use of the searchlights to pick out targets, would rise up through a formation, attacking planes from below. There was little the Lancasters could do to stop them; unlike the American B-17s, they lacked belly turrets.

Our plane was a specially inviting target, as it was at the very rear and side of the formation, and dropped steadily back to deposit us. The gunners at the rear and top stations turned in their mounts nervously. The crewman helping us looked up from his stopwatch every time one of the turrets rattled.

"Sixty seconds," said the crewman finally, and the nearby door was opened. Wind flew around—in my memory it is a tornado, thundering through the aircraft. I am swirled forward toward the door. I see Peterson grinning in front of me. I hear his words, his laugh. "We're up, Yank!" He laughs. He takes a puff on his cigarette, then, with it still in his mouth, he goes out the door.

I follow. It's much easier than it was over England. It is so easy that I know it was ridiculous to be afraid before. The parachute inflates slowly and I feel no jerk, hardly a pull. I remember this time to look up at the canopy, to make sure that it is full. I descend toward France and think that the parachute feels a lot like a swing under an old oak tree that once stood in my best friend's backyard.

That, at least, is how it is shaped in my memory. I know that as I fell, I could make out a village at the crest of a hill to my right. I was closer to the village than we had intended, but seeing it confirmed that we had been dropped very close to our target area.

The dark shadow of the ground rose to meet me swiftly. I stepped forward with my right foot and rolled, pretty close to the way I had been taught. My small kit had hit first. I gathered it up quickly, even before undoing the parachute lines. Had there been a wind, my doing so would have been a great mistake—I probably would have been blown all the way to Germany. But there was no wind, and the thing I wanted most of all, my Browning, came quickly to my hand. Strapped to my leg was a Colt .32 revolver that the commandos had given me, but it was my Browning I wanted. The gun was big and heavy; it felt more capable of doing damage if I were attacked.

I undid the parachute harness and began folding up the line, telling myself several times to go slow. I was about twenty yards deep in a meadow, hopefully in one of the farms along the road we'd targeted. The Resistance had been watching for us, but I didn't think about them until I got my parachute stowed. I expected Peterson to come up behind me at any moment, just as he had two nights before in England. When he didn't I was glad in a way; it gave me a chance to turn the tables on him.

Since he had gone out first, I guessed he had fallen to the northwest. From our practices I knew he could be as much as a half mile away. I got out the compass and reckoned the direction.

It was at that point, perhaps ten minutes into the mission, that I had to make my first real decision. The plan was to meet up with the Resistance people along the road to the village of Bois Clerc. I thought I had seen the road as I landed and that it was only twenty yards away. If that wasn't the road, it would surely lead to it, as the area for the drop had been chosen partly because there weren't many other roads.

I decided to look for Peterson rather than going to the road. It was probably the wrong decision, but in retrospect I doubt it would have changed much.

Parachute hidden beneath some brush, I set out with my gun in one hand and the signal flashlight in the other. I walked for exactly fifteen minutes, rising over a hill then down to another. The fifteen minutes, I reckoned, took me roughly a mile, though of course it may have been much more or much less. In my memory I walk with measured strides; in reality I probably was close to running. There were woods to my right, and I crossed two streams.

At the end of fifteen minutes, I realized I had gone too far. I also realized that it was very likely Peterson had found the road already and was waiting for me. I started back.

An hour later, I hadn't reached the road or found the spot where I originally landed.

Sometime after that, I found a small rise and sat at the crest, scanning around. There was a farm lane nearby, and what looked to be the roof of a house. I imagined that I could go there and get help simply by knocking on the door. I believed, in fact, that the entire French civilian population hated the Nazis.

Colonel Maclean had said as much. I started toward the house when I heard the noise of a car or a truck in the distance to my right, which by that time was to the south. I could see no headlights—it's possible they were blacked out—but at least now I had a direction.

A band of trees stood at the edge of the field and the road. I worked through them slowly, not because I expected the Germans, but because I thought Peterson might be somewhere nearby. I didn't want to be surprised by him.

He wasn't along the road, which though dirt was well packed and wide enough for two cars. I began walking northeast, which would be the direction of the village. About ten minutes after I started, I heard the noise of a truck coming up from behind me. I crouched behind some rocks—or maybe it was a tree trunk, or a low row of hedges—at the side of the road.

As the truck crested a low rise, the moonlight caught its hulk. It was a German transport.

My mouth probably hung open as it passed. I leaned forward, trying to see in the darkness if there were troops at the rear or if it was empty. Before I could quite focus, something slammed me hard from the side.

I believe the first thing the Frenchman said to me was, "You are a fool, Englishman."

It's not the words that I have questions about— or the sentiment. He might have been speaking for quite some time. The words were in English. The Frenchman called himself *"Loup"* or "Wolf"; later he told me his real name or what I took for his real name, Pierre or something, but it was *Loup* that stayed with me, the Wolf. He had been following me for at least ten minutes, certain that I was the man he was supposed to pick up, yet apparently hesitating because he thought the Germans were already trailing me. The Nazis had several patrols in the area; while these usually didn't amount to much—the Resistance had used this spot for drops several times before—there was always the chance that the raw troops charged with making the searches might get lucky. The troops quartered in Bois Clerc were absolute inferiors; there had never been veterans there, and any troops of any worth in the entire country had been shipped east to attack Russia months ago.

Loup told me all this as I rose to my feet, my head still scrambled by his punch.

So where was my companion, he wanted to know. I had to answer in French, *"Je ne sais pas"* (I don't know), several times before he understood. His accent seemed more British than French to my American ear; my American accent undoubtedly sounded even odder to him and made it difficult for him to understand me much of the time.

We made our way up the road. After we'd gone about a mile, he stopped suddenly, listened, then pushed me to the other side. A minute later, a woman came up driving a horse cart.

Her name was Oriel. It means bird, but the word doesn't begin to describe her any better than I can. To give you an idea of how beautiful she was I would have to cut out part of my brain, implant the cells that hold that vision of her in yours. Only then would you begin to feel what I felt—what I still feel, thinking of her.

There's no way I knew how pretty she was at that moment. From the side of the road I couldn't see her face, probably didn't even see her body. Yet I think of that moment now and I can feel her lips and the soft crush of her breast. I don't see them in my mind—I feel them against my body. I don't remember her, I know her, as if she has only just left the room.

She did something with her wrists that stopped the horses. Then, with barely a turn away, she reached and picked up a rifle, and said in French, "Out!"

"It's one of them," said Loup.

Oriel answered that of course she knew it, but that was no excuse. By that time I had emerged from the tree line at the edge of the roadway, my hands spread at my sides but not raised.

"Where is the other?" she asked.

Loup explained that he did not know. They began discussing what to do; at one point I worried that they were simply going to leave Peterson on his own. That frightened me not because I thought the Germans would find him, but because I thought he would get to the airfield without me.

"We have to look for him," I said.

Oriel turned, and perhaps it was then that I got my first real glimpse of her beauty. Her face was round, far rounder than her sleek body would suggest. Her hair was tied back and curled behind her neck.

I struggled to repeat what I had just said in French, thinking she didn't understand.

"We aren't abandoning your commander," she said in English. "Get in."

I climbed into the cart as they continued to discuss what to do. Finally, they decided to proceed up the road and look for the others who were out searching for us. Loup climbed up and sat next to her. I felt a pang of disappointment, like a high school kid who suddenly discovers the girl he worked up the nerve to talk to is going steady with someone else. But Loup didn't sit that close to her on the bench; they seemed no closer than fellow workers might be. Nor did either of the two men we picked up a short time later seem to have any romantic attachment to her.

They wanted to inspect a field they called black dirt; it apparently had been some sort of a swamp before being drained after the previous war. It lay on the other side of an intersection with a much wider road, and it seemed to me that we were quite a distance from where Peterson would have landed. I kept telling them that, gesturing and trying to sketch out a map in the air. They looked at me as if I were a crazy American, which I suppose wasn't that far wrong.

They tied the horse to a post near the entrance to the field, then sorted themselves into a search pattern to walk across. I stepped up to take a spot at the far right.

And so it was I who found Peterson's body face-down in the field. The moonlight had waned, and I nearly tripped over the back of his leg. I froze for a moment as I recognized the shape of a man. His parachute was still attached, but only to one side of his body.

I knelt near his feet. I should have been much more analytic and careful, but all I could think of was how impossible it was, that Peterson—*Peterson*—would die. I couldn't think of a more impossible thing than his dying.

I pushed at his side, hoping, I guess, that he had been merely knocked out. The body didn't move. I touched it. It must have been cold, but whether it was, whether it gave way or stayed stiff, I honestly don't know; all these memories have occurred to me from time to time, all seemingly real.

Did I turn him over? I think so, but perhaps not. Was he pale? What expression did he have? A smile at the end? A grimace of horror? I don't know for certain; it's possible I didn't know then, as that corner of the field was very dark.

Behind me there were shouts. I stood up, and bullets began flying near me. Instead of throwing myself to the ground or running back in the direction I had come, I began to walk, calmly and slowly, away from Peterson's body, toward the cart. It was a crazy, ridiculous thing, and only if you believe in God or at least predestination can you explain why none of the bullets hit me. At some point, one of the Frenchmen—it may have been Loup—pulled me to the ground with a curse.

"Peterson is dead," I told him.

And then we both got to our feet and began to run.

*   *   *

No matter what anyone ever tells you, the French Lebel was trash as a rifle. I was not an infantryman, of course, and I was hardly an expert shot, but I could tell as soon as I was given the gun in an onion barn the next morning that it was junk. A bolt-action rifle, to my eye it looked closer to the guns used during the American Civil War than a modern rifle such as the M1. But for the French Resistance fighters, it had the serious advantage of being available.

Loup gave me the gun the next day, telling me to be careful and make sure it was a German I was firing at before using it. Most of the people who lived in the area would not protect me from the Germans if I was discovered, he said, but neither would they turn me in. He went into no further detail, and I didn't ask for any.

I spent the day sleeping in the barn behind the horse stall. Built into a shallow hillside, the barn had three floors; I've learned since that it was an unusual arrangement for a French barn, but at the time I couldn't have cared less. Because it was built into a hillside, the bottom two floors opened out onto the ground, though at opposite sides.

The top floor was an open storage area. Whatever vegetables had been kept there were long gone, eaten over the winter as food became scarce. The bottom floor, which connected to the middle by a trapdoor, was a root cellar, with a wall of kegs used for storing apple cider. These, too, were empty. There had been a flood down there sometime before; the dank odor drifted up through the floorboards. The middle floor, where I spent most of my time, housed tools and the horse which had been hitched to the wagon the night before. He was a good sleeper; I swear he snored much of the day.

I sat against the wood of the stall, one foot propped on the wall. I had the rifle under my arm and a blanket over me. I fell in and out of sleep, but none of it was restful. I couldn't fathom how Peterson had died. I could do the mission alone— I knew I could do the mission alone—but not having him there lighting his cigarette and laughing, reaching into his pocket for his flask—how could that possibly be? He was the whole reason I'd come. He was the person I'd wanted to be growing up. He was my vision of a hero, my idea of swagger and authority and courage. And he was gone.

I told myself I should have reached into his pocket and taken the flask when I found him. I told myself I would go back that night and do so. The Frenchmen probably would object—Loup said I should wait in the barn a few days before moving, to make sure that the Germans had stopped searching, before moving on. Neither Loup nor the others knew what my mission was. For their safety as well as mine, I was to tell them as little as was necessary to accomplish it.

Somewhere in the afternoon I began to dream. The dream was a dark jumble that mixed different places and people together. One part had a Sunday service in it—my father stood before the congregation, speaking informally. Peterson was watching from the side, nodding. That surprised me. My father and my friend would not have agreed on much, and I doubt very much that Peterson would have listened approvingly to a sermon. But in the dream he nodded.

I was far in the back, and even though it was a small church, I couldn't hear what my father was saying. I wanted desperately to hear his words, but couldn't. Probably my father wasn't saying any-thing—the point of the dream, if dreams have points, might have been that I simply wanted to hear my father talk. But I kept leaning forward, and fi-nally I began to run toward the front. The rest of the church disappeared. The floorboards fell away, and I found myself back over France, falling in the moonlight.

She caught me. Oriel, I mean. Her hand—cal-lused from farm work—brushed across my cheek, and I landed in her arms.

I opened my eyes, and she was there.

"Easy," she said in English. "You're okay. You've been sleeping."

"You scared me."

She patted my leg indulgently. "I've brought you better clothes. And some dinner. Come, get changed." She stood up. If Peterson had been there—if I'd been Peterson—a few words would un-doubtedly have drawn her to my side. But I had none of his charm, only wished I did.

"There," she said, laughing and pointing as she paused at the doorway. A pair of pants, two sweaters, and some shoes were piled neatly beside the wall.

I changed awkwardly. The pants were a bit short, but the shoes fit perfectly. My automatic was easily hidden beneath the sweaters, and the .32 once again snuggled at my calf. I tied my clothes and boots into a bundle and took them out with me, rifle in hand.

"Don't shoot," she joked. She was standing next to the horse. She'd tossed a rope around its neck; to the rope was tied a kerchief and then another, and finally a sack. "Go leave the gun against the corner beneath the blanket where you slept," she said. "Can you ride?"

"A horse?"

"No, me," she said with a laugh. She led the horse outside.

I'd never ridden a horse before. This one was exceedingly gentle. Oriel threw a blanket over its back, then pulled herself up. She balled the fabric of her dress in such a way that she could move her legs; they were bare to midthigh, and if I hadn't already been beguiled, I surely would have succumbed then.

I climbed on behind her. My heart pounded so hard it must have bounced her back and forth as we started into the field behind the barn, crossing to a small lane that led to an orchard. I knew her leaning against me as we rode wasn't accidental, but I wasn't sure what to do.

I knew what I wanted to do. But desire thickened my throat to the point where I almost couldn't breathe, let alone talk. Even if I could have spoken, I wouldn't have known what to say. She was just too beautiful in that moment.

We stopped and she slid off the horse. I had lost my opportunity. I started down, swinging my leg over the animal's rear—then promptly fell as the horse jittered forward.

She pulled me up and kissed me. Exactly what happened then is lost to me completely. I think—I know—we made love. I know I held her breasts in my hands. I know I lined her hips with my fingers. I know these things in my soul, and no amount of time, no trick of memory, can take them from me or diminish their reality.

For how long? Forever maybe, and for only a moment.

One sharded vision, one moment of feeling comes to me when I think of that afternoon: Oriel, riding against my stomach, white cumulous clouds puffy in the sky above her, beautiful round breasts filling my hands. I close my eyes and see heaven itself, a black, endless space devoid of war and pain. She rides and I feel for a brief moment what God must have felt creating the world—I open my eyes and see whiteness piercing the black, then I see her face, smiling down at me.

I am certain of that; my memory cannot have changed it. And I am certain that at that moment, I loved her, and she loved me.

And yet it was she who betrayed me to the Germans.

Loup stood near the corner of the barn when we returned. He was frowning; I thought again he was Oriel's boyfriend. He said something to her I couldn't catch, and my muscles tensed, ready for a fight. Oriel slid down and began protesting. I jumped down behind her, but as I walked forward I realized they weren't talking about me or what she and I had done in the field.

Loup turned to me and said we had to leave. Now.

She didn't want to. She kept shrugging, and said this was a safe place. They traded the French word, *"sauf,"* back and forth.

And then there was a car coming into the farm-yard.

Two cars.

Loup smacked her across the face. I reared back to punch him, but he ducked, and with his left hand pulled me to the ground. As I rolled up I saw him running and started to chase him.

There were shouts behind me. German words, perhaps some French thrown in. There was no cover in the field, and for the first twenty yards as I ran I knew I would be killed. A trail of dust appeared on my left, tiny puffs as if miniature volcanoes were erupting there. I pushed my body right and some-how found myself running amid the trees.

There was another field beyond. It rose for about twenty yards. When I reached the top I threw myself down, rolling through dirt and rocks into a small stream. I ran across the water and then along its side.

There were more woods ahead. I ran to them. I reached for the Browning in my belt about the same time I got to the trees. I got the pistol out and as I ran it flew from my fingers. I had to stop and pat down the leaves and brush on my hands and knees to find it.

Loup whistled behind me. I followed as he ran through the thicket, then found a path. We crossed another stream, and just as we heard voices in the distance, the Frenchman grabbed a small motorcy-cle from a camouflaged hiding place behind some rocks.

It took forever to start. I sat behind him as he jumped up and down against the kick-lever. My hands had begun to shake; I gripped my pants with my left hand, trying to stop it, and folded my right, which still held the Browning, against my chest.

Dogs—there are dogs in the woods.

Gunfire—probably a burst from a machine pistol. Twenty or thirty yards away, no more.

Thunder.

The engine caught. In the first burst of acceleration Loup nearly toppled us. We pitched back to the right, and my shoulder smacked hard against a tree, but somehow we managed to remain upright. How close the Germans were at that point—if they were Germans at all—I have no idea. My eyes were closed against the dust and dirt and smoke that flew everywhere, and against the likely disaster.

We rode on the motorcycle for maybe ten minutes. Loup drove into a village—I know it wasn't Bois Clerc because the church lacked a real steeple. He parked the bike at the back of a building, then started to run; I followed. There was a truck at the end of the lane, and he jumped into the driver's seat and started it. I'm not sure whether he stole it or it had been placed there for his use; I didn't ask and didn't speak for more than an hour as we drove south, away from my target of course, though I wasn't about to tell him.

All of a sudden he began to laugh. He ducked his head down and turned it toward me and laughed.

I laughed, too. We laughed for a solid five minutes. He nearly ran over a donkey cart blocking the road, jamming the brakes and skidding a hair's width away from the old man trying to push with his back against the wheel. We laughed again.

By nightfall we had abandoned the truck and, starving, stolen some food at gunpoint from a poor man's kitchen. I had some money taped to my stomach and more in my pants and should have left it, but I was selfish, worried that I might need it to get back home. A few francs probably wouldn't have made a difference to me—as it turned out, they would have made no difference at all. To the home-owner, however, they might have bought food for a week or more. It would have been an act of kindness I regret to this day not having made.

Loup told me his real name that night, and something of his past. He had been a captain in the French army and had sneaked back to the Bois Clerc area after briefly escaping to England so he could organize the Resistance. As I listened I thought that he was telling me this as a way of somehow sharing my vulnerability—if he were captured I would be totally dependent on his not giving me away, and now he was similarly tied to me.

I told him the airfield where I had to go, but not what I intended to do there. He grimaced but immediately afterward nodded, and the next afternoon we set out.

We walked the entire way. It took the better part of five days. We would start around two or three o'clock in the afternoon, go until a little past six or so, rest, eat whatever we could find, then set out again, walking until past midnight. Once we slept in a cave formed by large rocks and an old tree, but the rest of the time Loup found barns or abandoned buildings. What sort of relationship he had with the owners I couldn't tell, though I guessed that, unlike the man we had robbed the first night, he at least knew who they were and could count on them not to turn us in. We saw a few patrols—once a black Gestapo car passed us as we walked along the side of the road—but for the most part we passed like ghosts across the countryside. It seemed no more troubling than a vacation tour, or at least seems so now. I can't remember the hunger that must have bit at my stomach, or feel how tired I must have been. The aches that probably came close to paralyzing my legs and the cold that pressed against the sides of my face and made my ears ring—all lost to me. I remember only walking and, as I walked, feeling not only safe but almost invincible.

At times I thought about Peterson. I had a vague notion that I must do things the way he would have. I didn't spend a lot of time thinking about how ridiculous it was that he had died, how worthless that was. As a pilot you see a lot of useless deaths, even during war.

Few deaths aren't useless, war or no war.

One afternoon we walked through a large field as a farmer was struggling with a horse to plow it. Loup pretended not to notice the farmer, and the farmer did the same for us. I thought he looked particularly inept, stumbling quite a bit behind an old horse. I imagined he wasn't really a farmer, or hadn't been until the war. We turned down a lane near the field, pausing as Loup grabbed a satchel near the fence. Inside were some crusts of bread and a small bottle of milk; we ate as we walked.

The lane turned right, but we went left, climbing over a small, rusted metal fence. As we climbed, I heard the drone of airplanes in the distance.

One of the things that made the early Fw 190 so formidable was its engine. I could give you statistics—

the two-row fourteen-cylinder radial BMW developed sixteen hundred horsepower and could pull
the plane to somewhere near four hundred knots,
depending on the load and altitude. Despite some
early problems with overheating, it was a solid, re-
liable motor that had the advantage, like all radials,
of being air-cooled, which meant there was no
radiator to be nicked by ground fire or during a
duel. Despite the fact that the engine literally
weighed a ton and had to be supported by a comparatively heavy airframe, it made the Focke Wulf
one of the fastest planes of its time.

But the statistics can't describe the sound the engine made, something that began like a whine and
turned into a guttural, ground-shaking roar as the
planes passed. If you can imagine a bulldozer in
the sky hurtling at the speed of a bullet, its throttle
buried at the firewall—that would be close to the
sound.

I looked toward the sky, trying to make out the
planes as they shot by to the northeast and began
spiraling upward. Loup finally yelled at me to come
away.

"I'm going to steal one of those planes," I told
him as we walked through the woods. "I'll need a
day or two to watch their routine. And then I'll take
it."

Loup said nothing. Perhaps he had guessed what
I was up to when I told him my destination, or perhaps he had already decided I was crazy. I kept talking; the sight of the planes had unlocked something
in my brain—sense, maybe.

"Most likely, they'll keep one or two of the planes
on the ground when the squadron takes off, as
backup," I explained. "That will be the plane to

take. Or I may just go in when the mechanics warm them up, sneak onto the field, overpower them, and take off. That was the original plan."

I thought of Peterson, and consciously tried to emulate his smile and shrug. "I'll take one of the buggers, no matter what."

Loup remained silent. We walked a short distance to a narrow dirt road, turned down it, and followed to the back of a small brick and tile factory. A highway lay on the other side. I waited in the woods while he went inside; a short time later he came out and led me around to a door at the back. Inside, I changed my clothes and went out into a large room with kilns all along the walls. Only one or two of them seemed to be working; a half dozen men went about their business without taking any notice of me.

The security I'd felt for the past few days left me. Every one of these men could betray me, I thought; every one might be a collaborator as Oriel had been. But I said nothing, keeping my eyes to the floor as I followed Loup to a staircase. We emerged on a balcony overlooking the main level; about half-way down we entered what turned out to be the manager's office. Loup told me I would spend the night there, pointed to the green leather couch in front of the walnut desk, then locked the door behind me with a key.

I didn't sleep. I paced back and forth, I checked and rechecked my guns, I listened to the noises in the factory. I realized how ridiculous and stupid the plan was. Steal a German aircraft? Parachute behind the lines and simply take it? What idiot had approved it?

What idiot had volunteered to do it?

That was the moment when I finally missed Peterson, truly. I didn't blame him for persuading me to come—I blamed him for dying. It was as if he'd abandoned me.

Somewhere during the night, I began to think of Oriel. I felt her body again—in my mind we made love.

Shouldn't I have thought of her as evil? She'd tried to have me killed. She was the worst sort of devil, a classic temptress.

But I thought only of her body. I am ashamed to say that I masturbated to the memory.

And still I couldn't sleep.

I nearly shot Loup with the .32 in the morning. He opened the door wearing a black German military uniform and smiled when he saw the gun in my hand.

The smile reminded me of Peterson.

"Here," he said, bringing in a large parcel from the hall. "Get dressed quickly, and we'll have breakfast."

I found Loup outside, standing in front of a German sedan with a large man who was holding forth on—from what I could tell—the great difficulties of making bricks during a time of war. People did not want even the most utilitarian of bricks, he said. As for his specialty, artistic bricks—*nein*.

He said the one word in German—the rest had been French—and then nearly doubled over laughing.

"The American," said Loup, gesturing toward me. He introduced his companion as Monsieur Renoir, like the painter. Renoir shook my hand, then opened the rear door for me to get in.

Maybe I looked too nervous or anxious—I hadn't slept so I must have looked both—but Loup changed his mind about having breakfast first and told Renoir to go directly to the airfield. Along the way, he explained our cover story. Loup was a major with the SS on special assignment to the Ministry of Information, which intended to put a radio station at the airfield. Renoir, in real life a contractor as well as a brick manufacturer, would look at likely plots of land and act as if sizing them up for construction. I was a French bureaucrat who would keep my mouth completely shut, while trying to get as good an idea of the general layout and location of the planes as possible. I could expect to be ridiculed as a fool by Loup, who called himself Major Rahn—a durable German surname that gave nothing away.

Loup's willingness to help me inspect the base went far beyond his brief, and I was immensely grateful. And yet, I was also fearful—I worried that his aim was not to help me but to betray me, and my heart began pounding wildly as we approached the gate.

But the Frenchman knew his business well. The first guards who met us at the gate seemed dubious until he mentioned Goebbels and produced a letter supposedly signed by the Reich Information Minister. From that moment there was no problem; if anything, the Germans were too cooperative, as two or three officers made it their business to offer to show him around soon after we drove through the gate. Loup deferred to Renoir as the expert on buildings. Renoir insisted he knew his business, but welcomed the men anyway, launching into a long soliloquy on the merits of bricks. We were soon left alone.

We got no closer than a quarter mile to the runway, and the aircraft were kept beyond that, but I was at least able to get a good notion of the general layout. Two things surprised me—one, that the fighters did not have any hangars at all, but instead were dispersed between trees at the edge of a wooded area, and two, while there were troops patrolling the fence, there were none that I could see near the planes themselves. Besides the thirty-odd Fw 190s, there were several Messerschmitt Me 110s on the field.

A small patrol group of two planes prepared and took off as we walked the field looking for a suitable building site. Only two dozen men were involved in getting the planes ready, not including the pilots, but there seemed to be plenty of others in the buildings on the other side of the strip and ramp area. More importantly, the Germans didn't bother preparing a backup plane in case one of the flight had trouble. They did, however, have the mechanics start the aircraft and warm up the engines before the pilots boarded them to fly.

I watched the two Fw 190s taxi across the open field to a cement apron, which they followed around a ramp to the end of the runway. The pilots paused at the end there, canopies open, apparently waiting for clearance before proceeding. It seemed to me that was their most vulnerable point. I could hide there on the ground until they came, then jump on a wing, rush the cockpit, shoot the pilot, toss him out, and take his place.

It was a ridiculous plan. So was the second I came up with, which I told the others as we drove away from the field for breakfast:

A dozen men would sneak in around midmorning when things were quiet, steal the petrol truck, fuel a plane, and take off.

"And then how do we escape?" Loup asked.

"We ram the fuel truck into the fence and set it on fire," I said.

Loup and Renoir laughed.

"You can tell he's an American," said Renoir.

I waited until they stopped laughing and asked Loup what he thought.

"I don't have a dozen men," he told me. "But I will help you as best I can."

"How many do you have?"

"Two or three," he said. It wasn't clear if he was counting himself and Renoir.

I hadn't formulated a better plan the next day, when Loup and I returned to the airfield with three men with surveying equipment. As they pretended to examine sites, I attempted to get a better feel for the operations at the field. They seemed to be timed around the usual approach of RAF patrols in the sector. (The U.S. Army's Eighth Air Force had not yet arrived in England.) At 1 P.M. sharp a crew began to prepare the planes; the mechanics wore black overalls and would swarm on one or two of the planes at a time, bringing them out of their parking area, checking them over, topping off fuel, and arming them. The planes were then started, rechecked, and turned over to the pilots, who lined them up at the edge of the strip to prepare for takeoff. They worked quickly; it was a little past two when the full complement of planes launched.

Soon afterward, Loup gestured that it was time to leave. I wanted to stay to see what happened when the planes came back, but he shook his head firmly. I watched the others pack up, then walked as slowly as I could to the sedan. As I did, a large aircraft made its way onto the runway. It was a three-engine Junkers, a general transport type. I ignored it, but Loup stared at it and waited for it to land and taxi; as a group of officers got out of the passenger area he pulled up a set of binoculars, a very dangerous thing to do.

"Problem?" I asked.

He shrugged and put the car in gear.

Watching the airfield had not inspired me with a new plan. If anything, I was beginning to think the task hopeless. But I couldn't admit that to Loup; instead, I told him I wanted to go back again and stay longer, so I could see whether the planes were refueled and relaunched after their first patrol. They might be more vulnerable then.

I was grasping at straws, but he agreed. This time, Renoir joined us, the idea being that he would suggest building auxiliary buildings for the fighters, which would allow us to get close to them. I wondered, quite frankly, if he didn't think he might be able to make a little money in compensation for the danger he was putting himself in.

I told myself that I wouldn't blame him if he did. He seemed to me the fat-cat type, though he wasn't particularly fat and, in fairness, was taking great risks.

He wore a pinkie ring. That was where the prejudice came from. He owned a factory and wore a pinkie ring—he must be rich.

We took a truck as well as a car to the field. This day, the Nazis were in a bad mood. They did not want us near their aircraft, no matter who had ordered us to find a radio station. A foul-tempered lieutenant met us at the gate and barraged Loup with questions. Finally, he simply waved in the man's face and drove away. For a moment I worried that the man in the truck would be too scared to follow, or that the lieutenant would take out his gun and shoot them, but nothing happened.

Loup decided to push things even further. He drove past the spot we had been looking at yesterday, down the dirt track beyond the runway, and out to the field near the dispersement area. The Focke Wulfs were parked less than ten yards away, with not even a single guard between us and the planes.

Two men with submachine guns came over quickly and demanded we leave. They spoke roughly to Loup even though he was an officer. They did not care for the SS, they said frankly, and if the French shit-eaters did not pack up their equipment quickly, they would all be shot, the major included.

Renoir tried to offer them a bribe, subtly suggesting that they might be thirsty, but the men didn't budge. Fortunately, another officer—I think he was the lieutenant's commander, a captain or *hauptmann*—came over. Loup unloaded his vindictive on him, demanding to see the base commander. Eventually another officer appeared, and Loup and Renoir went with him in Renoir's car to the main buildings. Just as they did so, I saw the crews starting out to prep the airplanes for takeoff.

I would like to say that I realized this was the moment to take the planes, but that I held off because I knew that doing so would leave Loup and his men stranded. I would like to say that I saw how it could be done easily—my small revolver in the one guard's face, his MP38 in my hands, the other guard down, the mechanics sprayed dead in seconds.

But I neither thought of taking off nor talked myself out of it for Loup's sake. I didn't even think of Peterson, who surely would have plunged ahead. The two guards scowled at the workmen and me, pointing their guns and making very unsubtle hints that they would shoot us if given the slightest reason. I kept my hands in my pockets and my eyes generally pitched to the ground. One of the guards said something about us being cowardly pigs, and I felt my face burn red.

Renoir and Loup returned a short time later with the German captain. Renoir had a large cigar in his mouth and he and the German laughed like old friends. In contrast, Loup was clearly worried; his forehead had furled downward and out, so that he looked like one of those dinosaurs with ridged facial armor plates. The German commander, it seemed, had invited everyone to lunch—the crew to mess with the enlisted men, Renoir, Loup, and I with him.

"Moi?" I asked. Loup, playing the role of the disdainful German officer, gave a snort of contempt,

then explained in slow French that yes, dignitaries did not eat with ordinary soldiers.

So we went along to the commander's quarters, which was a large house at the edge of the compound, closer to the perimeter fence than the runway. The parlor floorboards creaked and dipped as we came in, some part of their support obviously missing. Heavy, ornate furniture sat in the hallway; the thick cabinets and finely carved bookcases seemed to have no business there, as the house itself was rather small and modest. A butler—I believe he was French—met us as we came inside and ushered us toward a large, back room filled with upholstered chairs. Fine china lined the mantel, but the walls were badly in need of paint. There were several shadows where paintings had hung for years as the paint around them faded.

Renoir, Loup and I took seats, Renoir continuing his patter, Loup continuing his scowl. I stared at the floor as much as possible.

The base commander and one of his aides soon came down the steps. They strode confidently into the room, the commander snapping out a "Heil Hitler" which Loup returned with gusto. Renoir copied the salute—it seemed to me with a great deal of mockery—and I mumbled one myself. It soon became clear that, though I'd been invited to eat with them, I was a nonperson and would be ignored if I stayed more or less silent, which I did. Renoir expostulated on what could be done to the house if he were allowed a free hand. He then segued into the great difficulty of finding good architects and work crews, compared that to the trouble of locating

good wine. He somehow got the German commander—I wasn't quite sure of his rank—into a discussion of how much one might pay for 1930s
Burgundy or Medoc, should a case or two fall into
his hands. The commander, now smoking one of
Renoir's cigars, fell into the swing of things, ordering his butler to bring some cognac from one of the
cabinets.

It was some time before I realized that Renoir was
in effect telling the commander that he would be
taken care of if the project went ahead. Their discussion of wine was actually a way of haggling over
the size of the bribe.

I wondered again what Peterson would have done
in my position. This would have been his milieu,
surely. But I couldn't decide what persona he would
have taken—Loup's role as the German SS major
working for Goebbels, probably. If he had, he would
have added a bon mot or two about vintages, not
sat there frowning as Loup did.

I began to fantasize about Peterson's being there,
the part he would play. Somewhere along the line
he would mention that he was a pilot; he would ad-
mire the Fw 190. He would ask for a flight. He
would wangle his way into a cockpit, if only to sit
for a while.

And then he would be off.

I could do that. Surely, I could do that.

But how to go from the role of a toad to that
Peterson would play—a confident, cocky man?

He would simply move ahead, fill the space in a
certain way, just be there. I could not.

So how was it that he was the one to die, I
thought. Why him and not me? Without him, the

mission was hopeless—I might as well strike out for the coast immediately.

A dress rustled in the hall, stockings moving against a tight slip and skirt. I looked up and saw Oriel.

Not Oriel, not her at all.

But in the first glimpse of the silk dress as my eyes moved upward, that was whose body I saw. And when the face couldn't sustain the lie—when the face belonged to a blonde not a brunette—still I thought of Oriel. I see her now as I say this, feel her breasts folding against my chest.

The German commander introduced his wife, an elegant woman of thirty, ten or twelve years younger than her husband. She looked at us as if expecting adoration. Renoir promptly swept into a bow and kissed her hand. She glowed. I stared at her, then belatedly nodded.

We moved to the dining room. It seemed to me that the walls narrowed as we walked. I moved through the landscape of someone else's dream—someone's nightmare, perhaps, my fear growing. And yet I was perfectly safe, protected by the utter arrogance of my host. Some fliers were going to join us, he said—two men about my age, one a Captain Schmidt, the other a Lieutenant Weiss, came in as we took our places at a large circular dining table. They, too, were taken with the commander's wife, paying her homage with sharp heel clicks. I moved toward a chair the butler held out for me.

Three other men came to fill out the table. Two wore suits; the third, who came into the room last, was dressed in an *Oberstleutnant's* uniform.

It was Peterson.

*   *   *

I probably did not gag, though undoubtedly my face turned white.

I thought, what a genius he is, to have convinced them he is an officer, a lieutenant colonel.

"Arrest them," said Peterson. "They are spies."

In one of the outrageous versions of this scene that my imagination teases me with, I lunge at Schmidt, pulling him in front of me as I yank out my pistol. I fire two shots. One kills the commander, the other one of the men who came in with Peterson.

I extend my arm to fire at Peterson, but his expression freezes me.

There is firing outside the room, inside the room. A body flies face downward onto the table—Loup, shot by a soldier with a machine pistol.

I grab the commander's wife—Oriel with blond hair instead of brown. I force my way outside. The light blinds me, and something hot pushes into my side. She's cut me with a knife.

Of course, none of that happened, but I don't know exactly what did. Loup, I believe, wasn't shot until the next morning. I wasn't stabbed in the side. It is very likely, very probable, that I did nothing at all to get away. Perhaps I reached for the Browning beneath my shirt, or went to my leg for the revolver, and was struck on the head. It may also be that I simply bowed my head and marched with them to the basement room of a nearby barracks, where I was locked away.

The next morning, one of the men who had been with Peterson interrogated me. He wanted to know why I was there. I said nothing, of course. It was surprisingly easy. The man did not hit me, nor did he threaten me. He paced back and forth in front of me as I sat on a wooden chair in an otherwise empty room. I'd been taken under guard from the basement room where I'd slept and brought there; a guard stood behind me with his pistol unholstered but said absolutely nothing during the interrogation. There were no handcuffs or ropes binding me. After about a half hour of questions the man nodded, and I was taken back downstairs to the room where I'd spent the night. There I sat cross-legged on the floor against the wall. At times, I wondered how I would be killed. I imagined a firing squad, though I thought it might be possible I would be hanged.

Morning turned to afternoon, marked by a small plate of food left at the door by the guard who had brought me to the interrogation. As I stared at the wall I thought of Peterson, and I thought, inevitably, of Oriel.

While I knew that Peterson must be a double agent, part of me hoped that he was deep in disguise, that he had decided to give me up so he could complete the mission. I thought of what had happened in the commander's dining room. I'd done nothing to give Peterson away, said nothing about him. I was convinced that, if anything, my behavior had enhanced his cover story. At best, I'd acted exactly like a spy who should be arrested; at worst, I'd acted like a coward. Either way, it would help him.

I'm not sure why I thought of myself as a coward. I still do. There seems in my mind to be only black-

and-white choices—and a hero would have gone down in a blaze of glory, insisting to be shot. A coward went quietly.

As the afternoon went on I thought of Oriel. The fantasy quickly became elaborate. We rode in an open car along the roads Loup and I had walked to get here. Spring came. The war ended.

It seems odd that, raised by a minister, I didn't think of the Bible for comfort. I've heard of other prisoners reciting verses to themselves, passing time and keeping themselves from despair by recalling the Word. Perhaps if I had been kept longer I would have. Or perhaps in this, too, my memory is mistaken. But it seems to me that the thing I thought of almost entirely as time went on was Oriel.

Somewhere after eight o'clock—I'm guessing because it had turned dark outside—the door swung open and a pair of guards entered. These men were carrying rifles and wore full, heavy coats. They said something in German which I interpreted to mean I should come with them, and so I did.

Outside, there was a large transport-type truck, the kind that could carry a dozen or so men in the open back. The guards gestured for me to climb up; when I did so they followed.

We waited for about fifteen minutes for the driver. We left finally with a single motorcycle for an escort. Obviously, they weren't particularly afraid of me escaping.

As the truck passed the gate to the airfield, I felt relieved. Surely if Peterson was still playing his ruse, as improbable as that might be, my leaving took him out of danger. He could complete the mission. It was absurd, it was pathetic—and yet it was what I thought.

Squatting on my haunches against the low side of the truck, I thought I might be able to escape. The night was fairly dark; the motorcycle escorting us was in the front, not the rear. My hands and legs were still unbound. The German guards were alert, and I was very close to them, but surely the odds were good that I could get over the side before they could shoot.

A fifty-fifty chance to get down to the roadway, then perhaps a twenty percent chance to get to the woods, bad odds, but surely better than the one hundred percent chance of being shot or hanged wherever they were taking me.

I started looking for a chance. One of the German guards had his Gewehr 41 aimed directly at my chest. I stared at it, willing it away. I realized it was an automatic weapon because of the cartridge box below the stock. That meant he would have several quick cracks at me, but now that I had decided what to do I was determined to go on.

Then he moved his aim.

I locked my eyes on the gun. We slowed, then turned, and suddenly he swung the gun away.

I went over the side instantly. For some reason I had expected to hit the ground almost immediately and roll off to the shoulder of the road. But of course the truckbed was well off the pavement and it took forever to hit the ground. When I did it was with the elbow of my left arm, and the pain overwhelmed me. I heard gunfire and cringed and now maybe, maybe at that moment finally, I thought of a prayer—the Lord's Prayer, as the young minister back in England had urged on me.

Then something hot and wet warmed my back, and I realized the truck was on fire. I pushed off the road, dragging my hand and still on my belly. There were screams, and someone pulled me to my feet.

I thought it would be Loup, or one of the men from the brick factory. But instead it was Schmidt, one of the pilots who had been in the commander's dining room. I pulled my right hand back to punch him, when I heard a voice say no. Renoir came from the shadows across the road, waving his hand.

"Run," he said in French. His voice sounded like a flame shooting out an open window. Run, run, run.

And so we ran. There were several men running behind and alongside me, partisans who had engineered my escape. The motorcycle had been blown to pieces by a mine, the truck torched by small gasoline firebombs. A man with a bolt-action rifle appeared in front of me, pushing his arm to the right as if he were directing traffic at the main intersection of a city. I turned and crossed a stream, and on the other side found a clearing where the others were gathering.

Renoir was actually quite fast and beat me to the clearing. He gave orders to the others as I caught my breath. And then he turned to Schmidt and asked why he had come.

The German shrugged. They obviously knew each other; Renoir shook his head and turned to me.

"We can get you to the coast," Renoir told me in his thick English. "It will take time."

"Where's Loup?"

He shook his head. "The commander and others knew me, and since they were taken in by him as well, they believed it when I said I believed his story completely. Or perhaps they only wanted to believe me, since it was so worth their while. But now, I, too, will have to go on."

"I have to steal the plane," I told him.

"It's too dangerous," he said. "No."

Non, non, non. Ne sois pas bête.

No, no, no, it can't be done. Those were his words. And then, *Allez vous en.*

Go away. Except he didn't put it precisely that way.

"I will help you," said Schmidt in English, his voice almost a whisper. "Come with me."

There are men whom you meet for the first time and within a few minutes' conversation, with only a glance really, you know you can trust with your life.

Schmidt was not one of those men. Even if I had not been betrayed by Oriel and Peterson, I would not have trusted him, surely not at first.

He did have answers for my questions, most importantly: *Why did he want to help me?*

Because he was a Jew.

I am ashamed to say that, when he told me, I felt some revulsion. I would not like to admit that I was anti-Semitic then, and yet I did feel something like disdain for him.

See how I qualify it? "Some" revulsion. "Something like" disdain.

Here a man offers to help me accomplish an impossible mission, and I think of him with stereo-typical prejudice.

But at least I was wise enough to accept.

Renoir said he could have nothing more to do with me and let Schmidt take me in his car. We'd driven about a half mile when the German glanced casually in the mirror. He was letting me know we were be-ing followed.

"Who?" I asked.

"Your friend, Renoir," he said in German. When I didn't say anything, he repeated it for me in En-glish, and from then on we spoke entirely in my language.

"Why would be follow us?" I asked.

"He either wants to make sure I don't give him away, or he will have us killed because you're a fool."

"And you're not?" I laughed.

"I'm not a fool. Two days ago, one of my squad-ronmates accused me of being a Jew. It's just a mat-ter of time for me. Jews in Germany—do you know what is happening to them?"

"No."

"They are being moved east. Soon, there will be no Jews in Germany. You don't like Jews," he added, catching me by surprise.

I couldn't answer.

"You don't like Jews. You're an American. A Prot-estant."

"My father is a minister." I folded my arms, once again suspicious. Perhaps this was part of a convo-luted plan to find out whose side Peterson was really on. I thought of everything I had said since the truck had been blown up. What was the best course? To deny I knew him? To say as little as possible? To bolt from the car?

I thought briefly of grabbing Schmidt's pistol from him as he drove. But I hesitated, and soon we were driving down a winding road to a ramshackle farm building.

"Some of the black men use this cottage for trysts. You'll be safe during the day. At night, hide in the woods."

"Black men?"

Schmidt smiled. "The mechanics. They wear black overalls and we call them black men. They won't be interested in you, just the local whores. If you hear someone coming, hide in the woods back there, where you can see the path."

I got out of the car.

"I will be back tomorrow," said Schmidt.

The floor was dirt, and the place smelled of perfume and farm animals. I found a bed in the second room—there were only two—with some reasonably clean bedclothes. I wrapped the blanket around me and went outside. Though it was dark, I found a place not far from the house where I could watch the approach and not be seen, or at least not be easily seen.

How likely was it, I wondered, that Schmidt was a Jew? How likely was it that German mechanics needed to use a dilapidated farm building to screw?

Had the escape been staged? The gunfire and the explosions had certainly killed the guards. I'd seen the truck in flames.

But I'd touched Peterson as well. I had seen he was dead. I'd known he was dead until he appeared in the officer's room.

Had I touched his body?

Was it someone dressed to look like him?

It took more than an hour, but finally Oriel filled my thoughts. I remained cold and awake, propped up against a tree trunk, but gradually my fear if not my doubts subsided.

Schmidt did not return the next day. Around noon I began to get restless as well as hungry. I began to explore the area, very cautiously at first, gradually getting bolder. The woods directly behind the building seemed to go on for miles. I walked to the west, going about a quarter mile until I saw a freshly plowed field. I walked along the edge, but could find no house or any sort of building connected to it; I couldn't even see the road that a tractor or farm truck would take to reach it. It seemed bizarre, a field plowed into the middle of the woods.

My hunger had grown to the point where I actually considered stripping bark off some of the trees. Certainly if there had been leaves out, I would have sampled some. Instead I went back to the building where Schmidt had left me and looked inside it to see if there might be some food somewhere.

The first room had a door to a cellar on the right immediately past the main entrance. A third of the stairs were missing. I tripped over the next to last, falling into a shallow pool of water. The elbow that I had hurt the night before screamed with pain; I cursed out loud, and pounded my fist into the water, splashing myself with the muck.

I cursed again, then heard the car outside.

Schmidt?

I froze, unsure whether to go up the stairs or stay there. I heard voices—a woman's in French, a man's in German. It wasn't Schmidt.

They made love twice while I listened below, curled behind the steps. There were wide spaces beneath some of the floorboards in the second room, and light filtered through, light and shadows. The woman was a screamer, and she came several times while the German plodded away at her. Each time she screamed I moved a half step away from the stairs, deeper into the shadows.

I can think of no worse torture than having to listen to another man make love to a woman.

One worse—had the woman been Oriel. But then I wouldn't have listened. Then I would have rushed up the steps and killed him. I would have broken his neck with my bare hands, thrown him down into the muck where I'd kept myself hidden, then taken his place. I would have made love to her for hours and days, plunging again and again as she screamed, as she held my hair, as her teeth edged into my shoulder until they drew blood.

When they finally left, I was so exhausted and tired I went upstairs and collapsed on their bed. The smell of their sweat and juices nearly made me retch. Yet I fell asleep and dreamed I was back home, sitting in church, listening to my father preach.

Except that it wasn't my father, it was Peterson, whose lesson for the day was love thy neighbor.

A car on the gravel woke me. I got out of the house just barely in time to avoid being seen.

*   *   *

Schmidt returned the next morning. He got out of his car, whistled loudly three times, then walked into the house. It was no later than six. Stiff, I pulled myself up by clinging to the tree I'd slept next to. I walked into the building like a man with rusted metal legs.

"I have food for you," said Schmidt. "Eat it. And then I have news. News."

Now, I told myself, was the time to throw him down. I could kill him, take the car—and what?

Escape. Forget the plane. I had been briefed on the roads to take back to the coast; surely I could find my way. I could meet the boat sent to meet our collapsible canoe.

I wolfed down the two loaves of bread he brought without even pausing for a breath. Now, I thought, now I'll do it. But my legs and arms were still stiff.

"You look like a wolf," he said, laughing.

There was a bottle of water in the basket. I picked it up and began to chug it. I got about halfway through before I realized it wasn't water at all; it was wine.

"It was all I could find," he said.

I kept drinking.

"There is another plane coming this afternoon, an experimental plane. It will provide a diversion. We can take the fighters then," he said.

"We?"

"I'm coming with you to England. That's the arrangement."

"Whose arrangement?"

"My arrangement. You and I will steal the planes, one apiece. We'll fly to England."

The idea froze my brain, and I couldn't react. I barely moved for the next hour as he described the procedures the flight crews would take, told me how to time my approach so that the oil in the engine would be sufficiently warm for takeoff, but the pilots wouldn't have appeared yet. He was second-in-command of the squadron and would arrange everything. The leathers, helmet, and bright life vest were in the back of the car.

He told me I would have to be careful about getting onto the base since the commander and several of the officers would remember my face. And, of course, the guards would remember me. On the other hand, no one knew that I had been rescued; the truck and its escorts weren't due back for several more days from Paris.

A good thing, he said, that I was not considered an important enough prisoner to be taken to Germany. He laughed, as if that were the funniest joke in the world.

If I wore the pilot's gear and stayed away from the crewmen, I'd never be challenged, certainly not when everyone else was paying attention to the experimental plane. Two aircraft would be ready to fly as escorts. Schmidt would arrive, yell to me, and we would be off. A *Wort* would help me with my parachute.

A *Wort?*

A crewman, a black man, said Schmidt. He would make it seem as if I were a guest, part of the entourage that had accompanied the test plane to the base. It would be easy; all was arranged.

It sounded like a crazy plan. Obviously, he was setting me up.

"How do I get past the fence?" I asked.

"You'll have to kill one of the guards at the perimeter," he said. "It's the easiest way. Guards can scan the entire fence line, every other post has two men. But there are no telephones or radios. The small post at the northeast corner is one of six with only one man, and it's the most isolated of them all. So if you caught the man patrolling there, you could get in."

Ridiculous.

Schmidt began asking me questions about what I was supposed to do over the Channel, where I was to land. I lied and said that there were no specific plans, that he should follow me once we were in the air. I simply didn't trust him.

He nodded.

"You'll find a road two miles due north through the woods," he said. "Take it to the east. In a mile or two it will intersect with the road that runs along the southern side of the field. You'll have to get your bearings once you're there."

He went to the car and came back with the pilot's gear and a leather briefcase. He opened the briefcase and pulled out a Luger.

"Not mine." He smiled, handing it over. "I will see you at the airfield at three. Remember, say no more than a word at a time. And the commander knows you, and the guards at the gate. And Peterson, of course."

Peterson. Of course.

Some people draw a sharp distinction between what happens to the body and what becomes of the soul. I have never believed that there is an absolute sep-

aration. It's my heritage, I suppose; you can't grow
up listening to a Presbyterian minister practice his
sermons day after day and not think that what happens to you on the way to the druggist isn't a direct
result of God's desire.

I put on the clothes Schmidt had brought with a
sense of inevitable doom and set out. At first I wasn't
particularly careful about the noise I made or even
my direction. But then I began thinking of the
Focke Wulf, and what it would be like to fly it. The
intelligence people had given us ideas about it—
they were only guesses, of course, since the whole
reason for our mission was the fact that the plane
was essentially unknown. One compared it to the P-
40 Curtiss. I'd flown a Warhawk twice, and knew
from my encounter with the Fw 190s it was not a
very apt comparison. The British had also given me
several hours in a captured Bf 109, one of several
that had been used to develop adversary tactics the
year before. I knew this wasn't a particularly good
parallel either, though I hoped the instrument layout would be somewhat similar. The 109 was a tight
aircraft, even compared to the Spitfire, itself a bit of
squeeze. I imagined the 190 would be immense. I
imagined it would jump off the runway. I imagined
shooting over the Channel in mere seconds, met by
a pair of Hurricanes, who would realize who I was
and dip their wings. I'd land, and be a hero.

By the time I found the dirt road the sun had
climbed almost directly overhead. I could hear airplanes in the distance, and every so often I thought
I heard a truck or car coming. With the jacket, helmet, and vest tucked in my arm, I decided it was
better simply to walk along the side of the road than

scamper off to hide. No Frenchman would bother me, and I would just wave off any German who stopped. Whether it was a good idea or not was never tested, as the sounds I heard or thought I heard never materialized.

My anxiety returned as I reached the perimeter road. There was a shallow wash on the other side; at the top sat the fence to the airfield. Unsure exactly where I was, I walked first east, then west, a hundred or so paces. Still unsure, I walked a little farther in each direction, my heart pounding like the bit in a steam drill breaking through pavement. The day's heat seemed to build with every step. My arms and back were wet. Afraid someone would see me wandering on the road, I retreated back to the woods.

I'd just reached it when an airplane roared off the field. Its shadow came over the road about two hundred yards to the left of where I was. Finally, I could picture where I was. I mapped the base in my head, then started down the road again to my right, putting my hands in my pockets as if I were nonchalantly out for a Sunday stroll.

The guardpost sat above a slight bend in the road, giving it a decent view of both directions. It wasn't much of a post—there were a few sandbags for protection on the roadside, and just behind them a set of boards made a low-slung weather break. I could see a machine-gun mount, or at least something that looked like one, but there was no machine gun.

The guard stood a few feet behind the sandbags. His rifle was slung over his shoulder, and he was facing the airfield.

If it had been night, it would have been child's

play to get past him, or close enough to kill him. But during the day anyone crossing the road or coming up the incline would be in full view. His post was directly behind the fence; there was another fence beyond him, though I couldn't see it from where I was. Beyond the fence were a few trees, and then an open field to the area where the planes were stationed.

So this was the problem: a hundred yards of open terrain, culminating in a rock-strewn slope that would be hard to climb silently. Get past that, and I'd have to climb the fence before I could reach the guard.

I realized I hadn't decided how to kill him. If I used the pistol, surely it would be heard. But I had no knife, and the idea of taking him on with my bare hands wasn't realistic.

I'm not sure how long I squatted there. In my memory, it's a long time filled with wild plans of turning sticks into sharp, javelin-like weapons. More than likely, though, I was only there for a few minutes, long enough to watch him begin to wander around. I realized that the slope to my left, just around the bend, would be out of his sight unless he went in front of the sandbags. He seemed too bored to do that. I waited for him to turn around and look toward the woods. Instead, he walked in the opposite direction, toward the airfield.

I took a breath, and from that point on I stopped considering things. I simply moved, running across the road, then throwing myself down against the slope. My shoulder hit a sharp rock, but I ignored it, edging up as quietly as I could, watching the post. I took the Luger out of my belt; it felt so oily in my hand at first that it almost slipped. Then I began sliding upward along the slope, moving slightly backward to keep the crest of the sandbags just barely in view.

About halfway up, I saw a hole under the fence just to my right. The dirt was well worn there. I could crawl underneath, then have a clear run at the sentry, as long as he stayed away from the side of the slope.

I would hit him at the back of the head with the pistol. Once he was down, I'd just keep hitting him until he was dead.

And if I didn't kill him—if I didn't kill him I wouldn't much worry about what came next.

My legs trembled as I rose. I took a step—and the German guard appeared in front of the hole, no more than four feet from me.

He had a smirk on his face. Eight 9mm parabellum slugs erased it.

It was only after I'd emptied the magazine that I realized I couldn't hear. An aircraft had chosen that moment to thunder off the runway. It wasn't an Fw 190. I'm not sure what it was. It sounded closer to a diesel locomotive than an aircraft. It sounded like God's angels sweeping out from hell after vanquishing Satan.

I leaped onto the fence and jumped over. A pair of Fw 190s were just leaving the runway, following whatever had made the thunderous noise. I paid no attention; I saw nothing except the guard whom I'd just shot.

He was shorter than I, but at least thirty pounds heavier. Blood soaked his uniform shirt and jacket, but it appeared that only three of my bullets had hit him. One had gone square in the chest, another near the lapel.

The last hit square at his throat, hollowing it out. I pulled the man's body to the sandbags, then turned his face toward the ground so I wouldn't see his tongue, hanging out.

As I rose, I heard a car coming on the road beyond the inner fence. I ran quickly to pick up the soldier's gun. The car kept coming; it was open, some sort of convertible, a staff car or something of that sort, dully gray.

I drew the gun up to fire, then I saw that the driver was Schmidt.

He had someone with him. A woman.

Oriel.

Oriel, the beautiful demon. So it really was a trap.

I shouldered the gun. As I lined up the rifle I realized it wasn't Oriel at all, but the squadron commander's wife.

Schmidt pulled alongside the fence. I put down the gun and waited as he jumped from the car and ran over.

"What?" I asked.

"A change in plans," he said. "I'm going to steal the Messerschmitt."

"There are plenty of 109s. The RAF has plenty," I told him.

"No. The jet. I'm going to fly it."

In my memory, the Messerschmitt chooses this precise moment to pass overhead. It looks gray, and with its long, curved, empty nose the fuselage looks more like a shark than an airplane. Two long, cut-

off cigars hang down from its wings, which are thin,
almost narrow. It moves with a loud rush across the
sky.

I see it perfectly, but it seems to me too conven-
ient, and, besides, I did not yet know what plane
Schmidt was talking about.

"What about me?" I asked.

"Take the plane as planned. Choose your moment the way I said."

"But when?"

He'd already started back to the car. I waited until
he had driven away before I put down the gun and
climbed over the fence. When I got over, I realized
the Luger was empty and that I'd left the rifle behind. But instead of going back I turned and began
walking toward the dispersion area.

Two Focke Wulfs sat close to the concrete. Two
men were working on one; another man sat on the
wing of a second. They weren't paying any attention
to me. There weren't any pilots, either. The planes
seemed to have been refueled, but their engines for
some reason were not running.

It must have been then that I actually saw the
plane. The three men near the Focke Wulfs stopped
and stared at it as it landed.

I know now that it was an Me 262, the Messerschmitt jet fighter. The plane would remain in development for two more years, undergoing various
changes and improvements, but from what I saw on
the field that afternoon it was already an impressive
machine, far, far beyond anything we had in the air
ourselves. I've heard in fact that the plane could
have been operational later that year, except that

Hitler decided it should be a bomber instead of the fighter it was built to be.

The fool.

You could tell from the sound of it that it was fast. It came onto the long runway at a very good clip, and I imagine the pilot had to stand on his brakes to bring himself to a stop. The runway there was extremely long, which may have been why it had come. Even so, it took most of the length to stop, the tail wavering before finally settling down.

I envied Schmidt. I wanted to fly it. I stood and watched as the mechanics and a group of spectators ran to it. Two Focke Wulfs that had been escorting it landed; the crewmen who had been on the other planes went and began prepping them, but otherwise all eyes were on the jet. A fuel truck backed gingerly toward the plane, flanked by ten or twelve men. Many others milled nearby, craning their necks and bending to get a good view.

They were obviously going to run it back up into the sky as soon as they could. Which meant I had to be ready as well.

"An odd horse," said someone in German. It was one of the ground crew who'd been working on the Fw 190s. I grunted back in reply.

"We'll be servicing them in London, soon," said the German.

I laughed.

He asked for a cigarette. I shrugged and shook my head apologetically. He moved on.

At that moment, I felt as if God were protecting me. God wanted me to succeed. Truly, there was no other answer for my being here, or for the man neglecting to question me. I was going to succeed.

Cars crisscrossed back and forth near the Messerschmitt. I noticed two troop trucks parked nearby, and German soldiers were lined in a tight picket on two sides facing the fence.

By contrast, the Focke Wulfs were completely open and unguarded. All I had to do was wait for the crewmen to start one, then jump them.

But I had no weapon.

There was a toolbox nearby. I walked to it, glanced to make sure no one was looking, then scooped down to open the kit. My head is racing and I barely hear the car coming up behind me.

I have a pistol in my hand when the car stops. I can see it very clearly. It's an odd little thing, a Mauser M712, which has a square box magazine in front of the trigger. It's twelve inches long, about three pounds. There is a small lever switch on the left side of the gun, that at first I mistake for the safety, sliding it forward. The barrel hangs down awkwardly from my hand, the gun pitching forward because of its design. Finally, I realize the safety is at the back; I can't quite get it off with just my thumb, though, and must use two hands.

Where did the gun come from? Most likely from the toolbox. But as often as I try, I can't see it there, or remember precisely how it came into my hand. I only remember that I heard the car coming up suddenly, and I shoved my hand into my pocket, trying to hide the gun. The thick magazine hung up, and I stood with my palm against the back of it, half-sticking out from my clothes.

*   *   *

One pilot was in the sedan, dressed in flight gear. I watched the car stop. I thought it would be Schmidt, come once more with a change of plans because there were too many people near the jet. I could feel my heart pounding even harder, ready.

But it wasn't Schmidt. It was Peterson. We stood about eight feet apart, looking at each other in shock for a minute.

Then Peterson broke into his grin.

"Well, are you ready?" he asked.

I didn't know what to say.

"Come on. You take the plane on the right. I'll take the left."

He started for the Focke Wulf.

He must have seen the gun—it was hanging half-way out of my pocket. But he didn't say anything to the ground crew; they seemed to be waiting for him, and stepped back and saluted.

Another car started across the field behind me. A truck, too.

I started to run. I took the pistol out, staring at the back of it to make sure the safety was off. One of the ground crew tried to tackle me from the side, but he was easy to duck. I ran ten yards to the second plane, where a mechanic was just turning on the wing. I pressed the trigger of the gun. The muzzle flew up as I fired, but the bullet struck the German at the left side of the chest and he spun slightly, rolling onto the wing. With a leap I was at the cockpit.

Peterson, Schmidt, the man on the wing—they seem to vanish somehow. I hit the starter twice, three times, yanking at the lever that spins the engine even though it's already running. The fact that it's running doesn't sink in.

There's a screech at the side of my head. The man I shot claws his way up over the front of the plane, trying to grab on to the frame of the canopy and pull himself in. The throttle jumps in my hand—I can't get the engine to rev properly, and the plane shudders crazily. Then something in the motor seems to catch, and wind rushes across my face. The German throws himself down on me. My first thought is to go on ignoring him. I move the throttle to full but at first the plane remains in place, its wheel chocked, and perhaps I've left the brakes on.

The German punches the side of my face. I fall to the side, and at the same time, the plane jerks forward. I flail back at him, punching with all my might though I can't get much leverage—the plane's cockpit is actually extremely narrow, much tighter than I expected. I see the German's face, hatred welling up. I take another swing, and instead of hitting him I smash my hand on the metal spar holding the cockpit glass. Blood spurts out—it looks as if it comes from the metal, not my hand.

We're already moving, bumping along almost sideways toward the trees. I grab the stick and jerk the plane in the direction of the runway. I can't see forward very well—it was about as bad as looking out the front of a Spitfire.

Trim for takeoff. Schmidt told me I needed fifteen degrees on the flap and to keep the control column back or I'd start swinging wildly. I move in slow motion. The man on the wing is still draped over me, trying to grab the gear. I can see the compass on the instrument panel, but that's all I can see. The plane suddenly stops bumping, and I push the stick hard right, trying to steer onto the runway but I'm too late. The plane starts twisting, and there's a sharp pain in my left ear, then another, then something at my neck. The German is biting me, and, finally, I take my hands off the stick and with everything I have I punch him. I'm tired and drained and wondering where God has gone, and I pound him, I pound him as hard as I've pounded anything in my life.

The pain in my neck crumbles, and I'm on the runway headed in the wrong direction. A soldier fires at me. A bullet smashes through the armored glass at the side—it looks more like a bee than a bullet, wiggling through a spider's web.

The engine has steadied. I'm on the runway now. I'm starting, and I still can't see but it's sweet, oh so very sweet, and now I'm in the sky, climbing steadily.

A crank mechanism at the side closed the canopy. I couldn't get it to work. I must have fumbled with it for a good five minutes, perhaps even more. I didn't trim the wheels or check the instruments or even properly set my course—I fumbled with the crank, trying to get the cockpit snugged.

When it finally closed, I leaned back against the seat. For the first time, I checked the sky to get my bearings and see if I was being pursued. The Fw 190 had a good, high position for the pilot, much better than any other aircraft I'd flown. There was nothing behind me.

Another airplane flew about three or four thousand feet above me about a half mile ahead.

Peterson?

I nudged my stick back, climbing and angling slightly to get into an offset trail. I began checking the instruments. I had a full load of fuel. I'd made it. I'd pulled off the impossible.

I warned myself that there was still a long way to go. The Channel was a good thirty minutes to the north.

I'd practiced a lot with the radio of a Bf 109. This one seemed almost exactly the same as the unit I'd worked in England, but there was one problem—I didn't have a headset.

Peterson would.

Peterson. Thank God he found me.

When I look back, it seems odd that I accepted him so easily. I wasn't mad at him for giving me and Loup away. I might have rationalized that he had done so to save the mission, not himself. But I didn't. I didn't think about it at all. I didn't think about Schmidt or the jet either. I was too busy flying the unfamiliar plane.

Peterson climbed to about fifteen thousand feet. I remained a little lower than he, trailing off his right wing. Soon he began tacking westward, roughly in the direction of Dieppe. As I started to follow I spotted a group of fighters directly on the new course, flying at about twenty thousand feet, a good distance away. I thought they were RAF fighters on a sweep, or maybe escorting a reconnaissance flight, but as I watched them coming on I realized the planes had to be Germans. There were a dozen of them, a full squadron or *Jagdstaffel,* all Bf 109s.

More than likely, they'd ignore us, I thought. But if they didn't?

I checked the gun panel. I was ready to fire, if I had to.

Twelve on two, even in planes as disproportionately matched as these, were not very good odds. But they were survivable. Our best bet ultimately would be to blow right past, just run through the gamut and go for it—the Messerschmitts couldn't hope to keep up. I hoped Peterson was saying something to them, pretending to be German so they wouldn't bother us.

As soon as I saw the first plane at the far right begin to bank, I realized they were setting up an attack. I slammed my hand on the throttle and pulled the stick back—my aim was to take away some of the height advantage the first section of fighters would have, powering past the heads-on attack, then swerving as the other fighters came in from behind.

Peterson remained straight and level. Confused, I hesitated, then started to ease back on the stick so I wouldn't overfly him, sliding back into a wing position. As I reached to throttle back I saw the Messerschmitts breaking into what was clearly an attack mode—three elements, one on each flank, one head-on.

I held my wing position, wondering what Peterson was going to do. I had one hand on the throttle, ready to jump when he accelerated.

His left wing tipped and he dived toward the west. Of all the possible maneuvers, it was the one that made the least sense, or so it seemed to me—the Messerschmitts were still a good way off, and this would only give the squadron more time to flail at us. But I followed anyway, instinctually trusting my flight leader as I'd been trained. As I passed through ten thousand feet, the first pair of Messerschmitts began a front-quarter attack; they were at too great a distance and angle to pose a real danger, but the sight of their streaking noses rattled me. A little shock of fear grew in my throat; my shoulders felt heavy, and I started to yell at Peterson, demanding to know what the hell he was doing. As if in answer the gray rain of machine-gun fire from a Messerschmitt laced the air before me—a German had somehow managed to dive on my tail. I flailed right, but then came back quickly, Peterson now moving into the left quadrant of my cockpit glass. The gunfire was gone.

I craned my neck to find my pursuer, expecting him either to be behind me or, more likely, closing on Peterson. But he'd disappeared; I finally saw a plane recovering off to my right and figured it was probably the Messerschmitt.

Somewhere around here, I lose Peterson. I have a memory of him well off to my left, then he's gone. The sky around me is clear momentarily, then I have another Bf 109 in my face. Its wing guns are bright red, bullets flaring out in dark lines across the sky. I bring my nose up and for the first time fire my cannon.

If memory were something kind, I would see the plane blowing apart, exploded by the 20mm shells from my guns. But I remember clearly that my bullets missed. I can see them trailing downward and off to the left, far from the path of the oncoming fighter.

It takes me a few moments before I can reorient myself, before I can stop the compass from sliding south. Two more Messerschmitts take up the attack, this time on my tail. Their tracers bloom over my wings, and for a good twenty seconds I think I am doomed. Jittering to the right and left, I somehow duck the bullets. The Focke Wulf's engine finally drives me beyond them, and I'm in the clear.

Peterson is gone. Pushing up in the seat, I scan backward and forward, trying to find him and orient myself. There are two separate groups of planes to the southeast; they're climbing, not attacking, and they're far enough away that they won't be able to catch me. But I can't find Peterson at all. As I climb through fifteen thousand feet, I realize there's a pair of Me 109s at twelve thousand feet flying ahead of me, roughly three miles away.

I gun my engine and move to attack.

I was not being overly foolish. For one thing, if I had kept on my course the Messerschmitts would inevitably have seen me and launched their own attack. Striking them first kept surprise on my side.

I didn't stop to reason it out, though. I simply fell into the attack. The Messerschmitt closest to me was about a thousand feet higher than the other, and not quite parallel. As I came on I raked his right wing; it seemed to bubble as he turned toward my path. I let go of the trigger and pushed the stick hard to the left, the whole plane angling on its axis as I tried to pull the second Messerschmitt into my sights. But the pilot, who'd probably been the element leader and therefore more experienced than his wingman, turned his nose into my direction and

I lost the shot. The Fw 190 flailed as I started to turn with him, then realizing that would be a mistake broke hard in my original direction. The Focke Wulf, which had been so easy to fly until then, took my excitement very badly; the plane bucked and nearly pushed herself over into a spin.

My head jumbled, disconnected from my body. If the German fighters had been more powerful or better handled, they would have nailed me then. As it was the leader managed a pass from almost directly overhead, and probably the only thing that saved me was my utter confusion—I pushed the plane into a fierce dive with both hands. The Messerschmitt flew past without landing a shot.

Sweat pouring from my body, I recovered and found I was clear. My arms slumped. The muscles at the bottom of my neck and top of my shoulders stung.

But I could see water ahead. I wanted it to be the Channel so badly that I was afraid to decide it really was.

I had no idea where exactly I was anymore, but at that point I didn't care. There would be plenty of places to land, plenty of airfields from Manston over to Needs Oar. I was so anxious now that I let down the landing gear, one of the signs we'd agreed on to signal RAF interceptors that we were on their side.

As the gear trundled into place and my airspeed dropped, a typhoon exploded over my right wing. A black funnel whipped downward, and it was only the sudden deceleration of the plane that saved me from being hit as an Fw 190 crossed over my path.

As it arced back I saw the fuselage markings and realized it was Peterson.

I rocked my wings as he banked, trying to get him to realize it was me, thinking for some reason that he thought I was a *real* German in a *real* plane, not his wingman trying to complete the mission. He came at me hard, guns blazing. As the cannons lit, I shoved my aircraft hard left, ducking into a lopsided roll that nearly tore the gear off before I managed to regain control.

How did I know it was Peterson?

I can't recall the markings on the plane. I doubt very much that I had seen them before taking off or later in the sky. Logically, we both would have been moving too fast for me to get a good glimpse of them when he opened fire.

One Focke Wulf to me would be the same as any other. But I know it was him. That I know. That I know.

I leveled off at four or five thousand feet and immediately tried pulling the landing gear back up. But it had locked into position and wouldn't budge.

When I think of this part of the flight, I remember myself sinking into the seat, pulled down by the weight of my despair. The plane grows around me, the instrument panel towering above me. Black diamonds appear, crisscrossing in front of my wing. Something taps the backplate of my seat, rapping against the thick armor there. A white shroud seems to hover above the gunsight mechanism.

And then the Fw 190 streaks over my wing and

sails to the right. I stare at it, completely in awe, wondering why God has chosen to save me, and how.

In the corner of my eye, there is a gray blur. I turn the plane to the east, and as I do I see that Peterson is being attacked by a strange aircraft moving faster than any I've ever seen. Its shark nose closes in on the tail of the Focke Wulf. Peterson turns hard to the east, ducking his wing, but it is too late—the Messerschmitt 262 collides with his midsection and the entire sky becomes a brilliant red flame.

I'm sure Schmidt was the pilot. No one else would have deliberately flown the aircraft into an Fw 190, even if they thought it was escaping to the enemy. The Messerschmitt would have been too valuable.

And besides, few men are brave enough to kill themselves that way. I could never have done so.

For the next fifteen minutes, I flew directly north, reaching the water, making land. A pair of Hurricanes came out to meet me less than a half mile from the English shore. They acted immediately as if they knew who I was, though I found out later that in fact my mission had been for all intents and purposes forgotten. We put down at New Romney— I try to recall the landing, which cost me a broken arm, a sprained knee, and a smashed head, but I can't. The right landing gear collapsed, but whether I spun or slid or fell off the runway—it's just not in my head to remember. I was lifted from the cockpit and carried to a very cold room before falling into another void.

*   *   *

Days pass. My nurse is Oriel, whose body grows with my child. Her touch remains as warm and sensual, and my head floats above us as we make love.

Finally, one afternoon I see a woman in a white smock standing near me.

"Oriel," I say.

She turns. It's not Oriel. The woman is pregnant, seven or eight months at least.

"Madeline," she says. "Madeline."

"Yes, Madeline." And it is at that point my struggle with memory begins.

Colonel Maclean came by the next morning, with two men I hadn't met before. With a grim face, he congratulated me on my achievement.

"The plane is in excellent shape," he said. "You did remarkably well. Remarkably well."

They had taped my knee so severely that it was difficult to sit up in the bed. One of the men, a captain, helped prop the pillows and made a joke about how he only played nurse for heroes.

"I'm not a hero," I said.

They all laughed, then nodded solemnly.

"Do you want to know what happened?" I said.

"That's why we're here, son," said the other officer.

"Do you want to write it down?"

"We will," said Maclean. "We'll have a stenographer come around. For now, why don't you give us the highlights?"

So I told them the story, essentially as I've told it here. There may even have been more gaps. I forced the words out of my mouth as fast as I could, trying to bring back everything, as if saying it that first time would freeze it, preserve it in my head. I told them about Oriel, even the shame of masturbating in the factory. I told them of Peterson and Schmidt, the real hero. They listened with blank faces, standing all the while. Once or twice a nurse appeared at the door, but a glare from Maclean sent her away.

When I was done, Maclean shook his head. "You don't remember very well."

"I do. What I remember, I remember. There are parts missing, I know. Gaps, little details. But I'm pretty sure of what I said."

"You don't remember very well," he repeated.

I insisted I did.

"Peterson was a hero, chap," said the captain abruptly. "So are you."

"No," I said. "I did get the plane, but I was lucky."

"You're being too hard on yourself," insisted the captain. "Think of what you've been through, where you were. My God, man. If you're not a hero, who is?"

"I didn't save anyone's life," I said.

"The plane will," said Maclean. "It will, son. You are a hero."

"If it weren't for Schmidt, I never would have gotten on the airfield, or known what to do with the plane, or gotten away."

"Schmidt doesn't exist. He's been invented by your faulty memory," said Maclean.

I was so dumbfounded, I couldn't answer.

"We've made a careful check of the radar that day," explained the older officer. "Yours was the only plane that came over the Channel. The Germans don't have an aircraft such as you've described. They've been working on jet technology, but they're still far behind even the Italians."

My head had started to hurt about halfway through the story. Now it pounded at the top of my eyes, forcing them to narrow.

"I'm not a hero," I insisted.

They give me a medal anyway.

Were they right? Was it all an invention?

No. I'm sure it wasn't. After the war I read about the Me 262. That isn't proof, surely, but it fits, it fits. It has to be true. They were either wrong or protecting other secrets, or their choice of Peterson.

I know too well what memory does. Eighty-plus years have taught me that it can never be fully trusted. But it could not have invented the plane, not then, not now. It could not have invented Schmidt.

How could Peterson have deceived us so completely? He hadn't volunteered for a dangerous mission—he'd arranged to go back home.

It's not his betrayal that stings the worst. It's the fact that he thought so lightly of me. The airport hadn't even been alerted; he just assumed I wouldn't make it there on my own. Truth is, he was probably right.

If Schmidt had flown the plane straight on to England, he would have been the one with the medal. As it turned out, another Focke Wulf had been recovered a day or two before I landed, so my plane wasn't really that important in the grand scheme of the war. But imagine an Me 262 two years before it appeared over the skies of Germany. Imagine it reverse-engineered by the British or the Americans. How many lives would have been saved by such a plane?

When I had a choice, I followed Peterson, not Schmidt. I dismissed him entirely from my mind. How could anyone with such poor judgment be a hero?

And yet the Air Cross was awarded to me. And if I doubt my memory too much, if I give in to the temptation to believe this is all invention, I have only to open the bottom drawer of my desk and hold the medal and read the lie of the citation proclaiming me a hero.

I am old now, long removed from these events, at times estranged from my memory of them. It's been nearly a decade since I have given up my ministry, twelve years beyond the day my wife passed on.

I tell the story of what happened nearly every night, though only to myself. The main details remain steady, but small bits flash and glow and fade, falling away into the shadows. Sometimes they re-emerge, shards of glass from a window shattered long ago.

For many years, I told no one. Colonel Maclean and the others who heard it in the hospital room were the only people who knew it for many years. No stenographer ever came. There were two reports I was asked to sign, which I did without bothering to read them.

Then one day perhaps thirty years ago, when I was already past fifty, I tried to work the account into a sermon. But I fell short on the moral. If God had indeed saved me, as any good Presbyterian would say, what role had Oriel played? How could making love to her tell me so much about God, when surely she was in league with the devil?

Yet I could not tell the story without her. And so I never told it to my wife, nor my sons.

At times, I'm convinced Maclean was right, that my mind was clouded by the crash. That I really don't remember anything; that the past is all a figment of my imagination built from things other people have suggested. At other times I think I'm another victim of some uncharted mind disease similar to Alzheimer's, which substitutes one reality for another.

And then sometimes when I'm certain of this, I chance to see a young woman in a store or passing on the street. She turns her head slowly toward me, and I see Oriel again. Her soft weight presses once more against me in the field, and I look up to heaven and see the bright word of God shining past the blackness.

I fight my memory to remember this, and feel flushed from the victory.

AUTHOR'S NOTE

Aficionados of World War II aircraft are no doubt familiar with the sensation made by the Fw 190 when it first appeared in combat against the RAF, and probably know about the plan by Captain Phillip Pinckney and Jeffrey Quill to steal a Focke Wulf in June of 1942. "Operation Airthief" was dropped after an Fw 190 pilot became confused and landed in Wales instead of France, perhaps one of the most fortuitous combat mistakes of all time. Some details of the planned mission (which was to have featured a seaborne insertion and the theft of only one plane) are included in Dr. Alfred Price's *Focke Wulf*, a definitive book on the Fw 190, which was one of the references consulted for this novella—though I must admit I hadn't known of "Operation Airthief" until after I'd outlined and started working on the story.

The first versions of the Messerschmitt Me 262 jet fighter were being fitted and tested with jet engines at roughly the same time. As documented in J. Richard Smith and Eddie J. Creek's *Me 262*, all of the tests took place in Germany, not France, but would have had sufficient range and capability to perform as described here. Had Hitler not interfered, a production version of the jet fighter could have entered service in 1943, causing even more trouble for the Allies than the Fw 190.

Among the many other sources on period aircraft and the Luftwaffe, readers interested in seeing what the Butcher Birds looked like might look for Morten Jessen's *Focke Wulf 190*, which contains many photographs of the plane and their crews. I also found inspiration in a visit to the Imperial War Museum in London with my four-year-old son, where an Fw 190 is on permanent display.

While the technical and overall historical information is as accurate as I could make it, I've taken some liberties in the interests of storytelling, most notably in constructing and locating the airfield. Its description is a rough composite of three actual bases, not all of which were used by Fw 190s in the spring of 1942.

HANGAR RAT

DEAN ING

DEAN ING has been an interceptor crew chief, construction worker on high Sierra dams, solid rocket designer, builder/driver of sports racers—his prototype Magnum was a *Road & Track* feature—and after a doctorate from the University of Oregon, a professor. For years, as one of the cadre of survival writers, he built and tested backpack hardware on Sierra solos. His technothriller, *The Ransom of Black Stealth One,* was a *New York Times* bestseller, and he has been finalist for both Nebula and Hugo Awards. His more humorous works have been characterized as "fast, furious, and funny." Slower and heavier now with two hip replacements and titanium abutments in his jaw, he includes among his hobbies testing models of his fictional vehicles, fly fishing, ergonomic design, and container gardening. His daughters comprise a minister, a longhorn rancher, an Alaskan tour guide, and an architect. He and his wife, Geneva, a fund-raiser for the Eugene Symphony, live in Oregon where he is currently building a mountainside library/shop.

ONE

They claim it would be impossible to strap a teenage test pilot into America's hottest-climbing interceptor and get them both back intact. With the latest generation, they may be right. It was different in 1944, maybe because teenagers were different then, because their parents were; I reckon you had to be there. We learned a lot of things early, and some of them in strange ways.

For example, you wouldn't think Adolf Hitler could be explained by a stamp collection. My dad managed it, though. You also wouldn't figure that a guy raised on a peach orchard near San Antonio, and his father and grandfather raised on that same farm, would grow up fluent in German. Not unless you got to wondering where central Texas towns like Fredericksburg and Luckenbach got their names.

A lot of us, like the Rahms and the Mollers, fought Comanches to settle the region. Some kept up the lingo and correspondence with cousins in

the old country. My school bud Fred Moller and I
sometimes got ribbed for it, and by the time we were
in junior high it could get mean.

That's why, one day when I still had the cast on
my leg—that would make me twelve, so the year was
1938—I asked Dad about something so embarrass-
ing to him that it was never mentioned at home. "If
this guy Hitler is stampeding everybody out of Germany, why don't the people vote him out?"

He was torquing head bolts on a full-race Men-
asco in our shop, Rahm Rennsport near Luckenbach, at the moment, and he took his time
answering. Nobody rushed my dad, not if they
wanted testing and tweaking by Jurgen Rahm, the
best flight-test mechanic in the air-racing business.
But if you waited, you got the best. "Show you at
home later," he said finally, then motioned toward
a workbench, and I brought him the wiring harness.
Even then, I had been his hangar rat so long we
didn't always need words. I miss him still . . .

After supper, he had Mama bring a shoe box of
letters from our Stuttgart kin to my room, and with
a glance made it clear that she and my little sis, Elke,
should leave us be. I cleared a half-built Comet contest model from my drafting table, and he began to
sort through the box.

He didn't open any envelopes, but set one apart.
"Nineteen twenty," he said, and tapped the stamp,
an orange *zehn pfennig Luftpost,* the German equiv-
alent of a ten-cent airmail. He chose another;
tapped the stamps, one being an orange *dreissig
mark.* "Two years later," he said.

"Wow, thirty bucks," I said. I figured that meant
they were all getting rich over there.

"Wait," he said, and laid out another envelope. "Nineteen twenty-three," was his only comment. The stamp was green, labeled 400 marks—but overprinted 100 *tausend* marks. A hundred thousand bucks? I didn't quite believe it, until he showed me a pink five *millionen* and then a green fifty *millionen.* "I think they went up to *zehn milliard* or so eventually," he said. Ten—billion, with a 'b'—dollars to send a letter? I was flabbergasted. Those letters were a few years older than I was. Dad wasn't smiling as he carefully replaced the letters in the Keds box.

"They say longshoreman's wages in Hamburg were about twenty billion a day," he said slowly. "Men carried the cash home in wheelbarrows, and the government couldn't afford to pay its own printing office. Imagine that happening here, Kurt; the whole country in chaos. *Lieber Gott,* can you see why people were so desperate they'd vote for anybody who could lead them out of such a nightmare?"

"Did he? Mister Hitler, I mean."

Dad nodded. "His methods are vicious, but there's a recent *Deutsche Flugpost zehn mark* stamp somewhere in here. No more chaos in Germany today. No more freedom, either.

"They've exchanged nightmares. Too many people will forgive him anything for giving them confidence again in their money. And some of his top people are slick as Roscoe Turner, and just as good on the stick," he added. I got it. Turner was a fine race pilot, but mostly he knew how to hog friendly headlines. "*Und so,* now half the good people in Germany believe Hitler is the greatest genius in history in spite of all the Sturm und Drang. And the rest

are scattering like pigeons at the green flag because
Herr Hitler thinks he's Superman."

I had to smile. You could hide an air racer in a
two-car garage, but they had bodacious engines, and
when the green flag dropped and a half dozen Men-
ascos, Rangers, and Wright Whirlwinds cranked on
the horsepower for a race, you could hear their
thunder ten miles away, and that's not just tall Texas
talk.

And so I understood, vaguely, what was coming
when air racing was shelved after 1939. My heroes
were now designing and testing military planes, and
new engines were designed for reliability. Dad
didn't have much machining work for Mr. Moller.
The golden era of air racers was dead.

Between '39 and '41 Dad and I built a Hansen
Baby Bullet, a twitchy little bugger with responses
quick as a wink, the nearest thing you could get to
a race plane, from plans. We painted it my school
colors, red and white. After I soloed in a Piper, he
taught me to fly the Babe. And after that whenever
Dad tweaked someone's two-holer—more than one
seat—I got in some stick time with him.

Then he put away his tools and tried to work the
farm's orchard with one gimpy teenager. My left leg
never grew much after that fall from a ladder, so
the only letter I earned on the Fredericksburg Billies was for the javelin. But I made Dad proud in
school, flew the Babe now and then, and got a stiff
neck watching Army planes from nearby San Antonio airfields. I was a happy kid. The war was half a
world away, and my dad was the best man I ever met.

And our time together was running out. Pearl
Harbor changed everything. Almost everyone in air

racing put old contacts to use, building or flying
military aircraft. Fred Moller and I learned not to
use German words at school. Dad applied as a civilian, ferrying lend-lease Bell P-39s to the Russians by
the Alaska route, even before he realized how good
the pay would be. The idea was, this forty-year-old
could do his part and still spend some time at home.

For several months it worked fine. But there was
lots of bad weather in Alaska's interior, and some
very large rocks sticking up into it, and very few long
airstrips. One day they'll find which of those rocks
Dad's P-39 hit. The only reason I didn't go nuts then
was that, with Mama and Elke to think about, I
couldn't afford the luxury.

I graduated at sixteen, fully licensed with a flight
log to prove I could fly everything from the Babe to
a staggerwing Beech with retract gear. That was the
capper, I reckon, me being familiar with hot crates.
The Army was desperate for ferry pilots, and one of
Dad's old barnstormer pals sponsored me to fly new
AT-6s from the factory to Merced Army Air Field in
California.

Some cadets weren't much older than I was by
then. The T-6 "Texan" was a challenge, with retract
gear and an engine note that told everybody in the
county you were coming. Shoot, I'd have done it
free. I had a built-in grudge against Herr Hitler, and
the military didn't crave guys with a bum leg.

Mama signed her permission. I was the man, now,
with more cash than I'd ever expected to see. I was
a tad short, so I learned to talk down in my throat
and stand tall and wear a durn tie with my Stetson
around Merced because, if they thought you were a
kid, folks took advantage. And yeah, after some

Scheisskopf stood me a few beers in Fresno one night,
I got rolled. Once. Cost me nearly a hundred bucks
and a splitting headache. Fred claimed learning to
drink was a man's game, and set out to prove it after
his dad moved the machine shop to San Antonio
and set up an auto body shop, too.

People who made their living around high-
performance airplanes tended to have a thing for
cars, and I was no exception. The big thing in California then was hopped-up cars; foreign makes, engine swaps, weird fuel mixes—stuff I knew about. I
was itching to buy this gorgeous Alfa Romeo thing
until I found out it was Italian; the enemy—sort of.
Then some ferry pilot from Los Angeles had his girl
drive his Willys coupe to Merced, and it quit on him,
and I agreed to get it running. No wonder it
wouldn't run: Somebody had stuffed that poor little
coupe full of hot-cam Ford V-8 with a bad distributor.

I paid two hundred cash for the coupe, dropped
in a good distributor, and nearly passed out when I
lit it up. In Kentucky they'd have called it a rum-
runner. I drove back to Luckenbach pretending I
was flying the Pesco Special and baldied a brand-
new set of rear tires in the process. Ya-HOO, San-
an-Tone!

The ferry contract was running out in May of '44
when some colonel at Wright Field chased me down
by phone at the T-6 factory. I had a cold, which
dropped my voice even more. The colonel seemed
a bit flustered, like he was juggling three jobs, and
asked just the core questions. Was I the Rahm from

Luckenbach who could read German? How many
aircraft types had I flown and tuned? Did I know
that the test pilot who broke the B-26 of its mankilling ways and had sponsored me as a ferry pilot,
had now suggested me as engine man for a highly
classified crash program? Could I commit to a project that would keep me at Randolph Field, if they
paid me 250 dollars a month?

Randolph was seventy air miles from Luckenbach.
Stifling an urge to wet my pants I rattled off the
dozen or so hotter crates I'd flown, and said, "You
must've been talking to Frank Merrill, he's the one
who tamed that flying coffin." That's what Dad had
said, anyway. "And if he's on this new project, that's
good enough for me. Who else do you have on it,
and what *is* it?"

He couldn't say what, only that it was originally
out of Larry Bell's design loft, code name Pancho.
Whatever it was, I wasn't hiring on to fly Pancho,
just to help modify it under the guidance of some
educated civilian hotshot. There would be other
specialists for hydraulics, electrics, sheet metal, and
supply. A Georgia Tech grad aero designer named
Ullmer was in charge of the whole corral, and if I
showed up at the project hangar within three days,
I could sign on.

I took a deep breath. The P-39 was a Bell design,
and I'd heard rumors that Mr. Bell's outfit was working on something that flew, or might eventually fly,
with a jet engine. I'd have worked for nothing to be
involved with Frank "Bub" Merrill, who had flown
crates I'd helped soup up; with luck I might even
fly the Baby Bullet to Randolph to sign on, tie, Stet-

son and all. Was I gonna deliberately create slathers
of confusion by even hinting to this overworked colonel that there had been two Rahms from Luckenbach, especially with Merrill there to endorse me
when I showed up? Come onnn . . .

TWO

Landing the Babe at Randolph Field in May '44 wasn't like it had been when you could dip a wing and get a green light, before the air got full of cadets and radios. Even though I did radio for clearance, I was escorted off the taxiway in my civilian crate by MPs in an olive drab Plymouth with gun barrels poking out the windows. After a few phone calls from a shack out near the compass rose, they decided I rated a clip-on pass. I made a note to myself that it was edged with red tape, though in those days security was fairly primitive.

Then they led me a mile or two, pointed at a separated hangar-and-shop, and sped away, letting me set my own wheel chocks. Maybe I shouldn't have worn my old boots on a cross-country, but the heels were two-inchers, and this was Texas, and for my first time on the job I figured bigger was better.

The MPs were already calling Project Pancho's isolated little facility the wetback hangar, and its big sliding doors were closed. The civilian who answered my knock at the side door turned out to be the structures man, Roy Dee Ray, an old fella with watery blue eyes and a lip full of snuff. My pass spoke for itself, so he let me in. And I saw, over his shoulder, something to set the blood singing in my veins. It wasn't a jet, and I didn't care.

Designers put their signatures on planes with the lines they draw, and the solitary little beast getting a postflight inspection in one corner was a baby Bell, smaller brother to the P-39. But its nose was much too long, its engine cowl narrow as a knife blade, and its cockpit canopy bubble far back near the tail, exactly like the very last and hottest air-race specials. It reminded me of *Chambermaid,* the tiny screamer Russell Chambers had built in his garage a few years before, the one of which Art Chester said, "Ya forgot the wings, Russ." But this one had long-legged little wheels to clear an outsize prop, so I guessed the engine had to be a Ranger. I was instantly in love.

The wing was low and, as we used to say when no ladies were near, short as my *Schwantz.* I figured this crate should maneuver like a squirrel on tequila. And if that loosened cowling was like the rest of it, the durn thing was plywood.

Plywood? My head spun. Military crates were aluminum and steel. This gorgeous flying mite would be only one-third the weight of a P-51, maybe less, and should come off the line like a rodeo quarterhorse, with the slashing attack of a plywood wolf. If it held together, that is, just like the civilian racers, with a skin you could penetrate with a penknife. It was a sure-enough God-durn Army air racer from

hell, is what it was. I bet Jimmy Doolittle felt the
same way, first time he saw the mankilling R-2 Gee
Bee racer.

I had goose pimples. My eyes were misting
enough that I needed a few seconds to focus on the
fellas who had come up behind me. The short
young one in front, with hair he must've combed
with an eggbeater that day, was built square as a nail
keg, thick hairy forearms poking from rolled-up
sleeves, jabbering in double time with a mud-thick
Jawja accent. Something like, whothehail let that kid
in, this is a gawdam classified project, one hangar
rat in here's more'n enough, Hell's fahr, Roy
Dee . . .

But the guy behind him, taking long lank strides
in whipcord khakis tucked into tall lace-up boots,
cut through all that. "Whoa, Ben," he said, "he's one
of ours." Windburnt, early forties, Texas twang,
broad smile: It was Frank Merrill, and I guess that
B-26 Marauder program had aged him. More softly
he went on to me, "How ya doin', stud? Outgrown
your knickers, I see. You've shot up like a weed since
I saw ya last," and stuck out a callused hand that felt
like a mesquite stub. I had been sixteen, and
tongue-tied, when Dad introduced me before. And
I had purely hated those durn knickers.

"Much obliged, Mr. Merrill," I said, knowing he
had put me in line for this, and we shook while the
short guy stared.

"Aw, call me Bub now, you're entitled," said Merrill. "I hear you've been showin' those Merced cadets how it's done." He winked. Ferry pilots did
shoot some hot landings. Who was going to wash us
feather merchants out?

The short fella found his voice again. He made fists against his hips as he shook his head and squinted at my pass. "Rahm? This's Jurgen Rahm? Bub, if this is one of your Texas gags—"

"Kurt Rahm," I said. This time when I stuck out a hand, he shook it quickly like he didn't mean it. "Jurgen was my dad," I added. "I was his hangar rat from the git-go. Uh, and you'd be Mr. Ullmer, I guess."

He nodded. After a long silent moment, he said, more to Merrill than me, "Just won't do. I need seasoned men, not some kid I've gotta teach to read a print."

"I read blueprints in grammar school," I said softly, feeling like I was in knickers again.

"Bub, he'd be your power-plant man," Ullmer objected. "You gonna strap inta that thing over there with a full set of experimental mods this kid installed, and firewall it?"

"Did it when he was practically a tadpole; he never killed me but twice," Merrill drawled. I think he was starting to enjoy himself. "Larry Bell endorsed him, but shoot, what does he know?"

I had never met Mr. Bell. If he had done that, it had been at Merrill's urging. Ullmer growled, "This isn't funny, Merrill."

"Yes it is. It's the pot bad-mouthin' the kettle, and that's always good for a laugh. How old are you, Ben?" No answer. "If you're two dozen, I'm Mussolini."

"I've done graduate work, f'gawd's sake, that's why I'm here," said Ullmer.

Merrill grinned. "So has he, in the school of hard

knocks, and his professor was one of the best. That's why he's here."

I looked for a crack in the cement to hide in as the two faced each other. While Ullmer puffed and glowered, Bub Merrill laid a gentle hand on the younger man's shoulder, and said, "Let's drag this argument out in the open where we can see it. There's a secret crash program behind ever' prickly pear in Texas, or Bell and the Army wouldn't have to drop youngsters like him, and you, into the same bucket and shake 'em. I'll tell you something you didn't know: I wasn't the test pilot Bell wanted first."

"No shit," said Ullmer.

"None. He would'a borrowed Herb Fisher from Curtiss to fly this little chippie, but Herb wouldn't fit in the cockpit. Herb just likes his taters and gravy too much, that's a fact." Fisher was even more famous as a test pilot than Merrill was. Merrill's tone was soft, but for a proud man the facts were hard. "Anyway, we have to dance with who brung us, and if I can stand it, I reckon you can, too. If something goes wrong, it won't be you that finds out about it at forty thousand feet, or maybe at sagebrush altitude. It'll be me."

The casual mention of forty thousand, eight miles up, just about stripped my head bolts. It was my first hint of what Pancho was really about, and I silently guessed the little Bell would be strictly for unarmed, fast photorecon. Wrong . . .

Looking betrayed, Ullmer let his expression talk for him, and Merrill went on: "If you said the Army's already dealt the top tried-and-true professionals out to bigger programs, and is scrapin' the bottom of the barrel for these new projects, I wouldn't like it, but I wouldn't kick your butt for sayin' it. I don't know about our souls, but these are the times that try men's *cojones.*"

Ben Ullmer strained like he'd swallowed a june bug, and looked at me again, still talking to Merrill. "You think he can maintain an engine this tricky?"

"Check him out," said Merrill. "He's not in Timbuktu; he's right here."

When they both looked at me, I gazed at the sweet little wooden wolf in the corner of the hangar and thought out loud. "Not enough room in there for a big Allison or its heat exchangers," I said. "I figure it for a V-12 Ranger 770, air-cooled, blown for high altitude, prob'ly inverted. Cylinder fin ducting's a weird mess, but there's tricks to get around that. My hands are small." I held them up to him. "Replacing those plugs is a knuckle-biter, though, and if fuel metering's not perfect, we'll be swapping plugs every few hours of airtime."

Bub Merrill's mouth twitched. Ullmer stared at me until, "I'll be a dirty bastard," he said.

"Naw, just smudged a little," said Bub.

Something flickered behind Ullmer's eyes. "With little hands like those you oughta be a radio announcer," he told me. We stared at him. He continued, poker-faced: "You know, 'wee paws, for station identification'?"

"One more like that, and I'm callin' the MPs," said Bub, but they both were grinning by then, the tension broken, Ullmer nodding at me. "Well, I guess you'll do, and you're right about the spark plugs. It's clear you're more experienced than you look, kid. Let's try that handshake again—Kurt, is it? And I'm plain Ben except when the Army brass is on hand." He led off toward the dagger-nosed, wooden-hided little bird I had already fallen in love with. "Come on, let's show you what Pancho is all about."

The name Pancho was kind of a friendly insider's joke. Pancho Barnes was a woman race pilot in California, a familiar name to everyone in the fraternity. Close-coupled, well liked, so friendly to test pilots she'd give a man the shirt off her back, maybe before he asked—not to be too blunt about it. Point is, Pancho was unconventional and willing. Put in that light, the plane was well named.

While they watched me poke around in Pancho's innards, my bosses mostly filled me in about something else that scared me at first, and terrified me at last: the Junkers Ju 488. Nobody said it out loud, but the best Nazi aircraft outperformed ours. I couldn't avoid feeling a little weird about that, like there was a little pride stuck in me upside down. I could sure avoid talking about it, though.

Allied intelligence learned the Nazis had canceled their long-range bomber design work, a hint that they'd given up on mass bombardment of the U.S. But the Ju 488 was said to be already in development by then, a huge twin-tail, four-engine monster pressurized to fly at thirty-seven thousand feet. Some French mechanic had risked his tail forwarding pictures to prove that a pair were already being secretly built somewhere in France. Just two.

If its bomb load was light, the Junkers could reach New York City or Washington at 350 miles an hour, faster than a lot of our fighters at such heights. And another man had died to send the news that it had recently been uprated to a crash program. Bub reminded me that even with our Norden bombsight, dropping a few ordinary bombs from a single plane, from that high up, wasn't likely to hit anything with precision. The Nazis were nuts about secret terror weapons. What in God's name did they intend to drop on our cities that only needed one plane per city?

Our people thought they knew what, but, said Bub, they weren't telling. I thought about a story I had just read in the March issue of *Astounding* magazine, a small reading vice my bud Fred and I kept private to avoid the usual ribbing. But if there had really been anything like the uranium bomb in the story, surely a science-fiction magazine couldn't print short stories about it. It seemed likely the plane's load was like a bag of germs—cholera, plague, something of the sort.

If the Nazis were working so feverishly on the thing, said Ben Ullmer, folks in our new Pentagon building decided we'd have to cobble up something to intercept it. We wouldn't know it was up there until it was nearing our shores, which meant whatever we scrambled to meet it would have to climb about eight thousand feet a minute and maneuver at over four hundred miles an hour after climbing eight miles high. We needed to build at least two squadrons of these special interceptors, one to cover Boston and New York, the other protecting Washington and the Newport News shipyards.

In the entire arsenals of democracy, we had nothing that even came close.

I said, "Aren't we building jet planes that could do it? I heard rumors in California."

"If we are," Ullmer said, "nobody's talking to me about it. The rumor I heard was, our jet engines aren't up to it yet, especially at altitude. I'd be surprised if there's not another program like Pancho, though, somewhere."

Bub cussed the War Production Board because, he said, Lockheed had a P-38K that might have been modified to hurtle up that high, that fast. Some committee of fools had turned down the proposal. Meanwhile, there was this little screamer called the XP-77 at the Bell factory that had been designed to outclimb, outturn, and outrun the Misubishi Zero. It had been designed when we thought we'd have to skimp on duralumin, so Mr. Bell's boys used plywood, which worked perfectly on the British Mosquito bomber. Now, we had other planes that could whip a Zero. The XP-77 needed a new mission, and here was a mission that needed a wilder, woollier XP-77. And needed it yesterday.

Being a good guy, Bub urged me to climb into the cockpit, and I hopped in so fast you'd think I had two good legs. Pretty close quarters, for sure. The instrument panel had holes for extra gauges. I asked what they'd be for.

Turbocharger stuff, said Ben. I looked my next question at him. "Extra stuff," he said, and hesitated.

"He's gotta install it," Bub reminded him, and when Ben still didn't answer, the pilot said it for him. "Ben's waiting for some stainless tanks and lines, other stuff he's dreamed up. Ben purely hates that we're stealing tricks from the enemy. Pissed off that he didn't do it first."

"Awright, here it is," Ben said, as if someone were pulling each word out of him with a grappling hook. "Their new rocket bomb, and that tailless Messerschmitt rocket plane, use nearly pure hydrogen peroxide with permanganate catalyst to create gobs of steam. A little steam turbine can have more balls than a bowling alley. The rocket fuel turbopump alone puts out over five hundred horses for a couple of minutes."

I thought about the 3 percent peroxide that foams up when you pour it on a cut. Thirty times that strong would be comparing TNT to a firecracker. "Lordy! The whole Ranger engine doesn't develop much more than that. But you can't get to forty thousand feet in two minutes," I said.

"No, but we'll use a smaller rig and a bigger tank and hope we can stretch the peroxide to last fifteen minutes. That way we pick up an extra hundred ponies 'cause we don't have to rob the engine to run the blower."

"Boy howdy, that's a new wrinkle," I admitted. "So Pancho uses a chemistry set to run her supercharger. Sounds too good to be true."

"It's good news and bad—or could be," Bub cautioned.

I glanced from him back to Ben, who nodded. "The nice part is, the exhaust goes out a little belly nozzle near the center of gravity. Steam rocket boost. The drawings are locked up, but I'll show you later," he added, and I knew from the way he said it that this was Ben Ullmer's own idea.

"And the not so nice part," Bub put in lazily, "is that all that concentrated peroxide will be right

enough to be a rat. You figure it out," he added.

The little guy's ears weren't all that big, but I got it: Mickey Mouse. I wondered if the kid got it, too, and if he did, whether he enjoyed it. In the Southwest a lot of folks had their patronizing jokes about the TexMex citizens, and didn't extend friendliness to handshakes. I wasn't one of those folks, so I held out my hand, and said, "I'm Kurt Rahm, Mickey." To show Ben Ullmer I wasn't afraid of him, because I was, I added, "Us hangar rats may need to stick together."

"He's not much for contact," said Sparks quickly.

"Uh, he doesn't," Ben began, and then stopped as Mickey's scrawny little paw inched out to take mine the way a young raccoon would reach if you offered him a sugar cube. A quick, warm grasp without even meeting my gaze, and, "Much obliged," he said, with no accent I could detect. That's what you said to thank somebody for a favor, and I think that's just what Mickey meant for my treating him as an equal.

Then the moment was gone, except that Sparks gave a long quizzical glance to the kid, while Ben said, "Well, he doesn't, usually. Beats me."

They introduced me to my workbench, too, with a new skyhook, a tall, wheeled A-frame for jerking heavy stuff like engines up and trundling them around. I'd bring my own tools later, but it looked like a neat setup complete with a lockable cage the size of a bathroom for classified stuff. I expected to be wheeling that Ranger engine in there now and then, because no doubt it would soon be classified as secret.

It may seem weird, but I'll call it quaint: At the

start of June '44, civilian help and their kids pretty much got the run of the place, so long as they didn't do something dumb like wandering onto a taxiway or getting in the way of marching cadets. About all you had to do was keep your pass clipped where folks could see it.

They told me parking was behind the hangar, but I said, "I'd play the fool taxiing a Hansen Babe back there," which got a chuckle 'til Ben and Bub realized I wasn't ribbing them.

"How'd you get a Baby Bullet?" Ben asked, and I told him you build it with your dad is how, so it was my turn to show everybody my little red-and-white crate, which I did.

Roy Dee, who was more cabinetmaker than sheet-metal man, complimented me on the woodwork, and I admitted that was mostly my dad's doing.

Ben thumped the taut tail fabric and nodded. "Reminds me of the kid in Georgia who comes runnin' to his mom, and says, 'We kilt a bear! Paw shot it.' "

Bub let it pass with a look that said, you're on your own now, stud. "Well," I said, "my dad shot the Sitka spruce, but on everything else, I pulled the triggers."

"We got a few sharp corners to sand down, don't we, but none of 'em's on this airchine of yours," Ben said, grinning, and checked the brand-new Breitling watch on his wrist. He asked where I was staying, and I said it was just a puddle-jump to Luckenbach, and I'd drive my car down the next morning with my tools, maybe find a room with my bud, Fred Moller, whose family had moved to SanTone.

As Roy Dee and Bub helped stow my chocks, a car

came around the perimeter road, so low you
couldn't see the coachwork over the weeds, trailing
a python of dust that should have brought the MPs.
I know now why it didn't: They all knew that car
from a mile away, and had learned they were just
cops and he was the governor. Kind of.

The car had a rumble that got a man's attention,
like an aero engine. Then I saw the car, a low
swoopy futurecar the color of daffodils, and realized
it *was* an aero engine. "Holy cats; what's this?" I said.
Sure, aircraft people like airplany cars, but not many
cars looked or sounded so much like airplanes.

"Judging from the container I'd say our gearbox
has come," said Ben. A man-sized wooden box
jounced beside the man at the wheel as he pulled
up before the hangar with the multiple-horns
whonk of a Liberty ship.

"No, the car," I said.

"The man and the car," Bub put in, with an un-
readable expression, and he was right. The man had
wavy dark hair, a Gable mustache, and a great tan.
Of course a good tan's not much of a trick when
you drive around south Texas in an 812 supercharged Cord convertible roadster. I'd seen a couple on California highways, gobbling up the lesser
wheeled animals at a hundred or more, but never
up close. Lycoming aircraft-based V-8, chromed
dinosaur-gut exhausts coiling out from the hood,
which looked like a sun yellow steel coffin stretching
ahead of the driver. It was to be a long time after
the war before other American cars outran an 812
Cord. In California, they said, if you couldn't get a
date in a Cord, try trolling with a roll of hundred-
dollar bills.

"Ain't he your basic splendid vision," asked Bub, "and doesn't he know it? That's our supply officer, Major Dylan. His life story takes a while, and if you don't wanta hear it for the next two hours, stud, better prime your engine."

So Bub swung my prop over, and as I eased away light on the throttle to keep from blowing people's hats off, I waved. The tanned handsome specimen in the Cord waved back. That's how I met Major Athol Dylan, USAAF.

THREE

Mama wasn't happy 'til I convinced her that I wasn't joining the Air Corps and wasn't going to fly a warplane, which actually I was though I didn't know it yet. I decided against calling a girl I dated in town; there'd be time enough for that when I settled into the new project. We weren't going steady anyway.

I made a long-distance call to the Mollers, full of my news, but Fred wasn't home. No surprise there. He'd talked his dad into letting him have a second-hand Indian motorcycle to make deliveries for Moller Machining, and once ol' Fred got himself astride that thing he was, as he put it, as hard to find as an Austin virgin. In fact, I knew that's mostly what Fred hunted, though he always told his folks he was fooling around in Brackenridge Park in SanTone, because the University of Texas in Austin was just an hour away by Indian. Fred put a lot of miles on that velocipede.

Eugen Moller had moved his family about midway

between Randolph and Kelly Fields, off Rigsby in
South San Antonio. He didn't wait for me to ask
about a place to stay. "I've been wanting a chance to
meddle in that Willys hybrid of yours anyway," he
said, having seen it once and heard me romp it. He
knew there was something under that hood with lots
more beans than a little four-banger. Gene Moller
made more money now in SanTone than he had
working with Dad. He got piecework machining for
the military but specialized in making new parts for
special cars that pilots brought there to the cradle of
aviation. In wartime, parts manufacturers were otherwise occupied "for the duration," as the phrase
went.

I knew Mama and Elke would try to change my
mind, but it was nearing dusk, and I wanted to wake
up in SanTone, so I told Mr. Moller he could expect
me late that night.

After two hours and a few tears from the womenfolk I finished packing, nested my set of microm-
eters and dial indicators in the passenger's seat of
my coupe, promised to be back home in two shakes,
and lit out for the city.

Like many people running around the country
doing war work, I had a "C" ration card, and gas was
a dime a gallon. With a half-dozen military bases,
San Antonio was no longer the sleepy two-culture
reminder of Spanish America, and even late at night
the city traffic was as heavy as the blossom-scented
air.

When I pulled up in the Mollers' driveway, Fred
was just dismounting from his Indian. In my headlights he seemed even taller than before, with those

long legs and slender butt girls always seemed to favor. We would've hugged if young Texans had done that, but instead, Fred punched my upper arm lightly and offered me his hip flask. I took one sip. Gahh, gin.

The house was dark so we hung around a while in the backyard under a chinaberry tree, catching up, idling in the glider swing in air that felt satiny on my skin while locusts sizzled and lightning bugs practiced Morse code in the still, humid night.

Fred lit up a new vice, a pencil-slim cigar that smelled of rum, and wanted to know what I was doing at Randolph. Of course I could only tell him it was A and E—aircraft and engine—work. He was about half-bonked, cussing everything impartially because I wouldn't share military secrets, he didn't know whether he'd be drafted, didn't know whether he cared if he was, and didn't want to keep living at home where everybody bitched about everything a man did. He said he had plenty of cash in his jeans. I didn't remind him that his mama's cooking would keep anybody home, and that he was so flush because he was living rent-free with a salary paid by Moller Machining.

"Wish I had some sisters or brothers," he said, and drained his flask. "Give my old man somebody else to aim at. By the way, how's Elke doing?"

Fred could ride to Kerrville or Luckenbach just as easily as Austin. "Whatever she's doing, she's doing it sixteen years old. You stay away from that pasture," I said. Elke always turned quiet and shy around him, but I didn't really worry. Much. He liked 'em older. I was used to Fred's ways, with him half a head taller than me, and when meeting up with girls, Fred taking the pick of the litter like it was fated. He purely loved it.

He also loved telling about it, so I said, "How are all the other fillies in the corral doing?" It was just drugstore cowboy talk, the Texas way of being one of the crowd and young at heart. Older guys from Maine and Minnesota, new to the Southwest, picked the lingo up as soon as they could, like a joke everybody was in on and tried to improve.

So Fred told me his latest poontang story. I could discount about half of it, but I listened, and snickered in the right places. According to Fred, Austin had better cruising than SanTone, with fewer military bases and more college girls. He said you could just stroll across the tree-dotted green slopes flanking Barton Springs, Austin's biggest swimming resort, and beat 'em away with a switch; but you couldn't cut through the bushes without stepping on the bobbing butt of somebody who'd forgot his switch.

It sounded great, but it sounded a little trashy, too. When Fred offered to take me along next time, I said I'd pass on the Indian, a 1940 Sport Scout with the slick wheel valances. "I like some bodywork around me," I explained. And before he could suggest we go to Austin in the Willys, I added, "I'd like to drive, but with all those jury-rigged parts, I wouldn't trust my heap far from town." I don't know why I said that. What I mean is, I don't know why I was building an alibi to steer clear of doubling with my old boyhood bud.

Fred reminded me that his dad's shop took on problems like mine all the time. "Just in the past month they've fixed a Morgan three-wheeler, a Delahaye, a pair of Duesies, and the piss-rippin'est yellow Cord roadster you never saw."

I never saw, huh? I dived into the day's memories so I could one-up my bud. "You mean Dylan's," I drawled, casual as Adolphe Menjou. "The major's a purty little thing, isn't he?"

Ol' Fred got some smoke down the wrong way and, after hacking at it like a cat with a hairball, husked, "Damn if you don't get around. How come you know that Yankee?"

I hadn't even heard Dylan's accent, but just for fun I claimed him; laid it on thick. "Aw, he's one of ours. I expect I'll be drivin' that poor thing of his from time to time. The major's just one of the guys on our project," I said, as if I were a gum-swapping bud of a guy who, so far, had only waved at me.

"Listen, that high-stepper's on ever' project there is," Fred assured me. "I deliver a lot of stuff: Brooks General Hospital, Randolph, Kelly, Fort Sam, you name it. And the poon waves at him first. That sumbitch gets more tail than a bullfighter."

I didn't doubt it. "I guess a major must draw man-sized wages," I said.

"I guess. But there's lots of majors around, and not many yellow Cords. Nope, he's just got world-champ ways with five-card stud. Shit, he says so himself."

"He one of your new buds in town?"

"I wish." Fred chuckled, and yawned, and got up from the swing, adding, "I'm workin' on it."

That figured, I thought as we tiptoed into the house. If I could've been anybody I liked, it'd be a cross between my dad and General Doolittle. For

Fred it'd be Major Athol Dylan, USAAF, world
champion poker stud.

I was up and gone by seven, after raiding the icebox
for a glass of Mrs. Moller's famous homemade buttermilk. There was something more than flower and
tortilla scents in the SanTone air as I showed my
pass at Randolph, people standing in little groups,
carrying portable radios, so I turned on the coupe's
radio as I rumbled down the perimeter road.

Invasion in Normandy! Waves of excitement
crawled up my arms to tickle my neck hairs as
WOAI, San Antonio's clear-channel station, filled
me in on the thing the world had been awaiting for
so long, and now in the early hours of June 6 had
become a fact while I slept. I parked behind the
hangar and stayed put, listening.

The news confused me. Some of the early fighting
must have broken out before the Nazis knew it was
the sure-'nough kick-ass showdown at San Jacinto,
while I sat with Fred in that glider swing. The British, in gliders of an entirely different kind, had
landed troops at some bridge in Normandy—wasn't
that France? But Americans were coming ashore by
the thousands at beaches in Utah and Omaha,
which was still in Nebraska unless they'd moved it,
and the only big body of water I knew of in Utah
was the Great Salt Lake, and I didn't think we were
invading the Mormons, too.

I did what I always did in such cases: kept my
mouth shut and my ears open. The Elgin on my
wrist told me it was nearly eight, and I didn't want
to be late on this day of all days, so when Sparks
Fonseca parked his Studebaker and got out carrying

a portable radio, I got my armload of precision tools and went with him. He'd picked up little Mickey somewhere on the base, and instead of talking we just traded okay signals and listened to Sparks's radio.

Another radio was already on inside, and nobody was talking much. Everybody was full of beans in the shop, coffee beans at that, to judge from the aroma. Ben greeted us with a two-fingered "V" for Victory, half a cigar in his teeth, reminding me of a much older short guy in England. I wondered if Churchill was Ben Ullmer's hero. That gearbox the major had brought was free of its crate, its casing unbolted on my workbench, and Bub Merrill sat on a stool with sunlight streaming through a window to help him read a spec manual for the gearbox.

A lot of test pilots didn't bother with such details in those days, depending on the A and E guys to do things right. So they didn't always know how everything was supposed to work. Some of those pilots didn't live to Bub's age because, when something went belly-up under the cowl later, they didn't have a clue what it might be and didn't know whether to feather a prop, firewall the throttle, or step outside for a short parachute ride. Part of their mystique; part of the b.s. that was dwindling as our hardware got more complicated. I think Bub was still in one piece because back in the thirties he left the b.s. to guys who wore their sunglasses and scarf in the shower.

After I looked the gearbox over and set my feeler gauges out, Bub turned the manual over to me. He even asked how I wanted my coffee, and I sang out for cream and two sugars, and an hour later I knew

Mickey was a pearl among hangar rats because he'd been listening and, without a word, brought me another cup flavored just right.

We got the gears properly lashed by noon, and Mickey disappeared for a while with the coffeepot nickels, reappearing after what must've been a long trot to the PX with cheeseburgers and a pair of Three Musketeers candy bars for me. It happened that Three Musketeers was my favorite, maybe because in those days it was really three little bitty different-flavored bars side by side, connected under a blanket of chocolate. Somebody had noticed I'd come in without a brown bag or a lunch pail.

Fonseca told me the little guy loved chocolate but didn't care for the vanilla or cherry flavors, so I carefully broke off the chocolate third of each candy bar and gave it to Mickey. He said, "Hot tamale," a local joke on "hot dog," and winked, and then we all listened to Bub and Roy Dee discuss the Normandy invasion through bites of sandwich and swigs of Hires.

Roy Dee may have had a hard life, but he was worth listening to. Bub was hopeful that the Allies would take the town of Caen that day, but Roy Dee said they wouldn't if they didn't do it fast. While we ate lunch in Texas it was nearing sundown over Normandy and at dusk, he said, the Wehrmacht could bring in reinforcements our aircraft couldn't see to attack. Bub thought it over and agreed. I got the impression that, if Rommel's army got lucky, our guys could still get shoved back into the sea.

Ben was full of optimism about our beach landings until Bub said, "What we're hearing sounds good, young buck, but you notice they're not talking about Omaha Beach anymore. It's what they quit talking about that worries me." By then I understood about the code names, and knew that Utah and Omaha Beaches were near Cherbourg in Normandy. Cherbourg was still enemy soil, but as of that day, for a time at least, those beaches were ours.

Toward late afternoon, Major Athol Dylan showed up again, bringing special lubricants he'd had to liberate from Kelly Field. That was what a good supply officer did, cutting through red tape to keep deliveries on time. The stuff he brought matched the specs in the manual, and Dylan preened at our thanks.

That guy was really something: a little under six feet, careless grin and fresh haircut, the faintest tang of aftershave, tailored uniform showing off good shoulders, with his cap stowed rakishly under one epaulet. His tie? Knitted, the right color but about as regulation as an ostrich plume. His shoes? Shiny loafers, but in the correct rich brown, and unless somebody polished his ankles, he wore silk socks. From fifty feet off he was in uniform, but close up he was an illustrated manual for thumbing your nose at regulations. I reflected that if a man did a crucial job well and wore oak leaves, he could scorn the regs and not get jerked up by his short hairs. Yep, Fred Moller would just love him to death.

Dylan seemed more buoyant than any of us over the news on WOAI. "A whole new ball game," he kept saying, chain-smoking Pall Malls as he mooched coffee, often checking his foreign chronometer. He didn't have pilot wings over his single row of ribbons. I bet he wanted to, but Major Dylan was a supply officer and a finagler, not a flier. Wearing those wings without authorization, I think, would've been one nose-thumb too many. I had to admit he took his work seriously, delivering rush orders in his personal chariot instead of ordering some noncom to do it in one of those big Dodge Army trucks.

Presently, some switch in the major's head snapped, and he left as suddenly as he'd come. "Appointment," was his only explanation. I guessed his accent was New York, maybe Philadelphia, and I concentrated on my torque wrench.

Nobody quit at five, and we set up workstands around Pancho's nose to prepare for the new installation. Most wood-covered planes had steel tube skeletons, but the P-77 got most of its strength from its skin, like a big plywood egg. I worried when measurements showed we'd have to lengthen that skin a few inches up front, but Roy Dee tore a hunk of butcher paper from a roll and started making patterns. I felt right at home again because that's the way small outfits had to do it, in a pinch. Rough it out, trim it to fit, then transfer everything to new official blueprints later. It looked sloppy, but we could have Pancho in taxi tests while a big factory would've still been waiting for drawings.

I also knew by now what Sparks was cobbling up: a new skinny shape for Pancho's radio, so it'd fit back under the tail where Ben said it must. You can't fly a crate that doesn't balance—and you'd better not try—so extra weight up front meant relocating other things to the back. Pancho's battery and radio both wound up where they needed to be—near the tail—thanks to Ben's slide rule calculations and the new assembly drawings he cranked out on his drafting board.

By sundown, we had brought the prop gearbox into the hangar and slung it in place, ready for mounting. In the shop, with Howard Lacey helping because he still didn't have any fluid lines to install, Roy Dee had the durnedest rig I'd ever seen, actually bolted together from a kid's Erector set he kept in his tool kit. It made sense because it wouldn't stretch or shrink, and held a reinforced partial cone of new plywood skin in shape while the resorcinol glue set. He called it the dunce cap and nobody argued.

And on WOAI, they were mentioning Omaha Beach again, which relieved Bub more than somewhat. When I left, Ben was saying he wished now that they'd named Pancho the Screaming Eagle, to honor the 101st Airborne Division. That was my first full day on Project Pancho, and I went back to the Moller place and talked some more about the invasion. Mr. Moller asked only how I was liking my new job, and I told him it looked like a cinch. I suppose I took it for granted that my work would proceed like the Normandy beachhead, rushing from success to success. I had no idea so many things could go so wrong.

FOUR

Within a week after June 6, every man in the wetback hangar could draw a map of northern France
from memory, because we had one in full color, the
size of a daybed, pinned on the shop wall bristling
with pins and festooned with masking tape bearing
penciled notations. Major Dylan had liberated it, reminding us with that lopsided hero's grin of his that
we didn't know where we got it. We followed the
action in France the way I used to follow the play-
by-play announcer when the Fredericksburg Billies
played Tivy High and Fred Moller ran sweeps from
the single wing.

But as the second week of the invasion pro-
gressed, Pancho didn't, much. The Allies have
fought their way into Carentan, with, hot damn, a
pounding by sixteen-inch shells from the USS *Texas.*
There was no longer much doubt now that our guys
were headed for Berlin and not another Dunkirk.

In the hangar, we had the gearbox mounted and

ready for its pair of three-bladed props, which were overdue. Okay, they were special from Sensenich, but they'd been promised before this, and when Ben raised Cain over it, Major Dylan cussed a New York blue streak at the snafu in the delivery system. In desperation, Ben Ullmer finally started tracing the missing parts by telephone until, after two more days, the major dropped by with small packages.

"I hear you're shooting yourselves in the foot, Ullmer," the major said. "It's hard for civilians to learn the Army's motto, 'hurry up and wait,' but you've gotta stay in line. If you were a chicken colonel, you might get someone cranked up on minor parts delays."

Ben set up his conversational artillery and started firing away. "Propellers aren't minor parts. You can scrounge locknuts and safety wire, but next time you see an airchine take off, Major, look real hard at the front end. If it hasn't got a prop, it's bein' pulled by a towrope. And nobody's ever towed a glider as high as we're supposed to go."

"I sympathize, believe me, Ullmer. But this is the Army, and you have to go through the proper channels. When they take flak from a civilian, they can turn on you like an armadillo."

I was nearby with Roy Dee, helping measure Pancho's radio chassis mount for installation, and I turned my laugh into a cough, out of politeness. Dylan was trying to improvise his own Southwest lingo, but if he'd ever seen an armadillo he would know they were about as fierce as garter snakes, and lots cuter.

"You're saying they'd sabotage a crash program out of spite," Ben said.

"Hey, the Army doesn't want to hear that word, buddy." Dylan frowned, his voice with an edge now, standing a little too close to Ben for good manners. "I never said it, and I don't wanna hear it. But they're only human. If they're flogging a dozen crash programs, they might pay closer attention to a big one than a small one. A word to the wise, okay?" And presently, he left. Lacey, who was also waiting for some fluid lines, stayed busy helping out at the maintenance shops, but the rest of us had been an unwilling audience to their exchange. Nobody spoke, so the silence deepened. And then Mickey farted, and we had the chuckle we needed to go on with our day.

And we waited several more days for the props. Then one day Bub Merrill didn't show up 'til the afternoon, which was no problem because he wasn't scheduled for any tests that day. When he did come in, he called Ben off in a corner.

Ben's mood improved a lot in short order. It got even better when, a couple of hours later, he got a phone call and listened for a minute. Then, "Sergeant," I heard him say, "I hope you're beautiful 'cause if you're here with 'em by tomorrow, I intend to kiss ya." Then he muttered something to Bub, slapped him on the back, and returned to his drafting board, chewing that awful ruin of a cigar and humming.

Bub kept quiet but, "That's got to be the props," I said to Sparks.

"If it's not, don't let ol' Ben get you alone in the john," Sparks said. Mickey smiled because I did.

The rest of the joke arrived next morning, when a group of soldiers showed up in a truck with crated

props. If they'd been the wrong ones I reckon Ben
would've had himself a hissy fit. Three privates unloaded the big paddles as Ben supervised, fussing
like a mother hen because one little ding on a prop
blade meant waiting for a replacement. The driver,
a corporal, waved a set of papers at me. "Sarge says
to get these signed. And to duck if some feather
merchant named Ullmer gets too close." He was
grinning like someone had told him what Ben had
said.

So Ben signed, and we uncrated the props, and
for the rest of the day whenever Ben came near
somebody would yell, "Duck!"

We worked late to get those props mounted with
the right spacers, Roy Dee getting in the way as he
trimmed and adjusted the dunce cap so it wouldn't
disrupt airflow in such a crucial area.

The morning after that, I happened to be early,
and it was me who gave Mickey his ride to the hangar. He had cut across an open stretch near the
compass rose, where they were about to release what
we called a radiosonde. Once every day in early
morning, the base meteorology guys would inflate a
bright orange rubber balloon the size of a one-car
garage, and release it into the open. Carried beneath it like a limp bedsheet with a cage full of
clocks was a set of instruments and a multiband radio transmitter. The size of the balloon was because
of its heavy set of batteries.

The weather guys tracked the balloon until it
burst, many miles up, and when it popped, the radiosonde package floated back down to a gentle
landing. People recovered about half of the instrument packages for the reward. The others, for all I

know, might have ended up in the Gulf of Mexico.

While this goofy rig floated up and away on the breeze, and later while parachuting down, it constantly radioed back the information pilots needed: temperature and air pressure mostly.

When Sparks Fonseca came in ten minutes later, I told him I had picked Mickey up near the compass rose. He said those big orange balloons were a spectator sport for Mickey, who often hiked out to watch the radiosonde crew before the daily launch.

In midmorning the major showed up again, looking smug. "I found out how those parts went astray," he told Ben, while we were swarming over the airplane. "They were about to go into storage across town at Kelly Field. That's what happens when you have more than one airfield in town and some yardbird can't read a bill of lading. By the way, I need the copies you signed. Army files, you know."

Ben was busy like the rest of us, but little Mickey was sitting on a wingtip, out of the way, where he could watch us in hopes of being useful. He piped up, "I know where they are," and quick as scat he was off and running, the plane so gossamer it bobbed on its gear like a live thing when his weight was removed.

He came back with several sheets, pink and yellow, and after a brief look Dylan folded them into his jacket. Nobody had much time to talk invasion news with him, and I didn't know he'd gone until I heard the dwindling thrumm of the Cord's Lycoming.

With Mickey back on his perch, his head was about the height of a man, and next time I passed by him I thought I smelled booze. Now I don't give a durn if it was Jimmy Wedell—who was already dead by then, but he'd been proof you could fly a race plane drunk as a congressman—nobody, not even a kid who'd found a half-empty bottle, was going to drink around a project of mine. I went about my business and came back a few minutes later. "Mickey," I said, very softly but inches away from him, "if you've found some liquor someplace, you better ditch it. In any case, don't ever show up around here after you've been drinking it. Okay?"

"Okay," he said, "if I do, I will, and don't worry, I won't, but I haven't."

Which made me blink and then laugh out loud, and when Mickey snickered, too, I recognized the odor. Not alcohol; acetone. Great for cleaning stuff up, but not a potion people drank. "And you wanta be careful tasting anything else just because it smells good," I said. "Hyraulic fluid is poison, and acetone isn't much better for you. You understand me, Mickey?"

He nodded, his big dark eyes serious. Acetone was one of those highly flammable solvents found in every hangar, also used as a paint thinner. But there was something else about it, something to do with having it on your breath. I let my memory work on it and went on with my job. We still didn't have Ben's tricky steam turbine stuff, but now we could try out the props with the new gearbox.

When a Ranger engine first starts up, its exhaust is rich with unburnt avgas, and when you run it up you can fill a hangar in no time with choking fumes

that take a while to disperse. That's why we pushed
Pancho outside facing away from the hangar and
chocked her for Bub Merrill's tests.

Everybody, even Lacey, was on hand. While the
rasp of an air-cooled V-12 was an old song to me, it
excited me to hear an extra unfamiliar whir in its
music thanks to a pair of props, one right behind
the other, geared to turn in opposite directions. Ben
Ullmer rubbed his forearms—goose pimples, I bet—
and grinned like a hound dog chewing a caramel.
We weren't using two-way radios so we could only
watch Bub in the cockpit, splitting his time among
the controls, his instruments, and a clipboard. He
kept us in mind, too, giving us the okay after each
notation he made.

Finally, he let the Ranger idle and motioned for
Ben and me to approach, his canopy bubble yawning open. We crowded up behind the wing root, our
heads almost even with Bub's. "Checkoff list is complete, but, pard, I get a feeling she wants to taxi,"
he called out.

Ben took a big breath. "Not scheduled 'til tomorrow," he shouted. "You know that."

"Yeah, yeah; plan the flight, then fly the plan," he
quoted the test pilot's mantra with a flyswatting wave
of one gloved hand. "But the original schedule was
for last week, so we're behind the plan. Still, you're
the boss."

And while Ben looked at me as if I had an answer—so I did, with a thumbs-up—Bub sang out to
this much younger man, "Come on, Daddy, I'm only
goin' down to the corner," and gave the throttle a
momentary nudge like a kid in a jalopy.

That blast of propwash must've done the trick.

Ben slapped the plywood skin, and warned, "If that nosewheel clears the tarmac, no dessert for a week." He backed away, unable to see me giving another big okay from behind his shoulder, then we pulled the wooden chocks from the wheels as Bub sealed the canopy.

That nosewheel almost jumped off the instant Bub gunned the Ranger, but he throttled back, and we cheered as Pancho headed away from us, her nose nodding on the uneven tarmac. Bub made her swerve along, testing her brakes, then picked up his pace and briefly firewalled it. He must have been three hundred yards off, doing fifty or so in a moment before he braked and turned her around. He did it with the rudder, which needs fast airflow before it can turn the plane. When he brought her back I guided him with hand signals and waited for the props to fully stop before chocking his nosewheel. It was Mickey who huffed up dragging a little workstand, almost more than he could manage, for the pilot to step down on. Ben could've done it with one hand if he'd thought of it. That little hangar rat never missed a detail.

Bub didn't say much in front of the others, but after we pushed Pancho back in the hangar he had a little confab with me and Ben. The checklist showed no power plant squawks, but, "She's not pullin' like she oughta," he said. "Power's not down a lot, but I swear it's down. I can feel it here." He slapped his butt.

"Supercharger's not in the loop," I said.

"I factor that in," he said, frowning, then glanced at Ben Ullmer. "What? Why are you lookin' at me like that?"

Our designer was shaking his head in a "pity the poor morons" way. "You also factor in the gearbox losses?" Bub and I both dropped our chins; we had forgotten a small facet of the very thing we were testing. "The XP-77 wasn't built for contrarotation gearing. That engine's now running a whole 'nother subsystem without a blower to boost it. Gearbox friction, gents. We should be a little down on thrust, and we are. When we get a chemically driven blower crammed into this airchine we should be *way* up again. Next problem?"

There weren't any other problems we could see. It was what we couldn't see that would bedevil us.

Sparks Fonseca stayed late with Ben but the rest of us left on time that day, earlier than usual. I felt so good I called Moller Machining and told Mr. Moller I wouldn't be home for supper. Fred was there, so I offered to treat him to a movie that night, celebrate a bit, though I couldn't tell him why. He said celebrations oughta begin at the Buckhorn, and I said okay.

Without his usual ride, little Mickey had set off afoot, and I overtook him in the Willys. "Much obliged," he chirped, his pipestem legs too short to reach the floorboards. He didn't have much to say, as usual, pointing off toward some old but well-kept buildings not far from the Randolph tower.

I said, "Your mama work there?" He nodded happily. "That's a ways for you to walk, little guy," I admitted. "I don't reckon you have a bike, huh?"

"No. It's okay," he said, but I thought he sounded wistful. Of course a little TexMex kid whose mother mopped floors wouldn't see much spare cash for bikes and such.

Then I had an idea; actually, two ideas. The first one didn't exactly tickle my little friend. "Mickey, would it be all right if I talked to your mama?" From the sudden shift of his features I backpedaled fast. "Nothing bad, just a couple of things mamas like to know." This wasn't strictly true because I had remembered about an uncle in Bandera years before who'd smelled of acetone. Turns out he had diabetes.

After a moment's deep thought: "It would scare her."

"How do you know?"

More delay. Then, "It's what I think. Sparks knows; she doesn't like to talk much."

That, I thought I understood. In those days, Latin adults who didn't speak much English sometimes avoided us gringos to avoid embarrassment. What I mentioned next was the other idea. "You think it would scare her if you had a bike?"

"Why would it?"

"I dunno, buddy, that's why I asked. Some folks don't want their kids to get out on the range past the bobwire."

He said, "I could ask."

"Do that," I said, then we got too near little groups of guys trying to march in the streets of Randolph Field, and I let Mickey out and headed for downtown SanTone.

There were three places in town where you couldn't help but find someone you were meeting: the Aztec Theater, the Alamo, and the Buckhorn

Saloon, all three downtown. The Aztec looked like Hollywood's idea of a heathen temple inside. The famous Alamo looked like a pile of whitewashed limestone after target practice, which is exactly what it was; those were places where you met your girl.

But if you were meeting a bud, you did it at the Buckhorn. I wanted something on my stomach before I stepped up to that mile-long Buckhorn bar with Fred, and had plenty of time. Being cheap as a nickel haircut, I wasn't about to spend most of a dollar on my favorite weakness, a pair of cheeseburgers. I stopped near an old Mexican with a pushcart, one of hundreds on the streets of San Antonio all looking alike, and bought three of the only things he carried: sweaty, fat little beef tamales wrapped in corn shucks. The aroma near drowned me in my own saliva. I never knew what all was in them and was afraid to ask. Spicy as a scandalous joke, hot as the girls it featured, and at a dime apiece, twice as dear as what a street tamale had cost in 1942. By the time I walked into the Buckhorn my tongue was begging for a beer; one burp from me would've set fire to your curtains.

Any Yankee who thought Texas talk was *all* b.s. needed a wallop of bourbon after stepping inside the Buckhorn. The place had more homegrown stuffed animals than a pie-eating contest—big critters. In addition to a pair of stags with their antlers hopelessly locked up in the combat that had starved them, there was an entire longhorn steer, not just the horns. Oh yes: The horns spanned nearly nine feet, God's truth. And over the bar, among a jillion other trophies, including Russian boar some idiot had turned loose near Kerrville, was the mounted head of a mule deer. With seventy-eight tines. Okay, that ol' buck was a freak, but he was our freak. It's probably all still there today.

Fred and I punched shoulders, and after I breathed on him he accused me of munching a sen-orita, and two beers later he talked me into cruising Brackenridge Park. We took the Willys, parked it in tree shadows, and then walked.

Not too far off, some exotic animal cry reminded me of the sprawling zoo nearby. I flat refused to say exactly what I was celebrating as we strolled the bro-ken sidewalks under a canopy of pecan, between spiky-leaved hedges of what we called algerita. For once, Fred wasn't his cocky self and didn't pay his usual bird-dog attention to the girls passing in fluffy peasant blouses. I complained that he celebrated in funny ways.

He looked like he wanted to hit me. "Easy for you to say, Kurt. Look at you, happy as a two-peckered billy goat, war work that you like, good pay for the duration . . ." He broke it off and flopped onto a park bench with a sigh, long legs stretched out so his scruffy boot tops showed. He studied me in the dusk, lit one of those nasty little cigars, took a drag. "You're goin' places. Sometimes you're almost too much to take."

My jaw dropped. Big, outgoing, two good legs, both parents alive, a devil with the girls; the guy I'd admired all my life. "You're browned off because something good happened to us at work?"

"Naw," he said, and after thinking it over, "well, in a way, yeah. Not just today. It's your got-damn' life. You fly planes by yourself. You understand the math. You have a trade you love so much you

druther do it than drink, might plan your life
around it if you're a mind to. I would in your place."
He waited for me to answer, but he saw I was too
dumbfounded, so he went on. "You simple shit, you
mean you don't know how much I envy you? And
always did? I'd swap with you in a jiffy, bubba, leg
and all," he finished in a near whisper, like a prayer.

I don't know what he expected from me. What
he got was Dutch-uncle talk. If he wanted to learn
a trade, he might spend more time looking over his
dad's shoulder in the machine shop or the specialty
auto shop, and I said so. But he didn't want to sweat
over a lathe, he said, or bang his knuckles on other
guys' cars either. I made several suggestions, but the
trouble was, they all amounted to getting good at
something he liked.

It came out in a roundabout way, but the upshot
was, Fred liked what that hotshot major did. Not the
scrounging supplies, or keeping records. No, he
liked cruising around in a yellow Cord roadster and
stuffing his pockets with poker winnings.

"Join the Army before it joins you. Go to officers'
training," I said. "It's a start."

What he said next was something that had never
occurred to me in all the years I'd known him.
"Kurt, you know I got out of school after you did,
but do you know *how* I got through? I'll tell you how:
Because I romped and stomped in football and
baseball and track. They didn't dare flunk me out
if they wanted winning seasons. But you can't play
high-school fuckaraound when you're nineteen, it's
illegal. They just graduated me out of thanks, I
reckon. I can't understand half the crap I read in
Astounding, I do it because you do. But I got a stack

of Planet Comics that'd choke a horse. It's not that I can't read. It's that I can't understand. Kurt, little bud, I know for a fact I couldn't make it through college or officer's training."

We chewed on that a while. One thing I knew he was good at was leadership, and the Army needed officers for that, too. But the Fred kind of leader would risk getting his butt shot off, and I didn't want to suggest it.

He did that himself, though, and perked up when I mentioned the Navy or Coast Guard. "I do swim pretty good," he said, and gave me a piece of the old grin. "But it doesn't sound much like yellow Cord country." While I was laughing at that, he mused, "You know, I wonder if guys with cars like that just don't like each other."

"Why not? Seems like they'd have things in common."

"You'd think so. But if you'd seen what I saw in Dad's auto shop today, you might think again." And he said while the major's Cord was inside the shop for some tinkering with its supercharger manifold, that slinky blue Delahaye coupe pulled up outside. "I've seen it when I was making deliveries at Kelly Field. Driver's an older guy, long sideburns, snappy dresser. He starts into the body shop, then notices the Cord, and jerks his head like he was snakebit and spots Major Dylan talking to Dad. Dylan looks at the Delahaye guy and looks back at Dad. Mr. Delahaye spins around like he had wheels on his feet and chirps his tires on his way to hellandgone." Fred mulled it over, then went on, "Maybe they'd done some street racing, and Mr. Delahaye lost. You think?"

I shrugged. "They didn't nod or wave or say howdy?"

"Nope, I got the idea they didn't want hide nor hair of each other."

"It's a puzzler," I agreed. "One thing sure, the old guy's name isn't really Delahaye. Or is it?"

Fred's turn to shrug. "I could find out. Dad keeps records of what he does on those specialty jobs. You know that guy, too?"

I said I didn't think so, without a name to tag him, then Fred stretched and yawned and punched my shoulder again and said he was in a mood for a movie. We went to *Hail The Conquering Hero* since Eddie Bracken was always good for a smile.

And after he collected his Indian and led me home for buttermilk, I asked him to keep a sharp eye out for an armadillo. In what condition, he asked. In all four wheels churnin' condition, I said, I had no use for something he scraped off the highway. That might be tougher, he said, and what in the world for? I just winked and told him it was a military secret. I was sure it would be if Major Athol Dylan had anything to say about it.

FIVE

Seems like you can never find an armadillo when you really need one. Worse still, our schedule slipped again during the next week for lack of special parts. Meanwhile, Ben Ullmer got some rare photocopies direct from Wright Field where somebody rode herd on projects like Pancho, and they kept me busy. They were taken from Luftwaffe manuals, the negatives recently smuggled out through Switzerland. Now I saw why it was important that I could read German, though I just about read all the print off a dictionary translating some of it. When you come across *Luftschraubenregelgetriebe* you wish they'd just learn English like sensible folks. No wonder they were mad at everybody. I should be immune, but some of those jawbreakers made me a little testy myself.

For once, Ben was *my* student, and after seeing those photocopies he paid me more respect. That steam turbine, built to Ben's drawings, was overdue,

and the major swore he was tracking the delay, but
Ben wasn't so worried about his hardware. He was
nervous about the hazards of the chemicals that
would run it, and the real experts were in Germany.
Luftwaffe mechanics had to learn the handling dan-
gers, which could take a man's finger off at the
shoulder from what I read. Since practically anything including spit would make peroxide boil,
everything that it touched had to be stainless steel
with nary a blemish or rust spot. Roy Dee built some
expensive stainless versions of ordinary stuff like
funnels so we wouldn't have to order them and then
listen to Major Dylan's excuses for a month.

The day we lugged three hundred more pounds
of crate out of the Cord was another occasion for
applause. The major was all smiles, maybe the kind
of smile you strain through your teeth, until Bub
Merrill came over to check the papers. Nobody else
was beside them, and I was studying a photocopy
while Ben and Lacey tore into the crates on a workbench. The major said something I didn't catch.

"Had to be done," Bub replied calmly.

A little louder now: "How many times are you going to aggravate people up the channel, Merrill?"

"Many as it takes," said Bub in the same mono-
tone, like he was commenting on the weather.

"They tell me you've called in just about all the
IOUs you had in the system," said the major.

Bub never raised his voice, but, "I suppose 'they'
have names, Major," he said. "And if it's names like
Larry Bell or Colonel Kearby I'm interested. Otherwise . . ." He smiled, shrugged, and turned his
back on our military supply officer.

The major glanced around, and I tried to look like I hadn't been listening, but I think he caught me. Under his tan he was pale, little muscles in that handsome chiseled face twitching, and the look he gave me made me glad I wasn't wearing a uniform. I hoped he didn't have a dog because if he did, it was due for a few swift kicks. Before he brought his hands to his sides I saw his fingers had little tremors, like a fishing bobber when a perch tests your bait. And that made me curious, and gave me an idea for a harmless little experiment.

When the Cord charged off a few minutes later, Bub watched its dust wake from the window, hands on his hips, shaking his head ever so slightly. Then he heard Ben exclaim with pleasure over the contents of a box and strode across the shop with, "Listen to you; I swear it must be Christmas morning." I sloped over and looked past Howard Lacey's shoulder while they oohed and ahhed at what looked like brushed steel spaghetti, only thicker and twisted into shapes Ben had called for. Lacey could fudge 'em a bit if need be, but Ben had every curve memorized, and if he was happy, I figured they were right on the money.

It took us two days to find out, and yes, we had to reroute wiring bundles away from new pipes that, when carrying live steam, would be hotter than Terlingua chili. It all fitted inside Pancho, though, boosting my respect for Ben's design work.

Superchargers can scatter. That's a nice word for "explode," when a stray bit of hardware gets gulped by vanes whirling at several thousand rpm. Bub Merrill appreciated the shroud of armor plate Ben designed to keep scattered debris from shooting back through the thin firewall like a grenade into the cockpit.

"If this puts us overweight," Ben told the pilot, tapping the hardened steel shroud to get a "whonnnng" like a padded gong, "I can always haul it back out." He cut a sly glance at Bub.

"No you won't," Bub countered. "If we need to drop ten pounds, I'll just get circumcised." More Texas talk; seemed like Ben would never get used to it.

About that time we found that the new peroxide tank had been partially slosh-coated inside. Special coatings are sometimes sprayed on metal surfaces in processing, but this was no place for it. We had to take the tank back out for an acid flush and steam-cleaning. It was Roy Dee whose inspection spotted that coating after we'd installed the tank.

"Well, we'd have found out the second we ran a smidgin of peroxide in there," Ben said.

"I doubt it," said the sheet-metal man. "The coating is only near the top. Good thing I have an inspection mirror."

Ben paused, gnawed his lip, and nodded. "I'd put it stronger. You're saying we wouldn't get a chemical reaction 'til the tank was pretty much full. Right?"

"Most likely," said Roy Dee, then realized what that meant. "Oh, shit, shaw, Shinola," he added, meeting Ben's gaze. "Well, that tank won't jump back outa there by itself. I got work to do, Ben." And he went after his toolbox.

And Ben made some calls to the company that furnished the tank, because his drawings specified that the tank be flushed of any such remnants of processing. They claimed they'd flushed it. Ben told them to do it better next time. No, he didn't have time to send it back, and he couldn't explain the problem for security reasons.

Later, when he came back from the military maintenance hangars with the cleaned tank, Ben swore next time he'd add a new spec to the list on the drawing. Military specifications get letters and numbers. Ben said, "I'll add MIL-TFP-41. That should do it."

MIL normally stood for "military," but I didn't recognize the rest. "I don't know that one," I said.

"Make—it—like—the—fuckin'—print—for once," he explained in a growl. Designers had their own lingo, I guess.

That evening at the Mollers', I pecked out a note on Mrs. Moller's typewriter. I said everybody liked Miguel so much we hoped he was healthy, and we thought it was just possible that he might have a touch of sugar diabetes. If she needed someone to pay a doctor to find out, we would be glad to pay the bill. By "we," I meant me. I also asked if it was okay if we gave him a bike or candy, and asked Sra. Hernandez if she would write me an answer; Spanish would be okay, I said, figuring I could get it translated. I sealed the note in an envelope for Mickey and gave it to him the next day. I knew he'd give her the note because I told him no more Three Musketeers for him until she wrote me an answer.

On our hangar battle map, pins labeled "General Patton's tanks" advanced toward a town called St. Lo. The fighting was said to be fierce, with our infantry slugging it out in hedgerows against the troops of Field Marshal von Runstedt, with our P-47 fighter-bombers racing along at hedgehop altitude, mowing down enemy tanks and troops like deadly lawn mowers with their small bombs, rockets, and eight machine guns each. Our P-51 Mustangs were used to escort our bombers. Slower than jets, they had some luck in air-to-air combat but wouldn't have lasted long hedgehopping, with every soldier in the Wehrmacht trying to hit them. With the P-47 Thunderbolt it didn't seem to matter what hit it; the durn thing was a flying tank. Bub said a rumor had started up: If you want to send a picture to your girl, get into a sleek, gorgeous P-51 Mustang. If you want to come back in one piece, get into a fat, ugly Thunderbolt.

Rumors had it that our heavy bombers over Germany were sitting ducks for little Nazi jets, which made me worry more about whatever those Nazi long-distance Ju-488 bombers, Pancho's special enemy, might be carrying. We owned the air low over western France, but at high altitude over Germany it was another story. Our own Pancho had been dreamed up to help remedy that. Like the Nazis, we had to get our interceptors up fast and high near our own cities, but unlike them, we didn't yet have jet-propelled interceptors in production. According to Bub, Pancho might be almost as good, and in limited production lots sooner.

A year before, we'd have had a map of the Pacific on the wall, but the news from there was almost all good now, and in the wetback hangar we felt like our special enemy was in Europe. We cheered when WOAI announced our B-29s had started bombing Japan, and again when a U.S. task force caught half

the Jap navy in the Philippine Sea and whaled the
tar out of them.

Pancho's steam turbine, linked up to the supercharger, gave me fits when I installed it. In spite of
our joking, my hands weren't small enough to get
locknuts started on some of the bolts. Ben didn't
want me to use Mickey's little fingers until Roy Dee
reminded him they were using midgets in our aircraft factories for that very thing. Besides, I could
do the rest and test Mickey's work myself. So little
Mickey got to do some of the essentials on Pancho
in small ways. And in a very, very big way.

When Mickey brought my envelope back, I read
the reply and told him now we could pay him for
the work he did. Sra. Hernandez had printed, in
good English, that with many thanks, she did not
want Miguel to see another doctor. There was no
need for it. She made sure Miguel got his medicine,
and we could give him whatever we liked, and repeated that candy was okay.

I drove home that weekend, flew the Babe one
more time, then trundled it into our barn and pick-
led it for long-term storage. Then I oiled up my first
old Schwinn, the Mickey-sized one built low with
dinky wheels, and crammed it into the Willys's
trunk. I spent all Sunday evening with Mama and
Elke and, because I couldn't talk about the project,
I told them about the funny little TexMex kid who
was our own factory midget. Early Monday morning
I got on the outside of too many of Mama's potato
pancakes, then made tracks for Randolph Field, full
as a tick.

In a season of special days, that was one I'll never forget. First thing I did at the hangar was unload the old Schwinn, a scraped-up victim of many a spill I took when I was Mickey's size. The little guy acted like he'd been loaned a Cord roadster until I told him it wasn't a loan but his own property now, and then he was plain speechless. It was comically clear he'd never ridden a bike before. It took Mickey half the morning before he could get off it when he wanted to, instead of when it wanted him to, but the wiry little cuss never lost a patch of hide in his two-wheel rodeo. Ben finally told Sparks and me if we wanted to watch Looney Tunes, do it at a movie, though he was fighting a smile, too.

An Army olive Ford sedan drove up at morning coffee-break time, leading a truck at about ten miles an hour, and I was surprised to see Major Dylan get out of the Ford. It wasn't his place to say, but he told Mickey to stay away from the hangar.

Then someone said, "He did it. Remember, the major did it." I couldn't tell who had said it, but sure enough, he had finally done something on his own.

While Mickey pedaled away far enough that he didn't have to hear any more orders from head-quarters, Major Dylan told us what was in the truck, which I thought explained why he wasn't risking his big yellow boy toy. I gave him a point for having the nerve to escort that load. He got his papers signed and drove off a ways to park and watch.

The truck held several shiny tanks, each nested in a sponge-lined, wheeled wagon and carrying about ten gallons of peroxide. I wondered if the guys in fatigues got hazard pay; they unloaded those little wagons like they knew they weren't off-loading kegs of near beer. They didn't hang around when they were done, either.

The major came back after we wheeled the peroxide tanks to a hazmat shed near the hangar, and his hair was plastered to his forehead with dried sweat. It was then that I remembered my idea and came up to the major, tossed a couple of big ol' washers up, and caught them. They weren't A.N. parts, but common iron fender washers as wide as a tennis ball. Not many outlanders knew it, but the washer-toss was Luckenbach's version of horseshoes, and even Fred Moller had learned not to play against me for money. "Major, they tell me you're a gamblin' man," I said, and handed him the washers.

"So this is what passes for money in Texas," he said. "Funny, but they never anted up any of these when I cleaned out those guys in the Seybold Hotel."

"Nah, it's what *makes* money in Texas," I said. The Seybold, in Fort Worth, was the site of an ongoing poker game where cattlemen won and lost entire ranches on poker hands. "You dig a cup-sized hole, stand back a ways, and try to get your washer in it. I could show you how, if you had a dollar."

"I do believe I've been challenged," he said, hefting the washers, studying them as if there was a catch to it.

There is. The catch is, you've got to be good and steady at it, and I was. The worst that could happen was, I might lose a couple of bucks. Ben gave me the fish eye—this was work time—but he didn't say so, and he and the others came out to the parking area, where I dug a cup in that hard caliche dirt, then paced off the distance and drew a line.

I'll cut it short: I sandbagged a bit in practice and found that the major had good coordination, enough not to embarrass himself, and then we wagered an RC Cola. Because I skunked him we double-or-nothinged until he owed me a buck sixty, and when he wanted to double up again I asked if he had the cash on him. He pulled out a roll of bills that looked like a short snorter managing to look bored and determined and insulted all at once, and pulled off a fiver. I allowed as how I was satisfied, and then I missed the cup a mile—okay, a foot. I didn't feel like making an enemy of him but more important, for the first time he had a chance to break even. It was suck-it-up time. That was the point.

The major stood at the line, took a stance, and it was so quiet you could hear a meadowlark off somewhere in the distance. He finally took his shot, and beat me by an inch, and I pocketed the washers and shook hands with him and said now he was an honorary plainsman.

So Major Athol Dylan marched away from there with his head high and all his cash and his imagined honor intact. And the way his sideburns had begun to leak, and the way his hand had been shaking, if Major Athol Dylan ever won a poker hand at the Seybold Hotel it was with a bunch of blind tenderfeet who couldn't smell flop sweat. While the major might have been a lot of things, a poker stud wasn't on the list. He would take a risk, all right, but playing cards for money he'd telegraph more signals than Western Union. I pondered the notion of telling Fred about it; should I tell him his hero was all hat and no cattle? Maybe not.

Ben Ullmer knew a dozen reasons why we shouldn't rush a ground test of that peroxide turbine and only one reason why we should: The suspense was killing us. Not a man broke for lunch; we were too busy getting Pancho rolled outside with all her upper cowl panels off, surrounded by workstands. We learned that with our rig, gravity feed was the safest way to transfer peroxide. It was nearly four when we wheeled the workstands away from Pancho, Mickey again dragging that little stand up for Bub to use, and this time I shooed our hangar rat away to a safer distance even though we had put in only a gallon of peroxide.

Bub proceeded by clipboard as usual. He fired the Ranger up with me standing fire-extinguisher duty. It reached steady temperature quickly, also as usual. We had landing gear and wing tie-downs tight, which wasn't so usual, and it was a good thing we did. There was nothing ordinary about the canvas-rip screech of those props when Bub cranked on the supercharger, Pancho lunging against her tie-downs like a plow mule, landing gear skidding a few inches despite brakes, tie-downs, and all. That little beauty wanted to scat. I thought maybe Ben's thousand-horse guess was a little low. It was goose-pimple time.

But within ten seconds the duct temperatures were up to where they'd stay, and if you're going to have a steam leak, that's when you don't want it, so that's when we got one. Everyone else was looking below the plane where the steam exhaust rocketed out with a hoarse roar, but I saw a thin clear jet of something that became a steam plume between the turbine and the engine. If Pancho's plywood skin panels had been on, that clear live steam under pressure would've cut them clean through. I gave Bub the throat-cut signal: *Kill it, now.*

He did, and valved off the blower outlet so he could use up the remaining peroxide, because Ben had decreed that no peroxide would enter the wet-back hangar. We stayed late to seal that steam leak, and it must have been eight in the evening before I headed for the Mollers', wishing I could tell Fred what a heck of a day I'd enjoyed.

What I couldn't know was, my day wasn't over by a bunch, and I could have told Fred anything I liked because he was in no shape to hear me.

SIX

I whistled my way up the Moller front steps, noting that since the Indian wasn't parked out front where everybody could see it, Fred couldn't be home. Sure enough he wasn't, and I didn't smell the kitchen magic that said Mrs. Moller was trying to make us bust our belts. It was never completely quiet at the Mollers'; not until now. Humid summer days like that, people kept windows open hoping to catch a breeze.

I called a cheery "hi" inside, then did it again louder. "Out here," Gene Moller called from the backyard. He wasn't a talker, and said nothing more, sitting alone in the glider swing, watching as I trotted outside. He made his guess by the smile on my face. "You haven't heard, then," he said, and it was a croak.

He sounded a hundred years old, and my face fell. First thing I thought was, that durn Indian had landed Fred behind bars, but I'd never say that to his dad. I shook my head and sat down. I said I'd driven from Luckenbach straight to work and had a long day. Then I waited.

As a man of few words, Fred's dad made every one count. "My boy's not expected to live," he said. His eyes were dry, but they hadn't been for long.

Clapping my hands at my temples, I couldn't even start a proper sentence. What, I said, and then how, and then when, and then I held my hands out, begging.

It took ten minutes to get enough details for me to deal with it. Saturday night, Fred was supposed to be in Brackenridge Park. He wasn't; around midnight, some farmer on his way home from market-day called the police in New Braunfels, midway on the Austin highway. Heading north, the farmer had rounded a curve to see a ball of blackness surrounded by a big ring of sparks coming his way, and a pair of headlights next to it coming head-on at high speed. In his lane.

What he was seeing was Fred's Indian, flipping over and over on its way into the dry brush near the highway. The car he saw only as blinding headlights swerved back into its own lane and zoomed past without slowing. The farmer stopped with his lights on. At the end of a settling dust trail lay what was left of the Indian but even when the wreckage began to burn, the farmer couldn't find its rider. He got the cycle's license plate number and drove on to the nearest phone at New Braunfels.

And it was nearly three hours before they found my bud out in the brush with his skull stove in, compound fractures of both legs, and other stuff Mr. Moller said that I don't even remember. They thought Fred was dead at first. He was found 130 feet from the first highway scrapes. The ambulance brought him back to San Antonio.

Mrs. Moller hadn't left the hospital since they got the call at dawn on Sunday. Mr. Moller had come home for changes of clothes but was too shaky to drive back. "Must be after six," he said.

Way after, but I let it ride. "I'll drive you—if that's okay," I said. He nodded. I had to help him up.

I'd never seen Gene Moller scared of anything, but he was afraid of what he'd find at the hospital. On the way, he said, "Fred found you something Saturday morning. It's in that ol' varmint cage near the back steps."

I knew what it had to be. If I'd told Fred why I wanted it, he wouldn't have done it. "Armadillo?"

"Little fella, size of a cantaloupe," Mr. Moller said. "I put in a few table scraps."

"He'll eat it," I said. Whatever it is, and the bugs that it draws, it's all the same to an armadillo.

It was twilight when we reached the hospital. Mrs. Moller's news was good: Tough as a longhorn, Fred was holding his own. But he still wasn't conscious. "They worked on him some more. His head's the right shape again," she said, shaky-voiced.

About ten, a doctor came in. He said the signs were good but that we ought to go home until morning. He promised they'd call if there was any change, and I drove the Mollers home. I hadn't even seen my bud yet, and it drove me nuts that there was nothing I could do. Hours later, I decided there might be something, then I managed to fall asleep.

Tuesday was another big day. Mrs. Moller promised to call me at the number I gave her if she had news, good or bad, and I lugged The Major to work, cage and all.

At least it helped take my mind off my bud. Nobody had to ask why I named our little beady-eyed critter The Major. Mickey took its food and water as his mission, though at first it rolled up in its patented armor plate whenever we went near. In time, I knew, it would get used to us. Ben heaved a sigh deep as a well when he saw that we weren't going to let it go right away. As Bub Merrill told him, "Resistance is futile. Shoot, I'll adopt him myself."

We did two more run-ups on Pancho that day, the second a long one to make sure we'd cured the steam leak. Mickey stuck pretty close to me all day, helping to the point of getting in my way; somehow he knew I had trouble on my mind. Every time Ben's phone rang I crossed my fingers, but it was never for me. I'd told him a close pal was hurt, and after work I used the phone.

Mrs. Moller said there had been no change. I said I'd eat out and be home late, but I didn't want to say more. Actually, I didn't eat at all. I needed three calls to find where the wreckage of the Indian was, and saying I was Fred's little brother, got close directions to where it, and Fred, had been found off the highway. They wanted to know why I needed to know. I said Fred had been carrying a set of keys the family needed. Okay, I lied.

I couldn't actually get to the wreckage in the locked New Braunfels impound yard, but I could see through the cyclone fence that any paint scrapes from a car to the Indian would've been burnt to cinders. No help there, so I scooted the Willys up and down the highway 'til I spotted some recently burnt brush. From that point, the highway scrapes and caliche scars were easy to find.

And just off the highway shoulder I found a few little flakes of paint, gleaming in the late sun, and the color of the sun. I gathered them up, along with pieces of cylinder fin and other bits that had broken off before the Indian caught fire. Then I sat in the Willys and shook, thinking about it.

The pieces of the Indian had no paint on them, so I couldn't prove what I was thinking. I wasn't even certain those paint flakes were the same shade of yellow as a certain Cord roadster. Watching shadows stretch through the brush, I tried to make sense of my suspicion; why I'd had this gut feeling I hadn't ad- mitted to myself until I found bits of paint; why my bud might be racing his got-damn' hero; why Major Dylan might be on that stretch of highway at that time of night. I also wondered if telling anybody might, in some way, sabotage Project Pancho whether I was right or not.

I drove back to the hospital in twilight, and though they wouldn't let me see Fred, Gene Moller came out of his room with big tears rolling silently down his cheeks, and he was smiling. "He knows me," he said. "My boy's coming back." I pushed my dark thoughts away and let myself cry.

We didn't celebrate the Fourth much, as I recall. After years of salivating at fireworks stands I could barely see over, wishing for the day when I had the money for all the whistling red devils I could carry, now that day had come, and I had more important stuff on my mind. Made me wonder if life was really fair. For the first time in my memory I ignored the dozens of fireworks stands where you could buy Chinese crackers a nickel a pack, or a pack of baby giants for half a buck, or a rocket on a guide stick as high as your breastbone for forty cents. To look into the night sky that Fourth of July you'd have thought the war was being fought over SanTone. I didn't even stay up to watch.

Days later, they told us Fred was definitely improving. Not only that, but Pancho flew. Bub's flight card scheduled nothing beyond simple maneuvers in what we called a swing around the patch, but it was a long swing that would take him south over the scrub toward Beeville and Goliad. The transmitter was tuned for Ben's unit, and though Ben wanted something called a wire recorder to let him record Bub's transmissions, I guess those gadgets were too new for us to get one. We did the next best thing. Much as they hated to, Ben and Sparks both stayed in the shop with pencils and paper to take down everything Bub reported on the radio.

Pancho's takeoff wasn't any more wild and woolly than the last of the air racers until it was a few hundred yards down the runway, away from some cadet waiting his turn in a trainer. Mickey stood beside me at the mouth of the hangar. You couldn't pick out Pancho's engine note until a second after we saw a white trail erupt from below the fuselage. That meant Bub had cranked her up to METO, maximum-emergency takeoff power. And that meant a steam exhaust rocket assist by a turbosupercharger fueled from hell.

Now we heard it, a twin-engine note on the breeze, urgent as a hornet in heat, and Pancho leaped off the runway like I flat don't know what. I'm glad I didn't jerk when Mickey grabbed my hand in his and squeezed so hard it actually hurt. By now I was used to the fact that he always seemed to have a fever.

The guys had talked it over, and couldn't decide whether it would be less noticeable to stay low and get away from the field sooner, or climb like the devil and give anyone beyond the field less time to identify Pancho. Its weight and balance hadn't shifted from known P-77 habits, so Bub didn't have to feel it out so gently. The steam exhaust forced the decision. Ben didn't want anyone beyond the field perimeter to look up and see a tiny aircraft with a billowing white exhaust on its underbelly, without one of those new ten-second rocket bottles. So Bub Merrill stayed low only long enough to fully retract Pancho's gear, then, near the perimeter fence, turned her nose toward heaven.

And oh, Lord, Lord, how she climbed! I shouted for joy as she dwindled to a dot and became only a fleeting wisp of white, veering south.

While Roy Dee cheered, Mickey said, "Why are you laughing?"

I told him I had just remembered the one about the guy who had five cats and five entry holes cut in his back door. Why more than one hole? 'When I holler scat,' the guy says, 'I *mean* scat!' " I added, "Mickey, Pancho's for the guy who knows what scat means."

"You laugh at strange things," he said, and let go of my hand as if he were guilty.

We hurried back inside the shop, and, while listening to Bub, I took some notes in case the others needed them. Bub's gauges were all nominal as he leveled off at twelve thousand. Since we hadn't installed a new oxygen tank yet, he didn't risk climbing higher. Bub said his altimeter was reading ninety-five hundred after only sixty seconds off the runway. As far as I know, that was a record for props. Airspeed, once he leveled off, soon pushed past four hundred, and that was all the day's flight card called for.

"There's more on tap, Mother," Bub said, his voice made scratchy by vibration, "but if we adjust the exhaust nozzle, we might convert some of that into better climb."

"Roger, Wetback," Ben said. "How's the handling?"

"We're about to find out. Aileron roll to port in ten seconds."

Rolling Pancho with a tank half-full of hydrogen peroxide wasn't a maneuver I liked to think about. After an endless few seconds when no one breathed, we heard Bub's calm, "Sweet and steady. Aileron roll to starboard in ten seconds."

More silence, and Mickey's hot little hand crept into mine again. "This is a scary part, Kurt?"

"It is if there's even a speck of stuff to shake loose in the peroxide lines," I said, drawing a look from Ben that said, "Will you kindly take that kind of talk outside?" I shut up.

Finally, after a couple of shallow dives, Bub announced he'd flown the plan and was headed for the barn, and his only complaint was vibration. We wanted to start celebrating, but, as they'd said of the trickiest Gee Bee racer, even after you touch down you could wind up in a sack. I had to explain to

Mickey that, yeah, maybe we were a little superstitious about celebrating too soon.

Lacey made a quick trip to the maintenance hangars for hydraulic fluid, knowing it'd be a half hour before Bub came whirring up our taxiway. They both arrived back at the hangar at the same time, and we had our little soda-pop celebration. Then, while I was helping Lacey unload his fluid cans, he said, "Guess who I saw parked, watching Merrill in the landing pattern."

"Everybody," I said, still pumped up over our success.

"Yeah," Lacey chuckled, "and our supply officer was part of everybody. You reckon he's allergic to celebrations?"

As casual as I could make it, I said, "Could be. You notice if his roadster was looking spiffy as usual?"

"Didn't see it. He was off by himself, standing next to an Army-issue Ford," Lacey said. That would figure, I thought, if the Cord had body damage. I had been watching for the Cord without success. And of all the body shops in San Antonio, I was pretty sure which one would be least likely to repair that damage.

That evening I got to see my best bud take food through a straw. One eye was under bandages and both of his legs were hung up like trapped animals, but Mr. Moller said to ignore the colors of Fred's face because he was on the mend. The Mollers took my arrival as their chance to get something new to them: a genuine hospital supper. For a minute after they left us alone, I just stood there. I decided it was time for some questions. I said, "You tell the police what happened yet?"

The pain medicine kept him woozy, but his one good eye tracked me okay, and his voice was clear enough. "Nah. What would I say? Rat-racin' some yahoo in a pickup truck and sideswiped him? Hey, I just cut it too close, little bud. Like you always said I would."

I stood there some more and swapped long looks with Fred, and as I did, a kind of cold fever began to build in me. "So you do remember," I said, keeping it mild.

"Sure."

"Then you must remember the pickup's color."

"Black; maybe dark blue," he said.

"Yeah, or maybe a roadster, in fact. Yellow," I said. "The color of the stripe down a man's back when he runs you off the road and won't stop while your damn' Indian burns."

Fred swallowed and closed his eye. "Shit. He tell you, then?"

"In a way," I said, realizing Fred had just turned my suspicion into certainty. It wasn't fair to Fred, but I took advantage of the moment. "What I don't get is, how you two connected up where you were."

A long silence. Then, "We connected earlier in the evening." Fred was tiring now. "Austin, at Barton Springs. Spotted the Cord. Went over to say hi. Him and the Delahaye guy."

"You sure it was him?"

"Delahaye coupe's hard to miss," Fred said.

"You ever get his name?"

"Uh-unh."

Well, that was one thing I could maybe find out

myself. "So you egged him into a race home," I sighed.

"Not exactly. Major says, drop by later, we'll convoy to SanTone." Longer silence. "So I did. Kurt, we were just havin' fun. He didn't mean to, he must'a swerved around a chuckhole."

Swerved. Right. While they were blasting along at high speed. Well, whoever was at fault, you don't hit-and-run. "And you're afraid this would get him in trouble," I said.

The eye flicked open. "It would," he said. "Sure as hell."

"Sure as hell," I agreed. My bud looked like he'd talked himself to exhaustion, with my help. "Get some sleep. You look like the last rose of summer before last," I said.

"Whup your ass any day," he said. "Oh, you get my present?"

"Armadillo? Yep. Brung him to work. Thinking of training him for rodeos."

"Don't make me laugh; it hurts. What'd you name it?"

I pondered my answer because Fred wouldn't like the truth. "We call it Fred," I said, and left him shaking and cussing.

I linked up with the Mollers at their house. She was cooking a real meal, both of them still outraged at the uneatable suppers they'd walked away from at the hospital. "Take a seat," said Gene Moller. "Next time I spend a dollar thirty-five for a hospital meal, just wheel me straight to the loony ward."

I had the gut-rumbles anyhow, so I sat. Funny how hard it is to get around to asking a question you don't want the other guy to think too much about. Finally, without using its name, I asked him about that swoopy block-long foreign coupe I'd seen at the Moller shop.

"Delahaye," he said. "Looks like it could fly, doesn't it?" I nodded. Before I could phrase my follow-up, he went on: "But what else would we expect from a fella who owns the country's top aircraft factory?"

I thought, Boeing, North American, Bell? Oh God, *Bell?* The very idea made my stomach flop. Drymouthed, I said, "Which factory?"

"I forget," said Gene Moller. "It's not one of the big ones, just the best, according to him. Signs his checks Kevin Ireland, Esquire."

I nodded like it wasn't important, and watched Mrs. Moller serve up a real supper.

SEVEN

That vibration in Pancho's innards turned out to be a problem of prop-blade adjustment, which had to be reset and then monkeyed with on the ground. Mama used to say "Monkey isn't a verb." Dad would say, "It is when you work on race planes." Ben flew a consultant in to help, and I didn't get a chance to ask Bub Merrill about Mr. Kevin Ireland, Esquire, until later. I might've even asked Major Dylan, if I'd seen him around.

After I did ask Bub: "Funny you should bring up that name," he said, like he wanted me to explain.

"Why funny? He has work done on this terrific foreign car of his in town, is all."

"That's not all, but there's something called need to know. Ben needs to know more'n I do about these things, but I'm not sure he'd talk about it."

"What things, Bub? I say something wrong?"

"Naw. Let's just say Ben and Wolverine are competing."

That meant all of us were competing with Wolverine. But I didn't know what Wolverine was, and I said so.

"Well, they're kinda new. Wolverine Aero," said Bub. "A Michigan engineering outfit that reinvented itself after the founder went West," he said, using vintage pilot's jargon for "died." "They reincorporated a year before Pearl Harbor." He brightened suddenly, happy to be able to tell me something, I guess. "It's not a secret that old man Ireland left his middle-aged son Kevin a pisspot full of bucks and a bright design staff. Or that Kevin Ireland converted the business into his hobby, which is trying to build his firm a name in aircraft development. Only thing Ireland Junior was known for was, he threw the wettest parties for a favored few of the race pilots."

"Funny my dad never mentioned him," I said.

Bub laughed. "Favored few, I said. If Jurgen Rahm had been a high roller who won the Collier Trophy instead of a guy who made such things happen, he'd know Kevin Ireland, all right."

The way he said it I already didn't like Mr. Ireland. I also realized that I was hatching up some uncomfortable ideas about powerful men. "So what's he doing down here piloting a Delahaye coupe," I asked.

"I didn't hear the question," said Bub, and gave me a horsewink. "And if you shouted, I still wouldn't. I'm not supposed to know either," he added in a stage whisper.

I chewed that over for a moment. "So Mr. Ireland's down here in the aero business. We aren't talkin' civil air stuff, I suppose."

"You suppose right." Bub wasn't a guy to volunteer criticisms, and I got the idea he'd just as soon drop the subject.

But he wasn't a mealymouth either. I said, "So Ireland runs Wolverine Aero. Does he test-fly his own projects like, um, Howard Hughes?"

"Nope. But he hovers over his people like an autogiro, maybe on the theory that some expertise will rub off on him. And he wants to be Hughes or Larry Bell so bad he can taste it."

"You think he'll make it?"

Bub sighed, pushed his hat back off his forehead, and said, "All right, here it is, young stud: Howard Hughes has bags of money, a rage to succeed, a mind like a slide rule, and world-class talent. Take away the slide rule and the talent and you have Kevin Ireland. If you want him. Can we leave it at that?"

"Sure. Sorry, Bub." I looked apologetic for him, and he grinned to show it was okay. I spent a good part of the afternoon mulling it over while Mickey hung around me and let The Major out of his cage, tempting him with lunch scraps. Until then I hadn't tried to think like a detective, but it was past time I did. About the time I decided I should have already checked out the other body shops around San Antonio, I told Mickey to look out for The Major's sharp little digging claws.

"You're pretty smart," Mickey said. I winked at him and forgot about it for a while.

I didn't want to be overheard, and I didn't want to make Mr. Moller suspicious, so I asked to take off a little early to go to the hospital. Ben figured he understood.

A little after four, with a handful of nickels and a notepad, I used a hospital pay phone before seeing Fred. I'd never checked the Yellow Pages for body shops, but we used to say driving in SanTone was a dodge'em marathon. No wonder I used up nearly all my nickels. Without finding anybody who had a repair order for any 812 Cord of any color.

Down the hall, my big bud was feeling better even if his face was in Technicolor. I told him he looked like all the scenes in *Fantasia* shown at once, and he said I oughta see his shins, and I shuddered. Mrs. Moller sat in a corner with her knitting, so I tried to be sly. "Promise me something, Fred."

"What?"

"Trust me; you have to promise in advance."

"You're nuts, but okay," he said.

"Some of your hotshot buddies might be heavy on practical jokes. If any of 'em come around here, promise you won't see 'em unless one of us is in the room," I said.

He thought that over, while in the corner, needles clicked. Then he grinned, which looked just awful with his missing teeth. "Only one so far," he said, "is one I happened to run into recently."

"Here in this room?"

"Came after hours, but he talked his way in. Almost didn't recognize him. And durn if he didn't forget to leave the candy he brung me."

"He have much to say for himself?"

"Naw. Worried about me, of course. I told him what I told you: My own fault broadsidin' a ol' pickup truck."

"Just as well he didn't leave you any candy, Fred.

Too much sweets might not be good for you," I said, my gaze burning a hole in his.

"Well, he hasn't been back. Like I said, you're nuts, little bud," he joked, then changed the subject. But when I reminded him of his promise, he nodded, and I left it at that.

I spent some solo time that evening in the backyard glider, wiping sweat from my neck as locusts revved their engines in the mesquite, wishing for a breeze with half my mind while Fibber McGee cavorted on the Moller radio inside. With the other half of my mind I was thinking how lucky Fred was that, one, he had told Major Dylan he was sticking to his big lie about a pickup truck, and two, that the major hadn't left his candy. If Fred had barely recognized that scutter, he was probably wearing civvies using a fake name or something. And why would he do that, and him so proud of his almost uniform? I knew mighty got-damn' well why he might, but without a record of repairs to his car I couldn't tie it down to what cops call a motive. And my bud was too flat-ass bonehead dumb and loyal to say what needed saying. Probably call me a liar if it came to that.

We got Pancho's prop blades correctly reset on a Thursday, and on Friday, Bub let me do the engine run-up, leaning into the cockpit to talk in my ear as he stood on the workstand Mickey saw as his personal job. It pissed Ben Ullmer off, I think, to see me at the controls, but as Bub put it, a test pilot needs his crew chief to be at home in the business office. That's how I became Pancho's crew chief, signing off for notations in the flight log.

Bub went inside the hangar for some tape to mark a gauge. Mickey hopped up on the stand, and we grinned at each other like kids playing hooky. I nudged the throttle a tad just for fun, the propwash nearly blowing Mickey off his perch, and I made a big slow circle in the air with my finger like I intended to do a swing around the patch. Mickey laughed out loud, then gave me a funny look. He shouted, "Going to Austin?"

I shook my head, and shouted, "They'd shoot me down," seeing Bub on his way back out to us, and motioned for Mickey to hop down. And then I thought, *Why not?* I didn't mean fly there in an airplane I was scared to death to sit in, but if Major Dylan and Mr. Ireland were linking up there an hour away, Austin might be a place to check body shops. Tomorrow was Saturday, and since Ben was scheduled for a fast plane to Wright Field, we'd have all weekend off.

For the second time Mickey said, "You're pretty smart," and it gave me the willies not being sure exactly what he meant. He nodded to me, no longer grinning, then Bub was on the stand, slicing little bits of tape to put on the manifold pressure gauge. Bub's pocketknife was like mine, scalpel-sharp; most pilots kept them honed in the days before quick-release chute harness.

I intended to have a talk with our hangar rat, but by the time we shut down Pancho's engine and shoved her back in the hangar, Mickey had left. Sparks told me my little bud had zoomed off like he was late for supper, on the bike I gave him. I think Sparks was peevish because Mickey had sorta adopted me, but he never said anything, and they still worked together.

Now and then when the weather changed, like that afternoon with a curtain of harmless high cirrus clouds giving way to cadet-killer cumulonimbus thunderheads sweeping in off the Gulf, the meteorology guys would try and get off an extra radio-sonde balloon during the day before the wind made it iffy. I drove off watching little stick figures wrestle their big orange pear shape against fits of breeze. I think I saw Mickey there with his bike, but I figured there'd be other times, and I had other fish to fry.

First thing I did after crossing Austin's Congress Avenue Bridge to the middle of town was to find a parking place near the Driskill Hotel. Not only did they have no rooms, they said good luck finding one anyplace in town. I decided I was going to cuss out loud the next time someone gave me a sarcastic look, and said, "Don't you know there's a war on?" I knew, all right; I just didn't know who-all was fighting it. Yet.

It was already 5 P.M., and, from one of the hotel's pay phones, I managed to find four auto body shops still open. They weren't much help, and the other listings didn't answer. I thought ahead, tore out the Yellow Pages I needed, then had a brainstorm and tore out the page for paint stores. Luckenbach was a little closer than SanTone, and while I used my 'C' card to fill up with Esso Extra on South Congress, I got me a free Esso map of Austin. I was home in Luckenbach giving Mama a big hug before dark, and she didn't even complain when I said I'd have to be off again before breakfast.

I nearly had me a fit when Mama said Elke was on a date. A date? My little kid sister? And her only sixteen . . .

I called the Mollers to say where I was, fixed the back screen door and a leaky faucet, and gave Mama more money than she said she needed. Then I got on the outside of some of her leftover hassenpfeffer while I was doping out my next moves, circling locations of body shops and paint stores on the Austin map. Most of my circles were grouped near Congress and out East Sixth, with one on the Bastrop highway. I had just folded everything up when a Studebaker President pulled into the yard. I waited for what I thought was too long before strolling out on the porch—Mama said it was maybe ten seconds—to gape and stretch and pretend I wasn't trying to see into the car.

Well, Elke didn't even act guilty. The driver scrambled out and rushed up to pump my hand, and called me "Mr. Rahm," gabbing a mile a minute, and durn if he didn't act like I was visiting royalty. He had to get his daddy's car back by eleven, so Elke and I had a little time together. The way my little sis was filling out her clothes gave me prickly heat on my neck, but when I told her that blouse showed more Elke than somewhat, she told me off more than somewhat, and Mama settled us down with homemade peach ice cream. We made up, but I resolved to get home more often. Maybe buy Elke a blouse you couldn't stuff into the matchbox with my paint chips.

Those thunderheads had brought a sprinkle of early rain to the region, then moved on, the sun drying the highway as I drove. I was back in Austin before the body shops opened, dressed as flashy as I could manage, like a guy used to paying for his whims. In midmorning I changed tactics away from body shops because I figured stores that carried auto paint wouldn't be so hurried, and would want to sell me their stuff. At the third of my four listings, the salesman eyeballed the paint flakes in my matchbox and said he'd recently matched a special yellow chip like mine but didn't know what for. I paid him a buck to look up the record. It had been sold to the shop out Bastrop way. He warned me that they were a pretty pricey outfit, and that I could probably get just as good a job done in town. I thanked him and sauntered out.

A half hour later I parked the Willys again, jazzed its V-8 to get attention, and strolled into the shop with what I hoped was a devil-may-care grin. And a lie, since I didn't see the Cord anywhere.

I was tired of the Willys's color, I said. How much to paint it like my friend's supercharged Cord? The shop manager looked my coupe over while I tried to look patient. What color, he said. I took a chance: same color as the Cord you just painted, I said.

"Special job like that's gonna run ya a hunnerd-fifty. They'd sure see ya comin'," he said. "Though I'm playin' with a sorta orangy red you might like better than buttercup yella."

"Buttercup? You sure that was for Athol Dylan?"

"We don't need to match many special paints for 812 Cords, pal," he said. "But let me check." I bought me a red peanut pattie to give me something to bite while he thumbed over some bills. He finally frowned over one. "Nah. Fella's a Kevin Ireland, says here. Some other guy drove it here. Took it away yesterday."

"Tall guy, Yankee accent, looks like a movie star?"

"And perty proud of hisself," said the manager, nodding. "That's him. But the check was Ireland's."

"That ol' scutter," I said, like "Boys will be boys. The check clear?"

"Course it cleared."

"Well, they don't always. I'm gonna have some fun with this," I said, without the least idea what I was talking about but smiling my smile. "I'll give you a buck—no, two bucks, for that receipt."

I don't know what he thought I was doing, but he held up the receipt and smiled back. "Sawbuck and it's yours," he said.

And that's how I drove back to SanTone with proof of a left front panel repair and a buttercup yellow paint job to a Cord with Michigan plates. And for the five bucks, I got to stir around in the scrap pile where I found some metal Cord trim with paint smears that could've come from Fred's Indian.

Portrait studios in SanTone would've made me wait a week, but one lady said maybe I could get quick service from a place that did IDs and birth certificates, which I should've thought of to begin with. Cost me another five to get a pair of glossy prints of that receipt.

At the Moller place I bummed a big envelope and sealed the receipt and one copy inside with a note I made in my best draftsman's printing. I gave it to Mr. Moller for him and only him to open, and only if something ever happened to me. I also told him what I knew he suspected already: that in all innocence Fred might have made friends with some

wrong folks. And something else Mr. Moller probably hadn't suspected: If Fred had seen something
he wasn't intended to see, the accident might've
been an on-purpose, and they might try again, but
that Fred would never believe it 'til he woke up dead
one morning.

Then I hightailed it back to Luckenbach and took
my womenfolk shopping in Fredericksburg. No
point in doing it in Luckenbach, unless you could
wear a blouse made in the blacksmith shop. Which,
come to think of it, might've been a middlin' good
idea . . .

For the next day and a half, it was almost like old
times, only better and worse. Better because I was
fool enough to think I had a handle on what would
happen in the next few days; worse after Elke admitted she didn't care about high-school boys as
long as tall, handsome, romantic, poor, wounded
Fred Moller was still single. Lordy, Lordy . . .

I spent all Sunday, July 16, just hanging around
the farm. Seemed like everybody in town had to
drop by to see if I was still real. Near as I can figure,
I was burping Sunday supper's dessert about the
time when, six thousand miles away, other people
were turning Project Pancho on its head. After giving a lick and a promise to chores around the farm
I felt pretty good about myself, thinking of all the
power I had in my pocket. It wasn't much prepara-
tion for Monday, a day that would put old times
behind me forever.

EIGHT

Expecting Ben Ullmer to be back already by fast military flight, I was up with the chickens Monday morning so I could get to work an hour early. On my way I heard on WOAI that Marines were mopping up on the Pacific island of Saipan while, in France, our troops were fighting their way into St. Lo. It was easy to feel I was taking some small part in this global buttwhomp. Everybody on Project Pancho felt sure that, after Ben made his report, they'd have to clear us for those all-important flight trials to forty thousand feet. Maybe that very day!

That's why everybody but Mickey—and Ben, of course—showed up at the wetback hangar early. We all rolled Pancho outside, though a pair of us could've done it alone, and took extra care filling the peroxide tank. Bub, wearing his high lace-up boots with his gloves stuffed into his old flight jacket, helped me preflight Pancho.

Mickey leaned his bike against the hangar wall a

little before nine and came inside wearing an expression I couldn't translate. When Bub asked me to fire Pancho up and get the oil properly warmed, I just about busted my buttons with pride, and Mickey hauled his little stand out for me. In the cockpit I ran up the Ranger little by little and fiddled with the controls, pretending I was Bub shooting down a stratospheric bomber—but I shut her down when the gauges told me to and strolled into the shop, where Bub was checking his chute harness.

That's where we were when the phone rang and as acting project leader, Bub answered. You could see the set of his shoulders droop as he talked. Nobody else breathed.

It was Ullmer, calling from Ohio, and while he had to talk carefully on the phone, his news was not good. Listening to Bub, I gathered that Sunday afternoon they'd told Ben to proceed with the next phase, which we knew would be the stratosphere runs. Then Sunday night, before the flight back, the Pentagon sent a classified bulletin of some kind, and everything changed. They pulled Ben off the Wright Field flight line, all excited and secretive. Something happened just now, they said; hold everything.

Ben waited in a Wright Field ready room with a team he recognized as technical guys from Wolverine Aero, though they didn't mingle. A lot of coffee got drunk up, everybody tense.

Sometime after dawn they got hauled off again to different meetings. The upshot was, Pancho's next phase got canceled. Not delayed; *canceled.* Ben guessed from the gloomy looks that Wolverine's team got the same treatment. Bub listened a while longer, and didn't say much more, but meanwhile he took off his flight jacket.

When Bub Merrill put down that receiver he looked like he wanted to cry. "Gents," he said softly, "we've got the day off. Ben won't be back 'til tomorrow, but he says he's never worked with a better team. I won't tell you what that means, but you can guess."

Roy Dee spoke first, always thinking a step ahead. "We'll have to drain that hellbrew outa Pancho," he said.

Bub thought it over. "No, I'll use it up on some taxi runs and lock up the hangar, if Kurt will stay a while and help. That's still on the current phase of testing if I say so. You boys go have a few bottles of Pearl, if that's your poison."

I hadn't been on any previous military programs, so I wasn't sure how serious this was until I saw Sparks and Howard packing up the stuff at their workstations, quiet but reserved. It looked like they didn't expect to be working there anymore. Mickey kept tossing quick looks at me and Bub, without saying anything. But after the other mechanics left, the little guy said, "I'll leave your bike outside for you."

"It's yours, Mickey," I said. "Nothing's changed that."

"I think I'll have to go soon," he said, in what I'd later recognize as the understatement of the century.

"I think we all will, but that bike is yours, little bud," I said.

After some sad handshakes, though we expected to see the other guys the next day, the shop emptied, leaving Bub and me with Mickey. As we waved

Roy Dee off outside, I saw an orange dot disappearing into the sky, climbing fast, sliding westward on the wind. The meteorology crew was already driving away from their radiosonde shack. I had a sudden overpowering sense that we were the only people left in the world.

Not for long, though. Lost in my own thoughts, I began to pack some of my personal tools. I hadn't been back in the shop five minutes before I heard someone near say, "He doesn't know. Tell him."

I said, "Who doesn't know what," and looked around. Bub was away in the hangar, and through the window I could see Mickey outside playing with The Major, which was pretty tame now. Who the heck? Goose pimples again.

Then I saw the brilliant yellow flash of Major Dylan's Cord as it turned toward the hangar, and I forgot that voice, a stranger's but somehow familiar, that I'd heard before. I felt in my pocket. The photocopy was there.

Bub came into the shop from the hangar as Major Dylan entered from the outside door. "Boy, it's always something, isn't it," the officer said with a glum shake of his head. "Those damn' radio tubes have been held up."

Pancho's radio was on the fritz. I think it was frequency crystals, not tubes, we needed. Mickey came sidling in holding our tame armadillo like a kitten.

Bub took it all in. Generally the most decent guy you'd want to meet, he was already peevish. "Mickey, why don't you let The Major go, or take him with you wherever you're headed," he said.

Dylan frowned. "Let me go? What the hell are you talking about?"

"The armadillo," I said quickly. "That's his name: The Major."

Dylan peered closely at the critter Mickey held. "I thought they were dangerous," he said. Mickey backed out of the shop.

"They are," I said. "They're useless as tits on a boar hog. They make a whole career just scratchin' around lookin' busy. But you know how you see 'em squashed on the highway? They'll run alongside and sideswipe you at night, run you plumb off the road, leave you for dead. Sometimes they misjudge, though. That's why we call this one The Major, even if we didn't paint him yellow."

Dylan didn't move a muscle for long seconds. Bub blinked at me as if I'd starting spouting Swahili. Then Dylan smiled at Bub. "The kid's gone fucking crazy," he said, giving me the squint eye.

Bub's glance was still full of wonderment but, "Makes perfect sense to me," he said.

"I just dropped by to tell you, and I told you," Dylan said, turning. "You wanta watch your mouth, kid," he told me. I believe he actually thought he could bluff this one out.

"And you want to watch who you hit-and-run," I said, wishing my voice didn't shake. "I didn't want to do anything that might goof up the project, but that's all over, I reckon." As Dylan stopped, I added to Bub, "Somebody saw this son of a buck and Mister Kevin Ireland, Esquire, with their heads together in Austin, and he got sideswiped on the highway for it. Those two try real hard not to be seen together, and if you do, they'll try and smear you."

Bub cocked his head at Dylan, but just said, "That so?"

Dylan said, "I'll put that down to childish notions. Does my Cord look like it's been in a car smashup?" Then as he saw me pull the folded photo out, he sneered, "What's that, a homemade subpoena?"

Whatever that was. "You'll wish it wasn't what it is," I said, handed it to him, and turned to Bub. "It's proof he's just had that yella dog of his repaired and repainted in Austin after hitting an Indian motorcycle. I've got more proofs, too."

"Well, I be damn," Bub marveled. Without any hurry, he reached for his jacket and pulled his gloves from it. He was putting them on as Dylan, starting to sweat, folded the photo up and began tearing it in pieces. "And all for nothing," said Bub. "Guess you haven't heard our project got canceled early this morning. Don't figure on going anywhere, Major. Kurt, you want to hand me the phone?"

Major Dylan's hand took me in the gizzard like the end of a four-by-four as he grabbed the telephone by its vertical stalk and ripped it away from the desk, wires and all. "This what you wanted," he said, and threw it at Bub. I leaned against the wall doubled over and tried to draw breath, but I couldn't.

Our pilot ducked, but didn't advance. I guess he was more interested in clearing up details. "What I wanted was to believe you were just useless and not a saboteur," he said. "I couldn't figure where you got all the cash you throw around. You're no card-sharp. But Ireland has one skill: He knows how to spend other people's money. How much did he spend getting you to delay a war project competing with his, Major Ath-hole Dylan?"

"That's Ayth-ull, you Texas redneck," Dylan flared.

"I know an ath-hole when I thee one," Bub went on, savoring his lisp, and took a step forward.

Dylan licked his lips and tried once more. "Look, it's not sabotage. Anyway, I'm a patriot. I didn't even agree to talk to Ireland 'til I could see the invasion was a success. I'm not stupid. At worst, I may have screwed off a little." He put his hand in his pocket.

"Maybe attempted murder a little," Bub reminded him. "Your trouble is, you were just smart enough to get yourself shot after all this gets cleared up. Nobody can kid himself like a smart guy, Major. In wartime they have firing squads for this." And he took another step.

"Goddamn feather merchants," Dylan gritted, and I give him credit for the guts to meet an older man halfway. Still out of breath, I grabbed a scungy old coffee cup, but it flew past Dylan's head. For a man in his forties Bub got in a couple of good licks, but Dylan's right hand was full of something shiny now and my friend went down hard under a clubbing overhand right. I managed to grab an oak chair and stepped forward, swinging it around and over. It fetched up against Dylan's shoulder as he stamped on Bub's gloved hand while trying for his head, which just about made me crazy, and the impact swung Dylan half-around and the chair came apart, leaving me holding only its back and two legs so I was able to swing it around again and I reckon the son of a bitch figured half an oak chair beat what he held because he ducked away panicked and was out the door in a second, and he missed me with the set of brass knuckles he flung my way.

Papers and broken cups and a coffeepot and pieces of chair were underfoot, so I was late limping outside, still armed with what looked like a short oak ladder in my hands. Instead of jumping straight to his car, Dylan made for poor skinny little Mickey Hernandez, grabbing him up under one arm like a big doll. "I'll do him if you come after me," he snarled at me, dropping into the driver's seat and reaching toward his glove compartment, and then he made the ugliest sound I ever heard, like he was gagging.

He tried to leap up from his seat with our tiny hangar rat draped across his shoulder, and I knew Mickey's little monkey paws were strong, but what I saw was beyond belief. While one little brown hand gripped Dylan's hair, the other clamped into his throat; *way* into it. Dylan made another sound, half gurgle, half sigh, and his face started turning red and instead of hitting at Mickey he tried to pull the little guy's hands loose.

Mickey let himself be flung away across the roadster's sloping turtleback and scrambled down backward unhurt, his eyes round and fixed on this big scutter who had roughed him up. "Can you help him," was all he said when he was on his feet.

I didn't answer and I wasn't about to get too close while a guy who didn't like me, twice my size, was having himself a wild conniption. Dylan managed to stand, clawing at his throat, then flopped forward draped over his windshield and rolled onto his back. His neck was bleeding heavily from his own fingernails, his face an unlikely shade of maroon, and it was clear that he wasn't getting any air. His arms lost their strength, then his legs, and finally he slid down onto the doorframe faceup, his eyes open and blinking. It smelled like he'd soiled his pants.

"I can't do that. It's a crime," said the horrified Mickey.

"No it's not, you were just protecting yourself," I said, dropping the chairback to step near the major, who only twitched.

"Yes it is, no matter what. You don't understand our ethics," said Mickey in despair. I knew the word, but it wasn't one I'd ever expected out of a little kid.

I reached over and felt Dylan's chest. Then I wiped my hand on my pants. "Heart's beating," I said. "Mickey, how did you do that?" As I watched, the bleeding from Dylan's throat stopped.

"Scared." That wasn't what I meant, and it didn't seem like much of an answer to how you crush a man's throat. "He intended to kill us anyway. I knew in the night I'd have to go today, but I really have to go now," he added. "His heart stopped."

How could he know what the major intended? And if Mickey could know his heart had stopped pumping without being able to see Dylan's throat from where he stood, he was stranger than any little kid had a right to be. A whole slew of scary suspicions hit me at once that I wouldn't have had if I didn't read the magazines I did. "They'd ask me questions," he said, shaking his head, backing away. He turned and ran for the bike. "They'd bring doctors. No," he said.

But this last, he didn't say with his mouth. "You're not some little kid living with his mama," I accused.

"I volunteered for a project," he said. "We want to prevent a terrible mistake." His reply didn't sound like it was in my head, but it was. Mickey grabbed up his bike like it was a tumbleweed, easier than Fred Moller could've lifted it, and leaped on it. I swear his rear tire chirped from the power he applied.

I didn't want to touch Dylan again. I'm not sure why my eyes teared up then, maybe it was just seeing such a big good-looking healthy horse of a guy like him staring sightless up at the hot summer sky. Then I saw Bub Merrill lean into the doorway, holding one hand with the other, and I ran to him.

I wanted to drive Bub to get help for his broken fingers but he said he could manage. Besides, he reminded me, that would have left a secret project abandoned with Pancho sitting on the taxiway. As Bub drove away one-handed, I thought again of the way Mickey could talk to me. "Don't run, Mickey," I called, though he was nowhere in sight. "Can you hear me?"

His reply was faint but clear. "Not from very far. If you tell, no one will believe you."

Boy, that was no lie! I worried about what he might do if he got panicky again, and I was suddenly filled with questions. "What were you really doing here?"

Very faint now: "Watching, reporting. Helping when I—" Then nothing, and I realized there was a limit to his range, like a little Army walkie-talkie. I went into the shop and tried to fix the telephone cord to call somebody, anybody, but the receiver was broken, too. Surely Bub Merrill would tell somebody to come out to our remote hangar, though that might take a while.

My bandanna had seen better days, but I put it over the major's face to keep dust out of his eyes and mouth, I don't know why. And yep, in the Cord's glove compartment I saw a little automatic pistol, smaller than Army issue. I started pondering how Mickey usually seemed to know what folks around him were thinking. That was one of the things I'd be smart not to talk about. If my body temperature had been as feverish as his all the time, I wouldn't have wanted people to touch me much either—another don't-say-it.

And that acetone on his breath? That usually meant one thing, but in Mickey's case it could've meant another. Acetone—chocolate too, once I thought about it—might be as good an energy source as alcohol or gasoline, and the hangar had plenty of it. Did he drink the stuff? If he didn't have a mama nearby, he must've answered my note himself. No wonder his note had said not to put him in front of a doctor—a human doctor, that is. I leaned against the Cord and hoped the MPs would show up soon, wondering what I'd say when they did. Mickey had been gone nearly an hour while I fiddled with the phone and waited.

And then I saw the radiosonde balloons. Not one, but three in a tight cluster, drifting across overhead several hundred feet up and rising like somebody was chasing them. I've always had twenty-twelve vision, like my dad, and I could see the frame of a bike without wheels slung under those balloons. I don't need to say who was perched on the seat, holding on, and it explained why Mickey might have hung around the meteorology shack on early mornings.

"Mickey," I shouted, "listen to me. Those balloons will take you so high you'll pass out. Do you hear me? You'll fall."

"No I will not," was the reply, as sure of himself as if he were standing beside me. "Don't worry, Kurt Rahm. I will go away as soon as I have enough distance from your airfield. And you do not need to shout," he added, as if I'd said something funny.

"I know better than to tell about this," I said. "Where did you come from?"

"Far off."

"I have a million questions."

"I hear them. No, no one can know who will win, and we must not fight directly. But if you do not win your war soon, we fear—" His voice growing faint as before, then I heard only the breeze.

I shouted anyway. "Mickey! When those balloons get high enough, it won't matter whether you let go. They pop. Mickey, got-dammit, they pop!" What he'd been saying scared me. What could his people fear? And if he fell from eight or ten miles high, someone might find his body in the wreckage. He might not have thought about that. Had he counted on a water landing? The prevailing wind wasn't taking him toward the Gulf of Mexico. To the northwest, the direction he was going, there wasn't any water for a thousand miles bigger than a rancher's stock tank.

I had two perfect reasons for trying to save him, one for his sake and one for ours. A handgun like Dylan's wasn't any good beyond a hundred feet, though if I'd had a rifle I might possibly have been able to deflate one balloon so that he'd drift down slowly under the others. Tough as he was, that might save him. Maybe he'd thought of deflating one. Maybe not. He had already shown me that he didn't always do exactly the right thing when push came to shove. After all, he was only human. Well, almost.

It came to me then that, without a rifle, there was one and only one possible way I could still pop one of those balloons and save our gutsy little hangar rat. I could even wait until he was beyond San Antonio before I did it. And maybe get a question answered that was so important, it was worth ruining my career in aeronautics.

If I did it now, I might not be able to find him in that huge cloud-spotted Texas sky anyway. If I didn't, I flat-ass sure couldn't help him; not ever. And I thought—and still think to this day—he saved my bacon when Dylan was reaching for his pistol. That was all the goad I needed.

I was out of breath when I kicked the chocks away from Pancho's wheels and pulled the control locks off the ailerons. There was no time to go back and try to adjust Bub's chute harness to fit me. I had no radio either, but I had the hottest-climbing aircraft ever built in America. If I could take off from the taxiway, and locate that cluster of oranges again, and get close enough, my prop tips could rip through a balloon like it was a spiderweb.

I might even get Pancho back in one piece.

My run-up was brief because the oil was still half-warm, and also because I saw the dust devil of an Army jeep headed hell for leather toward the hangar. I sealed the canopy while taxiing and managed to cinch my straps, trying to recall the tidbits Bub had mentioned in casual debriefings.

Like any race plane with wings like afterthoughts, Pancho needed a lot of speed to take off and had tires too small to do it in comfort. I kept craning my neck to spot Mickey until I felt the rudder begin to work, giving me some control in what would have to be a slight crosswind takeoff. And as I eased the throttle farther forward, the props became less than a blur, acceleration pressing my head back against the headrest, and when I firewalled Pancho that Godhelpus peroxide turbine kicked in, and the shriek of contrarotating props met a hissing thunder from the belly's steam rocket boost and the airspeed indicator needle jumped like *I'd scared it*. That crosswind? I never noticed it.

In seconds I was so far beyond Bub's recommended takeoff speed I had only to ease back on the stick for Pancho to leap off the taxiway, and I needed a moment to find the gear-up toggle because I had never thought about using it. I got three thumps and green lights, spent a moment checking the sky, and nearly passed out from shock when I saw the needle sweeping past 250 knots. Randolph's perimeter fence was a thread far below, and I was headed in the wrong direction without clearance from the tower with who knew how many cadets piddling around in my way. Pancho's rearview mirror was mounted near the forward canopy lip left of center. It showed no hint of orange.

Scanning above and to my right I saw only one plane, a Vultee trainer, and I banked sharply intending to do it gently. With that much power, things happened a lot faster. Pancho carried me up and around so far, so fast, the altimeter seemed to

be lagging, and from this day on skyrockets would
be kid stuff. Ya-HOO, San-An-Tone and Luckenbach!

Soon I thought I'd be nearing Mickey's altitude,
which I judged might be eight thousand by now,
maybe ten, and the northwest edge of San Antonio
slid below as my airspeed climbed to 350. This was
completely out of my experience, but I had no time
to be scared about that. What scared me now was, I
saw no sign of Mickey, and with my speed still rising,
I horsed back on the stick and traded airspeed for
altitude.

Not until the altimeter showed fifteen thousand
did I realize I was starting to breathe faster, too fast.
I throttled back with the stick between my knees and
fumbled for the rubber oxy mask Bub had folded
into the map pocket near my right leg, its corru-
gated tubing hanging loose. By the time I got it connected to the oxygen supply I had spots of black
dancing in my vision, and I must have spent more
time than I thought getting the mask straps adjusted.

Maybe it didn't help to shout, but I did, and it
sounded strange to me with the mask over my nose
and mouth. "Mickey, I'm coming to help. Come in,
Mickey!" I kept saying it, banking clockwise again,
scanning between the fluffy little cotton-tops of
cloud three miles up that could hide him, or another plane, until too late. I'll say this: If Pancho
couldn't dodge in time, nothing could.

With my right wing dipped I could see the thread
of a highway passing through a small town northwest of the city; it had to be Boerne. No longer worried about oxygen starvation, I kicked Pancho's

pants again and sent her howling up to twenty-five thousand, spiraling to keep from leaving the region. Logic told me Mickey was a slave to the wind, and it could not have taken him this far away in such a short time.

So I knew I had overshot him, maybe in altitude as well as range. It was then that I had the sense to know I'd have a better chance of seeing that orange cluster against hard blue than against the differing hues of ranchland. I banked again toward the distant clutter of rectangles that was San Antonio, pushed the stick forward, and bulleted earthward until Pancho began to shudder. My airspeed was past redline, over five hundred knots, when I eased back and the shudder lessened to nothing and now I was below fifteen thousand feet, scanning up at the blue and patchy white with the city limits not far off. I resumed with, "Come in, Mickey," throttling back like a sane person and repeating it with less hope every moment.

Until, ". . . kill yourself, dear fool. Go away. How can I leave with you near? Yes, keep going. Land that amazing toy and—"

And nothing. He'd been near for a few seconds; maybe he could see me. I tightened my bank, throttled back, and used cloudlets to orient me back to a volume of airspace I had just left, climbing slightly. Pancho didn't like to fly any way but hot, like they said of a Gee Bee. I didn't know how, or if, I could handle her if I got into a spin. Good Idea Number One, my first in a while: Don't get into a spin.

It was then I spotted the orange tint on dirty white, a reflection on a piece of cloud, and thanked God and Mr. Bell for a winged bullet that could maneuver as tightly as Pancho. With my airspeed down around two hundred, in a very shallow climb while banking, I put myself in a corkscrew orbit around the balloons I saw emerging between small clouds, now standing out against the blue. "Gotcha," I said. We watched each other as I circled. He had something like a knapsack, only smaller, hanging at his side from his neck.

His shirt was torn all to tatters. Because his skinny little chest was swollen as big as Fred Moller's. "Yes, I adapt to altitude," he said. "You were not to see this."

"Shut up, Mickey, and listen. If I can fly by and pop one balloon, you'll come down gently out in the country. Or sooner or later all the balloons will pop. That's what I was trying to—"

"Shut up yourself, Kurt Rahm. When I say I will leave, I mean suddenly in a way I chose weeks ago, and safely. But anything nearby will not be safe, and the sound wave—You do not want to be anywhere near, Kurt Rahm. And I do not want another man's life, yours above all. Please."

I had a sudden surge of hope. "Is that a chute of some kind you're carrying?"

"No, but it is what I need. Do not ask."

"Okay. But you owe me this one. It's why I came."

"No it is not. You would lie to me, Kurt Rahm? But your question worries you. It worries us, too."

"Then tell me," I begged. A peek at my altimeter said we were at twenty thousand feet, gradually moving back toward Boerne.

"Last night, with one of us, brave men destroyed the bombers your enemy hoped to send with a ter-

rible weapon. No more bombers; no more need for
Pancho. I may be sent to help somewhere else because if you win soon, your people may cancel a
program that is terribly expensive and a huge mistake. We cannot see the future. We can only try to
help you create a good one."

"What mistake? You have to tell me!"

"I must not. If men are lucky, you may never
know. It is the same weapon your enemy hoped for.
It promises, and lies. In other places it has destroyed
entire peoples, sooner or later." His words held the
earnestness of a revival preacher.

To tell the truth, it sort of pissed me off. "You
know about it, but you expect us to drop it?"

"It is not too late. We were lucky. We first developed other, safer advanced ways to use energy. Ways
that helped us explore but did not let a few of us
endanger us all. Now please go away. Please!"

"I will," I said, "if you'll tell me a safer way."

With a return of something like humor, he said,
"You will hold yourself hostage? You are surely one
of your people. Very well: Study amplified light and
radio waves. And now I am in very serious trouble.
Go; *please!*"

"A deal's a deal," I said, and did an aileron roll
because—well, because I could. "I hope you know
what you're doing. Take it easy, Mickey."

Faintly, as I continued my climb, I heard: "Good-
bye, little bud. We love you. But go!"

I recall grinning as I firewalled the throttle into
another rocketing climb because Mickey had called
me "little bud," when he was no bigger than a Pack-
ard's hood ornament. I straightened Pancho out to

keep that blob of orange in my rearview as it dwindled to a dot, maybe a mile behind, when it was, instantly,

gone

I blinked and looked again. Still gone, and so was a segment of cloud near his location, a concave missing segment as if some invisible ball the size of a dirigible hangar had shouldered the cloud aside, and as I watched the remains of the cloud shattered, then rushed streaming back into the void, and another bit of cloud nearer behind me tore into confetti, which meant something I couldn't see was gaining on my race plane.

When the shock wave passed, it jolted Pancho so hard I got a whiplash, and I've heard thunder that loud but only once when I was a kid and the lightning bolt hit so near it created a warning sound like an artillery shell.

Bub Merrill had intended to do some more tests, and originally it included a climb to forty thousand feet. As long as I expected to be sent to Huntsville Prison, I figured on making it worth our while and the peroxide-tank gauge showed a third full. I didn't dare risk a bad landing with any of it still on board.

It turns out I had spent so much of the stuff chasing Mickey the tank went empty when Pancho was at thirty-eight thousand, the cockpit so cold that frost was collecting inside the canopy. So I never knew whether Project Pancho could actually put a prop-driven interceptor at forty thousand. But there was no question of it in my mind.

Getting that little bugger safely on the ground was mostly a problem in tactics because, with the stubby wing below and ahead of me, any landing would be part mystery and part Braille. I asked for clearance the way we did at airports without towers: flying around, waggling my wings, and waiting for a green light. After I got the green at Randolph I knew they'd warn other air traffic by radio, and I had upwards of two miles of real runway to land on. I almost did it with wheels up, but that's what warning horns are for, and with my fanny chewing washers out of the seat cushion I came in hot just above the perimeter fence and then let her settle. It was the worst landing I ever made, three bounces, but the great thing about the wetback hangar was, it was off near the end of the runway.

I was plumb out of spit by then. They tell me I shut Pancho down and climbed out alone before anyone got to me. I wouldn't know.

NINE

With all the medical teams stationed at Randolph Field to meet casualties airlifted from France, Bub Merrill found help right away. That's how come he was driving back to help me straighten out the mess with the major when he saw me taxiing toward the hangar. "Took me only an hour to figure out it wasn't me in there," he told me later, with Dutch-uncle sarcasm, after they found me near the plane sitting glassy-eyed on Mickey's little workstand.

He got some MPs to guard Pancho, and if he talked much to me while he walked me to the hangar with a bandaged hand over my shoulder, I don't remember it. I remember slopping RC Cola over my shirt as Bub helped me drink it from a coffee cup in the hangar. The Army officers around us didn't seem all that peeved at me. I understood why when I got my trembles under control and heard Bub say, "Were you afraid Major Dylan's friends would sabotage the plane if you didn't save it?" He was giving me an excuse, if I'd take it.

Coward that I was, I took it, nodding. Since all three officers were military cops and not pilots, and I was a licensed civilian pilot, they zeroed in on questions about the major. Bub stood by, trying to look friendly though I could see he wanted to punt me over the perimeter fence. When I told about Dylan tearing up the photocopy, a captain said he'd found it on the floor and pieced it together. Bub had already given his version of that, and a team was en route to check on the Cord repair job paid for by Kevin Ireland.

I told the captain he might send another guy to Mr. Eugen Moller's shop to get the rest of the story, since they probably wouldn't get much from the crash victim. A lieutenant asked me if the chairback near the Cord was what I used to crush Dylan's throat, and I said it might be, but I wasn't sure. "It all happened pretty fast. He was gonna shoot us, I think," I said, and I guess they thought by "us" I meant me and Bub. They'd found the pistol, too, and another lieutenant was taking notes. It wasn't long before they told us not to worry and took off, one of them driving the Cord, which I never saw again, or cared to.

Bub opened a Hires and sat on the edge of a desk and speared me with a firm look. "You are one lucky son of a buck," he said. I nodded. "How could I ever trust you again?" I shook my head. "Why? What in creation were you thinking?"

Tell him the truth? Not in a jillion years. "It was an accident," I began, trying to build a story that he'd accept. "You'd said you were gonna do some taxi runs to use up the peroxide, but when you left I thought MPs might take me away later; you know how those guys are. I didn't trust anybody else to fiddle with Pancho. Blow himself to smithereens."

"So you were gonna taxi up and down like a hot-rodder?"

If he'd buy that, I'd let him. Now and then a pilot does take off before he intends to, and I claimed that's what happened to me. I cranked my b.s. spigot on full force and sprayed poor Bub all over with it, saying I was scared to risk landing hard on a taxiway with that deadly tankful of stuff sloshing around, and once I was flying, all I had to do was keep boring holes in the sky until the tank was empty.

"Well, it worked," he said at last, "but don't— you—*ever*,—oh, hell, never mind. Far as I'm concerned, it never happened." He looked around. "Where's our hangar rat? Not that I'm too keen on having folks know he was underfoot so much."

"After the way the major treated him? I'll be surprised if he comes back for a while. He took off," I said. "On my bike." There was my understatement for the season.

I helped pickle Pancho for storage after Ben Ullmer got back, and Ben's recommendation got me another project at Kelly Field. I learned that during the night of July 16, French saboteurs got into the Latecoere factory in Toulouse and blew those prototype Nazi bombers to shreds, exactly as Mickey had told me. How he kept abreast of all that is beyond me. I don't even know where he slept, or *if* he slept.

And I didn't know for over a year about the weapon project near Alamogordo in New Mexico, the most expensive weapon of the war and the one the Nazis were hoping to build. But I saved every cent I could and in September of '45, after Elke got married, I hightailed it to Cal Poly for a degree in aero engineering.

Mr. Kevin Ireland was never convicted of anything, but Wolverine Aero never got another contract either. Last I heard, he was in bankruptcy proceedings.

Fred Moller wouldn't believe what anybody said about his hero, and quit talking to me. I wrote him a few times from school. He never answered.

I met Ben Ullmer a few times over the years at seminars. He stuck with aero research and development, projects he couldn't talk about. Always gliding along the cutting edge, he collected the papers I wrote on laser propulsion. Last time we met he told me Bub Merrill had gone West after retiring to Kerrville, not far from San Antonio.

Forget Mickey's last tip? Not likely. At Cal Poly I ran across scientific work on amplifying light and radiation, including one by Einstein back in 1917. I switched to physics at CalTech in the fifties, married an architect, did some work with Hughes, and managed to contribute when maser energy developed into lasers. The longer I live, the clearer it seems that Mickey was right about safer ways to use great whopping gobs of energy.

Before I retired I concluded that we can reach the stars propelled by amplified light—high-energy lasers—and with better fortune we might have done it without nuclear energy. It was just bad luck that the war lasted long enough that we took the nuclear energy option. I live outside Alpine now, in west Texas. I'm sure some of us will escape the mistake Mickey was so afraid we'll make, sooner or later.

EYES OF THE CAT

JAMES COBB

JAMES COBB has lived his entire life within a thirty-mile radius of a major Army post, an Air Force base, and a Navy shipyard. He comments, "Accordingly, it seemed natural to become a kind of cut-rate Rudyard Kipling, trying to tell the stories of America's service people." Currently, he's writing the Amanda Garrett techno-thriller series, with four books, *Chooser of the Slain*, *Seastrike*, *Seafighter*, and *Target Lock* published. He's also doing the Kevin Pulaski suspense thrillers for St. Martin's Press. He lives in the Pacific Northwest and, when he's not writing, he indulges in travel, the classic American hot rod, and collecting historic firearms.

She would never be called a beautiful airplane.

Her broad, twin-engined wing was pylon-mounted, set well above a flattened, boatlike fuselage well studded with a variety of bulges, turrets, and blisters. Likewise, her horizontal stabilizers rode high on her upswept tail.

As a fighting machine she also left something to be desired. Her designed defensive armament was light and her bomb load comparatively small. She was lumberingly slow and could be a cranky and notional flier at times, demanding that her pilots pay attention to their work and to her idiosyncrasies.

But she had her advantages as well.

She was versatile. In both her seaplane and amphibian incarnations, any body of water deep enough for her to float in could serve as an airport. If water wasn't available, swamp mud or snow could do. She also had range. She could span oceans or loiter in a single patch of sky for an entire day.

Lastly, she was tough. She had that uncanny rugged-

ness and survivability that American aviation designers have the knack of building into their creations. She could absorb battle damage that would kill any number of prettier aircraft and still, somehow, drag herself home again.

Her crews could forgive her much for that.

She was old for a warbird when her hour came. Her replacements were already on the drawing board. But when the world burst into flames in the fall of 1939, she was what was available. She was what was ready to fly and to fight and to meet the crisis at hand.

She was legion in the service of the Allies; the Americans, the British and Commonwealth Powers, the Dutch, the Russians, the Free French, they all knew and respected her, and she ranged over every sea reach of the Second World War.

She was never formally christened with a dramatic combatant's title like "Avenger" or "Dauntless." The United States Navy simply called her the PBY. (Patrol Bomber, with the "Y" standing as the government designation of the Consolidated Aircraft Corporation, her builder.) The British dubbed her the Catalina, after the island lying off her Los Angeles birthplace.

But in the night skies above the South Pacific, certain of her breed earned themselves another name, a name that would become intertwined with a legend.

They called them the Black Cats.

Lieutenant Meredith Leeland-Rhys, of His Majesty's Royal Navy Volunteer Reserve, was certain he was going to perish, and the close proximity of the enemy had nothing to do with it.

After four years spent in wartime England, he was quite accustomed to the potential of a sudden, violent death. This climate was another matter entirely.

He had left an early British spring to arrive in a late Solomon Islands summer, and the intervening ninety-four hours had not been near time enough for adaptation.

His tropic whites, the sole set he'd been able to borrow before enplaning, were sodden, both with sweat and with the blood-warm spray whipping back over the bow of the battered US Navy whaleboat. The spray served also to encrust his glasses and long-jawed features with sticky, half-dried salt. The smothering tropic humidity and pitching seas engaged in a conspiracy of nausea and dizziness, while the acetylene flame sun burned through both the crown of his uniform cap and his prematurely thinning hair. In the distance, beyond the body of water the whaleboat's coxswain had laconically called "Iron Bottom Bay," the mountainous outline of Guadalcanal Island shimmered, threatening to disappear in the heat haze.

Stripped to the waist, the mahogany-tanned boatswain's mate manning the launch's tiller seemed impervious to the environment. The Marine sentry assigned to Leeland-Rhys looked upon it merely as a good excuse for a nap, stretching out comfortably atop the equipment cases he was intended to guard.

Adding to Leeland-Rhys's discomfort, if such were possible, was the package he carried on his knees. The boat pool dispatcher had tossed it down into the launch just as they were casting off from the pier at Lungga Point. "Mind taking that across with you, Lieutenant? Commander Case has been bitching about this shipment all week, and they finally came in."

Leeland-Rhys had no objection to doing the favor.

He only wished that the parcel had not been quite so prominently marked.

MEDICAL STORES / US NAVY
CONDOMS / PROPHYLACTIC/ FIVE HUNDRED

Beyond the indelicacy of it also came the question of what his prospective hosts intended to do with them all.

Back aft at the whaleboat's tiller, the coxswain straightened and pointed. "There you go, Lieutenant. Tulagi Seadrome, dead ahead."

"We say *leftenant*," Leeland-Rhys murmured half-heartedly over the rumble of the engine. He twisted around on the hard thwart seat to look ahead.

The whaleboat had nosed into a sheltered cove in the flank of one of the smaller islands on the northern side of Iron Bottom Bay. A single vessel lay at anchor there, the glassy waters of the cove lapping lightly at its rust-streaked flanks.

Formerly a World War I vintage "four piper" destroyer, the little ship had undergone an APV conversion. Now reincarnated as a fast seaplane tender, most of its armament and two of its distinctive, slender funnels had been exchanged for the enlarged deckhouses needed for a suite of aviation service equipment and personnel.

Spotted around the tender were a number of seaplane-mooring buoys, half a dozen of which were in use by a flotilla of PBY-5A Catalina amphibians. Three of the aircraft were in the standard blue-and-gray livery of US naval aviation, their white star insignia prominent on their sides.

The other three seemed to bear no insignia at all

and were painted a dull, sooty black that absorbed the beating glare of the tropic sun.

As the whaleboat came opposite the APV's gangway, the coxswain popped the propeller into neutral. "Yo," he bellowed over the whine of the engine clutch, "got a load for the CO of Detachment Three! Whereaway?"

"Buoy Foxtrot!" The faint reply came. "The Black Cat straight off the stern!"

"Gotcha!" The coxswain got the launch under way again.

Leeland-Rhys was somewhat acquainted with the Catalina amphibians used by the Royal Navy. He'd assisted in the development of a number of systems for use aboard them. But the shadow-colored monster they now approached bore little resemblance to the airplane with which he was familiar.

There was a mottled effect to its dark paint that the Englishman had first attributed to some form of camouflaging. But as they drew closer, he realized that the mottling stemmed from a pattern of patches and dents on the combat-battered airframe.

A great many patches and dents.

The plane had been retrofitted with one of the new "Eyeball" nose turrets mounting a pair of thirty-caliber Brownings. Immediately below the turret, however, a metal plate had been bolted over the angled bomb-aimers window, a second and decidedly nonregulation cluster of heavy machine-gun muzzles protruding through it.

Reassuringly familiar was the set of antlerlike Yagi antennas that extended out from under the leading edges of the wings, the fittings for an ASV (Air-to-Surface-Vessel) radar. Those, at least, Leeland-Rhys could understand. The Catalina had been one of the first aircraft in the world to be outfitted with such a detection system.

The cowling had been stripped from one of the plane's massive Pratt & Whitney radial engines. A pair of mechanics tinkered with the exposed mechanism suspended over the water on a flimsy workstand draped over the engine nacelle. Other aircrewmen ambled over the top of the big plane's wings and fuselage, performing maintenance tasks with a monkeylike surety. Given the extremely casual and fragmentary state of their uniforms, it was impossible to tell officer from enlisted man.

One individual stood on a small work float tied off alongside the Catalina's bow. Dark-haired, of medium height and displaying the usual South Pacific Theater tan, he wore ragged, oil-stained khakis and a baseball cap, and apparently was of an artistic bent.

At the moment he was deeply engrossed in touching up the picture painted below the cockpit of the Catalina, a most striking and detailed rendering of an attractive and well-endowed blond bobby-soxer. Clad in nothing but saddle shoes and hair ribbon, the young lady sat astride a torpedo, her head thrown back and a look of ecstasy on her features, the name "Zazz Girl" slashed beneath her in scarlet.

On a more serious note, a double row of rising sun flags and bomb symbols had also been stenciled beneath the cockpit window.

With a satisfied nod, the artist turned away from his work and looked to the approaching whaleboat.

Wondering if he should be yelling "ahoy" or something else appropriately nautical, Leeland-Rhys called out. "Excuse me, but I'm looking for Commander Case."

"You found him. You the radar guy?"

"Yes, sir. Leftenant Leeland-Rhys at your service, sir. I have some equipment with me."

"Great! Come alongside at the starboard waist blister. I'll meet you there." The aviator swung up the side of the Catalina to vanish through an overhead hatch into the cockpit.

True to his word he reappeared in the open waist blister just as the whaleboat nuzzled alongside. "Watch that throttle, swabby!" he roared at the coxswain. "Don't scratch the chrome!"

Case tied the launch's painter around the base of the blister's gun mount "Careful with the footwork coming across, Lieutenant," he said, as Leeland-Rhys gingerly prepared to transfer to the aircraft. "You don't want to step on Fido."

"That's *leftenant,* sir," Leeland-Rhys said apologetically. "And Fido?"

Case pointed down between the boat and the seaplane.

Below, in the azure waters, something moved.

"Bloody hell!"

Six striped feet of disturbed tiger shark flowed out from under the Catalina, reversed lithely, and disappeared back into the hull shadow.

"We used to shoot 'em," Case commented conversationally, "but the blood in the water attracts the big ones."

At close range, the dominant features for Lieutenant Commander Evan Randall Case were a pair of piercing green eyes and a focused intensity of word

and action. "Right," he said, leaning in toward
Leeland-Rhys. "How much of the dope did they feed
you on the way in?"

The Englishman had to pause for a moment to
translate before replying. "Uh, not much at all really. I was simply informed that there was a problem
involving the location of a possible Japanese radar
facility. I was dispatched with what we hope is the
appropriate equipment to deal with the problem."

Said equipment was now being cursed into the
waist compartment by the plane's crew chief and the
Marine guard and coxswain from the launch. Case
had summoned the *Zazz Girl*'s other officers to a
conference with Leeland-Rhys in the amidships
crew's quarters. The cramped space had a set of
metal-framed, double-decked bunks on either side
of a narrow walkway, the upper bunk being latched
upright to provide a degree of headroom for those
seated on the lower.

"There's the bitch, mate," Case's copilot commented. "Nobody can call if there's a Christless radar station or not." Flight Officer Cyril Bates was an
exchange officer from the Royal Australian Air
Force, tall, lean, and intensely Aussie. Clad in boots,
baggy shorts, and a wispy blond beard, he'd en-
gulfed Leeland-Rhy's hand in a bone-crushing grip,
introducing himself as, "the native guide for the
bleedin' Yanks."

"One thing we can say," Ensign Phil Tibbs added.
"If there is a radar, the Japs have it damn well hidden." The *Zazz Girl*'s third officer was a striking dif-
ferentiation from her two pilots. Morose and
prematurely balding, he was heavyset to the verge

of fleshiness, burning red rather than tanned. His fellow aviators introduced him as Phillip-the-Navigator, spoken as a single word. "AIRSOLS has gone over every island in that area with a fine-tooth comb. They haven't found a thing."

"AIRSOLS?" Leeland-Rhys queried, something he sensed he was going to be doing a great deal of.

"Air Solomons Command," Case replied, "our lords and masters over at Henderson Field. The army fly-fly boys doing our photo recon claim we're just seeing things up the Slot. I'm saying they're *not* seeing something. That's why you're here, Lieutenant. You're going to prove which of us has a screw loose."

"It's *left*" . . . Leeland-Rhys caught himself and sighed. "Oh, bugger it! I suppose it really doesn't matter that much. You see, gentleman, I'm not actually a naval officer, professionally speaking that is. In truth, I'm an associate professor of physics at Cambridge, electromagnetic propagation and related phenomena. The military rank is a . . . convenience."

Tibbs chuckled dryly. "Don't let it worry you, Professor. I'm really an insurance salesman."

"Too right," Bates added. "My dad and me run a hotel in Rockhampton." A detached and dreamy smile crossed the Australian's lean features. "We have a public bar, a private bar, and a lounge, and all three of them serve beer, endless quantities of wonderful, beautiful, cold, beer."

Case snorted. "Oh, quit bellyaching, Cyril. If anyone has a bitch around here, it's me. Before the war it was LA to Reno three times a week for Western

Airlines and all the divorcées I could seduce. Anyway, Prof, welcome to the great South Pacific Amateur Hour."

Leeland-Rhys found himself smiling. This wasn't what he'd been expecting at all ... fortunately. "Thank you, gentlemen. I hope I can prove of assistance. Oh, and by the way, I have a parcel here," He awkwardly presented the carton of prophylactics. "They indicated over at the port that it was rather important."

Case brightened. "Damn square it is, Prof, at least to one of my guys."

"One of them?"

"Yeah. HEY, GUNS! WE GOT YOUR RUBBERS IN!"

The watertight hatch in the forward bulkhead swung open, and a bearded face under a blue-dyed navy Dixecup hat appeared. "Thank God for small favors, skipper." The sailor grinned. "My last set's totally shot. I didn't know what I was going to do for tonight."

Case tossed the package to the aviation hand. "Use them in good health, me son. And while you're at it, send the second Sparks back. I need words with him."

"Sure thing, skipper."

As the hatch closed Leeland-Rhys gathered himself to ask the question that had been nagging at him ever since he'd had the box of prophylactics tossed into his lap. Before he could speak, however, the hatch swung open once more.

"You wanted to see me, sir?"

"Yeah, Richie," Case replied, "I want you to give a briefing to the professor here on your scope ghosts. Prof, here's the guy who's really responsible for calling you out here, Radioman Second Class Richie Anjellico. He's our expert on, what'dyacall it, 'electromagnetic propagation and related phenomena.' "

Leeland-Rhys knew that all hands must be at least eighteen years of age to serve in the American Navy. The dark-haired youth in the sun-faded dungarees must simply look younger.

"It's like this, sir," Anjellico said, hunkering down on the duckboards that floored the compartment. "There's one sector out there where I keep getting abnormalities on my A scope . . . 'scope ghosts' the skipper calls them. To me, they looked like secondary spikes from another radar transmitter, like I get from the ASVs on the other Cats. But I've picked them up when the other planes haven't been around. I've even detected them when we've been the only PBY airborne over the Slot."

Leeland-Rhys frowned. "Possibly a secondary reflection of your own wave. Off an island or even a dense cloud mass."

The Englishman ran an annoyed hand back through his sweat-slick hair. Was this what all the fuss was about? Radar technology was still in its infancy, a tricky proposition at best for the most skilled of available operators. And the militaries were cranking out thousands of these . . . for lack of a better term, "children," with a bare minimum of training.

Anjellico shook his head emphatically. "No, sir! I know my set and how to use it. I performed all of the tests for false returns. I shifted frequencies and power settings, and I had Commander Case perform bearing changes. This was another active radar set cutting across my band. I'm sure of it."

"Have any of the other aircraft in your flight detected this phenomenon?"

"Not at first, sir, but I think I've got that figured out. I had the *Girl*'s ASV tweaked to work a skootch lower in the frequency range than standard. I seem to get a better surface return definition that way. That's when I started lifting the secondary spikes on my scope. When the operators on the *Hep Gee* and *Lazy Mae* pulled the same tweak, they started picking 'em up too."

Leeland-Rhys sighed . . . heavily. *God save us from the tinkering amateur!* Obviously it was a feedback effect of some nature, probably off the rectifiers. They should seal the bloody units when they leave the factory. He started to speak, then caught his arch comment before it could escape.

There were three other men present in the compartment. Three veteran combat aviators the Englishman reminded himself. And obviously they seemed to think the boy knew what he was talking about.

Case must have read his mind. "My guys all know their stuff, Professor." He stated slowly. "That includes Richie here. If he says something's cooking on his scope, then there is. If you don't believe me, there's a couple of hundred dead Japs who can give you references."

Leeland-Rhys decided that maybe things might not be quite so obvious after all.

"Is there any particular area where these phenomena occur?" He probed.

"Yes, sir," Anjellico answered promptly. "It only happens in one specific area. Right up in the guts of the Slot."

"Excuse me once more, but, 'the Slot'?"

"Yeah," Case interjected. "The Slot. Phil, you got that theater chart? Let's give the Prof a little orientation."

"It would be appreciated," Leeland-Rhys agreed.

Phillip-the-Navigator produced a well-worn map, unfolding it across the knees of the seated men.

"Here," Case indicated. "You see these three narrow islands up in the Bismarck Sea in a kind of a wishbone pattern? New Britain, New Ireland, and Bougainville, they belong to the Japs."

Case's finger whispered across the chart paper. "About 340 miles east-southeast as the Zero flies, you got this group of islands: Guadalcanal, Florida and Tulagi, Malaita, San Cristobal. They belong to us.

"In between, kind of connecting these two groups, are these two smaller island chains on either side of a strait formally christened New Georgia Sound. However, we who are on intimate terms with the place call it 'the Slot.' Choiseul and Santa Isabel make up the northern chain, Vella Lavella, Kolombangara, and New Georgia, along with a few odds and ends, make up the southern. These are the Central Solomons and exactly who they belong to is currently under discussion.

"The Japs have some little Podunk garrisons and outposts on some of the islands, and the Australians have coastwatchers and native guerrillas on some of the others. We aren't quite ready to move in and take over, and the Japs aren't quite ready to stop us.

Whoever gets ready first, wins. Get the picture?"

Leeland-Rhys nodded, peering down at the chart through his salt-speckled glasses.

"During the day, AIRSOLS aircraft operating out of Henderson Field on Guadal dominate the Slot. We can sink any ship the Japs send in, so they can't resupply and reinforce their garrisons conventionally. They have to rely on *daihatsus* and the Tokyo Express."

"Pardon?" Leeland-Rhys said, looking up.

"A *daihatsu* is a Japanese army landing barge," Case elaborated. "They're about fifty feet long, are made out of wood, and are powered by a small gas or diesel engine. Sort of like a Higgins Boat. The Jap barge yards crank 'em out by the hundreds. They use them to run a supply shuttle between their main bases at Rabaul and Bougainville and their Central Solomon garrisons. These *daihatsu* convoys move by night, hugging the island coastlines. By day they lie low under camouflage in little inlets and creek mouths, avoiding our regular air patrols."

" 'At's where we come in." Bates tapped himself on the chest with a thick-nailed thumb.

"Right," Case agreed. "Thanks to our radar, we can spot the little bastards, even in the dark. We bomb 'em, strafe 'em, and sic our PT boats on 'em. Killing *daihatsus* is our primary job around here. That and scouting the Tokyo Express."

"And what's the Tokyo Express?" Leeland-Rhys inquired, becoming steadily more intrigued.

"The other way the Japs have of moving personnel and equipment into the Central Solomons. They'll assemble a task group of fast warships, destroyers mostly, with sometimes a cruiser or two thrown in, at their big fleet base at Rabaul on New Britain. There, they'll load 'em up with a big deck cargo of stores, food, medicine, ammo, whatever. The task group will sortie and move right up to the edge of AIRSOLS daytime strike coverage. Then, come sunset, zoom! They head down the Slot, going flank speed and balls to the wall all the way to one of the Jap garrisons.

"Their cargo has mostly been loaded into watertight steel drums that have been ballasted to float, so when they reach their destination, the stuff can just be heaved over the side to be collected by small craft. Any personnel to be transferred get pretty much heaved over the side, too. Then the Express turns around and beats it back up the Slot, getting out of range before our strike aircraft can launch at first light."

"And your squadron has to, ah, derail this Express as well?"

"Oh, we take a shot at 'em now and again." Case grinned. "Mostly, though, we scout and shadow and leave the shooting to the big boys. Whenever we spot an Express assembling, we move one of our own cruiser-destroyer forces into position here at our end of the Slot. When the Japs come down, our guys go up. When they meet, things can get pretty interesting."

Leeland-Rhys arched an eyebrow. He suspected he was hearing a considerable understatement. "Back to the radar abnormalities. Where exactly do they occur?"

"Always right here, sir," Anjellico replied promptly, sketching on the chart with a fingertip "Kind of in a triangular area that runs from the northern coast of New Georgia to the southeastern tip of Choiseul to the northeastern tip of Santa Isabel."

A large gray cat rolled over in Leeland-Rhys's belly. "Just there and nowhere else?"

"No, sir, just there."

"Gentlemen," Leeland-Rhys said slowly, "I hope you will forgive me for coming into this matter with a somewhat dubious attitude. Especially you, Mr. Anjellico. But that is exactly the location one would cover with a search radar if one wished to control the Central Solomon Islands. And furthermore, that's the exact propagation pattern such a Japanese search radar would produce."

"Ha!" Case reached forward and swiped the grinning Anjellico's cap lower over his eyes, Bates, the copilot, adding a bruising slap on the boy's shoulder.

"Furthermore," Leeland-Rhys continued, "the Japanese do possess a surface search radar called the Type 22 that operates on the ninety-megacycle band. Conceivably it could interact with an ASV in the way you have described. We even have a working model of one in our hands. It was captured by your lads right over on Guadalcanal, so we know they are using them in this theater. But there is a problem."

"What's that, Prof?" Case demanded.

"You say that an air search has been made for a radar installation in this area?" Leeland-Rhys gestured to the chart.

"Yeah, both by photo recon and Mark 1 eyeball."

"Then something should have been spotted. You see, the Japanese do have radar, but their systems are comparatively crude compared to ours. Crude and large. To date they've got nothing like our air-borne ASV sets. They haven't perfected the cavity magnetron yet, don't you see ... Uh, you didn't hear that word, by the way. This Japanese Type 22 system I mentioned would require a large fixed-mast array rather like a British Chain Home station ... You chaps would call it a bedspring antenna ... and it would have to be located with clear direct view of the ... ah ... Slot.

"In fact, I'll go one better. To produce that conic propagation pattern, it would have to be located very prominently at one of the three node points mentioned by Mr. Anjellico here. The northernmost point on the coast of New Georgia ... the south-eastern tip of Choiseul or one of its smaller satellite islands, or the northeastern tip of Santa Isabel."

Case scowled and shoved his baseball cap to the back of his head. "One problem, Prof. There's noth-ing at any of those three points. Our blip jockeys figured out that propagation deal, too. Only no an-tenna. No installations of any kind anywhere where there should be one."

It was Leeland-Rhys's turn to scowl. "Nothing at all?"

"I can take you to the intelligence office aboard the tender and show you the aerial photography. I'll give 'em credit, the army F-5s went in so low you can count the land crabs."

The Englishman felt himself deflate even further. Again he found himself wondering just what he was supposed to be doing out here. Only now he found himself viewing the problem from the point of his own inferiority.

"That's why they sent for you, Prof," Case went

on, unaware he was rubbing salt in the wounds. "Our people are stumped. Either we're dead wrong about this, or the Japs have something new up their sleeve. You Brits are the whiz kids when it comes to radar. You invented the stuff. We figure you're our best shot at getting this sorted out."

Leeland-Rhys took a deep breath of humidity-dank air and let it puff from his lips.

"I certainly hope I can live up to your confidence, Commander. Firstly, I suppose we should see if we are dealing with an actual signal from a radar set. I've got something in my bag of tricks that might be able to resolve that question. It's called a passive intercept receiver, and it's designed to detect output on any of the known radar frequencies and verify that it is indeed an active radar sweep."

"How long will it take you to set it up?"

"Well, with the assistance of my associate"— Leeland-Rhys gave a nod toward Anjellico—"I believe I could have the unit installed and functional aboard your aircraft by this evening."

"That suits, Prof, because the Black Cats fly tonight."

Their takeoff run was long, far longer than for a land plane, the big twin radials thundering. The spank and jolt of the waves against the hull bottom shortened and sharpened as they slowly accelerated to flight speed. The wingtip floats lifted and, with a deliberate rock of the PBY's wings, Case broke the *Zazz Girl*'s keel loose from the suction of the water, and they climbed free.

The two other Black Cats of Detachment 3 followed in their wake. Cranking up their tip floats, the three night hunters closed into a loose vee formation. Circling once above Iron Bottom Bay, they lined out to the northwest, climbing slowly into the flaming sunset.

Leeland-Rhys had come forward to crouch between the two pilots' seats, and the airblast pouring in through the open cockpit side windows felt decidedly odd. It took him a moment to realize why. It was almost cool.

"Lord, but that feels good!" he exclaimed.

"Too right, Prof," Cyril Bates yelled back over the roar of air and engine. "That's one of the few benefits to this rum job. The luxury of not having to sweat for a bit. Wouldn't trade it for dollars!"

"How's your gizmo working?" Case inquired from the left-hand seat.

"Seems to be functional. I extended the antenna after takeoff and tested the receiver against the Guadalcanal defense radar. The trace came through quite clearly."

"Great. After the detachment disperses we'll set up a patrol area between New Georgia and Choiseul. The other guys will work farther north up Bougainville way so their ASVs won't screw up your readings."

"Excellent." Leeland-Rhys hesitated for a moment, finding it difficult to be delicate while yelling at the top of his lungs. "Commander Case, excuse me, but I simply have to ask. Those . . . medical stores . . . I brought with me this afternoon . . ."

Case threw his head back, and his laughter rang over the rumble of the engines. "It's okay, Prof. Eddie Dwarshnik, my ordnance hand, uses 'em on the Lahodney mount."

"Lahodney mount? I don't believe I know about that."

"No reason anyone not flying with the Cats should. It's something a buddy of mine, Lieutenant Bill Lahodney, cooked up. Bill's a Cat driver over New Guinea way, and he likes coming up with new ways to be mean to the Japs."

Case pointed under the control panel and down the access tunnel that led into the bow compartment. "You rip the bombsight out of the nose and replace it with a battery of four fifty-caliber machine guns fixed to fire forward."

Case then indicated a set of crosshairs and range scales painted on the windscreen in front of him. "The sights are done in luminous paint, and I have a trigger switch on the control yoke. It's great stuff for strafing, but you got to be careful of a few things. Like before takeoff, Dwarshnik tapes a condom over each gun muzzle so we don't get a slug of water down a barrel while we're taxiing."

Leeland-Rhys brightened. "I see. Most clever."

"Yeah, Dwarshnik is real religious about it. You see, he's also my bow turret gunner." The pilot pointed forward to where the head and shoulders of the ordnance man protruded into the Plexiglas dome of the thirty-caliber twin mount. "The only place he has to sit is astride the fifty-caliber tubes of the Lahodney on a burlap heat pad. Under those conditions you take barrel explosions real personal."

Leeland-Rhys could only agree. "Most understandable. But tell me, if you put machine guns in your bomb aimer's station, where did you put your bombsight?"

"On the bottom of the Pacific somewhere between here and New Caledonia. We heaved the damn thing over the side."

Case laughed again at Leeland-Rhys's nonplussed expression. "Let me clue you in on one of the great military secrets of the Second World War. The Norden bombsight's a piece of shit, at least for our kind of war."

"What do you use in its place?"

"We use what we call the TLAR, Prof," Bates interjected.

"The TLAR bombsight? I've never heard of it?"

"It's the best bombsight in the world, Prof."

The two Black Cat pilots grinned at each other in an ancient, shared joke. Extending their right fists ahead, they squinted one-eyed over an upraised thumb. "T . . . L . . . A . . . R . . . That Looks About Right."

Leeland-Rhys shook his head and retreated to the sanity of the radio/navigators compartment.

On the two-hour outbound flight to the patrol zone Leeland-Rhys prowled around the aircraft, taking the opportunity to reacquaint himself with the peculiarities of a Catalina's interior. Beyond fixing the location of the escape hatches and life raft in his mind, he peered up into the cramped confines of the flight engineer's station in the wing pylon. He crouched beside the observer-gunners in the waist blisters, and he peered down at the sea through the narrow confines of the tunnel gunner's hatch under the tail.

He most fancied the incredible view one had from the waist blisters. It was developing into a truly beautiful night at the war.

With the end of the dayfighter threat, the other

two Black Cats had sheered off about their occasions, leaving the *Zazz Girl* to fly alone through the settling darkness.

To the north and south respectively, the distant shadow mountains of Santa Isabel and New Georgia scrolled past, jagged against a ten-million-star horizon. Below, New Georgia Sound, the Slot, Leeland-Rhys corrected himself, shimmered in the light of a quarter moon, the coastal skirts of the islands like black velvet cutouts against the rippled pewter of the sea.

Leeland-Rhys sat perched on the ammunition bin for the waist guns, battered by the slipstream pouring through the open Plexiglas bubbles and totally entranced. He was rather sorry when Radioman Anjellico came aft to fetch him.

"We're coming in on the patrol zone, sir," the younger man yelled over the drumbeat of the engines.

It was time to get to work.

It was marginally quieter in the radio/navigators compartment. Likewise, much hotter from the tube banks of the radio and radar equipment and considerably ranker from the cigar puffed by the PBY's senior radio operator, the "First Radio," seated at the big GO-9 long-range transceiver.

Anjellico, the *Zazz Girl*'s Second Radio, sank onto the low stool positioned in front of the ASV radar. Donning an interphone headset, he passed a second pair of earphones to Leeland-Rhys.

The ASV was already operating. It lacked one of the new PPI screens with the 360-degree rotating sweep. Instead, it covered a fixed 90-degree wedge directly in front of the aircraft. A single horizontal

line glowed across the bottom third of its display,
the A scope. A vertical cone-shaped spike would appear in the center of the screen when the aircraft
came within range of a surface target, the height of
the spike indicating the range. A dial above the A
scope indicated the exact bearing of the target
within the sweep of the radar.

Even as Leeland-Rhys looked on, the scope spiked
decisively.

Anjellico grinned as the Englishman leaned forward.

"That's okay, sir. That's just a wreck piled up on
a reef off Wilson Point on New Georgia. It's a Jap
AK that got bombed and run ashore when we first
landed on Guadal. We use it for a radar navigation
checkpoint."

Anjellico adjusted the bearing dial. "We're coming up on it to port in . . . ten . . . five . . . now."

Leeland-Rhys peered out of the narrow lozenge-
shaped porthole on the left side of the compartment. Below, the gaunt and distorted silhouette of
the wrecked attack transport swept past under the
wing, the surf boiling around the broken-keeled
hull in the shimmering moonglow.

Leeland-Rhys looked back at the radarman and
issued a thumbs-up. The lad did know his business.

The Englishman deployed his own equipment.
Once more unreeling the long trailing antenna
through a transfer gland in the hull, he switched on
the oscillator of the passive detection receiver. Laying a pencil and notebook ready at hand, he began
to dial up and down the electromagnetic spectrum.

Hours crawled past like the sweat beneath his
shirt.

Zazz Girl flew a deliberate triangular course. Wilson Point on New Georgia to Rob Roy Island off Choiseul, across to Kokopani Point on Santa Isabel and back to Wilson Point once more, outlining the parameters of the search zone.

Once, twice, a third time . . .

The Japanese wreck became an old friend.

Shortly after midnight, Phillip-the-Navigator retired to the hot plate in the mechanic's compartment and produced a hot meal for all hands. A powdered egg and cubed Spam omelet, canned bread with bitter Australian marmalade, and powdered coffee. Leeland-Rhys found it surprisingly tolerable but was wise enough not to say so aloud.

The hunt continued. Cigarette packs emptied. Muscles cramped. Mouths soured. Twice Leeland-Rhys jerked to alert as a wave pattern flashed across the screen of the detector. Once it was a random touch of a distant RSV from one of the other distant Black Cats. The second occasion was a taste of the surface radar off a prowling American PT boat.

Anjellico proved to be a worthwhile relief from the tedium. Diffidently at first, but with growing enthusiasm, the youth pumped Leeland-Rhys with a steady stream of questions, not merely about radar operations but about physics as a whole. Strikingly astute questions.

A teacher as well as a scientist, Leeland-Rhys found himself responding with an enthusiasm of his own. It had been a long time since he had taught a class, even a class of one.

During a pause, he made a few inquiries of his own.

Anjellico shrugged, silhouetted in the green

scope glow. "I dunno. I want to stay in electronics after the war. I figure it's going to be a pretty big thing. They're talking about maybe giving vets college funding after the war. Maybe . . ."

"Maybe what?" Leeland-Rhys prodded.

"Maybe get into research. Become a real scientist like you, sir. That's what I'd really like to do. It's kind of a screwy idea, I guess."

"I don't necessarily think so, Mr. Anjellico," Leeland-Rhys mused. "This war we are fighting seems to be changing how we go about a great many things. Already I find myself involved in events that only a short time ago I would have thought very 'screwy' indeed.

"Very possibly we are entering a time when what one is willing to strive for is becoming more important than the conventional wisdom of what one may achieve. One can hope so at any rate."

"I guess one can, sir." The radarman's grin flashed in the dimness, then faded abruptly. A jagged spike lanced upward abruptly on the A scope.

"Radar to pilot!" Anjellico yelled into his interphone headset. "Surface contact! Bearing five degrees of port bow. Medium signal strength. Multiple targets. Range five thousand yards."

The *Zazz Girl*'s decks swayed with a course adjustment, the big patrol bomber nosing down slightly. "All hands! Man battle stations!" Commander Case's voice roared over the headsets. "Richie, make with the range and bearing!"

"Bearing now zero off the bow, range four thousand and closing!" Anjellico twisted around, looking back over his shoulder for an instant. "Mr. Rhys, get your antenna in right now!"

Leeland-Rhys didn't consider for an instant the incongruity of an enlisted radioman giving a commissioned officer of the Royal Navy an order. He just pounced on the reel of the detector set's trailing antenna, frantically cranking it back inside the aircraft.

Over his own headset he heard Anjellico calling out the distance to target to Case. "Range three thousand . . . Range two thousand, bearing still zero off the bow . . . range one thousand . . ."

"Stand by!" Case yelled back. "Targets in sight! FLARE! FLARE! FLARE!"

Something, presumably the cycling flare racks, thumped back under the tail section.

The night's darkness blinked out of existence, replaced by a dazzling flood of blue-white light pouring through the compartment windows.

Leeland-Rhys couldn't restrain himself. Abandoning the reel, he scrambled to one of the ports and peered out.

The piercing metallic glare from the magnesium parachute flares converted the sea into a rippling sheet of mercury crumpled by the wakes that trailed behind a trio of dark angular objects that swept past below the aircraft.

"We got *daihatsus*, guys," Case announced almost casually. "Prepare to engage . . . rolling in now."

Leeland-Rhys failed to note that everyone else in the compartment had taken a death grip on any solid handhold within reach.

Up to that point the flight of the *Zazz Girl* had been a placid, even a plodding experience. Now, however, the PBY's decks tilted to starboard almost a full ninety degrees. As the broad wing elevated, it lost lift, and the big amphibian fell out of the sky in a wild sideslip.

Leeland-Rhys skidded back across the cramped compartment, almost sliding under the equipment panels, before being caught by Anjellico and the radio operator. The airflow through the ventilators rose to a moan as the *Zazz Girl* reversed her course, diving under the dome of her flarelight and lining up on her revealed prey.

"Get a good hold, sir," Anjellico yelled. "We're going after these guys!"

Leeland-Rhys groped for words. "Is this going to be . . . difficult?"

"Depends, sir. *Daihatsus* always mount machine guns. But some times they'll fix one up with a pom-pom and a load of ammo and use it for an antiaircraft escort. It depends on if we have one of those gunboats down there."

Beyond the compartment windows, meteor-like streaks of light began to blaze past. Tracers, small ones, then much larger ones.

"We got a gunboat." Anjellico concluded.

Abruptly the quad fifty-caliber battery in the Catalina's nose cut loose with a stammering roar that shook the entire airframe, the stench of hot oil and gunpowder streaming back through the cockpit door in a lung-burning concentration. The bow turret was firing as well, the stuttering yap of its smaller rifle-caliber guns almost trifling when commingled with the deep-throated rage of the Lahodney mount.

Clinging to the electronics racks, Leeland-Rhys

felt the gravity pull as the *Zazz Girl* bottomed out of her shallow dive. At that instant, up in the cockpit, Cyril Bates screamed "Bombs gone!"

The Black Cat lurched delicately, and something flickered past the compartment windows, five-hundred-pound bombs falling free of the wing racks.

Zazz Girl lifted her nose and soared, converting accumulated speed into altitude. The hammer of the nose guns ceased, the clamor leaping aft as the waist and tunnel mounts engaged, ripping off short bursts as they overflew the enemy.

Thud! Thud!

Two heavy surges of pressure shoved hard against the aircraft. She skewed for a moment, then banked onto her starboard wingtip, coming around to the attack once more.

Leeland-Rhys caught a glimpse out of the starboard window. Formerly there had been three Japanese barges crawling across the sea beneath the flarelight. Now there were but two and a large spreading circle of debris and turbulence.

The TLAR bombsight was indeed quite effective.

The Black Cat aligned to dive once more, wheeling in like the vast bird of prey she was.

Damn it all! He had to see!

Leeland-Rhys found himself crawling forward to the cockpit door. Pulling himself up onto his knees between the pilots seats, he peered forward.

Case and Bates were each flying one-handed, Case with his left on the control yoke and his right on the throttles and propeller controls overhead. Bates flew with his right, the fingers of his left curled around the T-grip bomb release in the central cock-pit.

There was an eerie commonality of action between the two aviators. They moved as if they were a single four-armed entity, mastering the controls without the need of orders and reply. Their faces were al-most . . . placid in the harsh light that flickered be-yond the windscreen. Tradesmen, going about a comfortably familiar task.

"The gunboat?" Bates queried.

"Yeah," Case agreed. "Give him the last two eggs. We can gun the other guy."

"Righto."

The surviving pair of barges had turned in toward the coast of Choiseul Island, a meager half mile dis-tant, churning furiously toward the refuge of the beach. But the PBY was once more thundering in upon them like an aluminum storm front.

Almost washed out by the flareblaze, sparks of light danced near the low deckhouses of the *daihat-sus,* machine guns flaming defiance at their at-tacker. Amidships on one of the barges were the heavier, more deliberate muzzle flashes of a 25mm antiaircraft twin mount. Writhing tracer tentacles reached out for the *Zazz Girl,* closing around her, striving to crush out her life.

Leeland-Rhys heard a sound like nails being driven through tin sheeting and felt a series of faint, sharp taps radiating through the airframe of the Black Cat. It took him an instant to realize they were bullet impacts. Behind him in the radio/navigators compartment there was a burst of light like a pho-tographer's flashbulb going off and a sharp and angry crack over the sound of the engines. Someone swore savagely.

Leeland-Rhys couldn't bring himself to look around.

Case's thumb shifted on the control yoke, brushing a spring-loaded switch.

The Lahodney quad mount crashed and yammered once more, ejected shell casings spraying back through the bow compartment tunnel. The hot metal seared at Leeland-Rhys's legs, but he didn't feel it as he stared on awestruck.

The tracers from the multiple fifty-calibers didn't disperse, instead they cut a single tight tunnel of flame down through the night to the sea, the wave crests exploding at their touch.

With infinite deftness, Case rocked back on the control yoke, marching the boiling firestream up to the side of the gun barge.

The *daihatsu* vanished inside a cloud of spray intercut with a myriad of small, flickering explosions. Then, abruptly, from out of the heart of the mist cloud, a geyser of flame spewed into the sky as the barge disintegrated amidships.

"Dead one! Shifting target!" Case slammed the PBY's rudder bar hard over, skidding the *Zazz Girl* in midair, lining up on the last barge. From a slow, almost dreamlike deliberation, events suddenly accelerated madly, the barge and the surface of the sea leaping up toward the windscreen.

"Take him! Take him now!" Case yelled.

Bates hauled back on the bomb release. "Bombs gone!"

The PBY shuddered as the last pair of five-hundred-pounders fell free. Case and Bates both hauled back hard on the control yokes, hogging the plane's nose into the sky. Leeland-Rhys caught a last fragmentary impression of the targeted *daihatsu,* as the *Zazz Girl*'s bow swept over it, the barge's cargo bay crowded with Japanese soldiers firing their rifles at the Black Cat.

Thud! Thud!

This time she was closer to her own spilled venom, the patrol bomber staggering under the hammerblow shock waves of her own detonating ordnance.

The guns went silent, and the darkness returned as the parachute flares burned out. The pilots rolled the controls forward, leveling the aircraft, and Case pulled the throttles back to cruise power.

"Pilot to tunnel gunner," he said into his headset mike. "How'd we do on that last run?"

"Clean drop, skipper. We had Japs flying higher than we were on that one. The only thing still afloat is the gun barge, and I can see him burning real good. He's a goner."

"Okay that's a wrap then. All stations check for battle damage and report." Case glanced across at his copilot. "Sorry I threw that curve at you, Cyril. I shifted targets when I saw the gun barge blow. No sense wasting bombs on the guy after he torched."

"Right enough," the Australian replied. "Likewise, no sense coming around again for no reason. The silly bastards must have had one of the petrol power plants."

"Yeah, that or they were loaded with gas drums. Very obliging of them."

Bates noted Leeland-Rhys still frozen in the hatchway. "Oh hello, Prof. You had a seat in the boxes right enough. Quite the show, what?"

Leeland-Rhys didn't answer. He had lived with war for four years. He had fought it in laboratories and on the testing ranges. He had experienced it in the bomb shelters of the Battle of Britain and the Blitz, and he had lived amid its smoldering aftermath.

But he had never actually seen "war" before.

"Prof . . . hey, Prof?" It was Commander Case looking back at him now. "You okay?"

Leeland-Rhys mentally slapped himself in the face. "Yes, yes quite."

"We've gone through our bomb load and most of our strafing ammo. Unless you want for us to hang around out here a while longer, we're ready to head for the barn."

"Yes, I'm quite ready to 'head for the barn' as well. I don't think we're going to learn anything more out here tonight."

"I'd doubt it, too. We just had good kills, and the PTs are reporting some action down off Santa Isabel. Richie's scope ghosts never seem to show up on the nights we get the trade out here."

The random comment struck a chord through the numbness in the Leeland-Rhys mind. "Naturally. If you can see them. They can see you. They can warn their barges to seek for shelter . . . But they didn't tonight . . . not tonight."

Hands gripped Leeland-Rhys by the shoulders, moving him aside. "We heading for home, skipper?" Philip-the-Navigator inquired, squeezing past the Englishman.

"Yeah, Phil, studying on it."

"You better plan on a field landing at Henderson then." Outlined in the instrument glow, the navigation officer paused to pluck an inch-long splinter out of his hairy forearm. "We'll need a patch job before we can go back to the tender." Leeland-Rhys felt an odd draft tug at his shirttail and turned back into the radio/navigators compartment. Richie Anjellico was bandaging the scoured shoulder of the cursing First Radio by the light of a battle lantern.

In front of the detector set, at the approximate location where Leeland-Rhys had positioned his stool, a hole the size of a man's head had been blown through the hull and duckboard decking.

In the week that followed Lieutenant/Professor Meredith Leeland-Rhys learned a great many things.

He learned to despise powdered eggs and Spam as a diet. He learned that the state of not-sweating was indeed a luxury beyond price and that inflamed prickly heat was one of the tortures of the damned.

He learned to live . . . intimately . . . with fly and mosquito swarms and that Atabrine did turn a man's skin yellow. He learned that Fido was indeed not a "big one." He learned the ringing verbal satisfaction of "God damn son of a bitch!"

He learned that in a combat zone anything that one either wanted or needed was either difficult to get, out of inventory and on back order, or totally unheard of. He learned that mechanisms that operated flawlessly on an English laboratory test bench malfunctioned with a sullen vindictiveness in an equatorial environment.

He learned to drink powdered coffee not as a replacement for tea but because that was all there was and better than nothing.

He learned that Commander Evan Case was a skilled jazz trumpeter who had played professionally in a swing band before becoming an aviator. He learned that Richie Anjellico's girl back home was an American "cheerleader" still in high school, and that he wrote to her on a near-daily basis, and that Phillip-the-Navigator studied the biographies of the British kings as a hobby.

Leeland-Rhys learned that military discipline does not necessarily require shining insignia and regulation books, and that spotless uniforms and crisp salutes are not always the mark of an elite fighting unit.

Leeland-Rhys learned how to be "crew" and that there were far worse things in the world to be than "the Prof."

What he didn't learn was what he had come for.

For a full week, the *Zazz Girl* had launched every evening. Returning to the critical triangle of water up-Slot, they had electronically trolled for the phantom radar installation.

Leeland-Rhys combined his laboratory theorems with Richie Anjellico's field experience, the scientist and the teenage sailor becoming a team within a team. For long hours through the night they stared at the shimmering lines that bisected their cathode tubes, waiting to pounce on the first irregularity, the first hint of a radar sweep from an unknown source.

It did not come.

Another attack was conducted on another barge formation, with two *daihatsus* sunk in exchange for a hole the size of a football being blown through one wing. Half of one night's search was aborted in a hunt for a Japanese I-Boat reported prowling south of the Russell Islands. Another night's diversion occurred when a coastwatcher, desperately ill with dengue fever, had to be airlifted out of an isolated cove on a place with the unlikely name of Vonavona.

Beyond that, futility.

It was midafternoon on the eighth day and far too hot for any kind of sleep. The crews of the Detachment 3 Black Cats sweltered on the decks of their seaplane tender. Beneath the shelter of its grimy sunshades, they sipped lukewarm Coca-Cola, cursing the Solomon Islands, savoring few scraps of fetid breeze, and longing for the escape of nightfall and flight.

Evan Case emerged from the deckhouse and made his way to where the *Zazz Girl*'s crew sprawled. "Well, Prof," he said, dropping to the deck with his back to the gray-painted bulkhead, "I'm sure you will be pleased to know that you will shortly be leaving our august little group. It's been decided that we were seeing things and that you are too valuable an asset to waste on wild-goose chasing. You can expect your transfer orders back to England within the next day or so." To say that Leeland-Rhys had fallen in love with the South Pacific would be a massive inexactitude, yet there was a decided letdown at the pronouncement. In his own academician's way, he did not accept defeat easily.

"Damn!" He spat out the single oath.

Case comprehended. "Hell, Prof, it's not your fault. If the damn radar was there, you'd have found it, but apparently it's not."

"But that's just the point, Commander. There is a radar. I'm certain of it. All the evidence points to the Japanese having a powerful surface search installation in place to cover the Central Solomons. I've gone over your ASV from antenna to power source, and it's in perfect working order. I've also had plenty of opportunity to study the propagation environments, and there is nothing that could have produced a false return then that we wouldn't still be detecting now. If Mr. Anjellico says he saw an alternate trace on his set, then he did."

"But not lately, sir," the young radarman commented from his patch of deck. "We haven't picked up a single scope ghost since you've been here."

"Could be the Japs saw you coming, Prof," Phillip-the-Navigator commented wryly.

Flight Officer Bates sat up straighter on the ammunition can he was using for a seat. "Hang on! Might there be something to that? Are the Japs wise to this radar detecting bumph you've been about?"

Leeland-Rhys shrugged. "No reason they shouldn't be. As Mr. Anjellico has demonstrated, if you have a functioning radar set, you have, to a degree, a radar detector. Building a dedicated detector wouldn't be that much of a trick given you know the principles involved. We suspect the Germans are building them for their U-boats, and we know Germany and Japan exchange a certain amount of technological information."

"So, might be the Japs have just turned the bloody thing off so we can't find it," Bates countered.

Leeland-Rhys shook his head. "Doesn't make sense. The entire idea behind a radar is to use it to gain a military advantage. As you all have pointed out more than once, when the Japanese have their set operational, your kill ratios drop off. The Japanese can track your forces as they come up the Slot, permitting them to warn their *daihatsu* convoys of your presence and position."

"That only makes sense," Phillip-the-Navigator commented.

"What doesn't make sense is why we're not seeing it in use now," Leeland-Rhys continued. "Obviously, they have gone to some extraordinary effort to build and conceal this radar installation. Obviously, it's effective in protecting their logistic efforts. Obviously, it is of great value to their war effort in this theater. So why are they returning the advantage to you by not using it?"

"Could be their set just busted down on them," Richie Anjellico spoke up.

"For an installation of this importance one would assume they would have prepared for such an eventuality."

"What if they're saving it."

Case's words were a pronouncement, not a question. With eyes shadowed by the bill of his baseball cap, he was staring down at the decking as if a message of great importance were etched in its grimy steel.

"Prof," he continued, "call me if I'm wrong, but a big, fancy search radar like we're talking about can't just be plugged in and switched on like a table lamp. It has to be tuned up or something before it works right, right?"

Leeland-Rhys replied, "Quite so. An installation like a Japanese Type 22 might require several weeks of ranging tests before it's fully operational."

"That's it then." Case looked up. "Let's say the Japs have some kind of plan that involves using this radar, something big, beyond routine operations. They bring their set in, they set it up, and they start tinkering with it. As they're doing this ranging test stuff, they're tracking our operations in the Slot and they're using the plot they gain to warn their people off. Waste not, want not, right? This testing caused the scope ghosts we originally detected on our ASV."

"Yes," Leeland-Rhys said slowly. "But once they get their radar fully functional, they shut the system down, holding it in reserve for the day when they can use it against us as an aspect of this larger plan. A plan that must be of such a scale as to make the losses they are taking within their logistics pipeline acceptable in exchange for protecting the existence of the radar."

Phillip-the-Navigator scowled. "I wish to God that didn't make so much sense."

Case stood up abruptly. "Prof, you come with me. Let's go have some words with theater intelligence."

As with all of the other aviation facilities aboard the converted four piper, the air group intelligence office was a chronically undersized jackleg affair located in an off corner near the radio room. In the face of the feeble efforts of the ventilation system it was also steambath torrid to the point of the paint peeling off the bulkheads. A blackout curtain drawn across the center of the space concealed a clicking decoding machine and its sweltering operator and a hot and harried lieutenant commander crouched at a child-sized desk wedged between a set of lockable filing cabinets. He looked up annoyed as Case and Leeland-Rhys appeared in the narrow doorway.

"Yes?"

"Just fine, Ed, how's the world treating you." Case leaned against the doorframe as there was no room inside the office for an extra person. "I got a question."

"I hope it's important, Ev."

"It might be. It has to do with the radar problem the prof and I have been working on. Do the Japs have anything big showing on the boards? Any kind of a major operation?"

The expression on the intelligence man's face changed abruptly from annoyance to puzzlement. "How did you know? We only got the word down here a couple of hours ago. I'm working on your advisory briefing now."

Case and Leeland-Rhys lifted eyebrows at each other. "We're good guessers," Case continued. "What have you got?"

"An army B-24 out of Cooktown got a look inside Rabaul Harbor last evening. There's a Tokyo Express forming up."

The intel removed a wire photograph from a file on his desk, passing it up to Case.

The photograph was in black and white and taken from a low angle across a mountain-girdled bay. Its focus was a group of ships dispersed across the anchorage.

There were five in total, four of them with the distinctive raked stacks and twin-turret-aft configuration of the Japanese Fleet destroyer. The fifth and most distant warship appeared larger and of an older design, with three stumpy funnels set amidships on a low-riding hull.

"It looks like a standard Japanese destroyer squadron configuration," the intelligence man commented. "Four tin cans with a light cruiser serving as the squadron leader. About average for an Express run."

"The cans all look like early mark Fubukis," Case commented, studying the photo intently. "Do you have a make on the CL?"

"We think it's a Kuma class, but we're not sure. There's something funny about the silhouette."

Case brought the photo closer to his face, squinting. "Yeah, I see what you mean. Can I borrow a glass, Ed?"

The intelligence man handed up a powerful magnifying glass. Case put it to use with a Sherlock Holmesian intensity.

"You know," he said after a few moments, "I bet I know what this thing is. It's a Jap torpedo cruiser."

The intel officer scowled skeptically. "What in the hell would a torpedo cruiser be doing down here in Rabaul leading a destroyer squadron?"

"I've one better," Leeland-Rhys interjected. "What in the hell is a torpedo cruiser?"

"The surface torpedo attack is at the core of all Imperial Navy fleet combat doctrine, Prof," Case replied, lowering the photograph and the glass. "They consider the torpedo to be the decisive factor in any surface engagement. So much so that a couple of years back they took a couple of their old* CLs and

_____

(*Author's note: The IJN light cruisers *Kitakami* and *Oi*)

stripped about half of the guns off them. They replaced the gun armament with multiple torpedo tube mounts. Twenty tubes to a broadside, forty tubes in all. More torpedo firepower than any other naval vessel in history.

"Their theory was that in a fleet engagement, these ships would close with the enemy battle line at high speed, raking it with a series of massive torpedo salvos. Just one torpedo cruiser can launch enough fish in one pass to blow an entire battleship division out of the water."

"And that's why it's damned unlikely you'll find one leading the Tokyo Express," the intelligence man commented with a shake of his head. "The Imperial Navy considers the torpedo cruiser to be a strategic asset. They're all attached to the Japanese Combined Fleet, held in reserve for their general decisive fleet action of the war."

"Or at least that's what they've been doing with them." Case tossed the glass and the photograph back onto the intelligence man's desk. "Are we going to be counterpunching?"

"Tip Merrill's cruiser/destroyer force sortied from New Caledonia this afternoon, and is moving north to intercept. We figure the Japs should be ready to make their run in about two days. When they do, Merrill will be waiting for them."

"And vice versa. Thanks, Ed. Come on, Prof."

Leeland-Rhys followed Case back up onto the tender's main deck. The naval aviator was deep in silent, scowling thought. But the Englishman sensed that his presence was still wanted.

That there were still matters to be considered.

Moving back to the tender's fantail, Case leaned

against the rusting steel cable railing staring out across the sound toward Guadalcanal, the larger island a pale green day ghost in the heat haze. Leeland-Rhys followed suit.

"You know why they call that Iron Bottom Bay, Prof?" Case inquired abruptly.

"Because of all the ships that were sunk there, Japanese and American, during the battle for Guadalcanal."

Case nodded. "That's right. For every pound of Japanese steel down there, there's a pound of American steel rusting beside it. For every dead Jap sailor, there's one of our guys. In tonnage and in numbers it was a dead heat. We never beat 'em on skill, Prof. We just outlasted 'em. We could replace our losses faster than they could. We hung on and wore 'em down until they had to throw in the towel and fall back."

Case looked at the Englishman. "Never call a Jap no good, Prof. He might be a bastard and a son of a bitch, but he's as good a fighting man as they make."

"I've heard our lads express much the same sentiments about the Jerry. I presume you see how this is all coming together?"

Case nodded. "Yeah, it all fits now. That is a torpedo cruiser up at Rabaul. And Fleet intelligence is right on one point. The Japs wouldn't waste one of those ships on a Tokyo Express. This isn't a supply run. It's a setup. When Tip Merrill and his cruisers move into the Slot day after tomorrow, they're going to sail right into a bushwhack."

"Bush . . ."

"An ambush, Prof. They're going to be ambushed."

"Oh yes, quite. How do you think it will play out?"

"The Japs are the aces when it comes to night surface actions. It's their specialty. They've got good night optics, and, like I was talking about, they're great at torpedo work. Probably nine-tenths of our ships lost in this campaign have gone down with a Japanese fish in their belly. Some of us figure the Japs may have some kind of a super torpedo* that totally outclasses anything our navies have as far as range and hitting power goes."

Case snorted derisively and fished a pack of Camels out of his pocket. "Too bad we haven't been able to convince the brass hats back at the Bureau of Naval Ordnance of it yet. They seem to figure that if they didn't invent it, it can't exist. Smoke?"

"No thanks. I've my fixin's." Leeland-Rhys dug his tobacco pouch and briarwood out of his pocket and began the loading process. "The one advantage our forces would have in night fighting would be radar. Our ships mount sets. As yet, the Japanese don't."

"But this time around, the Japs will have radar. That hidden land-based set of theirs covering the Slot and the zone of engagement. Get the picture?"

Leeland-Rhys nodded, taking his first testing puff of his pipe. "Quite so. As our task force proceeds up the Slot, the Japanese will activate their radar and establish a plot on them, radioing the position, course, and speed of our ships to their own vessels. The Japanese task force commander will be able to

_____

(Author's note: Evan Case was correct, the infamous Japanese Type 93 "Long Lance.")

utilize this data to maneuver into a position of decisive tactical advantage. By the time the shorter-range radars aboard our vessels detect the Japanese, it will be too late. The 'bushwhack' will be an accomplished fact."

"You got it, Prof. Those early mark Fubuki destroyers are all strong torpedo ships as well. They have three triple-tube mounts on their centerline. Likely that's why they were selected for this mission. Add in the twenty-tube broadside of the light cruiser, and you've got a fifty-six-round torpedo spread. You could goddamn near sink Guadalcanal with fifty-six torpedoes.

Case snapped his lighter and touched it to the end of his cigarette. "It's going to be a slaughter, and that's the whole idea. If they can knock out one of our surface action forces, they can stall our offensive in the Solomons for months. Either that, or they'll make us weaken MacArthur in New Guinea or Nimitz in the Central Pacific, bleeding off replacement ships."

"Are you going to notify your superiors concerning this theory?"

The aviator shrugged "I suppose we can kick it upstairs for what good it will do. Problem is we still don't have any solid proof of the existence of that Jap radar. Besides, radar or no, Merrill is still going to have to contest the passage of the Express. Anything else means surrendering the Slot to Japanese control."

A speculative tone crept into Case's voice. "As far as I can see, we've only got one possible edge. To make this deal work, the Japs have got to turn that damn radar on."

"Indeed." Leeland-Rhys drew on the briarwood once more. "We've already got the passive intercept receiver mounted in your aircraft, and I've got a lobe-switching unit in my kit. If your squadron metalsmiths could assist me in running up a set of one-quarter-wave Yagi antennas, it wouldn't be much of a job at all to convert your ASV set into a kind of radar direction finder. When the Japanese activate their transmitter, one should be able to get a cross-bearing, fixing the set's location and giving one the opportunity to remonstrate with its operators."

"Remon . . . ?"

"Kick their ass."

Again Leeland-Rhys tightened the last screw on the new Yagi antenna hull mount, the dicky portside unit that he'd reinstalled five times that afternoon. "Test," he yelled up at the open cockpit window, gingerly stepping back on the narrow work float.

"Testing," the muffled reply came back. "Okay . . . that's got it . . . Switching off."

A few moments later Richie Anjellico stuck his head out of the portside cockpit window. "We got that antenna short beat, sir."

"At long bloody last." Leeland-Rhys stretched his aching shoulder muscles and dropped the screwdriver back into the tool kit at his feet. "That's as good as it gets then. We shall see what we shall see . . . literally."

"Give our bobby-soxer a pat, sir. It's good luck before a mission."

The Englishman reached up and gave the Black Cat's erotic nose art a pat on one creamy thigh. "At this late date I'm willing to take any help I can get," he commented wryly. "And speaking of that, Mr. Anjellico, this job would have been impossible without your good efforts and hard labor. I'm not quite sure as to how this medals business works in your navy, but I intend to see you put up for some kind of acknowledgment."

"Forget it, sir." Anjellico grinned. "I should be the one thanking you. It's been great working with an honest-to-God scientist. I've learned a lot."

A grin of his own tugged at Leeland-Rhys's face. "I've learned a deal myself, Mr. Anjellico. Have you given any more thought about your future?"

"Yeah. I think I'm going to go for it, sir," the radioman replied. "An electronics degree for certain, and maybe a doctorate."

"Very good indeed. I think you have the ability for it. I can give you the names of some of my American colleagues who could prove useful to you when you go looking for a university. And if you ever elect to study overseas, might I suggest Cambridge. I'd like to have you in some of my classes."

"You got a deal, sir. I'll see you after the war."

The chugging growl of a diesel engine became audible, and a cargo lighter rounded the stern of the seaplane tender, angling toward the *Zazz Girl*'s moorage buoy. Commander Case could be seen standing in the bow of the low-riding craft, guiding it in.

The lighter's engine whined into neutral as it came within speaking range. "Hi, Prof, how are we doing?" the pilot inquired, snagging a hull hardpoint with a boat hook.

"We have a functional direction finder, Commander, at least for the moment. How it will hold up under operational conditions is yet to be seen. I'd like another proving flight if we could afford it."

"We can't," Case replied flatly. "We'll have to prove it in combat. The word just come down from AIRSOLS. Like the Chattanooga Choo Choo, the Tokyo Express is rolling south on track twenty-nine. Ready or not, the show's on for tonight."

"Then I suppose we just have to assume we're ready. Was there a problem with my holding over for the operation?"

"No sweat. It was a simple three-point finagle. I swapped a Nambu automatic I had to the exec of a Kiwi corvette in exchange for a bottle of scotch from her wine mess. The scotch and I then met with a guy I know at Fleet personnel over on Guadal. He'll keep your transit orders lost until we want 'em found again."

"That's good, that's quite good." Leeland-Rhys shook his head in a detached manner. "Do you want to know something funny, Commander."

"I'm always up for a good laugh, Prof."

"To put it bluntly, I find that I am totally terrified motherless about tonight and about this mission." Leeland-Rhys glanced down at his hand amazed again to find that there was still no sign of a tremor. "And yet I also find that I'd rather die than miss this particular opportunity to get myself killed. It's really . . . most peculiar."

There was compassion in Case's responding chuckle. "Not really, Prof. Around here it's pretty much par for the course. I've never been able to figure it out either."

The aviator turned and jumped down into the

belly of the lighter. "Anyway, I brought back some presents from Guadalcanal." He hauled a water-soaked tarpaulin off the cargo in the lighter's belly. "The best the tender can give us are five-hundred-pound GPs and depth charges. I got the loan of these from a Marine dive-bomber outfit."

Two huge, lead-gray shapes lay chocked in place in the bottom of the boat, finned, sleek, and infinitely ugly.

"Semi-armor-piercing one-thousand-pounders," Case commented, "I figure that whatever we find out there tonight, we're going to want to kill it real good."

The long column of rakish ships was forelit by the last golden light of the setting sun. The black of their cast shadows angled off from the white of their streaming wakes as they steamed into the approaches of New Georgia Sound.

"Pretty damn things," Flight Officer Bates commented from the copilot's seat.

"They're giving Merrill the pick of the litter." Case dipped the *Zazz Girl*'s starboard wing to have a look. "Three brand-new Cleveland class light cruisers and four Fletcher DDs."

"It looks to be a fairly potent force. Enough maybe to handle the Express under any circumstances?" Leeland-Rhys inquired hopefully from his station between the pilot's seats.

Case ruefully shook his head. "In a nice, gentlemanly gunnery duel, those Cleveland CL's would murder the Japs. But tonight it's going to be like a shoot-out in a cow town saloon. The fastest on the draw wins."

He shook his head once more. "New ships mean green crews. I wish we had some of the old gang from the Asiatic Fleet down there. They knew how to fight Japs, the ones that got out alive anyway."

"Bow gunner to pilot." Edgy words sounded back over the headsets. "Aircraft at one o'clock high."

All three men in the cockpit snapped alert. After a few moments a dozen fast-moving specks appeared in the distance sweeping down the Slot, the twilight glinting on their cockpit canopies. The endmost dot closest to the PBY began to weave, banking steeply to display its unique twin-engined, double-fuselage configuration.

"Army P-38s, coming back from the last fighter sweep of the day." Case relaxed and rocked the Black Cat's wings in a pilot's reply. "Radio," he spoke into his lip microphone, "get on the horn with *Hep Gee* and *Lazy Mae*. Instruct 'em to go into a wide holding pattern around the task force and have them stand by for further orders. Nobody moves up the Slot until we get full darkness."

The aviator eased the *Zazz Girl* into a lazy bank around the ships in response to his own orders. "I've got a hunch we might have some little yellow-skinned pixies out this evening, looking to inflict FUBAR upon us cool cats."

He glanced over his shoulder. "You might as well go aft and put your feet up, Prof. Its going to be a lo-o-o-ong night."

"How soon before . . ."

"Four hours I'd figure. Just about four more hours."

In retrospect, Leeland-Rhys would find that he had lived shorter years.

* * *

Callahan, the First Radio, was on his fifth cigar of the night and the interior of the radio/ navigators compartment resembled a London coal fog. Leeland-Rhys would have told the crewman to, for Christ's sake, put the damn thing out, save for the fact he empathized highly with the state of the radioman's nerves.

Abruptly the radioman straightened. Pressing an earphone to the side of his head, he began to scribble onto a message blank, writing one-handed under the glowworm gleam of the radio desk's minute projector light.

"Skipper," he called over the intercom. "*Lazy Mae*'s got a contact . . . Stand by! . . . She's being bounced! . . ."

With the coming of full night, Case had sent the two other Black Cats of Detachment 3 ahead up the Slot to scout for the oncoming Japanese task force. Laden with its heavier bomb load, *Zazz Girl* had followed more slowly, moving into her old patrol ground between Santa Isabel, Choiseul, and New Georgia islands. There, they had held on station, awaiting the convergence of the two surface forces.

Leeland-Rhys put himself in position to snatch the message blank from the radioman and pass it forward into the cockpit. Case studied its content in the pinched glow of a pocket flash. "Phil, chart this. The Express is off Oka Harbor. Speed estimated at twenty-five knots, heading one-two-oh. Jake Tomlinson also reports that the Slot's crawling with Rufes west of Kolombangara. I was afraid of that."

"A Rufe is a Jap seaplane, Prof," Cyril Bates headed off the question. "A Zero fighter mounted on pontoons. Sort of our opposite number with the opposition. There's a flock of the little bastards operating out of the Shortlands."

" 'Nother signal from the *Lazy Mae,* skipper," the First Radio called. "They shook off the Rufes, but they've also lost the plot on the Express."

"They got this thing covered," Case said slowly. "With our scout Cats jinking around on the deck, dodging night fighters, we can't shadow the Jap ships on their run in. They're keeping us blind."

"Navigator to pilot," Tibbs cut in. "The last position fix we have on Task Force 39 puts them sixty-four miles south southeast of the Express. Speed twenty-five knots. Convergent courses."

"That's it. You've got around an hour, Prof. Start the music and get this ramble rockin'."

Leeland-Rhys didn't answer, he just slid back to his station at the passive intercept receiver. He had three other men seated within the sweep of his arm, but he had never felt so alone in his life. Deliberately, he cranked out the trailing antenna. Pausing for a moment to wipe the sweat droplets from the lenses of his glasses, he switched on the oscillator.

"Good hunting, sir." From his station at the A scope, Richie Anjellico gave him a thumbs-up.

It helped.

Slowly and deliberately, he began to comb the frequencies within the narrow confines of the surface search bands. At one nudge of the dial the entire circular screen fuzzed into a blur of dancing light. He had touched on the massed sweeps of the American task force, multiple search radars blasting into the night, probing for the oncoming Japanese threat.

A swift manipulation of the instruments squelched those traces, eliminating them from consideration and concern. He scanned on.

Another trace developed much fainter, wavering and intermittent; sometimes blinking out altogether. For long minutes he stalked it like a tiger might stalk through the jungle, not quite sure of the identity of his prey, not quite sure if he should make a sighting call.

"I'm getting trace spikes off the other Cats' ASVs sir? How about you?"

God forsake it! He'd wasted precious time pursuing the radar emissions of their own aircraft. *Idiot! Idiot! You've seen them before!*

"Yes, Mr. Anjellico. I'm seeing them," he replied, speaking through gritted teeth.

Maybe they were wrong all of them: himself, Case, Anjellico. Maybe there was no Japanese radar. Maybe it was all a glorious mistake, and he didn't have the lives of all those thousands of men in his hands. Please God, let it all come down to a sheepish laugh tomorrow morning.

And, then, there it was, a clean, shimmering band of green light cutting across the heart of the cathode tube.

"Got the bugger!"

"Me too!" Anjellico yelled. "I got scope ghosts! They just kicked on."

"Right on the 90 mc range! Sure as all hell that's Japanese Type 22! Commander, we've acquired the Japanese radar!"

"You've got the aircraft, Prof. Tell me what you want me to do!"

"Commence a slow wide circle to port. Mr. Tibbs,

stand by to take the bearing when the signal intensity peaks. I'll call it out."

The passive intercept receiver had done its job. It was now up to the jury-rigged direction finder capacity of the ASV radar. Leeland-Rhys hunched beside Anjellico at the A scope. "Go to automatic lobe switching and pray we've put this brilliant improvisation together correctly."

Slowly, the nose of the PBY drew a compass circle in the sky. The jittering spike in the center of the radar screen shrank to a minimal, then grew toward a maximal reading once more.

"Ready . . . ready . . . there! Bearing! Mark!"

Phillip-the-Navigator caught the bearing from the gyrocompass repeater at his chart table. "Bearing three-three-two true!" He positioned a ruler, and his pencil slashed across the map. "It's either Choiseul or New Georgia."

"Right! Commander, head to the southwest with all speed. We have to establish a baseline for a cross-bearing!"

"Roger"

The *Zazz Girl* banked steeply, her engines revving to full war power. Leveling, she raced through the night, seeming to strain against the resisting air as if she, too, sensed the urgency of her mission.

Three minutes crept past.

"That should be adequate, Commander. Reduce speed and give us another wide circle to port . . . Mr. Tibbs, I'll call the make again . . . Ready! . . . Ready! . . . Mark!"

Again the pencil slashed across the chart. "Bearing three-two-five . . . We got it!" Tibbs cried jubilantly. "It's Wilson Point on New Georgia!"

Abruptly the navigator's jubilation cut off. "But wait a minute. There's nothing at Wilson Point. Nothing!"

"There's got to be" Leeland-Rhys protested. "That's where the bearings converge. The radar has got to be located at that spot!"

Outlined in the chart table light, Tibbs held up a folder. "Look for yourself, this is the Wilson Point photo file from air recon. They freshened it yesterday. There is nothing there but beach and jungle."

"Christ!"

Feverishly Leeland-Rhys scattered the photo file on the chart desk, hunting for anything that looked like a radar mast. It would have to have a clean view of the horizon, it would have to have specific degree of antenna surface, and it could not be blocked or smothered by camouflage. Unless . . . unless somehow the Japanese had stolen an incredible technological march on the Allies.

"Prof, we're running out of time!" Case called back from the cockpit. "You've got to give us something now!"

"There's one possibility left!" Frantically Leeland-Rhys consulted the chart and ran a rapid calculation. "Steer a heading of 125 degrees south-southeast, retrograde along the radar bearing! We've got to follow the Japanese emissions to their point of origin."

"You mean use the Jap radar like a blind landing beacon?"

"Exactly! The Type 22 is monopolar with a non-rotating antenna array covering a single fixed sector. When we overfly the transmitter, the signal intensity will drop. We'll have the exact location of the site no matter how they may be camouflaging it."

Case's answer was in the tilt of the deck as the *Zazz Girl* pivoted on a wingtip, coming around to her new heading. The Pratt & Whitney radials snarled angrily as their throttles were once more rammed hard against their stops. The PBY began to shudder as she accelerated into a shallow dive, nuzzling closer to her red line maximum airspeed.

"All hands! Man battle stations! Radio! Contact AIRSOLS Guadalcanal. Tell 'em the Japs *do* have a radar out here! Give 'em the cross-bearing and tell 'em we're going in to attack! Then get on with Task Force 39. Tell 'em they're being tracked by the Japanese! For Christ sakes tell 'em they're sailing into a torpedo ambush! Send it in clear and keep repeating!"

Leeland-Rhys hunkered down beside Richie Anjellico at the ASV radar. "I knew I wasn't seeing things, sir," he kept repeating jubilantly. "I knew it!"

"You were right, Mr. Anjellico." Leeland-Rhys slapped the boy on the shoulder. "Point proven. Now, you must start feeding Commander Case bearing changes as we close the range. We must steer to keep the signal strength at its peak intensity right up until we overfly the transmitter. At that instant the scope spike will drop very abruptly to zero. Call out instantly when that happens."

"Got it, sir. Do you think maybe you should take the scope?"

"No, Mr. Anjellico. You started this job. It's yours to finish."

Leeland-Rhys crawled forward between the pilots' seats. *Zazz Girl* had burned off all of her altitude in her speed run dive and was skimming only a couple of hundred feet over the straits. The wave tops rippled and shimmered below her like wrinkled silver silk, and a dark looming bulk off the bow divided the sea from the star-spattered sky.

"New Georgia dead ahead, Prof," Case said. "How the hell do you think they have this thing hidden?"

"I haven't the faintest idea, Commander. All I can hope is that when we get close enough we'll be able to see the installation well enough for bombing."

"How about them seeing us, Prof?" Cyril Bates inquired. "You figure they got us spotted?"

"That's a very good question. The Type 22, granted that's what it is, is primarily an antishipping surface search system, not an air defense radar. But as we get closer, I presume they would become aware they have callers in the neighborhood."

"Radar to pilot," Anjellico interjected, "Bring her to port, skipper. Easy . . . easy . . . back . . . Hold that bearing! On the beam! Signal strength increasing."

The shadow ranges of New Georgia loomed closer, and Wilson Point reached out toward them like the low-riding bow of some mammoth ship.

"Still on the beam. Signal strength still increasing. Spike is peaking!"

"Not long now," Leeland-Rhys murmured. Over the sound of the engines he doubted if anyone had heard his words but himself.

A phosphorescence wavered on the surface of the sea ahead. Waves breaking across jagged coral.

"Coming up on the reefs," Case commented.

A dark blotch materialized in the surf line. Their old friend, the wrecked Japanese transport they'd touched base with on so many night patrol circuits.

They wouldn't be needing it tonight. It swept past beneath their starboard wing.

"Radar to pilot! Signal strength zero! We just lost the spike, skipper. It's gone! It's gone!"

The pilots and Leeland-Rhys all looked around wildly "What the hell's going on?" Case exclaimed. "We're still a mile off the coast! There's nothing down there but water!"

Realization came crashing in on Leeland-Rhys. "It's the wreck! The Japanese have hidden their radar aboard that bloody wrecked ship!"

It made sense. It made absolute sense! They would have their clear sea horizon, the antenna could be easily concealed within the tangled ruin of the transports king posts and upperworks, and all without leaving the telltale indications of a shore-based installation.

But there were other things that could be hidden on land far more readily than a radar site.

The night blazed white as concealed searchlight batteries snapped on along the shoreline, dagger blades of illumination slashing away the Black Cat's shield of darkness.

"Uh-oh." That single anonymous statement over the intercom came only a split second before the first antiaircraft salvo exploded around the *Zazz Girl.*

It wasn't like the *daihatsu* strikes. This time it wasn't merely autocannon and machine-gun fire although the sinuous tracer whips of the lighter weapons lashed at them as well. Heavy flak batteries had been positioned to guard the precious radar, Japanese seventy-fives intended and designed to kill a plane with a single hit or even a close miss. The PBY bucked and shuddered under the concussion, shrapnel ripping through her skin and ricocheting off her frames.

Quite possibly they would have died had they not already been flying firewalled at the PBY's maximum airspeed.

Their only way out was down. Case shoved forward on the control yoke and dived yet again until the amphibian's keel almost raked the waves, sinking the *Zazz Girl* below the fire and light of the gun and searchlight batteries.

Shell bursts still tracked them. Exploding overhead, they threatened to batter the Black Cat into the sea. The black sand beach of New Georgia materialized ahead, outlined by the flash of the shore break. The transitory flicker of the antiaircraft fire revealed a looming line of trees ahead and almost upon them, trees that towered *above* the surface skimming aircraft.

Leeland-Rhys found himself making some kind of a sound that would have been a scream had his throat and diaphragm not been paralyzed with starkest horror.

Case wrenched back on the yoke, lifting the Black Cat over the timber wall like a steeplechaser clearing a hedgerow. The big plane jerked and shuddered as tree limbs splintered against her belly, then she tore through and was clear.

But for a few deadly seconds her climb had carried her into the trailing edge of the flak curtain. Bullets *thwocked* through aluminum and 25mm shells exploded within the hull, venomous bits of incandescent shrapnel hissing and slashing. The cockpit windscreens exploded and Leeland-Rhys felt glass splinters slice at his face, then a spray of something hot, wet, and sticky.

"I'm hit! Christ! Christ! I'm hit!" Bates twisted in agony, the copilot clawing at a ruined shoulder with his working hand.

"Prof, for God sakes get him out from behind the controls!" Case yelled, fighting the yoke.

"Mr. Tibbs! Mr. Anjellico! Help me!" To his eternal amazement, Leeland-Rhys found himself able to move and act with conscious thought. Reaching around, he released the Australian's seat belt, dragging the shocked and injured man out of his seat and back through the cockpit door into the radio/navigators compartment. The rangy flight officer seemed to weigh almost nothing. Richie Anjellico and Phillip-the-Navigator were assisting now, the one helping to ease Bates to the deck, the other tearing open a first-aid kit.

"Prof, get back up here! I need you!"

Leeland-Rhys turned and scrambled back to the cockpit.

The night was dark again, blessedly, mercifully dark. They were beyond the reach of the Japanese gun batteries, and the maimed PBY was climbing slowly. Climbing faster were the hills of New Georgia; an arm of the island's central range rose to starboard, blotting out the stars as the aircraft fled down the landward length of Wilson Point.

"Prof, get in the copilot's seat."

Aghast, Leeland-Rhys stared at the pilot. "Me? I don't know anything about flying a bloody airplane!"

"I'll tell you what you need to know!" Case

snapped over the wind roar. "Get in the goddamn copilot's seat!"

It was no time for argument. The Englishman hunched into the seat. The slipstream slapped at him through the shattered windscreen, and everything, the seat belt, the control yoke, the headset he donned, seemed slick with congealing blood.

"Pilot to flight engineer, what kind of shape is the port engine in? . . . Pilot to flight engineer, report! . . . Franco! Talk to me, dammit!"

"Portside observer to pilot," a faint voice replied over the interphone circuit. "I'm up in the mechanic's compartment, skipper. The pylon's been hit, and the flight engineer's station is wrecked. Chief Franco's dead. But from the waist you can see the portside engine losing oil bad."

"Pilot to observer, acknowledged. Get back on your gun."

Leeland-Rhys could only see Case as a shadow play outline in the instrument glow, but in his headset he could hear the aviator swallow against a dry throat. "Prof," he said his voice level, "we've taken control surface damage, and we're losing hydraulic fluid. As they stiffen up I'm going to need your help on the yoke and rudder pedals. I'll tell you when. More important, I need someone on the manual bomb release.

"It's the white T-shaped lever next to your left knee. Arm it by rotating the T-grip ninety degrees from the horizontal to the vertical. When I give you the word, haul on it with all you've got. But not till I give you the word. Got it?"

"We're going back?" The answer was obvious, but he asked the question anyway.

"Prof, who the hell else is there?"

Obvious indeed. "Valid point."

"Coming about." The *Zazz Girl* flared and banked, doubling back on the course that had led out of hell.

"I'm not an expert at this, mind you," Leeland-Rhys commented, lifting his voice over the building wind roar, "But I've heard it mentioned that flying immediately back over a defended objective a second time is not generally considered a good idea."

"It is something to avoid if you can," Case yelled back, "But I figure we'll have a couple of things going for us. Most of the flak batteries that hosed us coming in were concealed in the tree line along the shore. They were aimed out to sea, covering the wreck out on the reef. By coming in from the landward side, the jungle will block their field of fire until we're almost out over the water. They'll only have that mile or so of clear firing arc between the coast and the reef to kill us in before we reach the target."

Case keyed the interphone again. "Pilot to gunners. On this next pass, do not fire on the searchlights. I say again, do not fire on the searchlights! That's an order!" Leeland-Rhys saw a wolfish smile gleam in the darkness. "You'll see why in a minute, Prof. Just for now those guys are *good* Japs."

The land flattened out beneath them, and they were racing across the New Georgia coastal plain. Outlined against the dimly luminescent waters of the Slot, the blunt, black tip of Wilson Point aimed them at their objective.

"Pilot to crew. Here we go again. See you on the other side."

The shadowed treetops flickered past beneath the PBY's belly as Case eased them as low as conceivable, holding off the inevitable to the last possible second. In the jungle below, keen ears would be hearing the growing thrum of the engines, and gun tubes would be swinging around, readying to unleash their barrage at the first possible second.

Forest . . . Forest . . . Forest . . . Beach! Surf! They were over water once more. And once more arc light and muzzle flame sprang up along the coast, converging on and tracking the Black Cat. Flying by a master aviator's instinct, Case dropped the *Zazz Girl* back to a bare man's height above the water, the PBY's wings slicing through the shell plumes that rose around her.

Leeland-Rhys suddenly saw the method to Case's madness concerning the searchlights. As the shore-based beams traversed, following the Black Cat out to sea, they also swung onto the hulk of the Japanese transport, illuminating it as it lay impaled on the reef, paving a silver highway through the night for the death ride of the *Zazz Girl.*

The waist gunners were firing back at the Japanese antiaircraft positions, the tunnel gunner was firing, the nose turret was firing. Case unleashed the hammering death of the Lahodney mount. Madly, the Black Cat clawed back at her enemies.

But there were gunners aboard the Japanese radar hulk as well. Men fighting for their lives against the great deadly thing that roared down on them from out of the darkness. Crouching behind their weapons' sights, they hosed death back at the ungainly silhouette outlined in the searchlight glare.

The bow turret exploded. Blood and tissue

streaked back over the nose and Dwarshnik, he of the condoms, was snapped out of existence in an instant, saving the lives of his fellow crewmen by absorbing the shell that would have wrecked the cockpit.

"Arm bomb release!"

Horizontal to vertical! Leeland-Rhys chanted in his mind as he twisted the T-grip. *Horizontal to vertical! Don't pull! Don't pull! Don't pull! Not yet!*

The rusting hulk of the Japanese transport was wedged across the reef at about forty-five degrees, and they were coming at it dead amidships.

"That . . ."

Tribarrel 25s were firing from camouflaged positions at its bow and stern and from atop the bridge.

"Looks . . ."

From this angle the outspread arms of the antenna array could be seen, artfully built into the crumpled midships deckhouse.

"About . . ."

Something crashed, and the aircraft bucked wildly under a heavy impact. A second, even more titanic crash followed as the *Zazz Girl* literally bounced off the surface of the sea, somehow recovering and regaining flight. Leeland-Rhys looked away for a single fragment of a second and caught an impression of the starboard engine, the propeller windmilling and golden flame streaming back from the shredded nacelle.

"Right . . ."

Looking ahead once more, the Englishman saw the side of the Japanese hulk fill the windscreen until there was nothing to be seen but rusted steel. Little antlike figures fled madly across the decks to nowhere, and Meredith Leeland-Rhys calmly accepted his own death.

"Now!" Case screamed. "Drop 'em now!"

Startled, Leeland-Rhys felt his hand jerk in instinctive response. A ton and a half of high explosives, two standard five-hundred-pound GPs and the two giant armor-piercing blockbusters salvoed from the racks. Freed from her burden, the *Zazz Girl* gave a leap like a bullet-stricken deer, clearing the mast tips of the hulk even as her bombs ripped into its belly.

Only the encapsulation of the explosions within the hulk saved the Black Cat from being swept from the sky by her own devastation. In the copilot's side view mirror, Leeland-Rhys saw the hulk, radar station and all, lift off the reef on a cushion of spray and flame.

"Bombs gone!" he whispered.

"Prof! Get on your wheel! Help me hold her!"

Case yanked back the throttle of the blazing starboard engine, feathering its prop. The two men fought the control yoke with all of their strength, resisting the wild swerve of the unbalanced aircraft.

"Can we fly her out?" Leeland-Rhys yelled.

"No chance! She's had it! Starboard engine's shot, and the port's got no oil pressure left. Best we can do is get as far out into the Slot as we can before she comes apart. Pilot to crew! Ditching stations! Rig for emergency sea landing! Radio! Send Mayday! We're going down!"

The *Zazz Girl* staggered on, not truly flying but riding the ground effect only a few feet above the wave tops. Case and Leeland-Rhys nursed her, prolonging the agony for another minute . . . a second . . . a third.

The portside engine balked, spat sparks, and started to seize. Case slammed the throttle closed and hit the kill switches. "Get her nose up, Prof."

They hauled back on the yokes, no longer fighting the asymmetrical drag. Sluggishly, the bow lifted, and, with a grateful dying sigh, the *Zazz Girl* settled on the water.

There had been no chance to lower the wing floats, and Case kept the amphibian balanced on her keel for as long as he could as the speed bled away. Finally, a wingtip touched, and they waterlooped around it, spray sluicing through the broken windscreen.

It was suddenly quiet, so very quiet. The only sound at all was the bubble of water through the punctures in the hull.

Case unstrapped and reached behind his seat, passing Leeland-Rhys a Mae West life jacket. "Come on, Prof. It's time to go."

The radio/navigators compartment was empty, at least of the living. A body lay slumped over the bullet-shattered radar chassis.

"Ah, damn it all. Damn it all to hell." Leeland-Rhys reached out and gently ran a hand over Richie Anjellico's blood-soaked hair simply because there wasn't anything else he could do.

Case's flashlight made a fast circuit of the compartment as he pulled the safety pins and snapped the switches arming the self-destruct mechanisms on the classified equipment. Lastly, he took the lead-covered codebook from its rack over the radio panel.

"We'll leave him with the *Girl*, Prof," he said quietly. "She'll take care of him."

The water was knee deep above the duckboards and rising by the time they reached the waist compartment. The remainder of the crew waited for them in the deployed life raft, the wounded Cyril Bates and the survival gear having already been loaded. Case and Leeland-Rhys rolled out of the open blister and into the rubber boat. Casting off in silence, they paddled clear of the sinking aircraft.

A few yards off they paused and waited, watching as the *Zazz Girl*'s bow sank and her tail lifted, a shadow against the stars. In a few moments more all that remained was the sheen of an avgas slick spilled upon the waves.

"She was a clapped-out old cow, wasn't she?" Cyril Bates said quietly.

"Yeah," Case replied. "It was about time the taxpayers bought us a new one."

From off to the northwest, something like heat lightning pulsed along the horizon, the sound of thunder following a few seconds later.

But then, to the southwest, a second storm replied in kind.

"Here we go, guys. Preliminary bout's over. Here comes the main event."

Star shells burst above the horizon, hot piercing sparks raining illumination on the sea battle bursting into life below, the bass drumbeat of heavy naval gunfire growing into a continuous rolling rumble.

"Were we in time?" Leeland-Rhys asked.

"Hard to say, Prof." Case shrugged and dug a crushed half pack of cigarettes out from under his life jacket, passing it around the circle of men spaced along the gunwales of the bobbing raft. "Likely we'll know who won come morning . . . by whoever it is that picks us up."

The thud and mutter of the guns continued for perhaps twenty minutes before trailing off. The flicker of muzzle flashes and star shells faded as well, leaving only a dim ruddy glow reflecting off the distant clouds as a ship burned in the night. After several long hours it, too, went out.

"Prof, hey, Prof! Come alive!"

Startled, Leeland-Rhys snapped his eyes open. Good Lord, was it conceivable that he had fallen asleep? He must have, for the sky was blue and spattered with fleecy clouds, and the sun was edging above the western horizon.

The life raft road easily atop the low swells and on the horizons the islands that flanked New Georgia Sound glowed a deep green against the sea.

Leeland-Rhys looked around at the other survivors of the *Zazz Girl* and noted that, most remarkably, every one of them was grinning.

"You want to see something real pretty?" Evan Case held out a pair of binoculars and pointed.

A column of tall gray ships was steaming down the Slot toward Guadalcanal. One of the cruisers rode low by the head with her bow distorted by a torpedo hit and a destroyer had its upperworks blackened by fire, but there were still seven.

Seven out. Seven back.

Leeland-Rhys felt his eyes sting as he handed back the binoculars. "All of this wasn't a waste then. Was it, Commander?"

"No, Prof, not a waste. And I guess that's about as good as you can do in a war."

The droning of aircraft engines echoed flatly across the waters, and two familiar high-winged shapes swept low across the Slot. The other PBYs of Detachment 3 had lingered into the day, searching for their lost sister. In response to the flare gun shell, they dipped their wings and separated, one patrol bomber climbing to mount high guard while the other lowered its tip floats to land.

The Black Cats would bring their own home.